A Reason For Dying

Wilfred Bereswill

P.O. Box 275
Boonsboro, Maryland 21713-0275

This novel is a work of fiction. Names, characters, places and incidents either are the product of the author's imagination or are used fictitiously. Any resemblance to actual persons, living or dead, events, or locales is entirely coincidental.

First Edition-June 2008
ISBN 1-59133-262-1
978-1-59133-262-6

Book Design: S. A. Reilly
Cover Illustration © S. A. Reilly
Manufactured/Printed in the United States of America
2008

To Linda, my wife and love of my life, for her unending support and for all the long walks that helped me through some tough times. Also to my daughters, Kelly, Kristen and Kaitlin for their patience in letting me talk endlessly about my new passion and giving me the time to write.

And finally, to my parents. I pray they are smiling on me from heaven.

Acknowledgements:

There are many people that played a part in the writing *of A Reason For Dying*, whether they know it or not. Inevitably, a writer's personal life is influenced by those around them and shows through in their writing. I owe a debt of gratitude to my friends, my foursome, business colleagues, acquaintances and pretty much anyone who cared enough to read, to offer suggestions, to listen and to talk to me--even the Clayton, Missouri policewoman that I cornered at Starbucks. Rather than slapping the cuffs on me when I asked to see her gun, she took the time to talk about her weapon of choice while sipping on a Caramel Macchiato. I also need to acknowledge the National Hockey League for the lockout during the 2004/2005 season that allowed me to focus on my writing.

I would like to thank Dr. Stephen Kurzweil for not only fixing my hernia, but for fixing my medical terminology. It's been a couple of years and everything is still where it's supposed to be.

A special thank you goes out to my blessed Aunt and Uncle, Bob and Mildred MacGuire, without whom I would never have believed I was capable of writing a work of fiction. Your prayers and support were not wasted.

I also appreciate the love, support and help from my wife, Linda and daughters, Kelly, Kristen and Kaitlin, my sister, Dona Sherwood and her family, Tom and Lisa and my in-laws, Ray and Virginia Meyer. Their constructive criticism and encouragement were key to bringing out the best in me and keeping me going.

When it comes to learning the craft of writing, I need to thank my friends at the St. Louis Writers Guild and the St. Louis Chapter of Sisters in Crime. I couldn't have done it without their assistance and support.

And finally to my editor, Shawn Reilly. The sincerest of gratitude for understanding me and sharing in my passion for my characters and my story and for helping me share it with you; the most important person; the reader.

Chapter One

Washington D.C.
November 28, 2001

There are over one-hundred and eighty species of chameleons in the animal kingdom. They survive by camouflage; approaching by stealth to destroy their prey, then melt into their surroundings before becoming prey themselves. There are chameleons in the world of humans as well. Using the same tactics for different reasons.

The '67 Mustang rumbled through the dark maze of streets that made up Washington, D.C. as if on autopilot, while Laura Daniels' mind pondered another crappy day. It had been nothing but a string of crappy days since arriving in D.C. a couple of months ago. The Mustang jerked to a halt between the white lines it called home and the big engine shuddered to a stop, letting out a sigh as it gulped a last gasp of air through its grimy carburetor.

Laura gathered her things and trounced up the stairs to her Forest Heights apartment. As she turned the key in the deadbolt, the concerns about her day vanished. There was no click and the familiar resistance was missing. Her mind shot back eighteen hours to when she left for work. *Did she forget to lock the door?* A forty-caliber Sig Sauer P-229 handgun appeared from beneath her lightweight jacket as she crouched to set the computer case on the hallway floor.

With the door pulled toward her to take the pressure off the latch, she turned the handle. A shake of her head evicted strands of short, blond hair from her face so she could peer through the thin opening, a near-full moon and streetlamps providing just enough light. The place looked trashed. Kitchen cabinet doors hung open displaying empty shelves. Dishes, pots and pans cluttered the counter. The trashcan in the corner of the room lay on its side spilling papers, open mail, and Chinese food cartons on the porcelain tile.

She pushed the door open and edged into the studio apartment. With gun extended, all five-foot four of her was taut and ready for anything. A circle of blue-white light swept the bedroom, both arms working in unison, gun hand supported by flashlight hand. Cosmetics were strewn about on the top of a small vanity near the bed with several bottles lying on the worn carpet. The closet door stood open and clothes were everywhere, except on hangers. File folders and papers covered the bed while the bedspread, quilt and sheet lay wadded in a heap on the floor.

"Well damn, everything's right where I left it."

She let out a long sigh as her shoulders relaxed and her gun dropped to her side. A quick flip of the switch on the wall illuminated Laura's life as Assistant Special Agent in Charge assigned to the Bioterrorism Division of the FBI. At just thirty-two, Laura Daniels was a youthful veteran, rising rapidly in the Bureau using her street-smart savvy, relentless work ethic and sheer grit. The depletion of manpower now assigned to 9/11 thrust Laura into the spotlight as the lead agent on the anthrax letter investigation. Her first big case and she was nowhere: no leads, no solid evidence, no nothing. Just seven letters written in a childlike manner, several grams of refined anthrax and five dead bodies—hopeless, just like her apartment. Like her life.

After retrieving her computer case from the dark hallway, she went to the small round dinette table and pushed aside this morning's mostly empty cereal bowl with a few Honey Nut Cheerios still floating like tiny life preservers in a shallow pond of skim milk. She carefully placed her pistol on the table and began her ritual of removing her shield, holster, cell phone and whatever else happened to be in her pockets where she could remember to reload everything in the morning before running out of the door.

She picked up the cereal bowl, dumped the souring milk and soggy O's in the corner of the sink, and stacked the bowl on the five other dirty ones. Looking in the empty cabinet, she concluded that she needed one more place setting to make it through the week.

"Susie Homemaker" was not her thing. She had been kicked out of her college dorm and when she tried to get her deposit back, the residence advisor said they were using the money to fumigate the place. In college, her excuse was schoolwork, now it was just work. Some things never change.

"Oh my Lord, I need a break...and a maid," she muttered, rubbing her throbbing temples. She threw last night's Lean Cuisine tray in the trash, booted her computer and tied into the secure FBI network. Her mind wanted to shut down, but the investigation prevented her from refreshing sleep. As she read the case files again, the words on the screen began to run together. Every lead a dead-end. Everyone makes mistakes, and these bastards were no different. Why the hell couldn't she catch a break and find one—just one.

Holding the "ctrl" and "alt" keys, she pressed the delete key and secured the laptop in the standby mode. She extracted her personal cell phone from her small purse and scrolled down the pathetically short list of names. She hesitated for a moment, began to flip the phone shut, and then pushed the talk button.

"Hello?" The voice on the other end was strong and soothing.

"Dad? It's Laura."

"Hey, Squirt, what are you doing calling so late? It must be one in the morning there."

"Yeah, it's late but I can't sleep."

"How's Shelby doing?"

"Not good, Dad. I don't think she's got long to live."

"Damn. How many miles?"

"I don't know. A hundred-seventy something. It's costing me a small fortune. I don't think she's going to see two-hundred thousand miles."

"Don't let her get away from you. Remember, I want her back."

"Okay, Dad."

"So how's my big shot agent doing these days? Anything you can talk about? Or would you have to kill me?"

"I'd have to kill you." The corners of her mouth curled up slightly as her father's reassuring voice brought a small wave of comfort with it. A warmth that quickly faded. "Dad...I'm...I'm ready to quit this thing. I think...I'm in over my head." Her eyes began to burn from the salt of gathering tears.

"Bullshit, Laura!"

The abrupt comment scared the tears back into her eyes. "Dad—"

"Squirt. We had this discussion when you signed up. You knew it wasn't going to be easy. You need to suck it up and buckle down. I don't know what you're working on, but I'm betting people's lives are at stake, or our freedom."

"Dad, listen—"

"No. You listen, Squirt." The voice on the other end became louder and more forceful. "I didn't raise no quitter. You've never quit at anything. I may not have been the best father for you while you were young, but I'm damn well not going to let you throw your career down the drain because you feel sorry for yourself. I'm not going to let you wallow in self-pity and then hate yourself for blowing your life."

Laura choked back the tears the same way she always did when her father directed his booming voice at her. She could see the deep lines in his forehead scowling at her through the receiver. "You're right, Dad. I guess I just need some sleep."

"Laura?"

"Yes, Dad?"

"I love you."

"I love you too, Daddy."

"Your mother would be proud...your mother is proud."

A loud buzz caught her attention. The secure cell phone on the table vibrated, dancing across the cheap wood veneer.

"I have to go, Dad. I have a call I have to take. Thanks for the pep talk." She flipped one phone shut and picked up the other. "Daniels," she spoke into the receiver.

"Laura, it's Mike."

"Mike, what's up?" Thoughts of sleep vanished. Mike Johnson, Special Agent in Charge of the Bioterrorism Division, didn't call to chat about the weather—especially at this time of night.

"A new lead. Trenton, New Jersey. Emergency response received a 911 call earlier this evening. It sounds like a young girl. She says she was forced to write letters and address envelopes. Some of the things she said couldn't have been known without inside knowledge. She gave an address to an apartment where they took her."

"Oh my God." A surge of adrenaline snapped her mind into overdrive.

"I'm downloading the call to your case file. Get to the terminal at Regan National. I have agents from the Newark field office heading that way."

"Mike, we can't let the locals interfere." She banged at the keyboard of her laptop to upload the file.

"Trenton PD has been directed to hang back a half mile."

"Good. I'm on my way."

Tires screeched as the faded blue '67 Mustang GT roared to a halt at the FBI terminal at Reagan National Airport. The throaty exhaust revved, clanked, and ran on before finally going silent. At the same time, the driver's door groaned in protest as Laura flung it open. With her computer case and overnight bag over her shoulder, she ran for the sleek Falcon 50EX waiting on the apron. The high-pitched whine of the engines and odor of jet fuel assaulted her senses as she approached the extended staircase. Within minutes, the small jet hurtled into the dark sky toward Trenton Mercer Airport.

Laura flipped open the Compaq laptop and pulled up the audio record of the 911 call. Fitting a set of headphones from her computer case over her ears, she centered the cursor over the play button and clicked.

Static filled the headphones and then an adult female voice. "911 emergency response. What is the nature of your emergency?" Laura adjusted the volume to seal out the drone of the jet engines.

Ten seconds of static and then a voice sounding like a young girl. "They took me from school and made me write things."

"What was that? What is your name, please?" the operator asked.

"I don't want to get in trouble."

"Honey, are you in trouble now? Are you all right?"

"Yes...I mean they didn't do things to me."

"That's good. My name is Kerri, Kerri Lambert, what's your name?"

"No...they said they would hurt my momma if I told."

"Where are you now?"

"At a phone, near a gas station."

"Where is the gas station? Do you know a street name? Can you see a name on the gas station?"

The clicking in the background must have come from the computer keyboard as the operator sent a dispatch to nearby police officers.

"They took me from school and made me write things on the anthrax letters. Bad things, I think."

"Honey, who took you? What school do you go to?"

"They took me to a room. I saw the numbers. They didn't know I could see, but I did. One...five...five...A...Lincoln Street." Background noise interfered with the legibility of the recording. Judging by her voice and the way she pronounced the numbers, African-American? Maybe eight to ten years old?

"One-five-five-A Lincoln Street?" The operator's voice seemed to remain calm, but Laura could detect the edge of stress creeping in.

"They made me write bad things, like...'death to America'...'death to Israel'...'Allah is great'. They made me put addresses on envel...ten...of the..., I count...I think some went to important people, uh...Senator..." The recording cut in and out as background noise drowned out her weak voice.

"Are you there? Honey, you need to speak up. I can't hear you very well. Stay where you are, the police will be there shortly."

There was a burst of static as the recording ended.

Laura listened to the recording over and over, taking notes, trying to focus on the voices, then the background noise, trying to determine the stress level in the girl's voice.

A loud thump and rush of wind noise announced their final approach to Trenton Airport. The intercom cackled. "Fasten your seatbelts." Several minutes later, the jet taxied to a private terminal where a white Ford Taurus waited with two men inside.

Laura trotted down the steps and approached the men, both wearing midnight blue Agency jackets.

The taller of the two stepped forward. "Agent Daniels?"

"Yes." She extended her hand. "And you are?"

"I'm Agent Taylor and this is Agent Aras." He pumped her hand once with a vice-like grip. Taylor's closely trimmed brown hair revealed a receding hairline. His pocked complexion accentuated narrow, squinting eyes, with thin lips that seemed incapable of smiling. Aras displayed a large set of white teeth that shone from the middle of his dark face. His only hair surrounded thick lips in a tightly trimmed goatee.

"Good to meet you. How far is the apartment?"

"About fifteen minutes from here," Aras said. "I have surveillance and assault gear in the trunk. Our mobile forensics lab is about an hour out."

"Great. Can you tell me about this apartment?" Laura asked.

"It's part of an old row of buildings recently purchased by a real estate company," Aras answered. "They plan on rehabbing it, but it's been vacant for about a year."

The car raced along the empty streets of Trenton toward the suburb of Franklin Park. The setting quickly turned from industrial to lower middle-class to semi-ghetto. Taylor brought the Taurus to a stop on Lincoln Highway just past Henderson Street.

"The apartments are right over there," Taylor said. "That row of old brick buildings. 155A is on the back corner, bottom floor."

Aras handed Laura a pair of night vision binoculars. The dark street turned ghostly green and black as she squinted to focus her vision. Several steps led to a small porch, slightly wider than the door. The amplified view revealed a crooked, weathered sign with the address; 155-A Lincoln Street.

"Crap! The windows are boarded up. Do you have infrared?" she asked.

"In the trunk—and directional mics," Aras said.

A few minutes later, Laura pulled on a lightweight, dark blue FBI Gore-Tex coat and watched a small screen while Aras aimed an infrared thermal imaging gun at the building. Taylor donned a pair of headphones and aimed an ultra-sensitive directional microphone.

"I'm reading several hotspots in the building. One is definitely a person. The others are static and appear to be smaller and hotter than body temperature," Laura whispered, her warm breath vaporizing in the cold night air. Fuzzy warm reds and yellows and blocky cool greens and blues danced around the small screen.

"I'm not picking up any voices, but there is definitely movement," Taylor added.

Laura reached in her coat, pulled out her gun and started toward the old building.

"Daniels, what the hell do you think you're doing?" Taylor whispered loudly.

"I'm going in. I'm not letting these bastards slip away."

"Agent Daniels." Taylor grabbed Laura by the arm, his stubby thick fingers digging into her coat. "You can't do that. It's against protocol. If there is anthrax in there, you'll be endangering yourself and others. We'll keep the place under observation and wait for environmental suits and backup."

Laura spun, yanking free of Taylor's grasp, her eyes glaring. "Taylor, who the hell do you think you're talking to? I'm in charge here. We're going in. Need I remind you what these terrorists have done in the past several months?"

Aras retrieved two M-4 Carbines from the trunk and held one out to Taylor.

"Aras, are you crazy? What the hell are you doing?"

"I'm helping Agent Daniels and following orders. My brother was killed at the Pentagon. I don't give a flying fuck about protocol right now."

Taylor reluctantly took the automatic assault weapon and watched Aras retrieve a backpack and three sets of body armor from the trunk. His eyes swept over Laura's thin figure. "Agent Daniels, I assume you're a small?"

She nodded, smiling briefly, took the black vest, removed her coat and pulled it over her head. After cinching it up using the Velcro strips on the sides, she headed to the old brick building in a crouched trot.

Concealed behind a battered, rust-gutted pick-up truck across the street from 155-A, she scanned the front entrance, peering around the side of the building. The cloud-covered pre-dawn sky cast no light or shadows. Steam wafted from the nearby sewer lid carrying a stench that curdled her stomach. The night vision goggles revealed no cameras or security.

"Taylor, take the back. Remember, we want them alive. Aras, blow the lock with the C-4 and I'll toss in the flash-bang. You take the right side of the room."

After creeping up the brick steps to the door, Laura tried the doorknob and, finding it locked, nodded at Aras to place a thin cord of plastic explosive around the strike plate. While Aras attached the detonator, Laura pulled the pin on the flash-bang canister and both agents crouched on either side of the front entrance. Aras lifted three fingers, and counted down. A small muffled pop, and the door swung open.

Laura tossed in the small grenade-like device and both agents closed their eyes and shoved their fingers in their ears. Following the explosion, they entered, weapons ready, eyes sweeping the room looking for movement. Aras yelled with a deep voice, "FBI, drop your weapon and come out!"

The dimly lit room was filled with pharmaceutical boxes and lab equipment. The air, still thick with the odor of cordite from the flash-bang, smelled of solvents. Plastic bags of white powder sat on a table in the corner of the room. As Aras crept toward the dark back room, Laura spotted a slight movement. She saw the muzzle flash of a weapon an instant before the report hit her ears. Aras spun around and hit the floor face down.

Diving behind an old stuffed chair, she trained her concentration on the doorway. A small dark figure appeared with a gun extended. "Got you, asshole." She squeezed off a round, leveled the gun from recoil and fired again. The first bullet entered the man's thigh causing him to fall backward and scream in pain. The second bullet missed its mark and pierced a can of toluene, then struck a boom box behind it. A spark ignited the extremely flammable solvent, rupturing the can, spraying a fiery rain over the wounded suspect.

The man screamed in anguish as his long stringy dreadlocks flashed, and solvent saturated clothing erupted in flames. The smell of singed hair and burnt flesh followed a wall of heat that pushed Laura back away. She stared helplessly as the dark man thrashed wildly on the floor—flames blistering and consuming his flesh. The back door banged open and Taylor raced in.

"Taylor!" she screamed. "Get one of the fire extinguishers in the corner. I can't reach them. We can't let him die."

The deafening screams rang in her ears as the man burned in front of her, thrashing against the wooden floor. A loud whoosh and cool rush of carbon dioxide licked at her face as the flickering flames died out.

"Don't you die, you fucking bastard," she screamed.

Chapter Two

Frederick, Maryland
November 28, 2001

Saif Yasin stared into the blackness, straining to see through the icy rain, silently praying to Allah to help him control his anger and decide if the American should die tonight. He parked the rental car on a dead-end street between rows of deteriorating warehouses, isolated from prying eyes. Raising his arm, he angled his stainless steel Breitling watch to catch a dim beam of light from the lone streetlamp. It was almost midnight.

Headlights blinded him briefly as they reflected off the streams of water cascading down the windshield. With his left hand shielding his eyes, his right hand instinctively slid beneath the overcoat to feel the cool textured steel of the nine-millimeter Israeli-made Jericho handgun. He slipped it out of the leather shoulder holster, pulled the knurled slide and listened as the hollow-point bullet snapped into the chamber. With the safety off, the gun disappeared into the map pocket near the floor in the driver's door.

The oncoming car slowed as the driver turned his gaze to Saif. As their eyes locked, Saif tried to gage the emotions of the American. He saw fear as the car passed. Red lights glowed in the rearview mirror before the car swung in a big arc and settled next to the curb behind him.

Saif reached up to turn off the dome light as the man ran toward him with his overcoat pulled over his head. The roar of the storm broke the silence in the car as the American hurriedly folded his tall frame into the passenger seat and slammed the door shut, once again muffling the torrent outside.

"Josef?" The man wiped rain from his eyes and forehead and squeezed water from his curly black hair.

"No, Dr. Bates, my name is Sam. You might say I'm Josef's boss. I have made the trip myself to see you." Saif casually flicked rain from his overcoat as he stared at Dr. Bates with sharp, calculating eyes. High cheek bones shadowed light brown skin and thin bloodless lips framed perfect English.

"But I was supposed to meet Josef."

"Let's just say Josef was demoted. You will deal directly with me now."

"Look, I know what you want. I told Josef six grams was the best I could do." Bates' voice wavered. "After 9/11, security got tight. I almost got caught."

Saif noticed Bates' hands were trembling. From the cold rain? Probably not.

"You promised us four hundred grams. We paid for four hundred grams. You appear nervous, Dr. Bates. Perhaps you thought you could accept payment and we would be happy receiving a fraction of what we paid for?"

Bates' eyes widened as Saif's hand disappeared into his overcoat. "Look, if this is about the money—oh please God, don't kill me. I can get it back." He pawed at the chrome door handle, failing to grasp it with his rain-slick hand. "I—I have a friend. She just got a job with the CDC. I can use her to get information."

Saif's mind pondered this new data. *Allah, what is your will? Give me your wisdom as I am your servant. This ignorant American should die for failing us.*

"Shut up, you fool." Saif pulled his hand free from the overcoat holding a white envelope with an address scribbled on the front. "You see what I have here, Doctor? There's a gram of anthrax in here—anthrax you supplied, with a letter naming you as our supplier. The handwriting will match the letters sent to the senators. That will be the first phase of your demise, unless you cooperate."

"I'll do whatever you want." Bates sweated profusely, a combination of nerves and the car's heater blowing hot air like a blast furnace.

"Yes, you will, and here's another reason why." Saif picked up a small digital camcorder from the floor in front of him. "Do you know where that pretty blond wife of yours is tonight?"

"She's at a cancer benefit..." His face twisted with comprehension. "Oh, shit. If you've done anything to her—I swear!"

"What do you swear, Bates? I don't think you're in a position to be swearing."

Surely the doctor's imagination was running amuck. He pulled his left hand up from his side and pointed the gun at the doctor's head. "Just watch the video."

The doctor fumbled with the camcorder, finally opening the small color video screen with fingers that were wet and numb with fear. The display flickered as the tape started, showing an empty bedroom.

"Do you recognize this place, Doctor?"

A man came into the picture carrying the limp body of a woman and threw her roughly on the bed. Her body bounced lifelessly on the mattress.

"What did you do, you fucking monster? And how the hell did you find her apartment? Oh Christ..." His voice cracked with anguish as tears glistened in the corners of his eyes.

"Careful, Doctor. It's amazing what you can find on the Internet. We've known for several months that your wife accepted a job with Johns Hopkins University and moved to Baltimore." After a brief pause, Saif continued in an eerily calm voice, "You know, Rohypnol is a wonderfully effective sedative. Surely you've heard of Rohypnol—you might know it as the date rape drug."

RAPE—such a powerful word that had the desired affect, causing the doctor's hands to shake so badly he could no longer hold the camera. His arms went limp and it dropped to his lap but his eyes didn't leave the screen. Saif's image now came into the picture and pulled the woman's head up by her long blond hair—the picture zoomed in on her beautiful pale face. Her mouth hung open, frozen, as if in a silent scream.

The camera pulled back as Saif removed a long knife from a sheath on his belt and flashed it in front of the camera. It looked like a hunting knife—smooth blade on one side, gutting hook and serrated edge on the other.

"Watch this part closely, Doctor."

With the tip of the blade pressed against her face, Saif traced a line down her cheek toward her chin. He lifted the blade, slipped it into her blouse at the top button, caught it on the gutting hook and pulled. The severed plastic disc flipped through the air, hesitated as if in slow motion, and landed on the bed next to her. One by one he cut the rest of the buttons off, and used the sharp point of the knife to pull the silky material of her blouse back, exposing a black bra with lacy trim.

"Oh, please, Lord," the doctor whimpered, tears dripped from his chin mixing with the raindrops on his coat. He balled his fists and clenched them against his forehead. "I...I can't watch this...I can't—"

The gun pressed hard against the Doctor's temple. "Watch the video." Saif looked to see that his eyes were open in thin slits, squinting at the screen.

The knife slid between her skin and the bra. With a quick jerk, the black material gave way—the screen went blank.

"Oh shit! What did you do to her? She hasn't done anything to you!" he screamed.

"No, she didn't, Doctor, but you did. She paid for your sins. Your greed. The sin of all America."

A sharp tortured howl filled the car. Saif shoved the Jericho against Bates' head, hard enough to pin him against the passenger window, silencing all but the whimpering sobs of resignation. His grip on the pistol tightened in rage. His hands shook with anger as he fought for control of his trigger finger. He so wanted to kill this man that had spoiled his mission. Moments passed.

The doctor's face contorted in fear. "Christ! Please, get it over with. I've got nothing...nothing left," he pleaded.

Yes, Doctor, your spirit is broken. You are mine now. Saif lowered the gun.

"Relax, Dr. Bates, I won't kill you yet. You may still be useful. And your wife hasn't suffered permanent injury. This time at least. She's probably still sleeping the drugs off. It's really quite easy to slip drugs into an unsuspecting woman's drink. They are so naïve, so vulnerable, aren't they?

Easy prey. Just waiting to be taken by a predator."

"Oh God, oh God," the doctor repeated, sobs still wracking his body.

"It's a good thing for you my associate was with me. Generally, Muslim men find American whores distasteful. They brashly show their skin, parade around like pampered bitches and act as if they are man's equal. But I find your wife very attractive and the next time I will have my way with her before shoving my knife into her stomach and opening her like a slaughtered animal. Of course, I will make sure you watch as she screams in agony, begging for me to end her miserable life."

"Please, I'll do whatever you want. Just leave her out of this."

Saif grabbed the camcorder and again pressed the muzzle of the gun to the doctor's temple. "You have my phone number. Call me if you find anything we can use as a biological weapon. Consider yourself on retainer—indefinitely. Now, get out of my car and call your wife—convince her not to contact the police. If I get the slightest feeling that you may betray us, this letter will be delivered to the FBI and you will watch your wife suffer a horrific death."

"Yes, yes, I will." He retreated quickly, running through the raging storm to his vehicle.

Saif watched the taillights disappear into the blackness as the spineless doctor sped away. He allowed himself to smile at the successful message that had just been sent. Now it was time to get back to New York and plan the next attack.

Chapter Three

Franklin Park, New Jersey
November 29, 2001

Laura sat in the driver's seat of the nondescript Government Issue Taurus, head resting on the steering wheel as she replayed the death of her only suspect over and over. His screams reverberated in her ears as his body blistered and burned in her mind's eye, the investigation incinerating with it.

"Goddammit!" She shoved the door open hard enough for it to bounce back and catch her leg. "Shit!" With her leg throbbing, she surveyed the impoverished setting of Franklin Park on the outskirts of Trenton, New Jersey. The long rows of aging brick apartments were narrow and most were attached. Graffiti-covered plywood nailed over broken windows offered anonymity to the interiors. What was once a working class neighborhood was now a harbor for the underworld.

Eric Wassel, the forensics team leader, sat on the brick steps in front of the building partially shielded by yellow plastic ribbon. Being a large man, his bulbous body stretched the seams of a white Tyvek suit. His puffy lips spoke quietly into a digital voice recorder while he referred to pages of handwritten notes. Seen in a casual setting, he would be stereotyped as a donut-eating slob. Although he was considerably overweight, he was far from being a slob—at least as far as his work was concerned. Meticulously organized, Eric Wassel was one of the FBI's best forensic specialists.

Laura slammed the car door, shutting up the incessant dinging of the car's alarm, and limped up the walk. "What'd you find?"

"It was a meth lab, Laura, not an anthrax lab."

"You're missing something, Eric."

"We've been through it twice, for Christ's sake! I've been doing this awhile, Laura. I'm telling you we're wasting our time here. All the supplies inside add up to methamphetamine, nothing more. As volatile as the atmosphere was from all the solvents, I'm surprised you didn't blow the fucking place up with the flash-bang. All the white powder you saw in the front room was crystal meth."

"What about prints?" she asked. "What about the payphone?"

Eric scratched at the scrubby stubble on his chin. "We located the payphone—completely clean. Looks like it was wiped down with a cleaner—rubbing alcohol or acetone. As far as the apartment, it'll take us a few days to lift all the prints out of there. The prints we took off your cadaver match the prints on the glassware. The rest probably belong to distributors and junkies all over Trenton."

Laura's normally piercing green eyes were dull and offset by dark circles of fatigue and faint lines of stress. She pulled at strands of short dingy blond hair being blown in the cold wind. "The toilet. Did you check under the toilet seat or the flush handle?"

"Yeah, yeah, your cadaver raised the lid and took a piss before you toasted his ass. Don't tell me how to do my job, Laura."

"Goddammit!" She turned abruptly and muttering under her breath, hurried to the car. Without turning to face him, she yelled, "Go through it again!"

Eric rolled his eyes, shook his head and shouted at her retreating back, "Goddamn you, Laura. When did you become such a bitch?" He pushed himself up and went inside the apartment to give his crew the bad news.

Laura dropped into the front seat of the Taurus and slammed her fists against the steering wheel. The first real lead in the case and it was looking like a dead end. "What the hell do you do now, Laura?" She jammed her slender fingers against her temples. "Think!"

Twisting the key in the ignition, she brought the Taurus to life, slammed it into gear and jammed down on the accelerator. The car leapt from the curb, tires grasping at the pavement and raced north along Lincoln Avenue towards Trenton Police Headquarters on North Clinton. She jerked the car into an open space, scraping the tires and grinding the alloy wheels against the curb without caring.

"I need to speak to Kerri Lambert." Laura flashed her FBI badge as she approached the desk sergeant.

The white haired officer looked up from behind the counter to see an attractive young woman with delicate features and a triangular shaped face with high cheekbones. He squinted through cheap reading glasses that were barely hanging on to the tip of his nose to read her shield. "I'm sorry, Agent...Daniels, Miss Lambert is covering the phones right now."

"Get someone to cover for her. This is a national security issue."

"Yes, ma'am. I'll get her right away. Please wait here."

"I need a place to make a private phone call while I wait."

"You can use that office in the corner if you like, Agent Daniels." The officer flashed a grandfatherly smile, pointing to a small office in the corner of the big room.

She watched him limp away and then headed for the office, punching a speed dial number into her secured, encrypted cell phone as she went.

"FBI, Mike Johnson."

"It's Laura. The news isn't good."

"Damn—talk to me."

"Nothing makes sense and so far there's absolutely nothing we can use."

"That seems to be the way this case is going. So, what now?"

"I'm going to question the emergency operator who took the call—see if there's anything I didn't catch on the tapes. I'll have a few of the agents canvassing the other apartment buildings go over to the pay phone and look for witnesses."

"Yeah, okay."

"Unless something comes up, I'm coming back to Washington tonight."

"I'll see you in the morning then."

She flipped the phone closed and went back to where Kerri Lambert was waiting, running freckled fingers nervously through flaming red hair.

"Ms. Lambert, I'm Laura Daniels, Assistant Special Agent in Charge with the FBI in D.C. I'm leading the investigation of the recent anthrax letters. We spoke briefly on the phone and I have some more questions for you."

"Of course, Agent Daniels. I'll help any way I can."

Laura led Kerri back to the small wood-paneled office. Dusty blinds clattered when the door slammed shut sealing in stale, smoky air. She pulled a notebook and pen from her jacket and settled in the worn secretary chair behind the desk as if it were her own.

"Can you talk me through the call one more time? Try to remember every last detail: ambient noises, inflection of her voice, background voices or noises. Start by trying to describe the girl from her voice."

"She sounded young, maybe nine or ten. Black, I think. I have a seven-year old and this girl sounded slightly more mature in the words that she used." Kerri had her eyes closed as if trying to conjure up an image in her mind.

"Good. Go on."

"She said that she wrote the *antrax* letters, I assumed she meant anthrax. She said a bad man made her do it. She was sort of...whimpering."

This woman is observant, Laura thought. *Whimpering? Scared, or just an act*? "Did it sound like she was being coached or told what to say?"

"Not coached, maybe coerced, her voice was shaky, scared. She may have been reading. Her words sounded...measured."

"Hmmm, what else?" Laura wrote furiously in her notebook without looking up.

"She said the man picked her up from her school and took her to a building on Lincoln Street. Then she gave me the address saying the numbers one at a time. She said the man made her write bad things like 'death to America,' 'death to Israel' and 'Allah is great' and he had her address envelopes."

As Kerri spoke, Laura's mind hung on every word, analyzing, searching for unspoken clues or hidden messages. *Those were the words—the exact words on the letters. That's pretty detailed. Maybe too detailed. This is a young girl.* "I wanted to ask you about that. On the taped conversation it sounded like she said ten envelopes. Is that what you heard?"

"Traffic noise was drowning out her voice, but that's what I thought she said."

"You know there were only seven letters received so far."

"Yes, that's what I read."

"What else do you remember?" Laura urged.

Kerri tapped her front teeth with her finger. "Well, she told me that the bad man told her not to tell anyone or he would hurt her mommy. Then the call was disconnected."

"Yeah, it's suspicious that she waited so long to call. Anything else? What about background noises?"

"No, no other voices, nothing but traffic noise and the call trace identified the pay phone in Franklin Park not far from the apartment. When the squad car got there...maybe three minutes after I'd lost her, the place was deserted. No security or traffic cams cover the phone and no witnesses."

"Thank you, Ms. Lambert. Here's my card, if you think of anything, anything at all, call me immediately."

Laura stood and left without looking back. She was disgusted that such a promising lead turned up as another roadblock. Every girl in the three nearby elementary schools was being questioned with no luck so far. Parents were also being interviewed to see if there were any unexplained absences.

The door of the rented Taurus slammed shut and Laura headed for the airport. *Where were the other three letters? Was she being set up? This case had to be solved soon before more people died. This was more than her career. This was about preserving American freedom.*

Chapter Four

New York City
December 2, 2001

The plush apartment in Greenwich Village sat a few city blocks from the rubble of what was once an icon of the New York City skyline, the twin towers of the World Trade Center. If Saif Yasin craned his head out the window far enough, he could see the billowing clouds of dust from the massive clean up. This morning he was busy browsing the Internet for biotech company research projects on his laptop computer when his cell phone vibrated across the expensive cherry-wood desk.

"Hello?"

"Is this Sam Yasin?" the deep voice at the other end grumbled.

"Yes, yes, this is Sam." Sam was the alias he chose to attract less attention.

"We will meet at the regular place at the prearranged time. You will give an update on your progress." The line went silent.

Saif flipped the phone closed and began to rub his temples. There was no progress to report. Afghanistan was not a place he desired to be called back to. Even though he hated Americans, the conveniences of a modern society were too appealing to give up. This dichotomy of ideals continually confused him and challenged his beliefs.

Born in the United States, his birth mother was Spanish. His father was a Saudi and a quiet Islamic extremist. Saif's close-cropped black hair framed a clean-shaven, angular face that resembled his birth mother's Latin heritage more than his father's Saudi features. Ten years ago, his mother had disappeared. Even though he missed her immensely, he somehow knew not to ask where she went. His father raised him strictly, bending the words of the Qur'an to mold his mind in anticipation that he would one day be allowed to serve Allah.

A sleeper until a year ago when his father returned to Saudi Arabia, he was recruited for a specific task and given a cell of five men, all of them trained in specific areas and all long-time citizens of the United States.

A product of the finest private schools, Saif graduated summa cum laude with a master's degree in biochemical engineering from Rutgers University. In June of 2000, shortly after graduation, Saif received orders to travel to a remote ranch in Borger, Texas, where he spent six months with his cell on weapons training, covert communications, and commitment to Allah. His mission was to find and deliver a biological threat immediately after 9/11. Although not a total failure, the anthrax attacks were not nearly as effective as desired. His cell failed to appropriate enough anthrax spores to carry out the original plan.

Josef Mohammed, Saif's second-in-command, had found Dr. Reed Bates working for the army at Fort Detrick. The corrupt doctor claimed he could deliver four hundred grams of weapon grade anthrax from the army's infectious disease research program. Instead, he delivered six grams and only two were refinable to weapon grade. The capricious doctor then had the audacity and stupidity to demand full payment, saying more anthrax would follow. It never did.

Josef was a fool for trusting the American. Furious when he learned of the doctor's failure, Saif pressed the muzzle of his gun to the side of Josef's head. Josef stood calmly looking back with blank eyes while Saif's hand shook with anger, his finger lightly squeezing the hair trigger. Josef's body was disposed in several landfills. It wouldn't be found. Not enough of it anyway.

The original plan called for two attacks that would shake Americans to their core, making them afraid to leave their homes and doing irreparable damage to the economy. The first attack was to be on September 23rd at the Georgia Dome during an Atlanta Falcon's football game. The spores would have been dispensed into the ductwork during the national anthem.

A second attack would come the following week at a Washington Redskin's game using a crop duster. A Minnesota cell was investigated by the FBI after checking out crop dusting equipment in Florida, grounding flights for several weeks during September and October. However, unknown to the government, there was a capable pilot and a Thrush 550 crop duster in a concealed location at a small grass airstrip just outside Washington, D.C.

The attacks would have been devastating, but instead, because of the infidel doctor, the plan had to be scaled down to ten letters, with a half-gram of anthrax in each one. Making matters worse, the inept American mail system lost three of the letters sent to the media. Letters to CNN, the U.S. office of the BBC, and the *Washington Post* were never mentioned in the news.

Using the girl to address the envelopes and make that phone call had been brilliant. The little street waif from the Bronx would never be missed and never be found. She did not look all that scared when Azzim pulled the blade across her neck. Actually, her and Josef were not that far apart now.

For Saif, failure meant certain death. Not a death of honor, but a death of disgrace. After fidgeting for hours, he pushed himself away from the desk and retrieved his heavy winter coat from the closet. There was a report to give. Taking the elevator to the lobby, he hustled the two frigid blocks to the Starbucks on Broadway. Opening the dark green metal and glass door, the warmth and smell of fresh brewed coffee calmed him—just a bit. He ordered a decaf mocha latte with hazelnut from the overly-pierced new-age hippie clerk. *Stupid American youth*, he thought, shaking his head imperceptibly. *They call it freedom of expression. It is disrespect to our maker. Another reason American society must pay for their crimes. Disrespect is ingrained in their culture.*

While the barista prepared the concoction, Saif let his eyes scan the store. In the corner, a well-dressed middle-aged man of Middle Eastern descent browsed expensive coffee mugs. Saif took his latte to a small, isolated table that was in the same corner as the mugs and his superior.

No eye contact was made. Saif lifted his paper cup, grasping the cardboard insulating sleeve, and felt the cup collapsing in his shaking hand. He used both hands to steady it and raise it to his mouth. The steam rising from the small hole in the lid hit his nostrils as he sipped. With the cup covering part of his face, he let his eyes drift toward his contact.

The man walked to the counter and ordered something. Something simple. The barista offered a weak smile and quickly handed a small cup to the man with his change and receipt. He turned—his black eyes and dark face surveyed the small store and then strolled toward Saif.

"You have something to report?" the man asked, speaking quietly.

"Sit down, please," Saif whispered.

The man sat and leaned in close as Saif continued in a soft voice, "The doctor in Maryland has been convinced to apprise us of new opportunities. We are also investigating private clinics doing research. Patience will reward us soon."

"Very well," the man said, turning away from him. "Perhaps we brought you along too quickly."

I have disgraced Allah and my superiors. A sharp pain flashed through Saif's head making him wince slightly. "We are ready for another assignment now, if that is your will. We will not fail this time."

The man held up his hand. "Keep vigilant but do nothing without my approval. We will look for a new mission for you and your brothers. One that, maybe, you can handle."

The man stood up quickly and walked out the door leaving Saif with that last sentence echoing in his head. *One that, maybe, you can handle.*

Chapter Five

Washington D.C.
FBI Headquarters
December 3, 2001

God, traffic in D.C. sucked. Laura Daniels unlocked the door to her office and threw her purse and keys on the credenza behind the desk. The key ring hit the simulated wood-grain top, skipped and came to rest against the wall. They hung there for a moment as she lunged—too late. They disappeared in the small gap.

Shit! So this is how my day starts? With the light freezing mist falling from the sky this morning, it took over an hour to travel the short distance from her overpriced apartment. She let herself drop into the green leather chair with a sigh as her eyes scanned the top of the desk for the morning reports. They were right where they should be, stacked neatly in offset piles in Megan's organized fashion—summaries from the night staff on top. If it weren't for Megan, her office would look like her apartment—a mess. Laura used the toe of her shoe to flip the switch on the power strip under her desk to start the computer boot sequence. The Windows logo made a ghostly appearance on her screen, assuring her that the docked laptop was coming to life. Looking deeper into the monitor, she caught her faint reflection.

"Damn." She opened the top drawer to retrieve the ragged red and gold makeup bag left to her by her mother and fished out a small mirror. Shuddering at what she saw, the tips of her fingers traced the outline of the vampire-like circles beneath her eyes that hastily applied make-up was unable to hide. Since 9/11, there hadn't been any time for her to take care of herself and it was beginning to show. It depressed her to see this haggard old woman staring back at her.

She reached in the bag for a bottle of foundation. *Screw it, no time now.*

"Laura!"

Startled, she dropped the mirror and looked up quickly to the sight of Mike Johnson, standing right in front of her.

"Have you reviewed the nightly summaries yet?" he asked.

"No, Mike, I was just getting to it," she answered, stuffing the case into the drawer.

"Get on it. The president is on a tight schedule today and I need to have the briefing ready in an hour." He disappeared as suddenly as he had appeared, followed by the clack of his customary quick stride as he hurried down the hall.

Retrieving the mirror from the floor, she hastily slid it back in the case and slammed the drawer shut. Taking a moment to lean back in her chair, she glanced around the small, windowless office. Barren white walls stared back. In three months, with the exception of the picture of her father and late mother, she still hadn't done anything to personalize the office. She picked up the silver frame and stared at her mother with her swollen belly wrapped in her father's arms, beaming. The picture was taken two months before Laura's birth and her mother's death. Leaning forward she gently replaced the picture, grabbed the summaries and started jotting notes.

Fifteen minutes later, she took her seat in the small conference room, secure from the outside world with recycled, filtered air canceling active noise.

"Okay, people, let's hear it," Mike began. There was never any meaningless chatter in his meetings.

The four section agents took turns giving updates on bioterrorism security risks around the world. It amazed Laura how skillful Mike was at listening to the verbal reports, weeding out the noise and summarizing them for the president and his staff. It didn't hurt that he was easy on the eyes with wavy brown hair and dark mysterious eyes. At well over six feet, his muscular physique made him intimidating, even to his own staff.

"I've got two hits. One, I believe, has potential significance," Laura said when it was her turn. "Two people broke into a private research lab used by the Mayo Clinic in Boston. It appears they were trying to steal or destroy mouse embryos being used for research, but there were vials of Hantavirus being held at the clinic for a special immune research project. The intruders, a young man and woman, were caught and arrested by the clinic's security force before they reached the secured areas. Police in Boston are holding them until the clinic confirms that nothing was taken or sabotaged. A background check shows they have ties to PETA."

"Also, there was a letter sent to the *National Enquirer* with a death threat and a white powder," she continued. "The powder turned out to be an inert silica material used to filter yeast cells in the brewing industry. The handwriting on the note and the envelope didn't match the anthrax letters from September and October. Sounds like a hoax, but we have a field team investigating."

"Okay, Laura," Mike said, standing up. "Thanks, everyone. Good job. I'll pull this together and get it to the White House."

He turned to walk out the door, stopped and looked back.

"Laura, I'd like to see you in my office at ten." By the time she looked up, he had disappeared.

Walking back to her office, she was bothered by what Mike might want. It wasn't so much what he said, but how he said it. Her stomach did a cartwheel. She'd been working around the clock on the anthrax letters for almost three months and there were still no leads on the origin of the anthrax or who sent it. She knew that all seven letters were in the same handwriting and contained at least two grades of anthrax.

The first group of letters sent to various media offices contained a low grade or cutaneous anthrax. The second two letters, sent to the senators, contained refined weapon grade anthrax.

Even though the grade was different, the anthrax came from the same strain. The strain was very similar, if not the same, as the type used for research by the U.S. Army Medical Research Institute of Infectious Diseases at Fort Detrick, Maryland. However, the weapons grade anthrax was refined into an extremely fine powder with low surface cohesion that would disperse and stay suspended in air, which made it easier for unsuspecting victims to inhale or ingest.

The current theory was that the first letters were meant to get attention. The second wave was meant to kill. No terrorist groups had yet claimed responsibility for the attacks and now five people were dead. The country was still reeling from 9/11 and it didn't need more uncertainty.

Laura tried to dismiss the trepidation she felt at Mike's comment and slipped behind her desk to start scanning e-mails. She phoned the field office in Boston to have the research lab break in investigated. At ten o'clock she pushed back from her desk and walked down the corridor to the corner office, passing by Mike's receptionist.

"Close the door and have a seat," Mike said, waving her in.

Crap, nothing could churn a stomach faster than those words. The pictures of the past two presidents handing Mike service awards did nothing to alleviate her nerves.

"Sure thing. What's going on, Mike?" she asked, trying to put on an upbeat front.

"I have a few things to discuss with you." He shifted in his seat and leaned forward, resting himself on his elbows with hands clasped in front of him. "Laura, I know you've heard the rumblings. The Hill isn't happy with our lack of progress on the anthrax case. Well, whenever some hotshot senator is unhappy, a shit storm hits."

Oh crap, she thought, then countered, "You know we've done everything we can. It's harder than finding a needle in a haystack."

"Believe me, Laura, I know. I really do. But here's the deal. We're taking everyone that's worked on the team and placing them in field offices around the country. The chiefs think that it would be better to scatter the expertise in the field in case we have another incident."

"Yes?" Laura said, nodding her head.

"You're being reassigned to Seattle. You'll report to Robert Williams, the head of the office, but retain your bioterrorism investigation duties and have a dotted-line relationship with me."

"Seattle? Sir, that seems a little remote. Why would you—?"

"First of all, it wasn't my decision. You were chosen for this location because of the number of high profile targets and because we feel the next attack will be at a more unsuspecting and unprepared location. Actually, the territory is pretty large and consists of Washington, Idaho, and Montana." He settled back in his chair. "You leave Monday. Pack as much as you can and we'll relocate you when we find a break in the action."

"This is a crock of shit and you know it, Mike! I've run this investigation exactly the way it should be run."

"Christ, Laura, you killed your only fucking lead! Freak accident or not, you can't question a fucking corpse. Yeah, he may not have had any info, but we'll never know now, will we?"

She stood and headed for the door before the tears started.

Chapter Six

Seattle, Washington
April 1, 2004

April Fool's Day! It was no joke to Laura that she happened to still be stationed in Seattle. Even after repeated pleas and reassignment applications, she remained firmly rooted in the Seattle field office. Even with a large window office on the twentieth floor of an upscale building, she longed to get back to the other Washington. Washington, D.C.

Yeah, Seattle—the hotbed of bioterrorism. The people here are so laid back they wouldn't know or even care if there was a bioterrorism threat. The only things these damn people seemed to care about were spotted owls and old growth forests. And the weather sucks.

Robert Williams, the chief of the Seattle field office, walked by Laura's office and stood in the doorway. "Good, I was hoping I'd catch you at your desk. We have a conference call in five minutes in the quiet room."

Bob was short, carried a few extra pounds and had a baby-face despite nearing retirement age. He could have been a poster child for Rogaine with a few wispy threads of brown hair forming a thin curtain around the back of his head. His right cheek carried a scar from being shot while on a field assignment in Russia during the cold war. The bullet was meant for his partner, but Bob spun the wheel of the car, smashing into the KGB agent's car as he raised his gun. The bullet shattered the passenger window, whistled by his partner's face and tore through his cheek, shattering his jaw. It was his badge of honor.

"What's up, Bob?" she asked, putting down her sandwich.

"Don't know, but it's with Mike Johnson in D.C."

"Okay, I'll be there in a few minutes."

Laura finished her lunch, grabbed her notepad and chewed up pen, and headed for the quiet room. Located in the interior of the building, the quiet room was a secure conference room with passive and active noise cancellation and signal blocking.

Bob punched a button on the encrypted conference phone. "Mike, you there?"

"Yes, Bob, we also have the San Francisco and L.A. offices coming on. Is Laura there?"

"I'm here."

"Good, good."

There was a soft beep, "John Driscoll, L.A. here."

"Okay, L.A. we have Seattle, we're waiting for—"

Another soft beep.

"This is Jack Davis, San Francisco."

"Okay people, we're all here," Mike started. "Listen carefully. We've just received reliable information that there is a credible threat of terrorism likely on the west coast of the United States. Let me explain and then you can ask questions."

"The army, working with the CIA, orchestrated a sting of sorts in Iraq. A fake, heavily armored supply convoy was sent from Bagdad to Tikrit, Hussein's hometown. The army put Predator and Pioneer drones in the air for reconnaissance above the convoy while the NRO positioned satellite surveillance." Mike continued, "The route took the convoy through a residential area in north Tikrit which was suspected to house al Qaeda controlled insurgents. The convoy's route was intentionally leaked at the last minute to known spies so there wasn't enough time to plan anything fancy.

"The insurgents took the bait, attacked the dummy convoy and ran. Between the drones, satellite and ground surveillance, their hideout was quickly located, stormed and taken by allied troops. The Iraqis were caught off guard and the troops found a trapdoor leading to a communication's center where considerable intelligence was obtained."

"Do we know how current the information was and did it suggest specific targets and timeframes?" Bob asked.

"We don't really know how old the intel is, but we believe it's fairly current. At least we think it was received in the last two weeks. The specific targets mentioned were three baseball stadiums: L.A., San Francisco, and Seattle, and the convention centers in San Francisco and L.A. However, it appears these were suggested targets, so we can't rule out anything."

"Well, regular season baseball doesn't start for another two weeks. That gives us time to get extra security in place. Mike, is there any indication what we might be facing?" the L.A. agent asked.

"No. There was nothing. Sorry, but based on what happened in 2001, chemical or biological would be my best guess—anthrax, Sarin gas maybe. That is if they don't resort to a dirty bomb. We will have daily conference calls and I want a report on action plans from each of you by tomorrow afternoon. That's all."

The conference phone went silent.

Chapter Seven

Chicago, Illinois
April 5, 2004

Dr. Brandon Stiles left his spacious and sparsely furnished town home in Oak Park, Illinois, to begin the forty-minute commute to Interex's home office. There were still thin sheets of snow on the ground from the weekend, but with the sun finally shining it was disappearing rapidly.

Pushing the button on the garage door opener, he squeezed his Toyota Land Cruiser through the narrow opening allowed by the too-close walls of the small garage and the hulking size of the SUV. The Land Cruiser was one of the few things he had left since the divorce from Janie over 2 years ago. At a mere 12 miles per day to the train station and back, it should last forever.

Brandon graduated thirteen years ago with a doctorate in Paleontology from Yale University. His unique theories on the viral demise of prehistoric life landed him a prosperous job at Interex, a large oil and gas exploration company headquartered in Chicago, Illinois. He took repeated abuse from his co-workers for taking mass transportation instead of driving, but the time on the train relaxed him. Plus it made him feel a little bit better about driving that gas-guzzling dinosaur of an SUV.

This morning the six miles went quickly in light suburban traffic. With his computer backpack slung over a shoulder, he headed for the platform. Being a creature of habit, he headed for the last car, folded his six-foot-three frame onto his usual seat and closed his steely blue eyes. This morning, Brandon's mind played back a different snippet of memory. Rather than his tumultuous trip to China less than seventeen months ago, it drifted back to his days in college.

Brandon started his academics at the Colorado School of Mines studying Geotechnical Engineering. During his sophomore year, he took a five-hour geology course and met a man that would change his life. Professor Hamlin would have been considered an odd fellow by most people's standards, but he loved geology and his exuberance rubbed off on his students.

Hamlin snared Brandon in his web of enthusiasm and shifted his interest from engineering to geology and paleontology. After completing his undergraduate studies, he applied to the prestigious Yale Paleontology Program, and was offered a partial scholarship and a job in the Peabody Museum to pay the remainder of his tuition and expenses. Working hard to maintain excellent grades, he became good friends with Dr. Andrew Burch, Department Chair, and participated on digs over the summers and worked in the museum through the school year.

Six years later, Brandon presented one of the most controversial doctoral dissertations in the history of Yale's Paleontology Program. It was as controversial—maybe even more so—than Burch's own dissertation theory, that dinosaurs were related more closely to birds than reptiles. Brandon contended that the dinosaur population had been decimated by newly formed deadly viruses bringing them to the edge of extinction.

His undergraduate degree and dissertation, however, won him job offers with almost every oil and gas exploration company in the world—lucrative job offers.

The train slowed as it neared the LaSalle Station and his internal clock snapped him awake. Again, by habit, he ran his fingers through straight-brown hair in a vain attempt to smooth it down, then tugged at the overcoat draped over his narrow shoulders to pull out the wrinkles. Joining the crowd of people squeezing through the train's sliding doors like lemmings, he followed them in an orderly line to the escalator. Again his mind flashed back—*there were no orderly lines in China, only semi-controlled chaos.* Once on the surface, he pulled his jacket tightly around him to ward off the chilly wind that always blew between the buildings and rushed to Interex's world headquarters two blocks away.

The lobby was spacious and had become a museum of sorts, displaying the history of oil and gas exploration. There were pieces of equipment from the oil rush in the late 1800s and early 1900s. Brandon loved the sharp contrast of the rusty, aged equipment with the glimmering stainless steel railings, modern fixtures, and marble floors.

He opted for the stairs instead of the elevators, finding the four flights started his heart pumping and provided a kick-start for his morning cup of green tea, a habit he picked up in China. He pulled the computer out of his backpack, snapped it into its docking station and pushed the power button. As he grabbed the *Tribune* from his pack, his eyes swept his travelogue wall, covered with pictures of the places he had visited: Patagonia, Africa, and China. His favorite picture was positioned in the center of the collage: Hukou Falls, where he met Ling Mae. Every morning he gazed at Mae sitting on top of a ragged but brightly adorned donkey standing on an ice pack in front of the magnificent waterfall. Every morning he was reminded of the happiest and saddest moments of his life. Before the computer could boot up, the intercom line began flashing.

"Yes?"

"Brandon, Jeff would like to see you right away," the feminine voice on the other end said.

"Okay, I'll be there in 5 minutes." He pushed the release button on the phone and turned back to his computer monitor. There was an e-mail message from his old friend, Dallas Wheeler.

Doc. Vegas is great. Especially the showgirls. Well, them and the strippers at The Crazy Horse. The craps tables are being gracious. Remember the five-hundred mile rule: what happens in Vegas stays in Vegas.

Brandon smiled. Dallas was a guy that could find fun in any city he spent the night in. He stood and stretched his long arms and walked down to the corner office to see the president of Interex, Jeffery Hargrove.

Jeffery Hargrove was a pure businessman. Neatly groomed black hair graying slightly at the temples, he always looked the part. Whether he wore one of his many thousand-dollar suits or a polo and slacks on the golf course, he looked like a millionaire. And he was. His office looked like a million bucks as well and it probably cost that much to decorate.

"Brandon, I just got off the phone with our lobbyist in D.C. and have some great news."

"The project got approval?"

"Well, not quite, but we've been called before the National Energy Subcommittee to discuss it. The president himself instructed the committee to listen to us. He *wants* the project, Brandon. It's amazing what high gas prices can do. Mama can't afford the gas for her oversized SUV, uh, sorry buddy, and suddenly there's an oil crisis. I'm thinking this is just a formality, but we need to convince them of the viability."

"That's great! When do you go?"

"You mean, when do *we* go? It's your project—we go together. Our flight leaves at six, so I'd advise you to wrap things up here, go home and pack. Bring a nice suit. You do own a suit, don't you? Tell me Janie didn't take all your clothes too."

"Ha ha very funny, Jeff. Hey, do you think we should take our environmental guys with us? If the committee attacks anything, it'll be the environmental impacts."

"Hmmm. Always thinking about the environment, aren't you?" Jeff hesitated, tapping his pen on the desk. "Good idea. Bring John. And dust off that presentation we gave to the board of directors. There might be some information on volume estimates and maps that we can use."

Brandon made it home, packed an overnight bag and met Jeff and John at O'Hare. The plane ride was uneventful and after a half-hour wait in the taxi queue, the trio crammed themselves into a cab on their way to the Hyatt Regency on Capitol Hill.

"Brandon, you've been fidgeting all evening. You've got to learn to relax a little." Jeff watched as Brandon flipped the zipper on his backpack back and forth tirelessly. He reached over and grabbed Brandon's hand and squeezed. "Relax, buddy."

"I know. I know. I'm just a little apprehensive about this hearing. This has been one of the toughest energy subcommittees ever."

"Yeah, and look at the shape we're in. Domestic natural gas supplies are being depleted at an alarming rate while imports of expensive liquid natural gas from Algeria are increasing. Soon we'll be as dependant on foreign supplies of gas as we are on foreign oil." Jeff reached up and squeezed Brandon's shoulder. "*You're* the expert here, remember?"

Brandon went back to flipping his zipper.

"Okay, when we get to the hotel I'm sending you a couple of cold Budweisers to calm your nerves."

Two hours later in the plush hotel room, he lay back with his cold brew and watched CNN cover the Iraqi war, which was the current excuse why gas and oil prices had gone through the roof. After an hour of car bombs and innocent civilians being carried off bleeding in stretchers, he fell into a fitful sleep.

The next morning, the trio endured a barrage of intensive security screening at the entrance to the capitol building before being escorted to a meeting room near the senate chamber. Senator Macmillan's young brunette page greeted them with a carafe of coffee and a disinterested glance.

"Senator Macmillan's committee will be in very shortly. Can I get you anything in the meantime?" she asked, using her most professional voice.

"No thanks," Jeff said. "I think we're good."

Senator Macmillan was the quintessential politician and a fixture on the Hill. Pushing seventy, he was legendary for facial expressions caught on camera and displayed on CSPAN. Recent injections of Botox rendered his once lively features expressionless and a silver rug carefully covered his balding head. Once tall and strong, arthritis and age hunched his back. His once thick, steady hands had transformed into frail, thin-skinned, trembling claws. Although his body was failing, his mind and personality remained razor sharp.

After introductions, the committee sat on one side of the large ornate wood table, leaving the Interex staff on the other side, providing the setting for a confrontational atmosphere from the start.

"The national energy subcommittee will now come to order," Macmillan said as be banged his gavel on the cherry desk. "Gentlemen, thank you so much for being here today. As you know, in light of our present energy situation, the president wishes us to explore a proposal that Interex has brought to the table."

"We're very happy and excited to review our proposed project with you. I know there are some concerns, but after you see our projections, I believe you'll be able to recommend this proposal without hesitation," Jeff said.

"Mr. Hargrove," Macmillan said, dramatically clearing his throat. "I have read the projections. You make some pretty hefty claims here. I'm just a little curious about how you came up with these outlandish figures."

"Sir, I assure you they are not outlandish. We have solid scientific data to support our research and estimates."

The senator glanced down at some notes pretending to read something, then raised his head to glare at the three men from Interex.

"Ah, yes, Dr. Stiles, I suppose you wouldn't mind explaining to this committee why on earth we should allow your company to take heavy drilling equipment into such a pristine environment and adulterate nature with a bunch of oil wells and pipelines that will pollute the ground and devastate the natural beauty?"

"Senator, first of all, I assure you that we do not intend to devastate the environment." Brandon looked up from his notes into the sharp eyes of the aging Macmillan. "We will take all precautions necessary to make sure there will be no pollution as a result of this project. We've prepared a comprehensive mitigation plan to bring the environment back to its original condition when we're through."

"Mitigation? Dr. Stiles, the very term mitigation implies that you are indeed planning on destroying the environment. But let's not put the cart before the horse here. You see, Doctor, I did a little research of my own. I understand that you have some...well let's just say, unconventional theories that lead you to the conclusion that there *may* be oil reserves in this region." The senator seemed to have a knack for hanging on words for emphasis and was now staring at Brandon over his reading glasses, causing Brandon to look down at his notes.

He took in a deep breath and continued, "Sir, you see, there must be exacting conditions in order for a petroleum pool or gas pocket to form. First, you need organic material. Fossil records in the area indicate this was one of the most active areas for prehistoric life in the world. Second, you need layers of porous rock for the oil and gas to migrate into large pockets."

Come on, Brandon, layman's terms. This guy's an asshole, but you can't sound condescending. "The layers of rock that formed in this area of land during the Jurassic and Cretaceous Periods were primarily loose shale, sedimentary rock and sandstones—which are perfect for the migration of liquids and gases. Third, you need an impervious cap so the lighter-than-water petroleum doesn't float to the surface, and the gas doesn't migrate and dissipate into the atmosphere as it does in modern day landfills."

Again, Brandon paused to gather his thoughts. "There is a dense layer of igneous rock, primarily granite, which formed over the project area that makes for a perfect cap."

"Let me stop you there, Dr. Stiles. Gentlemen?" Senator Macmillan turned his head to make eye contact with his committee. "Are there *any* questions thus far?"

The glassy-eyed trio of junior senators shook their heads from side to side in unison.

"Okay, I have one then," Macmillan said. "Doctor, why here? Why on earth can't you move your blasted project a hundred miles north or southeast? Why do you have to drill between Yellowstone National Park and Bighorn National Forest? President Ulysses S. Grant is likely rolling in his grave with the consideration of the degradation of the oldest national park in our country's history."

"Sir, the area of land where both these parks are located had been either placed under the huge burden of super-volcanic activity, or up-thrust, or heaved over time. That would allow the methane gas and petroleum to migrate to geologic structures that were not under pressure. In other words, the creation of the mountains that now form Yellowstone and Bighorn squeezed the oil and gas, much the way you would squeeze water out of a sponge, into the Bighorn Basin. The impervious layer of granite nearer the surface now protects the largest oil and gas field not lying a thousand feet beneath the ocean."

"This site has been on the top of my priority list since my dissertation. The size should rival those in the Middle East, China, and Russia. It will help this country become energy self-sufficient for at least fifty years and at a reasonable cost. And to calm your fears about cluttering the countryside with oil pumping rocking horses, newer pumpers are being made that are almost unnoticeable. The scenery in Yellowstone and Bighorn will be preserved, after the actual drilling that is."

"Yes, yes, Doctor. Now I understand why the president is so enamored by this proposal. You do weave an alluring tale. As I understand, and have alluded to before, you have an interesting theory about the extinction of dinosaurs. You say they all died at once from, uh hum, a *nasty cold*." The senator's remark brought some feigned coughs from several of the committee members, as they raised fists to their mouths and tried to stifle their laughter. "In fact, if my sources are correct, Doctor, you were almost thrown out of the highly regarded Yale Paleontology Program when you presented your doctoral dissertation on the subject."

Brandon felt his face burning. *Maintain control.* "Well, Senator, it was more like a flu bug than a cold, really." He decided to hand the senator's smugness back, bringing laughter. Even the elderly lady recording the proceedings cracked a smile.

"First off, I believe that the dinosaurs had a reason for dying, other than a meteor impact. And that reason for dying was a virus or viruses. One of the smallest forms of life was responsible for killing off the largest forms of life. Although I do not think viruses alone caused the extinction of dinosaurs, large populations were killed off quickly as the victims of diseases. Those large quantities dying off rapidly have formed large oil and gas deposits. My successful finds in the Four Corners Region of the U.S., Africa, Patagonia and China are proof that there is credence to my theory,

Senator."

Brandon stood up. "Bubonic Plague, smallpox, Spanish Flu, Hanta Virus, Ebola, SARS, I could go on and on, have killed hundreds of millions of people and animals throughout time." Pausing for emphasis, he continued. "Senator, did you know that the Spanish Flu pandemic in 1918 killed over eight million in Spain alone? Can you imagine the biomass of thousands of creatures the size of dinosaurs lying together in a graveyard?"

The senator sat expressionless, staring at Brandon.

"We've been able to effectively wipe out smallpox because researchers developed an effective vaccine and the virus wasn't able to mutate and change in order to survive. Flu viruses, on the other hand, continually mutate and that's why we can't eradicate them. There are some viruses that can survive outside a body, in soil or suspended in air. You see, a new virus can ravage an unprotected population and these creatures never had a chance to develop the necessary immune systems."

"So not only are you an engineer and paleontologist, but you are a medical doctor as well?" the senator asked.

"Sir, I saw first hand what a new epidemic can do. I was in China when SARS hit. I was in the very province where it emerged. I lost a very close friend to it. I've also done considerable research in the area to support my theory."

"Yes, Doctor, I have read about your deportation from China. But since the details are classified, I won't go into that here," the senator said.

Brandon took a deep breath. He couldn't let the memories come pouring out. Not here. Not now. "Senator, have you heard of Leonardo, the mummified Brachylophosarus, or duck-billed dinosaur found in Montana two years ago?"

"No, I haven't."

"The curator of paleontology of the Phillips County Museum in Montana is a friend of mine. He invited me to come down and have a look. You see, actual soft tissue was found preserved with the skeleton—an extreme rarity. Dr. Kurt Edmonds found Leonardo and is intimately familiar with my theories. Leonardo was so well preserved that even the contents of his stomach were intact. We were able to tell that Leonardo ate ferns and a variety of a magnolia plant just before he died. Pollen of over forty species of plants was identified in his stomach and we were able to ascertain that there was, in fact, an unidentifiable virus present."

"Okay, let's stop this right here," Senator Macmillan said, holding up his hand. "For the record, I have been instructed by the president to make this project work. This is an election year. It's time for the president to run for re-election and he feels he needs to start addressing high gas and oil prices. Therefore, this committee will approve your project and recommend its immediate commencement."

Macmillan took off his reading glasses and leaned forward, staring hard at the men across the table. "Gentlemen, this approval will *not* come without stipulations. You *will* work with the Department of Interior and the Wyoming Department of Environmental Quality and Fish and Game to ensure there will be no environmental impacts. You will be closely monitored by the agencies and shut down at the first hint of environmental damage. You will have one shot at this. Do I make myself clear?"

Senator Macmillan stood suddenly and walked out of the room without so much as an acknowledgement. The junior senator from California opened his binder and took them through the details and stipulations of the approval. After an hour of questions and answers, the trio from Interex strutted from the capitol building beaming with smiles. They were about to make their stockholders very happy.

After the flight attendant served Jeff and Brandon lukewarm Budweisers, Jeff turned to Brandon, speaking very softly. "Brandon, I'm confused. You told Macmillan that you lost someone to SARS."

The words hit him like a punch in the stomach. "I wondered if you'd catch that. I shouldn't have let it slip..." Brandon wiped at his eyes to stop the tears from running down his cheeks.

"Hey, if you don't want to—"

Brandon raised his hand. "Jeff, Ling Mae died of SARS."

"Oh shit. I'm sorry, Brandon. But...you said she decided not to leave her parents after they sent you home."

"That's what the U.S. Embassy made me say."

"Oh, God, I didn't know. I would have never asked. Maybe someday, when the time is right, you'll be able to fill me in on what really happened over there." Jeff reached over and patted Brandon on the shoulder.

"Thanks, Jeff. There's not a day that goes by that I don't think about her."

The muted roar of the powerful jet engines filled an awkward silence until Jeff broke it. "Do you have any problems bringing Dallas Wheeler on as the drilling supervisor?"

"Is he available?" Brandon asked.

"He is now. That piddly well he's working on now is nothing."

"You know I love Dallas like a brother."

"Yeah, but he was there. He thinks Ling Mae left you as well."

"I'll never forget those eight months, Jeff. So, having Dallas around again may just be good therapy."

"Anyway, I want to strike hard and fast on this one. I don't want to give the Middle East Cartel a chance to catch wind of this and give Macmillan a reason to change his mind. Do whatever you have to do to get this thing moving."

Brandon extracted his computer from under the seat and began typing a list of things to do.

Chapter Eight

Billings, Montana
April 15, 2004

Two weeks passed with a flurry of activity and twenty-hour days, and with Brandon and Jack "Dallas" Wheeler finding themselves in the 1940's vintage Big Sky Motel. Crumbling mortar held irregular chunks of pink granite forming drafty walls around faded blue doors. Chimneys made of the same pink stone poked through the slate roof and blue wood shutters flanked cloudy, single-pane windows. A small stone cabin in the opposite corner of the parking lot served as the owner's living quarters and office.

"What a dump!" Brandon stomped on a roach hustling across the fraying area rug covering chipped squares of floor tiles. The squish of the bug's body being ground into the carpet caused his face to scrunch in disgust. "This place reminds me of the Bates motel in *Psycho.* I expected to see Norman Bates dressed in an old granny dress standing over me in bed wielding a butcher knife last night."

"Ah, com'n Doc. Ole' Normie only killed people in the shower. We've stayed in worse. Besides, how many hotels have you stayed in with these quaint stone fireplaces?" Dallas said in his slow Texas drawl.

"Yeah, right. The damper was stuck open and I nearly froze from the wind whistling down the flue. Nights are still pretty cool up here." Brandon looked around the makeshift office. "I expect this crap in China or Africa, or some other third-world country. In the United States I expect a little better. Damn bugs are everywhere."

"Just a 'lil Montana wildlife. At least the manager is a nice guy. I mean, he's pretty much kissed both your butt cheeks since we moved in."

"What? He moves the bed out of a room and brings in a couple of beat-up tables and he's kissing my ass?"

"Don't forget the DSL line *and* the extra phone line for the fax."

"Whoopee do. Well, do me a favor. Find an exterminator and see how quick you can get him here. Interex is paying the bill. Christ! You should've seen the size of the roach that walked up my arm last night while I was sleeping." Brandon shivered just thinking about it. "Ugh! Talk about getting a case of the willies. I was afraid to close my eyes the rest of the night."

"You got it, Doc." Dallas pulled himself to the edge of the overstuffed chair with a grunt and reached for the small dust-covered phone book sitting under the night stand in the corner of the room. A few minutes later, he flipped the cell phone closed. "Doc, I got 'The Bug Man' comin' out in about an hour. I told him we'd make it worth his while."

"Excellent. So what's the situation with the equipment?"

"There're plenty of land-based rigs available. Not much drillin' goin' on these days. Wyatt's knockin' the rust off his big rig and should be on his way by the end of the week. I got us a local dirt movin' contractor headed out Monday. That way we can start working with EPA on the mud pit. Let's see...what else?" Dallas tapped his wrinkled forehead as if trying to dredge up thoughts. "Hopefully with any luck, we'll have the bit in the ground by May 1st."

"Okay, I'll call Mr. Evans and tell him that we'll be bringing in equipment Monday or Tuesday. We'll treat him to a big steak dinner. Although, he's going to be a rich man from the royalties he'll collect." Brandon added things to his to-do list as he talked through the project with Dallas.

"Doc, if Evans asks ya to get into a friendly poker game, just say no. Ya know he won that spread in a game of five card draw."

"I didn't know that."

"Yep, that's the scoop. Drew four sixes. So I'm guessin' we got the right-of-entry agreement squared away?"

"Evans signed it last night. The fax arrived this morning. Sounds like the Four Sixes Ranch will be the site of our new well," Brandon answered. "Things seem to be going according to plan. This'll sure as hell be a first. Now, let's just hope there's actually some gas or oil down there."

"Doc, I've drilled for a lot of lame-ass desk jockeys in my time. There's none I trust more than you," Dallas confided.

"So I'm a lame-assed desk jockey?"

"That's just it, Doc. I don't consider you a desk jockey. You actually know what it's like out here because you spend your time in the patch."

"Thanks, Dallas."

Dallas had shaved his thinning gray hair into a crew cut, which seemed to deepen the weathered crevasses in his forehead and around his eyes. His square jaw and hooked nose gave him the look of an aging drill sergeant. He still had a barrel chest and thick arms that the ladies loved, but age and beer were starting to build a spare tire around his once muscled gut. Interex Exploration's top drilling supervisor had been working with Brandon for the past twelve years. He was born and raised in west Texas and had worked in the oil patch all of his life. A tireless worker, Dallas knew the field aspect of the oil and gas business as well as anyone.

"Hey, by the way, Montana Gas is starting a twelve-inch pipeline from the West Continent Main Transmission Line to the drill site," Brandon added after a pause. "They'll take the equivalent gas in transportation charges to supply Billings. That way we won't have to worry about constructing a pipeline for the gas right away."

"So where's the petroleum going?"

Brandon scratched his head. "Well, that's a bigger problem. The liquids are going to have to go southeast to the AmerOil pipeline near Casper. That's quite a haul and I hear AmerOil is in the process of getting the permits for a twenty-inch pipeline. In other words, we have a lot at stake in this dig and a lot of people are spending a lot of money gambling on us. If we don't deliver...well, let's just say I'll never work in this town again."

Chapter Nine

New York City
May 1, 2004

Saif Yasin headed north on the subway, taking the Eighth Avenue Local from his apartment in Greenwich Village to the 96th Street Central Park West Station. Pushing through the thick subway crowd, he made his way up the stairs to the street where his nose was free of the stale perspiration-tinged air. Dodging mothers jogging behind three-wheeled strollers, he maintained a brisk pace through the park, making quick turns and glancing over his shoulder. The sounds of car horns grew louder as he neared the east boundary of Central Park. Two short blocks later, he trotted down a long escalator and boarded the Lexington Avenue Local and rode the distance to East Tremont. Back on street level, he hailed a cab and backtracked to Castle Hill Avenue.

Flipping a twenty at the driver, he swung the door open and exited the cab without saying a word. His paced slowed considerably the last two blocks, carefully pausing and looking around every hundred yards or so. From where the cab dropped him, Saif's dark eyes were alert. This time, he was not watching for a government agent, he was watching for his own safety. This neighborhood was overrun with junkies and their suppliers, whores and their pimps, and gangs.

After climbing the stairs to the front entrance of a run-down apartment building, Saif stopped to pat his pants pockets pretending to look for keys that weren't there. After a final survey of the street, he was certain he wasn't followed. He quickly ducked in the door and buzzed apartment 4B.

"Yes?" a voice crackled from the intercom.

"This is Sam. I have your package."

"Come." There was no emotion in the voice from the brittle speaker.

He hurried up the stairs rather than risk being trapped in a rickety elevator. Saif surveyed the hallway. Graffiti-covered paint flaked off the walls and the air reeked of cigarettes and urine. At the door marked 4B he took a deep breath and rapped his knuckles on the door frame, twice.

The door creaked open to a well maintained and comfortable flat—quite a contrast to the neighborhood and the building. The four members of his cell waited patiently. Unlike Saif, the others were obviously of Middle Eastern descent, but all were clean-shaven, meticulously groomed and dressed casually, but neatly. All of them possessed nearly accent-free English.

Growing up in the United States, Saif never developed a Middle Eastern accent. In order to remain as veiled as possible, he enlisted a speech pathologist to rid himself of his slight New York speech pattern. He dressed neither flashy nor trashy. Like a white Honda Accord blended into a parking lot, Saif's life depended on melting into the background. Every move he made was carefully calculated, including his tardiness to flaunt the power he wielded as cell leader. He shook each member's hand and pulled them close for a manly hug slapping each man on the back. He dragged a cushioned kitchen chair to the 'L' shape of the tan leather couches and straddled it, resting his arms on the back.

"Let's get started. I have an appointment in three hours that I must keep. Azzim, is there any word from the doctor in Virginia?"

Azzim was a killer. His specialty was weaponry, but he could kill efficiently with anything, including his hands. He was dark skinned and tall with bulging muscles covered by thin skin. A loyal follower, he was not very bright and needed specific instructions.

"I spoke to him last night. He insists that the security has been tight. He no longer has access to the virus research area, but he claims to be cultivating a close relationship with one of the researchers there." Azzim leaned forward. "He says he is being very cautious not to raise suspicions. He also mentioned his friend at the Centers for Disease Control in Atlanta will call him on outbreaks."

"Do you think he is lying to us again?"

"I don't think so. Not since your message long ago."

Saif raised his hands to form a triangle in front of his face as if pondering something of great interest and importance. "I received new instructions early this week. Our superiors are trusting us to succeed this time. We have an encrypted web site with our new orders." He slid a paper across the table. "There is a URL on this paper. Once there, place the cursor in the center of the logo on the page and hold the 'alt' and 'shift' key while clicking the mouse. You will be redirected to the site with instructions."

"What is it, Brother Saif?" Azzim asked.

"We have been instructed to build and detonate a radiation dirty bomb. There are instructions for each stage. First we must collect the radioactive material. There is a list of radiation sources which may not be as secure as most."

His gaze shifted to Ahmed Halid. Halid stared back with shadowed dark eyes that shouted evil. Even early in the afternoon, dark stubble erupted around his chin. His thin, short physique concealed steely muscles. "Ahmed, I have an assignment for you."

Ahmed, a new addition to the cell, spoke softly. "Yes, Brother, what is your will?"

"A Muslim guard working for a security firm in Spokane, Washington, has the first stockpile of devices we must acquire." Saif recalled the data from memory. "There is a large stockpile of smoke detectors with Americium-241 radioactive sources being stored for installation in a new apartment complex. The sources are small, but they will go unnoticed if they are missing."

"I know these types of devices, Saif," Ahmed said. "I worked with these types of sealed radiation sources for my former employer."

Ahmed graduated in Iran as an electrical engineer. He took a job with a German manufacturer of radiation devices before being transferred by the company to the United States. Two months ago, he quit his job and moved to New York. His employer thought he quit to return to his family in Iran. Instead he stayed in New York and was recruited by Saif's superior.

"Yes, I see now why our superiors sent you to us. That knowledge will serve you well. Look at the list on the web site. There are other possibilities in the area around Spokane that you may be able to take while you are there."

"What do you mean? What other possibilities?"

"There is a pipeline project being built near Billings, Montana. The United States department of transportation requires that the welds of pipelines be x-rayed. The x-ray companies are normally very sloppy with their equipment. I looked on the NRC website and read many incidents of these x-ray companies and what they call well loggers that lose radioactive sources. They transport sources in their trucks from job to job. One of these sources is larger than the whole shipment of smoke detectors," Saif finished.

"Very good. I will leave immediately."

"If you have an opportunity to take the additional sources, you must be very careful. We must complete this mission. It shouldn't take longer than two weeks. Take Ali with you." Saif extracted a thick envelope from his jacket and handed it to Ahmed. "Here is enough cash to get you through."

"We will," Ali said. "It is an honor to be chosen for this task."

"Very well. Fear Allah as He should be feared, and die not except in a state of Islam. Remember, whomever Allah enlightens will not be misguided and the deceiver will never be guided." Saif bowed his head slightly toward Ahmed and Ali. He then turned to the last member of the cell. "Fahid, it will be your job to build the detonation device. You are the only member to have that knowledge."

"Yes, Saif." Fahid's flabby cheeks jiggled with a shake of his head. His chunky body ended in rock-steady hands with slender fingers that were perfect for working on explosives and triggers.

"You must be mindful when and where you obtain the materials. You will let me know your plans before you proceed. We must be careful because the government and people are now vigilant." Saif flashed Fahid an approving look. "Our superiors will be pleased to know we are proceeding quickly. To fail would be to dishonor Allah and ourselves. That must not happen."

Saif pushed back from the table, and motioned to Ahmed. "I wish to speak to you in private."

Ahmed followed Saif into a small bedroom and shut the door. Saif sat in a chair in the corner of the room and motioned to the bed for Ahmed to sit. "Ahmed. I do not know much about you, but I trust my superior's judgment. He said you were a capable leader. We cannot tolerate mistakes. Our last mission was not as effective as we hoped. As Josef discovered, that will not happen again. You must plan each step carefully and execute each step with extreme care."

"Do not worry, Saif. I will not fail you. Before I left my homeland I trained rigorously for a mission of this type. I know these devices and how to handle them. What can you tell me about Ali?"

"Ali is committed to our cause, but watch him closely. Patience is not a virtue he possesses. Do not allow him to act independently. He is a generalist and is clever—street smart. He is good with weapons and especially effective with a sniper rifle. He catches on to things quickly, but must be given strong direction." Saif stood and slapped Ahmed on the back. "Remember, keep me informed."

He opened the door and left without looking back.

Chapter Ten

Four Sixes Ranch
Bighorn Basin
May 6, 2004

Brandon stepped out of the rented office trailer to stretch his long legs and was met by a view that caused his jaw to drop—one that was spoiled only by the massive drilling rig, the clanging of pipes and roar of the generators and rig engine. This truly is God's country, he thought.

The Four Sixes Ranch, located in the Bighorn Basin near the Greybull River, sprawled in a large natural depression surrounded by the majestic Tetons to the west, the Bighorn Mountains to the east and the Owl Creek and Bridger Mountains to the south. The Tetons and the Bighorn Mountains reached over twelve thousand feet into the heavens. Well above the tree line, the pinkish hue of granite and copper-tinted sandstone displayed a wondrous range of colors and moods as the sun swept across the sky.

A loud, high-pitched ringer interrupted his serenity. Only a handful of people knew the number of the satellite phone. That would be Jeffery Hargrove checking on the progress of the well.

"...as usual, things are behind schedule. The environmental permitting for the generators didn't get approval on time and the drilling mud pits had to be rebuilt with an additional polyethylene liner. I may be paranoid, Jeff, but I'm convinced Senator Macmillan has the Wyoming Department of Environmental Quality doing everything possible to delay the project."

"Hang in there, Brandon. I'll see if there's anything I can do on this end."

"Thanks. We'll keep plugging away here."

Brandon pushed the end button as Dallas strolled up to him chewing on a big wad of bubblegum. "Bee-u-tee-ful, ain't it, Doc?"

"It's quite a sight. I especially love the sunrise." His mind pictured the brilliant orb of the sun edging over the lower peaks of the southern Bighorn Mountains and spreading yellowish-orange light on the jagged Teton Peaks. Thrust from the earth's core, the crystalline fragments in the fire-forged rock reflected the sun like diamonds flashing in firelight.

"Now I know why the senator had such a hard-on about stopping the project," Dallas drawled, gazing in the distance.

"Yeah well, people have their priorities in life and gas guzzling SUVs and minivans are more important to the voting soccer moms of the world than preserving the beauty of nature. Oh sure, if it doesn't directly impact their lives—"

"Hey Doc, not to call the kettle black or anythin', but how many gallons to the mile does that Land Cruiser of yours get?" Dallas quipped with a smile that transformed the weathered creases in his face into shadowed chasms.

"Look who's talking, Mister I'm Driving a Hummer."

"But I'm not the one waxin' rhapsodic 'bout the environment."

"Yeah, yeah, it's a gas hog, but I only put about two-thousand miles a year on it. You drove almost that far just to get here from Dallas, Dallas." Brandon giggled at his own joke.

"You're full of crap, Doc. It was only fourteen hundred miles." The loud hollow clank of pipes banging together filled the air as the steel drill pipes were pieced together into a single stem pushing the bit deeper into the earth. "Aw, shit, I forgot, I came over to introduce you to our well loggers." He had to yell over the deafening roar of the rig motors that started suddenly spewing a big puff of black smoke.

They walked over to a specially built truck which looked like a small moving van, where two rather rough looking middle-aged men stood. Both sported ragged beards and long stringy hair. Besides one being a little shorter and wearing slightly cleaner clothes than the other, they could have been twins. *Well loggers were an odd lot*, Brandon thought as they approached. Dallas always did contend that the radiation killed off their brain cells after a while.

"Hello, I'm Brandon Stiles. You know we won't be ready for you for another week." Brandon extended a hand.

"Hey there, my name is Billy Goller and this here is Jimmy Buck." The cleaner of the duo stepped forward, grabbed Brandon's hand and pumped hard. "We've been up in Bismarck loggin' a gas well and thought we'd swing by and scope things out. We're on our way down to the home office in Laramie to drop off our Americium sources. They're pretty much depleted. You expectin' this to be a big reservoir?"

"Everything points to that. And we're sure as hell hoping it is," Brandon answered. "I want a sonic and a nuclear run. If you don't have a generator, we can provide power."

"Ten-four. Good meetin' you, Mr. Stiles," Billy said as Jimmy stood in the background shifting his weight from side-to-side staring at the ground and chewing on a big chaw of tobacco.

"We'll call you when we're ready," Dallas added.

As the two men walked back to their truck, Dallas turned to Brandon. "Well, Billy looks okay, not sure about that other fella though. From the look on his face, you'd think there was somethin' earth shattering about that little patch of ground he was starin' at. I'm tellin' ya Doc, the radiation musta done killed his last brain cell."

"I think I remember those two from *Deliverance*," Brandon quipped. "And I don't mean the guys in the rafts."

Dallas erupted in a big belly laugh and walked away.

The sun was just dipping behind the Teton peaks when Brandon and Dallas began their drive back to the Vista View Condominiums in Cody bouncing down the dirt access road in the company Humvee. *Cody must have been a quaint little town thirty years ago. Now it was overly commercialized and looked out of place in the countryside. Being so close to Yellowstone may have brought prosperity to this town, but destroyed its charm in the process.*

"Buffalo Bill Bar, Doc?" Dallas asked, bringing Brandon back to reality.

"Sure, why not. The bison burgers are growing on me. By the way, I'm going back to Billings tomorrow. I have a meeting with Montana Gas on the status of the pipeline and the tie-in schedule to West Continent's pipeline. I've also got to answer a bunch of e-mails and touch base with the office."

On their first visit to the Buffalo Bill Bar, the proprietor told them the history of the bar while pouring moonshine whiskey into shot glasses. He explained that it was an original venture of Buffalo Bill Cody, one of the founding fathers of Cody, Wyoming. The bar looked like it belonged in a Clint Eastwood spaghetti western, with its wood façade and swinging saloon entry doors that hid the inner energy efficient glass door.

Inside, well-worn wood planks formed the floors with tables that matched. There was an ornate hand-carved bar that ran along the entire back wall with hundreds of bottles of liquor sitting on shelves, flanked by a large mirror that could have come right from a Hollywood set. Stuffed wild game adorned the walls and a large buffalo head stood sentry over the bar. An obligatory jackalope hung in the hallway leading to the bathrooms.

Neon and backlit beer signs were absent from the walls. There were no televisions and the large chandeliers hanging from the ceiling were fitted with natural gas flames instead of light bulbs. All the rest of the lighting was indirect so it appeared that the bar was an authentic 1890's saloon. Even the bartender and waitresses were dressed in Old West attire. The place was only half-full when they arrived. Not quite tourist season, the town seemed relatively deserted.

"You know, Dallas, this place would be great if it weren't so damn smoky. Seems like everybody in this town smokes." Brandon waved his hand in front of his nose as they walked through the swinging saloon doors.

"Well, Doc, you know this here's Wyoming where men are men and sheep are nervous. Up here, real men smoke. You know I gave up smoking cause of your allergies."

"Bullshit, you gave it up because Alice cut you off until you did."

"Yeah she did, but hell, she's always cuttin' me off for some odd reason."

An attractive full-figured forty-something woman, face thick with make-up and trailing the scent of perfume, greeted them at the door as they entered. Her face, stature and even her voice reminded Brandon of Rosie O'Donnell. "Hey, Dallas. Hi, Doc. You're later than usual. Just the two of you tonight?"

"Yeah, Delores, I figured it was time the Doc here met the late crew." Dallas slipped his hand around her cinched waist and pulled her in for a hug. She whispered something in his ear and pulled away, playfully slapping him on the shoulder.

"Well, you'd be the man to make the introductions, you big flirt. Follow me." She led them to their table, swinging hips that were accentuated by the tight corset around her midriff. "Debbie will be your waitress tonight."

As she walked away, Brandon asked, "Don't tell me. You're doing Delores?"

Dallas grinned. "She's one wild babe in bed, let me tell ya."

"I should've figured."

"Remember the fifteen-hundred mile rule, Doc."

"Yeah, yeah, what happens in Cody—"

"Stays in Cody," Dallas finished.

"I thought it was the ten-thousand mile rule."

"It is when you're in Hukou, China. Funny thing about that rule, it's time and space dependant. Damn, I haven't thought about those Chinese massage girls in a long, long time." Dallas' grin spread from ear to ear.

Brandon opened the leather-bound parchment menu that he had memorized. The list of wild game dishes dominated the pages, save for a few standard items for big city folk. The house specialties were alligator tail and bison burger.

"You know, Dallas, I can make the connection to the bison burger, but I'm pretty damn sure there aren't any alligators within fifteen-hundred miles of here," Brandon said.

A waitress sauntered up to the table. "Hey, Dallas, who's your handsome friend?"

"Debbie, meet Doc Stiles."

"Oh, you're a doctor?" Debbie's eyes widened a bit.

"Yes, but not the kind you're thinking of. Please, call me Brandon."

She gazed at Brandon displaying a big smile and held eye contact a little longer than he was comfortable with. Finally, with a hint of a western drawl, she said, "You have the most interesting eyes, Brandon. What color are they? It's hard to see in this light."

"Uh, that's a good question. My driver's license says blue, but I think they're more like gray."

"May I?" Debbie asked, already leaning in. Without waiting for an answer, she reached for his chin and raised and turned his head for a good look. "I don't think I've ever seen eyes that color—kind of a bluish-gray...no, almost silver, but brighter than most. Sorry for being so forward but I have this thing for men's eyes. Windows to the soul, you know. And yours...well, there's wisdom and maybe some sorrow there." She blinked as if she were roused from a trance and continued, "Anyway, the specials are on the board and we're out of the elk ribs for the night. Can I get you something to drink?"

They placed their drink orders and as Debbie walked away, Dallas rolled his eyes. "Damn, Doc, she sure likes you. She never looked at me like that. She wants you bad. I'll bet she could take your mind off your worries for a night."

That brought a chuckle from Brandon. *It was nice to be noticed by a woman again.* It had been a long time since his romance with Mae, and Debbie was pretty, although not beautiful, and had a natural, sensual aura about her. Her smile...it was her smile that really grabbed him.

Brandon had always been a bit self-conscious about his looks. He had a good natural complexion, but he thought his nose was a bit big and his face too full. The Chinese called him "da bizi" or "big nose." The term wasn't used in the derogatory sense; it was just fact among a race of flat faced people. His brown, medium-length hair was very straight and unruly and was beginning to gray around the temples. However, he knew his eyes were his best feature.

"Hey, Doc, I was meanin' ta ask. I mean ya don't hafta answer if you don't want to..."

"You mean Ling Mae?"

"Yeah, I do. Whatever happened? I mean ya'll seemed so into each other when I was there."

Brandon glanced around at the empty tables next to them in the no-smoking section of the Buffalo Bill Bar. "Dallas, I wanted to tell you. But I was under a gag order. Mae died."

"What the fuck?" Dallas blurted.

Brandon shushed him, looking around to see that nobody noticed them. "She died of SARS, Dallas. Not long after you left." The look on Dallas' face was one Brandon hadn't seen before.

"A week after you left I took Hank Chu to investigate the shoddy piping that was being installed in the village. I was worried that someone would blow themselves up. The Chinese government decided to give gas to the local villagers so they didn't worry about losing their coal mining jobs and sabotage the wells or the pipeline." Brandon hesitated, trying to sort out how to tell his friend the story. "You remember how crappy the welding was over there. Well, there were gas leaks everywhere."

"Yeah, but that had been going on for a week before I left."

"Well, anyway, Mae had returned from a weekend at her parent's home in the village and I had her sign the paperwork for the marriage and our trip to the States. The next morning she woke up real sick. I got her to the medical clinic in Hukou. God, the conditions were deplorable." Brandon winced at his memory of that day.

They had bounced along the dusty, dirt road for twenty minutes before arriving at a small building in the center of the village. A dirt path led to a dilapidated structure of stacked, crumpling brick. It looked centuries old. A tilted, weathered sign with the Chinese characters for "Hukou Medical Clinic" hung above a splintery door propped open with a brick that had dislodged from the front of the building.

Patients lined the dirt path leading to the open door. Some of them, mostly village elders, looked on the verge of death—squatting, waiting patiently.

Inside the clinic, the conditions were worse. Dirty, ragged patients, jammed into a small waiting area in the single room, stared at the American with blank almond eyes. A makeshift curtained cubicle set up in one corner served as an examination room while a new natural gas space heater occupied another corner. Judging by the dirt outline on the floor, it recently replaced an old coal-fired heater. Hank had argued with a nurse standing behind a small counter made from milk crates and old wood planks.

"Hank got them to take Mae right away. They took one look at her and ordered me to take her to Beijing."

"Beijing? Shit that was a long way from Hukou."

"Six hours by van to Linfen and thirteen hours by train. And the train station...some things are burned into your brain. The sick were everywhere. The concrete boarding platform was like a living, moving floor. There were no seats and most of the people seemed too sick and weak to stand. They squatted or lay on the concrete. The sounds...oh my God, Dallas, I can still hear the moans of agony that filled the air as I made my way to the ticket counter. The ticket office was jammed with hoards of people desperate to purchase tickets." Brandon shook his head.

"It was a fucking mob scene, Dallas. I was scared shitless. When the train came, it was mayhem. People surged forward, using what little strength they had, jamming on that train. It looked like a thousand got left behind."

"When we got to the People's Hospital of Peking University, they took Mae through a secured steel door and I never saw her again."

"Holy shit, Doc. Why didn't you tell me all this?"

"I wanted to, Dallas, I really did. But I couldn't. Shit, I'm not supposed to be telling you now."

Dallas scratched at the stubbles of gray hair on his head. "Why?"

"I waited for hours to hear about Mae. They wouldn't tell me anything. I got sick of waiting. I watched a doctor punch in the security code to the door they took Mae through. On the other side was some kind of large courtyard with three massive tents, like circus tents, only these had airlock entrances. There must have been thousands of people dying in those tents. Dying of SARS, Dallas. Christ, I can still see their frightened faces."

"Wait, I thought it wasn't all that bad." Dallas continued scratching at his head.

"It's a Communist country, Dallas. They control the media. Shit, they control everything, including the American Embassy. That's why I'm under orders not to talk about it. I got caught looking in the tents. A guard cracked me over the head with the butt of his rifle. I woke up days later at the American Embassy. The embassy negotiated my release; otherwise I'd be rotting in a Chinese jail."

"Jeeesus," Dallas drawled.

"The U.S. didn't want to jeopardize China's place in the World Trade Organization so they turned their back on the SARS cover-up and quietly shipped me home with orders not to discuss it with anybody. I'm telling you, Dallas, there were literally thousands of people and then there were the people that were left on that train station platform in Linfen."

"Geez, Doc, I'm speechless."

"Hmm, that's a first." He shot Dallas a forced grin attempting to break the somber mood just as Debbie returned with their food.

"I hope you enjoy it, Brandon." Debbie turned, shot a quick wink over her shoulder and sauntered off.

After finishing dinner, Brandon and Dallas headed back for the condo. The accommodations here were much better than the motel in Billings, but the cell phones didn't work well and there was only dial-up Internet connectivity. Brandon had rented the three rooms at the Big Sky Motel in Billings for the month, so he opted to leave the equipment there as a more permanent office. They maintained the satellite phone at the trailer for emergencies.

Dallas pulled the yellow Humvee next to the Jeep that Brandon rented in Billings. "This condo was a great idea, Doc." Dallas pulled the keys out of the ignition. "I thought the motels here would be worse than Billings, but this place sure beats the shit out of most places I've stayed."

"Thank the travel agent. She stayed here on vacation last year," he said to Dallas as they crawled out of the beastly vehicle. "I'm leaving at about five-thirty and I'll probably spend the night. Let me know right away if anything comes up."

"You got it, Doc. G'night." Dallas gave his partner and friend a wave as he set off down the dimly lit path to his unit.

Brandon paused a minute to gaze at the star-filled night sky before heading to his room. The sky here seemed as big as it was in Montana. After a minute of reflection of how amazing the universe really was, he trotted up the steps to the spacious condominium. He wondered how he would feel after getting the whole China issue off his chest. It felt good to talk about it—cleansing.

He needed to update the project status spreadsheet so he could fire it off via e-mail as soon as he arrived in Billings. The digital pictures made it too large to send over the slow phone connection. As his laptop booted, Brandon's mind shifted to the electric feel of Debbie's touch, bringing a slight smile to his lips. "*It's been a long time. Too long*," he muttered.

Chapter Eleven

Seattle, Washington
May 7, 2004

Laura Daniels sat at her desk immersed in security plans submitted by biotech companies located in Seattle and Portland. Since 9/11, the Department of Homeland Security required companies that stored large quantities of hazardous materials to develop detailed security plans, but left it to the FBI to review the damn things and pick them apart, and they could be complicated. She reached for the stainless steel travel mug filled with a Starbucks Caramel Macchiato, extra hot.

"Laura."

She jumped and knocked over the tall mug, spilling a dribble of creamy, light-brown liquid on the Siltex haz-mat plan.

"Oh, shit, Bob, you startled me." She grabbed the mug with quick reflexes and sopped up the spilled coffee with a wad of napkins.

"Sorry, but I need you to check out something in Spokane." Robert Williams walked through the doorway to her office.

"What's that?"

"Well, a fairly large shipment of smoke detectors is missing from a construction site."

"Smoke detectors? Why is that a concern?"

Bob went to a chair next to Laura's desk, handed her a file and sat down. "Radiation threat. Many smoke detectors have small radioactive sources in them and being so small, they're nearly unregulated. Which makes them easily accumulated for a dirty bomb."

"Wait—smoke detectors have radioactive sources?"

"Yeah. Well, the missing ones did. They have a small ionizing chamber in them that uses an Americium-241 source tied up in a gold matrix. It would take a huge amount of smoke detector sources to present any real radiation danger, and even then, the blast from the bomb would do far more damage than the radiation, but it's the psychological effect terrorists are after. Explosion goes off, Geiger counter reads trace amounts of radiation and people get scared." He stood up. "It's probably nothing more than a crooked contractor trying to scam the insurance company, but we have to investigate to make sure. It shouldn't take more than a day or two. The info's in the file. I've contacted the Spokane police chief and he knows you're coming. Let me know what you find."

Three hours later, Laura was on the short flight to Spokane, Washington.

The modern brick and glass building housing the Spokane police headquarters sat in the northern quadrant of the downtown area off Main Street near Riverfront Park. Laura entered the large open atrium and approached the information desk in the center of the brightly lit lobby. She showed the officer at the desk her credentials and asked to see Chief Reynolds. The disinterested officer pointed to a waiting area and asked her to have a seat.

Ten minutes later, an elderly black man wearing an impeccably tailored three-piece, blue pin-striped suit strolled up to Laura and introduced himself as Chief Reynolds. He was tall and still carried and athletic build. The swagger in his stride alerted her that she was in for a turf battle.

"Ms. Daniels, it's nice to meet you. Please come with me to my office."

His forced smile and use of the title Ms. instead of Agent, made it clear he didn't recognize her authority. She followed Reynolds up a flight of stairs and through a glass door to his office.

"Please have a seat, Ms. Daniels. Now can you tell me why the FBI is interested in a pissant case like this? Construction sites are ripped off every day."

Obviously, Chief Reynolds was not one to beat around the bush.

"It's *what* was stolen that's the concern. You see, smoke detectors have small radioactive sources in them. Smoke detectors, certain glow-in-the-dark exit signs, some medical devices and well, the list is rather long, but these items are on the FBI watch list because they could be used by terrorists to build dirty bombs." She was thankful that she used her time on the plane to read the information in the file. "The fact that the only thing missing was a large number of smoke detectors raises a red flag."

"Well, it's your time, not mine, Ms. Daniels." Chief Reynolds picked up his desk phone and dialed an extension. "Yeah, Harrison, the FBI is here." He sat the receiver in its cradle and stood up. She was being dismissed without so much as an offer of a cup of coffee. It was sad that so many government agencies couldn't seem to play well together. A short rap on the door and the chief waved in a young and very attractive man before sitting down and turning his attention to a stack of folders.

"Hello, I'm Detective Harrison. I'd be happy to assist you in any way I can." Harrison extended his hand.

Laura met his firm grip and introduced herself. "I'm Special Agent Daniels, FBI Seattle Field Office."

"Nice to meet you, Agent Daniels." Harrison smiled warmly. He held the door open as they headed for the stairs. "Would you like to go directly to the scene? We can talk about the details on the way."

"That would be great. Is there any place I could get a cup of coffee before we leave?" Laura asked, still not able to take her eyes off Detective Harrison.

"We can stop on the way. The coffee here sucks. There's a Starbucks with a drive-through right around the corner if that's okay—my treat." Harrison smiled and added, "We get a nice discount."

"Starbucks would be great."

Detective James Harrison was tall, at least a head taller than Laura, not thin, but not thick, and obviously took care of himself. His short black hair framed a handsome, square face. The only visible flaw was a small scar above his left eye which only served to draw attention to a pair of sparkling hazel eyes accentuated by heavy black eyebrows.

Harrison led Laura to a plain maroon Chevy Impala and followed her to open the passenger side door. *Well, chivalry isn't dead after all*, she thought.

After a quick stop at Starbucks, Harrison pulled out onto Monroe Street and headed north. "Agent Daniels, the apartments are just over the river—about ten minutes from here."

"Please call me Laura. Can you tell me what you found out so far, Detective?"

"Sure, but if I have to call you Laura, you have to call me Jim. All we really know is what the site superintendent's statement says. They were locked in one of the apartments along with lights and doorbells and other electrical equipment. He said the electricians reported the missing equipment shortly after they arrived in the morning. The doors to the hallway entrance and into the apartments were forced open—probably a crowbar."

Laura watched Harrison closely as he drove. He appeared nervous, tapping his finger on the steering wheel and bouncing his left heel to a beat that wasn't there. The car's radio had been removed in lieu of a scanner and on-board computer.

"How big is this apartment complex?" she asked.

"Pretty big. Uh, let's see, maybe two to three hundred units."

"And there are no security guards?"

"Uh, that'll be a good question. So far we haven't done much except taken statements." Harrison's face was now red with embarrassment.

"This theft took place almost two days ago and all you have is statements?"

"Yes, ma'am. But a theft of less than two thousand dollars doesn't get a high priority investigation."

"Detective Harrison, that is *exactly* how a terrorist would operate—flying under the radar, patiently collecting supplies without attracting attention until he's ready to strike. If they walked in and stole a hundred pounds of uranium from a nuclear power plant, every law enforcement agency would be turning the country inside out to find them."

"Please don't lecture me, Agent Daniels. I don't make the SPD policies," Harrison responded sharply. "There's the apartment complex right there. Let's get the information you need."

Suddenly she had gone from being called Laura to Agent Daniels. *Well that was the story of her life: a female exerts a little authority and she's automatically labeled a bitch.* As they pulled into the driveway, Laura noted the guards at the gatehouse fogged in the dust from two bulldozers leveling the future parking lot. Harrison flipped open his badge for the guard and drove through.

"Well, there's your answer, Agent Daniels."

He parked the unmarked car next to the construction trailer and approached the waiting construction manager. Eduardo Salvio's hardhat added several inches to his stature and he still appeared short, even to Laura. Everything about him was dark: his hair, his skin, his eyes and his clothes. "Mr. Salvio, I'm Detective Harrison of the SPD and this is Agent Daniels of the FBI. We have some questions about the theft you reported a couple of days ago."

"FBI? Of course, have a seat in our luxurious conference room." Salvio pulled out a metal folding chair at the large homemade plywood table in the center of the trailer. The trailer walls were papered with blueprints, safety policies and human resource bulletins. "What would you like to know?"

Laura spoke up. "Mr. Salvio, we couldn't help but notice that you have security guards watching the site. Do they work twenty-four-seven?"

"Yeah, or at least they're supposed to," Salvio responded.

"Supposed to?"

"Yeah, I think I know where you're going here. I had the same question." Salvio rocked back in his chair, nodding his head. "I talked to Secure Systems, our security company, and apparently the guard assigned to our site Wednesday night called in sick at the last minute. They didn't get a backup guard out here until after ten."

"Can we take a look at the storage room?" Laura asked.

"Sure, follow me. It's one of the unfinished apartments on the ground floor."

They followed Salvio the short distance from the construction trailer to the main building, where Laura noticed the new door at the entrance. Salvio turned to them as he pulled open the door. "I had to replace this door. It was pretty dinged up—looked like they pried it open. The old one is still in the scrap-metal bin."

Salvio turned to the left, went to the first door on the right and pulled at the large retractable key ring hanging on his belt. "This door got the same treatment. I replaced it too."

They entered the unfinished apartment where the drywall was hung and the joints were taped but not painted. A rudimentary light fixture was attached to the center of the ceiling with a bare light bulb screwed into it casting hard-edged shadows. The room was full of electrical equipment, expensive tools, light fixtures, spools of wire, stacks of conduit, boxes of switches and receptacles, but no smoke detectors.

The sharp odor of wet limestone from the curing drywall mud stung Laura's nose as her eyes swept the room. Dirt and drywall dust were tracked all over the floors. The wall around the light switch was smudged with greasy fingerprints. There were sawhorses in the middle of the floor with metal shavings under the conduit cutter and threading machine. Dust outlines marked the location of where the boxes had been stored.

"As you can see, the electricians use this room for storage and as a fabrication room," Salvio explained.

Laura asked, "Mr. Salvio, have you made an insurance claim on the stolen equipment yet?"

"I reported it to the parent company, but my only losses are the doors and time," Salvio explained. "The electrical subcontractor placed a lump sum bid. They get paid one price for the project, so the smoke detectors were their loss, not mine. And honestly, the replacement cost wouldn't be worth the deductible."

Both investigators were scribbling on small notepads. Laura decided to take the lead and Harrison didn't protest. She took a minute to walk over to the door and carefully examined the doorjamb and the light switch that lacked a switch plate.

She looked carefully at the greasy fingerprints surrounding the light switch. "Do you know what this substance is?"

"Pulling lubricant," Salvio answered.

"What?"

"Electricians coat the wires with a lubricant so they can pull the wires through conduit. As you can see, it gets messy and it's damn hard to paint over."

She scanned the walls and ceiling again and then looked at the floor between the door and the empty place where the smoke detectors had been stacked. Footprints were everywhere and going in all directions. The scene was completely compromised. There was little use in standing here any longer.

"Can you put us in touch with the security company?" Laura asked, flipping her notebook closed.

"Of course. I have their card in the trailer," Salvio said. "However, with the exception of their dispatcher, the office is closed now."

Chapter Twelve

Billings, Montana
May 7, 2004

Ten miles south of Billings, tucked away in a small stand of pine trees, Ahmed sat in his rented Buick Century with an expensive pair of Nikon binoculars pressed against his face. He had been watching the construction site all day, taking mental notes on the x-ray technician and the radiation source. The device seemed rather primitive, with the radiation source housed in a metal container about the size of a paint can. The way the technician lugged it around, leaning to one side for balance, the can must be heavy with lead shielding. Attached to the container were two flexible conduits that looked like plumber's snakes used to unclog drains and sewer pipes. At the end of one conduit there was something that resembled a fishing reel on steroids.

He watched as the technician used bungee cords to hold strips of protected x-ray photography film around a weld joining two sections of pipe. He then attached one end of the other conduit on the side of the pipe opposite the film. After unwinding the flexible conduit until he was a safe distance away, the radioactive source was reeled out of the paint can to expose the film. After about a minute he reeled the source back and removed the film. A simple operation.

The entire crew quit for lunch right at noon and drove off somewhere to eat. Just before leaving, the x-ray technician coiled up his radiation device, locked it in the back of his truck and drove off with a co-worker in another pick-up truck.

Making sure nobody was around, Ahmed carefully walked to the x-ray truck to have a closer look. *The lock could be easily chopped with bolt cutters*. The cab of the truck had some manuals thrown about on the passenger seat. *Not worth the time to pick the lock for*. A cloud of dust rose in the distance and was heading in his direction. He looked at his watch—12:40. Half an hour for lunch. Not much time to take the source.

When the technician returned, Ahmed carefully watched him remove the coiled machine and gauged its size. Yes, it would fit in the trunk of the rental car. As he prepared to leave, a small caravan of vehicles approached. Ten people got out and milled around. They all donned new orange hardhats and walked up to one of the construction trailers. It seemed like some sort of inspection and with only a few un-welded sections of pipe stacked near the trailer, the project appeared to be nearing completion. Ahmed put his car in gear and drove off slowly, heading back to the hotel.

Brandon got out of the car, walked back to the trunk and picked out a new, orange Montana Gas hardhat. He was with the project manager, some of the engineers and three representatives from West Continent Transmission Corporation.

West Continent's main transmission pipelines ran from the oil and gas fields in Montana, Idaho, and North Dakota, west to Spokane and Seattle then south to Portland and San Francisco. Their customer base was one of the largest in the United States. Eventually, most of the gas from the new field would be metered into West Continent's pipeline and head west for the big markets.

"So when will the tie-ins be complete?" Brandon asked, turning to the Montana Gas project manager.

"We'll be tying into our distribution line in two days. The tie-in to West Continent will be scheduled later. The piping, conditioning plant and skid-mounted booster compressor will be done early next week. West Continent needs to find a time when they can lower the pressure and isolate this section of the line. We'll have to play it by ear, but we'll have our contractor standing by and the tie-in will be done the next day," the project manager explained.

"Well, I guess it's up to us to deliver," Brandon said as his cell phone vibrated on his belt. "Excuse me, gentlemen. Hello?"

"Brandon. It's Jeff. I need you back in the office. We're in negotiations with the Brazilian government for your project near Porto Alegre. They're sending some delegates from their energy department and I want *you* to sell it to them."

Brandon could tell from Jeffery Hargrove's voice that he was excited at the prospect of another job.

"Jeff, can't we delay? The bit's in the ground and we're making good progress."

"The delegation is on its way. Besides, you know as well as I do that Dallas can handle the drilling. Get on the next flight and let me know when you get in. We have to go over the game plan and put together a presentation for them." Jeff was persistent. "Oh yeah, do you remember the name of that Brazilian barbeque place on the lakefront?"

"Jeff, they're from Brazil, they don't want to eat Brazilian food in the U.S.," Brandon responded, shaking his head. *Jeffery was a brilliant businessman but sometimes he needed help with the simple things.* "Remember the Cape Cod seafood restaurant at the Drake Hotel? Have Janice get the private room—it has a gorgeous view of Lake Michigan and it's quiet. I'll get packed and call you when I land at O'Hare."

"Good idea. See you soon." Jeff hung up without asking about the well.

"Well, gentlemen, it looks like everything is going great here. I just found out I have to get back to Chicago. I'm sorry I have to rush off, but can you please send me e-mail updates daily?"

"Of course, Dr. Stiles—" The project manager began to answer.

"Brandon. Please call me Brandon."

"Sorry…Brandon, let's go. I'll drive you back to the hotel."

Brandon said his goodbyes and headed out.

Chapter Thirteen

Four Sixes Ranch
May 8, 2004

Dallas made his way back to the trailer from the drilling platform with the daily progress logs. He let himself drop into the heavily-padded, vinyl swivel chair in his office at the end of the trailer. Pulling up the mud-stained legs of his Carhartts, he unlaced his muddy boots, pulled them off and let out a sigh. *These new work boots were hot and tight.* With his shoes off, he leaned back in the chair and swung his feet up on the desk, then strained forward to grab the log sheets lying on the desk next to his feet. *God, he had to start taking better care of himself.* The long hours coupled with his age led to a sedentary lifestyle.

The thoughts of gloom fled his mind when he looked over the data. *Finally, ahead of schedule.* "Yeeeah. Now that's the way life ought-a-be," he hollered to the empty trailer.

There was a quick rap on the door a moment before it slammed open, bringing a gust of chilly wind with it. Jerry Muckler, the muddy rig foreman stuck his head in. "Hey, Dallas, we just hit the cap rock. Judging from how the bit is chattering, it's pretty damned dense."

"Thanks, Jerry. Put a screen on the mud flow. The Doc's gonna wanna see what this rock looks like," Dallas said with a groan, taking his feet off the desk. "I'll phone him and let him know."

Jerry Muckler's bald head disappeared from the open door followed by a loud slam as the stiff breeze blew the door shut. Dallas bent over to start the tedious process of lacing up his boots. It was hell to have to hold your breath while bending over to tie your shoes. And these work boots required three long breaths just to get one tied.

He grabbed the satellite phone from the desk drawer and dialed Brandon's number. "Interex, Brandon Stiles speaking."

"Hey Doc, it's Dallas."

"What's up?"

"We hit the cap. Started chewing on it just now."

"Get me a sample, will you?"

"I knew you'd want one, so I already told Jerry to put some screens on the mud flow to collect some chips for you."

"Great! Thanks. I should be back out there Monday afternoon. If you break through the cap before I get there, get the well loggers started. There are a lot of people with a keen interest in the size of this field."

"You got it. When's the meeting with the Brazilians?" Dallas asked. "I'm looking forward to laying on the beach for a change."

"This afternoon—wish us luck."

Chapter Fourteen

Spokane, Washington
May 8, 2004

What the hell? Laura sat up abruptly, sending the room into a brief spin. *Where am I?* Her emotions reeling, feeling a mixture of confusion and apprehension, she looked around the small beige room. A loud ringing snapped her back to reality. She reached across the king-size bed and fumbled for the phone on the nightstand. A pleasant, female voice on the on the other end announced, "Good morning. This is your wake-up call. Thank you for staying at the Holiday Inn Express."

She grabbed her watch off the nightstand and squinted to see the dial in the dim light filtering between the small slits formed by the heavy curtains that didn't quite overlap. *Six-thirty.* She had an hour and a half before Harrison would pick her up. Arms stretching overhead, she swung her legs out of bed and headed for the bathroom.

Picking through a couple of Bic disposable razors and half-empty sample tubes of skin lotion in the small toiletry bag, she retrieved her own soap and shampoo. She could never get the shampoo in those little hotel bottles to lather and they weren't very fragrant. She reached into the bathtub and turned on the water. Immediately her hair and back were drenched with cold water rushing from the showerhead.

"Dammit! Is this some sadomasochistic ritual they teach in maid school?"

Shivering, she redirected the shower head, pulled the curtain closed and slipped off her wet and well worn FBI academy tee shirt and gym shorts. She turned to inspect her image in the full length mirror. *Not too bad*, she thought, letting a smile cross her lips. Since moving to Seattle, she exercised more and the workload at the field office was lighter with much less pressure, allowing more time to spend on personal things like the bi-weekly appointments at her day spa.

Flexing her arms like a bodybuilder, she checked the skin under her biceps. *Nice and firm.* Stepping back from the mirror she eyed her stomach and hips, noticing everything was in the right place and taut. Then turning around and twisting her head as far as it would turn, she examined the backs of her thighs. Satisfied with what she saw, she adjusted the water temperature and let the tension drain away with the flowing water.

After showering, dressing and carefully applying makeup, Laura was sitting in the lobby when Harrison drove into the parking lot. She shoved the last bit of bagel in her mouth, ran outside and tapped on the driver's window.

"Good morning, Laura." He smiled at her as the window slid down with a hum.

Hmmm, well, back to Laura again. "Park this thing. I'm driving today. That's my Grand Am over there."

"Uh, sure," he stammered. "I hope you had a good night's sleep."

"Yes, I did, thank you. Now park so we can go."

Harrison obediently swung the Chevy into an empty spot and jumped out of the car. Laura had already started the Grand Am when he opened the passenger door and sat down.

"How was your night?" she asked.

"Uneventful as always."

"Could I interest you in Starbucks this morning?" She put the car in gear and drove off. "My treat."

"Sure," he said. "So, what's the game plan? What exactly are we after?"

"Well, we get the name and contact information of the sickly security guard, then we pay him a visit. Does Secure Systems know we're coming?"

"Yeah, I called the dispatcher after I dropped you off last night. The office manager, Mr. Jenson, is going to meet with us."

"Thanks for the help, Jim. You know, I was thinking, why don't you introduce me as Investigator Daniels and leave off the FBI part for now, unless he specifically asks."

"Why's that?"

"At this point, I'd rather downplay the terrorism inference." She turned and looked at Harrison. "I don't want this guy calling the security guard and giving him a heads-up that the FBI is investigating. He might just decide to make a quick exit."

"You *really* think this is a terrorist plot, don't you?"

"More now than ever. The smoke detectors were the cheapest things in that room. There were light fixtures, tools and equipment that were worth a hell of a lot more and left untouched. It just doesn't add up. Somebody broke into that room wanting those smoke detectors."

Harrison glanced at Laura as she concentrated on the road. Something was different. Her skin seemed more vibrant and her eyes brighter and sexier. She really was an attractive woman if you could get by the overwhelming personality.

"What?" Laura asked, snapping Harrison out of his thoughts.

"Huh, what, what?"

"You were staring at me."

"I wasn't staring." His cheeks flushed. *Damn, caught red-handed.*

"Okay, maybe not staring, but you were checking me out. Admit it."

"I'm a detective, remember? They pay me to be observant. Turn left here."

Laura turned into a small strip mall with a handful of storefronts and parked in front of the security office. Secure Systems was no more than a small room with a few dispatchers and an office in back. Harrison showed his badge to a young lady working near the door. "We're here to see Mr. Jenson."

Harley Jenson was tall, black and casually dressed in jeans and a sweater. His hair was short with gray sprinkled throughout. His face was wide with a broad flat nose. He stood up to greet them as they approached. The office was cramped with two desks with computers, another radio system and a large white board with about thirty names and locations written on it.

"What can I do for you, Detective Harrison?" Jenson asked, as he motioned for them to have a seat at the empty chairs in front of his desk.

"We'd like information on the guards assigned to the River Chase Apartment construction site. The evening of May fifth one of your guards called in sick at the last minute. Later that evening, there was a theft." Harrison took the lead.

"Yeah, I remember that. We got coverage out there in less than four hours, but some equipment was missing the next morning, right?"

"Yes, we'd like to get the names and contact information for both of the guards that were involved that night."

"Why do you care about the guard that called in sick?" Jenson asked. "He doesn't have any information."

"We're covering all the angles."

"You don't think this was an inside job, do you?"

"Again, Mr. Jenson, we're not insinuating anything. We're just gathering information."

"Okay, okay. It'll take me just a minute." Jenson turned his chair around and pulled a keyboard drawer towards him. He moused his way through a few menus, clicked one more time with an exaggerated gesture and an aging laser printer came to life with a few clunks and a loud hum. He got up and grabbed the paper that was still working its way out.

"Here you go, the first name is the guard that covered and the second one is the guy that called in sick. But my sick guard is still out sick," Jenson said, handing the print-out to Harrison. "I haven't heard from him in days."

"Thanks, Mr. Jenson. And one other thing—can you keep this confidential? We'd like to talk to them unawares."

"No problem. I'm not happy with them anyway," Jenson answered, shaking his head.

They got to their feet and shook Jenson's hand. On the way to the car, Harrison handed the paper to Laura. She glanced at it and stopped abruptly. "Did you see the second name on the list? *Mohammed Atwah.*"

Chapter Fifteen

Billings, Montana
May 9, 2004

Ali Atif had just gotten out of the shower when Ahmed called and asked to see him. Ali was the jack-of-all-trades of the cell. He was small in stature with dark skin and black curly hair. His bushy eyebrows almost bridged the gap above his nose, shielding large brown eyes. He had a soft-spoken façade that hid an explosive hate for Americans.

After entering the small hotel room at the Comfort Lodge, Ahmed sat in the threadbare chair in the corner, sipping on a bottle of water. He motioned for Ali to have a seat on the corner of the small, too-soft mattress.

"Ali, how much longer will it take you to finish with the smoke detectors?"

"I worked all day and into the night yesterday. It is tedious work dismantling them carefully and putting them back together. The lighting in the storeroom is poor and there are no outlets for a lamp. But this way, if they are found, it will take additional time to discover that the radiation is missing."

"You haven't answered my question, Ali."

"I have removed about one hundred sources. I think two or three more days at most—if my fingers last that long." Ali held up his hands displaying bandaged fingers. "The parts are small and have sharp edges."

"How long did you rent the storage room for?"

"I paid for a month when I dropped off the rental van. I told the owner that we were storing some excess inventory from our supply business."

"Very well. I will inform Saif of our progress," Ahmed said. "I need to decide if I can take the radioactive source from the pipeline construction. I would be more comfortable if we were ready to leave this place, but it appears that the construction work is about over and I do not want to miss this opportunity. That one source is much more powerful than all the smoke detectors together."

Ahmed rubbed his face with the palms of his hands. "I was planning to take the device from the construction site during their lunch break, but I think I will follow the x-ray people to see where they stay the night. If we take it during the night, it will give us time to be out of town before they discover it missing in the morning."

"That sounds like a better plan, Ahmed. Have you heard anything of our Islam security guard brother?" Ali asked.

"Nothing, but I have not listened to the television news much."

"Well, I'm going back to the storeroom to work." Ali rose from his seat. "I will try to be back by dark."

"Okay Ali, may Allah guide your hands," Ahmed said solemnly.

Chapter Sixteen

Spokane, Washington
May 9, 2004

Laura's mind raced as she headed back to the River Chase Apartment construction site. It couldn't be coincidence that the security guard responsible for the gap in coverage at the apartments had an Islamic name.

"Bob, I have some information and need you to run a background check." Laura cradled the small cell phone between her ear and shoulder while guiding the car down the four-lane road, weaving in and out of the heavy traffic. She glanced over at Harrison who clutched at the dashboard with eyes wide in fear.

"What have you got, Laura?"

"A lead, maybe. The construction site is being guarded by a small security firm, Secure Systems. The evening of the theft, the guard scheduled for night duty called in sick. The day shift guard had already left, leaving the entry gate unsecured for four hours. The security guard that called in sick was a man named Mohammed Atwah. He's not returned to work since."

"Okay, the last named spelled a-t-w-a-h? Do you have an address?"

"Yes, on both accounts," Laura answered and gave him the remainder of the information. "I was going to question the guard, but I think maybe we should check his background first and then put a surveillance team on him."

"Let's run the background check first then we'll decide. What about the scene?"

"Completely compromised. I don't think there's anything we can get from it, but I guess it's worth a shot. I'll talk to the local PD to see if they can send a forensics team in." Laura hesitated and glanced at Harrison. "On second thought, I doubt I'll get that kind of cooperation. Chief Reynolds made it clear that he doesn't share our sense of urgency here."

"I understand. We'll send our own ERT in. I'll call Reynolds and let him know. So what are you doing now?"

"I'm heading back to the scene to see if I can figure out what type of vehicle they needed to transport the stolen smoke detectors. Who knows, maybe our thieves rented a truck for the heist. Then I'll check with rental agencies and see if anything adds up."

"Good idea, Laura. I'll call you on Atwah when we have something. Do you need any other help?"

"I will if we decide to post surveillance."

"Alright, keep up the good work," he said.

Laura flipped her phone closed.

"So you don't think my boss is sincere in his support of the FBI?" Harrison displayed an exaggerated look of surprise.

"Chief Reynolds doesn't seem to appreciate the FBI—especially a female agent working in his territory." Laura used her most diplomatic tone.

"Just between us, Chief Reynolds is an asshole. He used to be a top-notch detective. Now all he cares about is covering his ass and sucking up to the mayor and city council so he can keep his pension."

Laura drove through the security gate of the River Chase Apartments and parked next to the construction trailer that housed Eduardo Salvio's office. They hustled up the makeshift wooden steps and knocked on the door.

"Come in!" The voice was faint, but audible through the insulation of the trailer and over the roar of large graders leveling the future parking lot. "Ah, Inspectors, uh, Danson and Harrison, right? What can I do for you?"

Laura spoke up. "It's Daniels." She noted the recognition mixed with a touch of embarrassment in Salvio's face. "Mr. Salvio, we're trying to get an idea for the size and type of vehicle needed to transport those smoke detectors."

"Well, you're in luck, Inspector *Daniels*," Salvio said, grinning. "The replacements came in this morning. I can tell you they could have fit into a cargo van, but I'll let you look for yourself."

Following Salvio back to the storage room, Laura studied the five boxes. Too big for a car, but yes, they could definitely fit in a van. It would have been easier to check for larger rental trucks.

"Mr. Salvio, is it possible to ask the workers to stay out of this room for a while? I have a forensics team coming in to check it out. It'll make their job easier if it isn't used."

"No problem, the electricians are done roughing in the wiring. They only have one guy out here doing some miscellaneous repairs. He may need some equipment, but I'll make sure he stays out as much as possible."

"Thank you, Mr. Salvio. They'll also have to print the electricians and anyone else that had access to that room."

Back in the car, Harrison asked, "Where to now?"

"How about some lunch, then back to the station?"

"Sounds good to me. There's a diner that has a variety of food right down the street from the station."

"Let me guess," Laura smiled, "you get a discount."

Without waiting for a response, she retrieved the cell phone from her purse, flipped it open and dialed Bob Williams' number.

After two rings he answered "Robert Williams."

"Bob, it's Laura again. All the smoke detectors could fit into a vehicle the size of a large cargo van."

"Okay, I know you're running around out there, so I'll have Shirley initiate a search for rented vans and small trucks within a two hundred and fifty mile radius of Spokane. I have the feeling we're going to get a lot of hits."

"Can we filter by Middle Eastern names? Any rental car firm is going to require a driver's license and maybe it'll list his real name."

"Good idea. We'll put our standard list of Islamic names in the search parameters."

"Did you turn up anything on Atwah?" she asked.

"Nothing yet. Oh yeah, I've got surveillance and ERT getting their equipment together. They should be headed your way first thing in the morning. I'm dispatching the Falcon jet to speed things up. You were right by the way, Reynolds was less than cooperative."

"I'll be ready for them. I already talked to the construction manager at the apartment complex. He's going to minimize the disturbance in the storage room until the team arrives."

"They'll call you when they hit the ground. Keep me informed."

"Let's eat. I'm starved. I'll fill you in at the diner." As Laura reached for the car door handle, Harrison grabbed her arm.

"Can I drive? You make me nervous as hell."

She shot him a look that conveyed a clear message. "Just get in the goddamn car."

Chapter Seventeen

Billings, Montana
May 9, 2004

Ahmed parked his car behind the same stand of pine trees he'd used before. The sun hung low on the horizon as he watched the construction workers gather their equipment and secure it for the night. The x-ray crew and the supervisors were the last to leave.

The door opened on the back of the x-ray truck and the technician stepped out carrying a handful of long negative filmstrips. He disappeared into the construction trailer for a moment before returning to his truck empty-handed, locked the back and drove off.

Ahmed started the car and followed him, keeping a considerable distance along the rustic county roads. It was easy following the trail of dust from the gravel roads. As he neared the city, he closed the gap. They crossed the Yellowstone River on a small two-lane bridge, went through Riverside Park and under Interstate 90. A left on King Avenue and a mile later, he pulled into the Big Sky Lodge. Ahmed drove past the motel parking lot and settled the car against the curb within visual range. Contractor's vehicles and welding trucks were parked all along the old style, single-story u-shaped building.

He watched as the technician jockeyed his truck into a tight spot between two welding trucks. He climbed out of the vehicle, walked to the back and tugged on the heavy lock, then let himself into the room directly in front of the parking spot.

The motel lot had only one street lamp next to the office on the other side of the building. There were lights above each door that would shine out onto the parking lot. The back of the x-ray truck was clearly visible from the street. As Ahmed's eyes swept the blacktop for more information, he noticed a larger vehicle that looked like a small moving truck. He recognized the universal yellow and magenta radiation warning symbol plastered on all sides. Bringing the binoculars to his eyes, he read the sign on the door of the truck: *Wyoming Test Labs, Well Logging Division*. The x-ray truck was from the Pipeline Support Division of the same company.

Ahmed still had the binoculars to his eyes when he heard a whistle and spotted a rough looking man with long stringy hair and beard walking toward the truck, waving. He put down the binoculars and saw the x-ray technician come from his room to meet the waving man.

They shook hands, had a brief conversation and drove off in the larger vehicle. Ahmed followed. The two men parked near the small central business district and disappeared into a small tavern. He hurriedly pulled his car to the curb and walked back to the tavern, looking around to make sure nobody noticed him. The window facing the street had been painted black to keep the bar darkened throughout the day. However, there were enough scratches that Ahmed could see in. Most of the patrons were tough-looking biker types and he immediately knew this bar did not cater to Middle Easterners. He would stand out—something he was warned about. It was hard enough being Middle Eastern and blending in out in the West.

There were only a handful of customers and the two men from the x-ray company were sitting in a booth near the middle of the room. He could see their dirty, greasy hair above the back of the booth. The two chatted with a waitress briefly and the x-ray technician stood and followed her toward the doors at the back of the bar labeled *BULLS* and *HEIFERS*. The other man sat with his back to the door. Taking the opportunity, Ahmed quietly entered the tavern and slipped into the next booth with his back to the men he was watching.

Still feeling trepidation about his surroundings and keeping his head down to avoid being noticed, he was startled when the barmaid sauntered up and asked in a loud voice, "Hey, stranger, what can I get for you?"

"I'll just have a pop," Ahmed answered quietly, staring at his hands.

"Pop? Darlin' I suppose you mean Coke?"

"Yes, yes." Ahmed nodded his head.

"You wanna little Jack in that, darlin'?" The barmaid stepped to the other side of the booth and bent down with her elbows on the table. She wasn't wearing a bra and her low cut top was loose, exposing most of her breasts.

"I'm sorry, a little Jack?" Ahmed asked, trying to focus his gaze on anything other than the woman's cleavage.

"Well, you really ain't from around here. Jack Daniels, sweetie. You know, whiskey?" She shook her body a bit causing her dangling breasts to jiggle in a flirtatious gesture.

"No, just Coke please."

"Suit yourself. Comin' up, sweetheart."

Damn that American bitch. He was trying to remain calm and unnoticed, but she had rattled him with stupid questions and incessant flirting. He heard the x-ray technician come back from the bathroom. The man was slightly taller than Ahmed. His light brown hair was long, over his ears, and continued around his chin in a short beard. He appeared to be in his thirties, but had the skin of a man who made his living outdoors.

"So, Billy, what's new back at the office?" the x-ray technician asked.

"Same ole shit, Walt," Billy answered. "Not much business, so everybody's on the rag down there. Lucky this new well and pipeline came up or you and me would be shovelin' crap for the ranchers."

"Anythin' on the oil pipeline going south?"

"Bids are in and they're lowballin' it. Shit, they ain't no other x-ray hands near here, so we should land it." Billy grabbed his beer and took a long swallow.

"Hey, how's that sidekick?" Walt asked grinning.

"Jimmy? Shit, Jimmy's Jimmy. A bit slow, but he's good at the manual stuff and I don't need to tell him what to do." Billy said. "Hey man, I forgot ta tell ya. Got me some new big sources."

"How hot are they?" Walt asked.

"Real hot. Makes me a little nervous. Each one is five hundred millicuries." Billy wiped fake sweat from his forehead for emphasis.

"You shittin' me?" Walt asked. "I thought two-fifty was the max."

"I wouldn't shit you, Walt. You know you're my favorite. Hey, I don't set em up, I just use em."

"Damn, don't let Jimmy get too close, he'll fry his last brain cell. It would be a public service if it made him sterile."

"Nah." Billy brushed the thought away with his hand. "Jimmy's a bit spooky at first, but he's got a really nice wife and two cute kids. I've had much worse."

"Kids? What? With a round head, big ears, sittin' around on the porch all day playin' the banjo?"

"Ah, come on, Walt. Give 'em a break."

How could these two American stooges sound so dim-witted one minute and talk about nuclear radiation sources the next, sounding reasonably intelligent, then revert right back to unintelligible drivel? *Allah led me here for a reason*, Ahmed thought in amazement. Each of the well logger's sources was two hundred thousand times the size of all the smoke detectors together. A smile crossed his lips. *Saif will be pleased.* The bar maid interrupted his thoughts and sat across from him.

"Here's your Coke, honey. Can I get you anything else?" she asked, putting on a sexy smile.

"No, can you leave my check please?"

"Goin' so soon? You just got here." She pouted as she stood up.

"Yes, I have an appointment and needed to kill some time. Now I must leave."

"Okay, honey, it's a buck fifty," she said with her hand out.

Ahmed reached in his pocket for his money clip and peeled off two-one dollar bills. He handed them to her without looking up. She snatched the money from his hand and walked away. Now he could focus on the conversation behind him.

"So where's this well we're headed to tomorrow?" Walt asked.

"Down near Cody, on the Four Sixes Ranch—'bout thirty miles southeast on the Greybull River. We got reservations at the Wyoming Inn in Cody."

"Shit, I'm gonna hafta follow ya. I mean, I know where Cody is but I get lost out in the wilderness," Walt said.

"Yeah, me and Jimmy checked it out last week—kinda hard to find." Billy slammed his empty can on the table and motioned to the barmaid for two more. "Talk about a lucky sonofabitch, this dude that owns the ranch, won it in a poker game ten years ago. Winnin' hand was four sixes, now he's gonna be a freakin' billionaire with the oil wells."

Ahmed heard all he needed. He got up quietly, pulled his collar up in a feeble attempt to conceal himself and without looking back, made his way to the door. The door swung open, bringing a rush of cool air with it. He cleared the doorway and headed down the sidewalk toward the panel truck with the radiation placards displayed on all sides. He wanted to inspect the back of the truck as he walked by. The lock looked like a heavy deadbolt built into the door. *This one wouldn't be as easy*.

As he swiveled back, he slammed into what felt like a brick wall and stumbled back.

"What the fuck, towelhead?" The voice was heavy and loud.

The two men were huge, both wearing tattered black leather jackets and ragged jeans. The mountain that Ahmed had run into had a heavy chain clipped to a belt loop that curled around and disappeared in a denim pocket. Long, stringy black hair was covered in a red and white do-rag. His cratered face sat atop a thick neck that sported a tattoo running under his dirty white tee-shirt. Ahmed couldn't see clearly the other man standing behind the monster that came toward him.

"I'm sorry. I don't want any trouble." Ahmed's voice was a little shaky.

"Well, then you should watch where the fuck you're walking."

"Look, I just want to get to my car and leave quietly." Ahmed's mind raced. He couldn't afford to get in a fight. He couldn't afford the attention.

"Yeah, I'll bet you want to leave." The monster turned to his buddy. "Whattaya say we send this asswipe back to fuckin' Iraq?" The other guy just laughed. The sound bounced off the empty, dark street.

Deciding he better do something, Ahmed tried to turn and retreat in the other direction, but the biker was quicker than he calculated. A searing pain tore through the top of his head as a big hand grabbed him by the hair and yanked him back. A thick fist smashed into the side of his head, causing his vision to go white an instant before another blow caught him in the lower back, driving the wind from his lungs. He was being pummeled by both of the ruffians. Biker two grabbed Ahmed in a bear hug before he could go down. The stench of sweat was horrific as Ahmed struggled to reach the gun that was in the back of his waistband. The loudmouth that he ran into swaggered up to face him.

"You ready to visit Allah?" Crooked yellow teeth flashed as he drew his fist back. Everything slowed down. Ahmed could feel the butt of his gun, but couldn't get his fingers around it. The big man lashed out, landing a blow on Ahmed's jaw, causing his head to jerk to the side and his legs to buckle. As the biker let go, Ahmed collapsed onto the pavement, blood running from a gash above his eye and another on his high cheekbone. With the taste of warm blood pooling in his mouth, the dim light began to fade. If Ahmed lost consciousness, the entire operation could be in jeopardy.

Somewhere in the distance he heard one of them say "Let's finish this fucker."

This was his last chance. He reached behind him and felt the cool steel of the Jericho nine-millimeter. With his hand wrapped around the grip, he tugged with his remaining strength. The gun caught in his waistband. He tugged again as he felt himself being lifted. With everything he had left, he yanked the gun free and pushed the muzzle into the face of the thug that had him by his jacket.

"Oh fuck." The gravelly voice came with a stunned look.

What Ahmed wanted most in the world right now was to pull the trigger and see this American bully's face disappear. But if he did that, the operation would be over for sure. His body shuddered with anger and pain as he gasped for breath.

"Tell your friend to back away or I will send you both straight to hell."

Biker number two took a step back with his hands up. The shrill wail of a siren sounded in the distance. Ahmed pulled the gun back and swung hard, jamming the muzzle into the mouth of the biker. Teeth splintered with a crack, sending blood spraying in the air. The biker fell to his knees and grunted as Ahmed backed away to the refuge of his car. A moment later he drove away shaking, knowing that he almost ruined the operation with his carelessness. Somewhere on the drive back to his hotel room, he decided that he and Ali would be going to Cody, Wyoming.

Chapter Eighteen

Chicago, Illinois
May 9, 2004

Brandon ran to retrieve the ringing cell phone from the kitchen counter of his Arlington Heights townhome. "Hello."

"Hey, Doc, it's Dallas."

"Hey, Dallas, how are things going out there?"

"We just punched through the cap rock. It wasn't as thick as our models showed. We're into some voids and, let's see, how did the foreman put it? *Mushy stuff.*"

Brandon chuckled for a moment and asked, "Mushy stuff, huh? Okay, take it down another fifty to a hundred feet, or whatever you can get by midnight. Then call in the loggers."

"Loggers are on the way, Doc. They'll be here in the mornin'."

"Great, I'll see you around noon."

"Noon? Did you sprout your own wings and stuff a rocket up your ass?"

"Jeff freed up the jet to bring me out. A couple of guys from Contracts are coming with me."

"Since we're going to be here all night, will the company splurge for a big tip for the pizza delivery guy?" Dallas asked.

Brandon got a good laugh, imagining his friend giving the pizza delivery boy directions to the site. "Dallas, I'll send you pizza from Chicago if you get me another hundred feet tonight."

"Deal. See ya, Doc."

Brandon thumbed the disconnect button on his cell phone, sat it down on the kitchen counter and returned to the sparsely furnished bedroom. He had his suitcase half packed for the trip. Being a fastidious packer, everything had a place. It had taken years to find the exact suitcase to fit his needs.

He unzipped one of the compartments on the front of the Tumi case and reached in, not knowing what he was looking for. He was expecting an empty pocket, but fished out a folded slip of paper. His heart sank with remembrance as soon as he saw it. He knew the note had been written by Mae. *Oh my God, Mae.* He felt the crushing blow of depression as tears trickled down his cheeks.

It had been a little over a year since he'd lost her. He had tried to contact her parents unsuccessfully. They lived in a small village without a phone or television. Brandon had written several letters and even had an interpreter write in Chinese characters for him and included a postage paid envelope, but he never received a response.

He sat on the corner of the bed and unfolded the paper.

Dearest Brandon, I want you to know you make me very happy. When I am with you, I feel very rich with life. It will be hard to leave my parents, but I want to be with you forever. I will miss you while you are away from me.

Love you, Mae

Brandon wept, putting the paper to his face in clenched fists. Mae had written this shortly after she moved into the Jin Pu Hotel with him. He had to go to Linfen the next morning to meet with the SinoPec management team, so he took the afternoon off to show her Hukou Falls.

Mae had been astonished by the beauty of the falls. She had lived her entire life only hours from the rugged magnificence and had never really seen it. She stood on the icy bank and held onto him, watching the mesmerizing water drop a hundred feet into a canyon. She told Brandon the Legend of the Dragon's Heart.

That's when they met the Donkey Man. An elderly man in traditional Chinese robes with a long curved wooden pipe clinched in his teeth approached Brandon and Mae with a ragged looking donkey in tow. It was quite a sight standing on thirty feet of ice above the rushing waters.

The man told Mae that the donkey was famous, but never said what it was famous for. He pointed to the brightly colored blanket with Chinese characters and English letters: *Famous Donkey of Hukou Falls.*

The old man accepted ten yuan, about a dollar-twenty, for Mae to ride the donkey on the icy banks. On the way back to the hotel, they talked about getting married and Mae moving to the United States with him. When they returned to the room, they made love and held each other until dinner, making plans for the future. Her only concern was for her parents.

It had been a day Brandon cherished—watching the awe in Mae's eyes as she experienced the wonder of the falls. She talked about it until she got sick and left him alone and empty inside. "Oh, Mae, I miss you so much."

Chapter Nineteen

Spokane Washington
May 10, 2004

It was 7:00 a.m. and Laura had already put in her two-mile run and showered. She was waiting in the lobby of the hotel when her cell phone rang.

"Agent Daniels."

"Laura, it's Ty Desmond with ERT. We're on the ground in Spokane and loading up the van. We should be on our way to the River Chase Apartments in a half hour. Can you clear the way for us?"

"No problem, Ty. Do you have directions?"

"Monroe Street, just north of the river." Desmond read his notes.

"That's right. How about the surveillance team?"

"Johnny Campisi has two men with him. They'll be on the way to SPD headquarters about the same time."

"Have him ask for Detective Harrison when they arrive."

"Okay, Laura. I'll call you as soon as we find anything."

As Laura flipped the phone closed, she turned her gaze to the parking lot and spotted Harrison in his maroon Chevy. Grabbing her briefcase, she headed for the door and bounded down the steps. Harrison was already out of the car and opening the door for her.

She approached with a smile saying, "Well, that's a nice gesture. Such a gentleman."

"I'm here to serve, my lady. By the way, I had a great time at dinner last night."

"It was nice, and no discounts either."

"Oh, nothing but the best for the FBI," Harrison said, displaying a large smile.

As he guided the car out of the parking lot, Laura turned to him. "Jim, I really appreciate the company last night. Hotel rooms seem to close in on me after a while. I'm not one to go barhopping by myself and all the shopping malls start to look the same."

"Don't give it a thought, Laura. It was my pleasure." Harrison turned briefly to meet her gaze. "Hey, are you checking me out now?" He watched as Laura flushed before changing the subject.

"Well, let me tell you what's going on. The Emergency Response

Team and surveillance are on the ground. ERT is headed to River Chase and surveillance is coming to police headquarters."

"Do we have time to stop at Starbucks?" he asked.

"I insist."

Arriving at SPD Headquarters, Laura found a glassed-in conference room, sat her extra hot Caramel Macchiato down and pulled the laptop from her briefcase. She started building a timeline on the case, leaving blanks for the information that Johnny Campisi was bringing from the field office on Mohammed Atwah. But, based on her last phone call with Robert Williams, that wouldn't be much.

A commotion at the main information desk announced the arrival of the surveillance team. Harrison was already trotting to the desk to greet the team and escort them to the conference room. She closed the lid of her computer and took a notebook from her briefcase.

Harrison led Campisi into the conference room with Agents Aldo and Jackman following closely. Johnny walked over to Laura, and shook her hand. "I hear you're broadening your horizons and working a real case."

"That's me, Jill of all trades," she replied, grinning.

Johnny Campisi's physical attributes labeled him as a mafia thug. *Pretty* wasn't a word that came to mind when you looked in Johnny's direction. Thick muscled forearms, a stocky frame, black hair and pocked face hid a keen intelligence. The cover of the book brought to mind the cliché "dumb as a box of rocks," but in addition to his graduate degree in criminal psychology, he was considered street-smart and was an expert in surveillance and forensics. Johnny and Laura had gotten off on the wrong foot when she was transferred to the Seattle Field Office two years ago. She had made it known that her assignment to Seattle was temporary and would soon be heading back to D.C.—words that she came to regret.

Campisi was assigned to surveillance on her first project in Seattle and made it clear that he didn't like her holier-than-thou attitude. However, near the end of the project, Laura sat down with Campisi over beers and told him about her involvement with the anthrax case and how she was hung out to dry. Now she considered him a friend and enjoyed working with him despite his gruff exterior.

"I guess you guys met Detective Harrison?"

"Sure did. Here's the file on Atwah." Johnny handed a thin file folder to Laura. "It's not much. He's Saudi and came to the states two years ago. He moved to Spokane to be with his nephew. Since then, the nephew has moved to San Francisco, so he lives alone. He's tried to obtain citizenship for the last six months with no luck and has been with Secure Systems for a year and a half. There's not so much as a parking violation with his name on it. That's it."

"So, what's your plan?" Laura asked.

"We've requested a list of calls to and from his home phone for the past six months. He doesn't have a cell phone registered in his name. The phone records are being faxed here, to you, and should be showing up by nine or ten. Bob Williams is getting a tap placed on the phone." Johnny hesitated, putting his finger to his dimpled chin. "We're going to visit his apartment. Aldo here has a Washington State Electrical Co-op jumpsuit. If he's not home, we'll have a look around the apartment and place some bugs. If he's really at home, we'll post a watch and listen with a long range microphone."

"Sounds like a plan," Laura said.

"Agent Campisi," Harrison spoke up. "If there's time before you leave, I'd love to see your equipment."

"My equipment?" Campisi boomed, placing a big hand over his crotch. "Geez, not in front of the lady."

"Your *surveillance* equipment." Harrison's face turned bright red. "The department's gear is getting old and I'd like to see what kinds of toys are available now. I mean, you FBI guys must have all the best stuff."

"Sure thing, man. We'll try to touch base before we leave. Well, Laura, we're off. Call me if anything comes up."

As the surveillance team headed for the exit, Harrison took a seat next to Laura and started looking through the information on Atwah.

Forty-five minutes later, Laura resigned to refilling her Starbucks cup with the station's watery brew. She retrieved Atwah's telephone records from the fax machine and had just settled down to look through them when her cell phone chirped. Her forehead crinkled a bit noticing Campisi's name flash on the display.

"Laura, it's Johnny."

"Hey Johnny, what's going—"

"Get down here right away and bring your detective friend with you."

Chapter Twenty

Four Sixes Ranch
May 10, 2004

It was a late night for Dallas, so he didn't bother going back to the condo in Cody. Instead, he unfolded an old cot he kept in a closet and slept in the trailer. The drill crew made one hundred feet below the cap by 1:30 a.m. The well casing was completed and the welding crew was working on the connection to the Montana Gas pipeline that would take the gas to Billings and West Continent's Mainline and a number of towns between. The well loggers were on the way and would start work later in the morning.

Everything was ahead of schedule. The cap rock was supposed to have been at least a hundred feet thicker—which is what the schedule was built around. The dense cap rock took twice as long to drill through as the softer sedimentary rock above and the sandstone and shale below.

He woke at six in the morning, unable to sleep on the lumpy thin mattress. He slowly pushed his way out of the cot, feeling like he had been hit by a truck. After banging his elbows and knees in the small shower enclosure, he grabbed a couple of slices of cold pizza from the refrigerator and wolfed them down. The door to the trailer flew open, startling him. "Hey, Dallas, you gotta come see this!"

Dallas followed the rig foreman, Jerry Muckler, down the wooden steps. "Just another beautiful morning in paradise." He stopped and looked around with the Teton Mountains as the backdrop for the vast expanse of the Four Sixes Ranch. "What are we lookin' at?"

"I had one of my hands cleaning the mud screens. He came running up to the platform stinking to high heaven. Drug me down to the pit and...well, shit. You have to see it for yourself."

Dallas followed the foreman along the path to the mud pits. They were at least a hundred feet away when the stench slapped them in the face.

"Holy shit!" Dallas held his nose with one hand and waved his other hand in front of his face. "Smells like a rotting cow in a pile of elephant shit."

They hurried to the edge of the pit to see one of the laborers wearing chest waders knee deep in drilling mud. Earplugs were stuffed in his nose and his tee shirt was wrapped around his face covering his mouth like a bandanna. He was shoveling large chunks of something off the screens and had a small pile of it on the ground at the edge of the pit.

"Oh my God, that's the most disgusting shit I've ever smelled. And I've smelled some pretty disgusting shit in my time." Dallas struggled to get the words out between retching gags.

He got up close, bent over and touched the substance with his finger—slimy and soft. Instinctively he pulled his finger back and smelled it. He thought it felt like it looked and smelled like...rotting flesh?

"Crap, you don't think some animal got in there, do you?" Dallas asked, standing up.

"Fuck no. That's no animal. There's no head, no fur, well hell, I don't know," the foreman answered.

"I know it's a crap job, but have Stinky there in the waders wrap that shit in some plastic sheets for the Doc to look at. He likes that kinda stuff. I can't take this anymore." Dallas turned and hurried back down the path toward the trailer.

The stink seemed to permeate his clothes and skin. Dallas neared the trailer, stopped and sniffed. "God, make it stop!" he yelled at no one in particular while looking up at the sky.

The stench followed him into the trailer, so he grabbed the overnight bag he kept tucked in the corner of the office, locked the trailer door and stripped down. His clothes went in a plastic trash bag and he disappeared into the tiny shower at the other end of the trailer for a second time in less than an hour. Stepping in the stream of cool water, he felt refreshed. Scrubbing himself from head to toe, this was probably the longest shower Dallas had taken for as long as he remembered. It would have been great if he hadn't kept banging his elbows, head and ass on the walls of the tight confines.

He stepped out and took in a deep breath. "That's better." He thought about that poor laborer in the mud pits, and again, speaking out loud to nobody, said, "And that, my friends, is why I went ta college."

After pulling on his favorite pair of broken-in Carhartts, he was tying the plastic trash bag shut when there was a rap on the door. Dallas threw the bag in the corner thinking that it should probably go right into the trash. He unlocked and opened the door to see Billy Goller.

"Hello, Mr. Wheeler. We're here to start the logging. Looks like you're ready for us."

"Yeah, don't want to waste any time. What's your schedule?" Dallas asked.

"We'll run the nuclear tool first, then the sonic. Take a day for each." Billy used his fingers to count them off. "You were sayin' that we could hook up to your generator?"

"Yeah, there's a panel on the rig. Help yourself."

"If you got anything else for us, give us a yell. You're welcome to watch as much as ya want."

"The Doc and I will stick our heads in now and then. Oh yeah, safety first!" Dallas said, pointing to a big poster on the wall. "Hardhats, hearing protection and safety glasses the moment you set foot out of your truck, understand?"

"Yes, sir," Billy said, looking down.

"You do have safety equipment, don't you?" Dallas asked in a boss's voice. He could see that the stringy haired technician was embarrassed.

"Yes, sir, Mr. Wheeler, we do. I'm real sorry." Billy turned to go, then turned back, "Oh, I brought the x-ray technician with me. He'll be startin' on those pipeline welds shortly."

"Okay, tell him to see the pipeline supervisor to make sure everyone's outta the way. I want the area taped off so's nobody walks up on that source while it's reeled out. I don't want anyone's gonads fried. Especially mine."

"Yes, sir." Billy disappeared from the doorway and the door slammed shut.

"I'll be damned if anyone gets his ass killed on one of my jobs." Dallas had a habit of talking out loud with no one to hear.

Just then the door swung open. "What's that you were saying, Dallas? People's asses are dying to get off your jobs?"

"Hey, Doc, good to see your sorry ass. Hey, by the way, the rig super's got your lunch wrapped up for you." Dallas wore as serious a face as he could muster.

"What the hell are you talking about? Are you suffering from sleep deprivation?" Brandon asked.

Dallas's serious expression broke into laughter. "No, seriously, some god-awful shit came out of the hole and got caught on the screens. Stinks to high heaven." His fingers went to pinch his nose as he walked to the corner to retrieve his trash bag. He tossed it to Brandon and said, "Here, Doc, take a whiff of this."

"You want me to smell your trash? What have you been smoking out here while I was gone?" Brandon's brow furrowed in confusion.

Dallas pointed at the bag. "Just untie that doodad there and take a sniff. Oh yeah, and stand by the door will ya?"

Brandon looked confused as he twisted the wire tie. "Holy crap! What the hell did you fall into?"

"Shit, Doc, I didn't get all that close to it. Have you ever had anything like this come out of a hole before?"

"You know, Dallas, I did, I think." Brandon snapped his fingers, "Wait. You had already left, but in Africa...something hit the mud pits right after we penetrated the cap." He resealed the plastic bag. "I never got a chance to see what it was, but the whole area smelled similar."

"Well, you got your chance now, by God. I got it all wrapped up real good for you."

"Excellent. But *what* is that smell? I mean besides being the most offensive odor I've ever encountered."

"Ya know, Doc, I hunt a lot in the off-season," Dallas said as he sat on the corner of the desk. "I've seen me some rotten animal corpses. Similar stink. Hell, that smell is the only thing that makes me gag and I'm tellin' ya, I gagged my ass off smellin' this shit. You don't think this could be some undigested million year old critter, do ya?"

"I never thought of that, but I suppose it's possible. Hold my calls, Dallas—I'm going to take a look."

"Uh, Doc, you got an extra set of clothes with ya? I've got extra trash bags."

"Two weeks worth. I've got to check this out."

Brandon ran out the door only to return with an old pair of jeans, an old Harvard tee shirt and his paleontologist tool kit. "I may be excited, but I'm not stupid."

"Hey, Doc, ain't that your favorite college tee shirt?"

"I went to Yale, you goofball. We hate Harvard." The office door clicked shut behind him.

Chapter Twenty-one

Spokane, Washington
May 10, 2004

Laura pushed back from the table and leaned over the atrium rail at the main level of the SPD headquarters. She spotted Harrison hunched over a pile of papers on his desk. Above the buzz of activity she called, "Detective Harrison, we need to go."

"What's going on?" Harrison asked, catching up to her at the base of the stairs.

"Mohammed Atwah is dead. The surveillance team found his body in the bathtub. Shot in the back of the head—execution style." They hurried down the corridor as she talked. Once in the car, Laura snapped her phone from her belt holster and found Ty Desmond's number.

"Ty, it's Laura."

"Yeah."

"I need you at another location ASAP."

"We're not done here," Desmond said.

"I guess I didn't make myself clear. Johnny's team found Atwah dead in his apartment. Keep the rest of the team working at the apartments and get over there, now."

"Laura, we can't take jurisdiction over that crime scene. This is Spokane's issue."

"Listen, Ty, just get in the van and get to Atwah's apartment. We'll worry about whose jurisdiction this is later. I'll text you the address. Plug it in your GPS."

"Whatever you say. You're the boss."

She jabbed at the end button on the phone and muttered, "Yeah, then why the hell do you keep questioning my authority?" She looked over at Harrison, whose eyes shot up at the confrontation and snapped, "What?"

"Nothing," he said, before turning back to the road trying to hide a grin.

Desmond gathered his personal equipment and dug his GPS locator out of the case. He entered the street address and realized he was only about ten minutes from Atwah's apartment.

“Hey, guys, keep working. I need to check on something with the surveillance team. I’ll be back as soon as I can.”

Ten minutes later, he spotted Laura outside the apartment complex chatting with Johnny Campisi. The conversation broke as he approached and Johnny led the trio into the apartment complex. The apartment was neat and clean, but the putrid odor of decay fouled the air. They entered the small bathroom off the hallway between the two bedrooms. Desmond reached in his bag and pulled out a small jar of camphor cream. He unscrewed the lid and smeared a small amount on his upper lip, then passed it around. The smell of death still made him sick. It was something he’d never get used to.

It was a typical windowless apartment bathroom with a small single-bowl sink sitting in a Formica countertop atop a light oak cabinet. The toilet was lodged between the sink and the bathtub. A blue bath towel hung on a towel bar opposite the toilet. The light blue shower curtain was draped in the tub and drawn halfway. Spattered blood splashed on the shower curtain created silhouetted splotches. Other than the mess in the tub, the bathroom was spotless.

After donning a pair of talc-free rubber gloves, he leaned over the bathtub where Atwah’s body lay face down and felt around the entry wound in the back of Atwah’s head. His eyes shifted to the blood splatter on the ceramic tile wall. He gently lifted Atwah’s head a few inches and leaned over to see the remnants of his face.

“Okay, it looks like he’s been dead awhile—several days at least. It’s likely he was kneeling in the tub when he was shot. Looks like a medium caliber gun, maybe nine-millimeter. Using his hand like a gun, he positioned it in the air behind where Atwah’s head would have been as he knelt in the tub. “Shooter was here. The bullet went through and took a chunk of his forehead with it—there.” He pointed to the chipped tiles spattered with blood and flesh.

“Judging from what I observed on the way in here, he was preparing dinner when it happened. There’s no sign of a struggle,” Desmond added.

Johnny spoke up. “Yeah, we looked around a bit. This guy went without a fight.”

“So there’s no way this was a suicide?” Harrison asked.

“No way. Besides the obvious, no gun—he couldn’t have shot himself at that angle, even if he were double jointed,” Desmond said. “There doesn’t seem to be powder residue near the entry wound, so it’s likely the gun wasn’t pressed to his head.”

“What kind of person gives up his life without a fight? I mean if someone with a gun tells you to kneel in the bath tub—well, you have to know what’s going on,” Harrison said, scratching his head.

“Someone who’s not afraid to meet their maker and willing to die for a cause, that’s who—a religious fanatic. Whoever stole those smoke detectors came here, had Atwah call in sick, then killed him,” Laura said.

"It fits," Harrison agreed.

"I'm going out to the kitchen and phone this in to headquarters," Laura said, grabbing a handful of paper towels from Desmond to wipe the camphor from her lip.

"Bob, we've got a dead Saudi on our hands." Laura sat at the kitchen table with her notebook open. "Looks like it may have been done by whoever stole the smoke detectors. I'm going to need you to call the chief here so we can take jurisdiction of this case."

"All right, Laura, I'll call the attorney general and city attorney. There shouldn't be any problem with this looking more and more like a national security issue. I'll notify headquarters and the Office of Homeland Security. By the way, did you talk to Shirley yet?"

"Shirley? What about?"

"She came in about ten minutes ago and told me she may have something on the rental van angle. Do you want me to patch you through?"

"That's okay, I'll call her in a few minutes."

"Okay, I've got some calls to make."

The line went silent and Laura called the team into the living room to inform them that the FBI would have jurisdiction. Then she and Harrison left to return to police headquarters.

"Laura, I'm going to have to tell the chief about this or I'll get my ass fired," Harrison said.

"I know, Jim. Hopefully my boss is already laying the groundwork. I'll go in with you to make sure it's clear that we have jurisdiction."

They pulled up to police headquarters and stepped out of the car into a beautiful spring day. Laura didn't notice the cool breeze or the sunshine as she hustled into the building. She looked forward to seeing the look on Reynolds' face when he found out that he didn't have jurisdiction in this murder case.

At Spokane Police Headquarters, Chief Reynolds watched Laura and Harrison trot up the steps through the glass front of his office. He waved them in and motioned for them to sit. "I understand. Yes, sir," he said, setting the receiver back in its cradle. He looked up at Laura and Harrison. "So we have a national security issue here?"

Laura spoke up. "It looks that way, sir."

"That was Mayor Wilkins. I'm sending over a couple detectives to watch, but the scene is yours, Ms. Daniels," he said calmly. "As well as the River Chase theft."

"Yes, sir," she responded.

"Okay, you can go, Ms. Daniels. Detective Harrison, please stay and close the door," Reynolds said in a tone that was too calm for his normal demeanor.

"I'll be in the conference room," Laura said to Harrison. She closed the door behind her.

"Harrison, what do you think? Is this really a national security issue or is the FBI trying to shove this thing up our asses?"

"It looks legit to me, Chief."

"You wouldn't be saying that because she's a head turner now, would you?"

"I hadn't noticed that, sir." Harrison shot the chief a grin.

"I want you to stick with them and keep your eyes and ears open. Make sure they stay in line. You might learn something."

"Yes, sir."

"You know, Jimmy, you've got potential to be as good a cop as your father."

"Thank you. I know he respected you and would be proud that you succeeded him as chief." Jimmy turned and left the office.

Laura closed the door to the conference room and dialed Shirley Olsen at the Seattle field office. Shirley was a mid-level analyst, skilled at searching records and transactions.

"Shirley, it's Laura Daniels." She hit the speakerphone button and set the cell phone carefully on the desk.

"Hi, Laura. I heard it's getting a little tense out there."

"Things are definitely heating up. What do you have for me?" She picked up a pen and opened her notebook, hoping for a solid lead.

"First, I ran the search for vans and trucks in a two-hundred fifty mile radius around Spokane. I thought it seemed strange when I didn't get many hits. Then I realized that Seattle is just outside the range, so I widened the search to include Washington, Idaho, Oregon and Montana. I started with rentals after May first. There were over two-thousand hits, so I filtered the data for Middle Eastern names and unbelievably came up blank."

"Blank?"

"None. We kicked it around a little and realized that a lot of cargo vans and small moving trucks are rented by small firms not on a networked system, so we broke it by state and started calling small rental firms." Shirley paused and Laura heard papers being shuffled on the other end.

"We found ten rentals. But there's one that sticks out."

"Sticks out how?"

"A van was rented in Billings, Montana, by a man named Ali Ibrahim Atif. Atif is on the FBI watch list, Laura. He is suspected to have been involved with terrorist activity in London and we last had him living in New York."

"Can you e-mail the file on Atif, Shirley?"

"Sure, but I'm not finished. The owner of the rental firm, a man named

Seth Gates says Atif and another Middle Eastern man rented the van on May fourth and returned it on May seventh. When they returned the van, they rented a storage unit for a month. Atif paid with cash, which the owner admitted seemed a little suspicious, but he said the men were very nice and polite."

"Good work, Shirley," Laura said.

"One more thing—Atif rented the van again yesterday."

Chapter Twenty-two

Cody, Wyoming
May 10, 2004

Ahmed followed the white cargo van into the parking lot of the Buffalo Bill Villas. He stopped the rented Buick Century in front of the small corner office, squinting as the overhead sun glinted off the statue of Buffalo Bill Cody standing guard. He adjusted the rearview mirror to check out his face. The gashes above his eye and on his cheekbone were bandaged and purple blotches covered the right side of his face. It still hurt like hell, but the swelling in his lower lip was starting to go down.

Earlier that morning, they abandoned the careful, time-consuming removal of the smoke detector sources. The last fifty were cracked apart with a hammer and screwdriver, and the pieces thrown in a box. All the sources were now in the trunk of Ahmed's rental car. They locked the storage room and left for Cody without checking out of their hotel rooms in Billings.

Ahmed stretched his arms and legs as he extracted himself from his vehicle. His back hurt from the hour of kneeling on the concrete floor of the storage room, whacking the smoke detectors with a hammer. As Ahmed entered the office, he heard a soft bell meant to alert the manager of prospective business. At the far end of the room, an elderly lady reclined in an overstuffed lounge chair watching a soap opera on an old, console television.

The old lady slowly pushed her way out of the oversized, heavily cushioned recliner. It appeared as if the chair held onto her with invisible arms as she tried to break free from its grip. With a huge effort and loud grunt, she pushed herself to the edge of the chair and stood up. She turned to look at the man who was interrupting her peaceful rest, giving him a forced smile.

"Can I help you?" she asked, her voice weak and grandmotherly.

"Yes, I'd like a room for the night."

"Sure, okay," she said as she limped behind the counter. "You'll have to excuse me—darned arthritis is flaring up this morning. What kind of room would you like? We have one and two bedroom villas. They're quite nice with a fireplace and color televisions in each bedroom and the sitting room. The televisions in the rooms are a damn sight better than the one I have to watch."

"I'll take a two bedroom unit for me and my associate," Ahmed said.

"Okay, let's see. Fill in this registration card. How will you be paying? We take Master Card and Visa. No American Express, they charge five-percent. Did you know that Mr. uh, Halid?" she asked, glancing at the registration card Ahmed was working on.

"I've heard something about that. I'll just pay in cash if that meets your satisfaction," Ahmed said with a warm smile.

"Oh my, yes, but we can't give a discount for cash."

"That's quite all right," Ahmed said, still smiling.

He took the key and strolled to the car, spinning the large keychain on his finger. *Just a few more days and we will be back in New York with more than enough radiation sources for the bomb. Allah and Saif will be very pleased.*

Although the x-ray tool would fit in the automobile's trunk, Ahmed's Internet research led him to believe that the well logging tool was about eight feet long with two radiation sources. He thought with all the protective shielding the tool would be difficult to handle by himself. He also needed Ali to punch out the lock on the well logger truck while he cut the lock on the x-ray truck.

He planned to steal the radiation sources sometime after midnight and return to Billings before daylight. They would dismantle the devices at the storage room as much as they dared to and pack it all into the rental car. Then they would return the van and leave for New York. It would be a long drive home but the thought of returning to the city relieved him.

Their work would not be done until Fahid built the explosive device for the dirty bomb. Perhaps after fulfilling their mission, they would be allowed to return home to be reunited with their families. Or maybe they would be chosen for the honor of detonating the bomb that would strike fear into the hearts of their enemy. Being allowed to give their lives for a cause so great would be the ultimate reward.

Chapter Twenty-three

Four Sixes Ranch
May 10, 2004

Billy Goller and Jimmy Buck had their logging gear in place. The nuclear tool hung above the double-valve well casing. The two valves operated much like an air lock on a submarine. Billy closed the bottom valve at ground level, climbed back up on the rig platform and cracked opened the pressure relief valve. Gas from the well hissed through the valve and into the atmosphere.

Billy watched the shimmering light through the natural gas as it swirled around him. Gas created from prehistoric life millions of years ago and trapped in the bowels of the earth enveloped them until the light wind carried it toward the laborers and pipeline crew.

"Ah, come on, Billy, what'd ya do? God, you stink," Jimmy said, waving his hand in front of his face.

"That's not me, you idiot. It's the gas from the well."

"I never smelled no gas like that except from your ass," Jimmy laughed, still waving his hand trying to shoo the smell away.

All of the men working downwind of the well looked around yelling, "Who cut the cheese?"

When the pressure was released, Billy closed the relief valve and opened the big ball valve on top. The nuclear tool was lowered into the well using the remote control for the large winch attached to his truck. Jimmy clamped a rubber seal on the well casing and secured it to minimize gas loss as they ran the surveys. Then he climbed off the platform and opened the big valve at ground level and the process began.

Billy ran to the back of the truck and flipped the switches that would open the shutters on the nuclear tool releasing the gamma radiation from the Americium-241 sources. The radiation would penetrate the rock surrounding the well casing and sensitive scintillation tubes would read the returns and record the properties of the rock formation.

The winch hummed to life and the heavy tool started its downward journey, very slowly, to the bottom of the well. In the corner of the truck, a computer hard drive stirred and a circular chart recorder sprung to life taking readings from the sophisticated measuring devices housed between the two potent radiation sources at each end of the cylinder.

Meanwhile, Brandon picked away at his smelly specimen. He opened the plastic and almost passed out from the odor. Unable to control himself, he turned and emptied his stomach of the bagel he'd eaten on the corporate jet.

After the heaving ceased, he quickly cut samples off the mass of oozing material and rewrapped it. He placed the samples in large zip-lock plastic bags. The heaving started again, only this time there was nothing left to come up. His stomach constricted again and again. Finally regaining control of himself, he took the sample bags back to the trailer. Not hindered by modesty, he stripped down outside the trailer, put his clothes in a trash bag and sealed it shut. He scrambled into the trailer and right to the shower.

"New hobby, Doc?" Dallas yelled, seeing Brandon streak by. He heard the water start flowing and various bumps and bangs followed by a curse word or two.

Shaking his head from side to side with a broad grin in the shower, Brandon couldn't think of anything witty to say to his friend.

Chapter Twenty-four

Spokane, Washington
May 10, 2004

"Bob, this is Laura," she spoke into the small cell phone cradled between her ear and shoulder.

"What do you need, Laura?"

"I just talked to Shirley and they came up with a lead in Billings. I'm on my way to check it out and I'd like to take Campisi and his team with me."

"That's fine."

"Can I use the jet?" she asked, crossing her fingers.

"It's at your disposal."

"Okay, Bob, thanks." She flipped the phone closed, then opened it again and called the government hanger at the Spokane airport. It would take about a half-hour to file a flight plan and fuel the Falcon 50-EX.

Next she called Johnny Campisi. "Johnny, we have a change in plans."

"Shit, what now?"

"We may have identified our bad guys. A man named Ali Ibrahim Atif and another Middle Eastern man rented a van in Billings, Montana, several days ago. Atif is on our watch list. I've got the jet warming up."

"I'll get my guys and leave Desmond's team combing through the crime scenes."

"See you in about a half hour. I've got to go back up to tell Chief Reynolds what's going on."

"Good luck."

As Laura flipped the phone closed, Harrison appeared in the doorway.

"Did the van rental angle yield any results?" he asked.

"As a matter of fact, yes. I'm leaving for Billings as soon as I can get out of here."

"You're leaving?"

Laura thought the look on his face was disappointment. "Yes. The forensics team is staying behind, but I'm taking Campisi and the surveillance team with me."

"But you just told the chief—"

"Things just changed, Jim. I'm sorry. I need to go back to see Chief Reynolds and let him know," she said, standing.

"I'm going with you."

Reynolds spotted Laura and Harrison trotting towards his glassed front office. He held up a finger with the phone cradled in the crook of his neck when they entered.

"Okay, thanks, Mr. Williams, I'll tell them. Yeah, uh-huh, you have a good day too." He looked up at the two of them. "I'll make this quick, Agent Daniels, because I know you're in a hurry. Detective Harrison is going to accompany you on this investigation."

"What? But we're going to Montana, sir. Spokane PD has no jurisdiction there."

"I know where you're going, Agent Daniels. I just hung up with your boss. He called me as a courtesy to thank me for my cooperation. He also let me know you were headed to Billings. Mohammed Atwah was a Spokane resident killed in Spokane. You're tracking his murderers. Harrison is going with you. It's been cleared with your boss and will be shortly with the Montana governor," Chief Reynolds said. "Harrison, get your things together and get your ass on that jet."

"Yes, sir. I'll see you downstairs, Agent Daniels. I live on the way to the airport." He turned and left.

Laura turned toward the open door to leave.

"Agent Daniels," Chief Reynolds said in a softer voice, "Harrison really is a good detective. Maybe this experience will be good for him. Send him back in one piece."

"Yes, sir." Laura turned and left, a grin spreading across her face. She gathered her things in the conference room and ran downstairs where Harrison was waiting at the door.

"Welcome aboard, partner," she said, patting him on the back.

They boarded the Falcon jet and taxied out to the runway immediately. A minute later they were wheels-up for their short journey to Billings.

As they entered the austere government jet Harrison said, "Wow, this is nice."

"Well, it's convenient," Johnny said. "Compared to other private jets, it's a Plane Jane. Get it? Plane, as in airplane?"

"Oh, yeah, ha, ha. Well, it looks nice to me," Harrison said, checking out the comfortable leather seats.

"Johnny, I need your team to find out where Atif and his accomplice are, or were, staying. Jim and I will visit Billings U-Store. Williams called the Billings PD so they're expecting us," Laura said, above the roar of the jet engines.

She opened her laptop computer, linked to the wireless network on-board and downloaded her e-mail and the file on Ali Atif. There were several pictures of Atif, mostly taken in London roughly three years before. The young Middle Easterner didn't look particularly dangerous with his bushy eyebrows and medium build. But they never do. The most dangerous of all were the ones that fit easily into society. After printing out the contents of the file, she chose the clearest photo and printed out several copies on the plane's color printer and passed them out.

"Here's one of our suspects and all the data we have on him."

Thirty-five minutes later, a loud thump announced that they were on final approach. "Fasten your seatbelts" was the only announcement.

There was a white Ford minivan and a white Taurus waiting at the hanger. The team gathered their tools and luggage and loaded the vehicles. The surveillance team took the van, leaving the Taurus for Harrison and Laura.

"I'm driving." She smiled at Harrison. "Not that I don't trust you."

"Hey, I'm not above lounging in the passenger seat."

Johnny Campisi drove the surveillance team directly to the Billings Police Department. They climbed out of the van and entered the old single story building with rusting steel bars at the windows, a leftover from Billings' wilder days. Inside, the station looked just as rustic: dark wood paneling on the walls, crumbling, water-stained ceiling tiles and bare concrete floor.

"Excuse me, I'm Agent Campisi, FBI Seattle. I believe someone here is expecting us," Johnny explained to the officer at the desk.

"Yes, sir, that would be Inspector Todd. That's him, with the cue-ball head in the corner." The desk officer pointed to a bald, older man sitting at a desk in the far corner of the room. "Hey, Todd. The FBI is here."

Todd stood, stretching his lanky body and limped toward the FBI agents. Johnny took a step toward him and held out a thick hand.

"I'm Agent Johnny Campisi. Nice to meet you, Inspector Todd. This is Agent Bart Jackman and Agent Tommy Aldo."

"Welcome to Billings, boys," he said, shaking their hands. "I know you're in a big hurry, so let's go to that table over yonder and find out what we can do for you," Todd said, with a big smile.

Stick a lollipop in his mouth and you have Kojak, Johnny thought. They followed him to the worn and scratched table out in the middle of the open room. Todd used his arm to sweep the salt and ketchup packets to one end and sat down.

"Inspector, we're trying to locate a couple of suspects. They are Middle Eastern and one of them is named Ali Ibrahim Atif. We believe that they arrived sometime around May fourth and probably stayed at a local hotel. They may have checked out today, although that's speculation. They may still be here."

Johnny paused and then said, "Although they may be using an alias, we are fairly sure Atif is using his real name. He rented a storage room and van from Billings U-Store using his real name. We have two agents checking that out now."

"Cocky bastard. Just what did these two do?" Todd asked.

"They're suspects in a theft and murder in Spokane. We think they may be associated with a terrorist cell planning to build a dirty bomb," Johnny explained.

"Well, let's find these bastards. We can do a computer search, but there are a lot of bed and breakfast places and small lodges that don't have networked guest registration systems. We're going to need warm bodies to cover them all. I can bring in three off-duty officers to help. Let me get a list and we can split it up," Todd said.

"Inspector, I suggest we prioritize by hotels that will rent rooms for cash without requiring a credit card for a security deposit."

"All righty, I'll be right back." Todd walked to the desk sergeant and began politely barking orders.

Johnny watched how the uniforms respectfully took orders and figured that even with Todd's gruff exterior, he must have a soft spot inside. *Why couldn't they receive this kind of cooperation everywhere?*

Laura and Harrison pulled into the opened gates that protected the Billings U-Store facility. A gravel lot surrounded three long storage buildings situated in rows. The wind howled down the long rows, kicking up dust from the gravel lot.

Each building had twelve orange roll-top garage doors on each side. Two small white moving trucks and one white cargo van with Billings U-Store painted on the doors were parked in the front corner of the lot next to an unmarked GMC pick-up truck.

Getting out of the car, Harrison looked down the driveway between two of the buildings. All the doors were shut and he could see the eight foot chain link fence at the end of the row with two strands of barbed wire protecting the top. The middle building housed the rental office. Harrison turned the knob on the door and lost his grip as the force of the wind caught it and slammed the door inward.

The door banged open, slamming into a cow bell hanging from the ceiling. The dull clanging announced their entry. He reached in and held the rental office door for Laura, bringing a smile and approving glance from her as she passed by, her hair flying in the strong breeze. A chest-high counter separated the customer area from the business side. Behind the counter was a closed door with a small window leading to a private office. Closed mini-blinds prevented prying eyes from spying the interior of the office.

Laura stepped to the counter and pushed a doorbell labeled *Push for Service*. They heard the muffled buzz from behind the office door. After a minute passed with no response, she pushed the button again. No sounds, save the buzzer, emerged from the office. She rang the bell a third time—

nothing. *That's peculiar*, she thought, looking at the hand-written sign boasting *Round the Clock Security*. The gates and rental office were open.

Back outside, Laura pointed to Harrison and then to the right. She pointed to herself and then to the left. Harrison nodded and they separated, each going to peer around the corners of the buildings on opposite ends. There was nothing down the long rows of buildings. They came back to the office door and Laura pulled her gun, hidden under her jacket. Harrison did the same.

"I'll go first," Harrison whispered. Opening the door, careful to hang onto the knob, they entered the office again. Harrison ducked under the counter and positioned himself with his back to the wall next to the private office while Laura watched, with her gun drawn, standing next to the entry door under the swinging cowbell.

"Police! Is anybody in there?" Harrison said, loud enough to be heard through the closed door.

No response.

Harrison reached for the doorknob and turned it. The door swung open and he peered around the edge of the door frame, pointing his gun in the office at the same time.

Empty. Although messy, there was no apparent foul play. Harrison looked over to Laura, shook his head from side to side and entered the office.

She heard a click behind her. Before she could react, something slammed into her back, throwing her to the tiled floor. Her gun flew from her hand and skidded to the far wall as she tried to brace herself. She couldn't tell if the ringing she heard came from banging her head on the ground or the cowbell clamoring in the howling wind. Her training took over. Sliding forward, with her hands outstretched, she reached for the gun spinning on the tile floor near the wall. At the same time she twisted her body around to see her attacker, and brought her Sauer P-229 in front of her, fingering the trigger.

A large man rushed toward her, his black hair and beard flying wildly in the wind. For a moment, Laura thought Hagrid from Harry Potter was rushing toward her.

"Freeze!" Laura shouted.

"Oh my God, I'm sorry! Oh shit, whoa, slow down, missy."

The man's eyes were open wide at the sight of the young lady sitting on the floor holding a gun at arm's length, pointed right at him. He threw his hands in the air.

"The wind pulled the door out of my hands, is all! Oh shit, are you okay?" The man looked as confused and rattled as Laura was.

Harrison came running from the office with his gun pointed at the man and asked, "Laura, are you okay?"

"Yeah," she answered, then asked the man, "Who the hell are you?"

"I'm Seth Gates. I own this place. Who the hell are you?"

Getting to her feet, Laura pulled her ID from her waist and said, "Agent Laura Daniels, FBI. This is my partner, Detective Jim Harrison from the Spokane Police Department."

Harrison and Laura lowered their guns and placed them back in their holsters both letting out a quiet sigh of relief. Laura's heart was still pounding as was the back of her head from the door slamming into her.

"Are you okay, missy? I'm real sorry. The wind blows hard from the south this time of year. You'd think I'd be used to holding onto that doggone doorknob better."

"I've been better, Mr. Gates, but I'll live. Where the hell were you? Are you in the habit of leaving your storage facility unattended with the gates open?" she asked.

"No, ma'am. I was cleaning unit 312 down there on the end," he said, pointing to the far end of the property. "I closed the door most of the way to keep the wind out."

Gates lumbered to the counter and ducked his humungous torso under. "Is this about them A-rab gentlemen that rented one of my rooms and truck?"

"Yes, sir, it is. What can you tell us about them?" Laura patted the pockets of her jacket to locate her notebook and pen.

"Not much to tell." Gates retrieved an accordion file folder from under the counter. The hairy giant thumbed through rental contracts pulling out several and placing them on the counter. "Let's see here. Mr. Atif and another gentleman rented one of my small trucks, a cargo van, on May fifth. They returned it on May seventh and put one thousand fourteen miles on it. He said he was going to his Washington supply warehouse," Gates said, gazing through his bifocals at the first contract.

Picking up the second contract, he continued, "When he returned the van, he rented unit 113 and paid for a month up front—cash."

"Then this morning, he rented my other small truck. The stamp here says he went out at 9:30 a.m.," Gates said, looking back at them. "That's about it."

"I'll need the information on the van they rented: year, make, model, color, vehicle identification number and license plate number."

"Hold on. I keep a file handy in case one gets stolen." He bent down and pulled several file folders from under the counter. Thumbing through them, he extracted one folder and handed it to Laura. "Here—there's even a picture of it."

Laura took the file and said, "Thank you, Mr. Gates, can I take this to the police station and make copies?"

"No need, I have all the information in the back office. If you happen by again, and you don't need it, just drop it off."

Harrison spoke up, "You said there were two men. Can you tell us about the other man?"

"Oh, I only seen him once. Want to hear a little secret?" he said, and chuckled. "I couldn't tell 'em apart." His eyes almost squeezed shut from the broad grin that spread across his hefty face.

Laura pulled the photo of Atif from her jacket pocket, "Was this one of them?"

Gates took the picture and turned his chin up to study the picture through his bifocals. "Looks a bit like him. But like I said, they all look a bit alike to me. I know that's not PC to say these days."

Harrison took his turn, "Can you recall the other man's name or is there anything you can remember special about him."

Gates took off his glasses and stuck the temple piece in his mouth to chew on it. "Hmm, I sort of remember. Let's see, Ackmen, or Akman. Maybe Ahmed. Yeah, Ahmed, because I thought he was saying amen, like in the end of a prayer. Didn't catch a last name though. You want to take a peek in their storeroom?"

"I would indeed, Mr. Gates, if you don't mind," Laura said.

"Well, I'm not supposed to—but you being the FBI and all…I guess I don't have a choice." Gates reached for the big key ring on his belt.

"Renters are required to purchase their own locks. But I require them to give me a key in case there's a fire or something. Hee, hee. I also sell locks in case someone needs one. I make a few extra bucks that way. Watch the door on your way out."

Gates opened the door and led Harrison and Laura to the end unit on the northeast corner. He bent down, unlocked the door and rolled it up.

The room was empty except for four boxes, a folding table and a chair. There were small screws on the ground around the table, a box of bandages and a box of tissues. On the floor there were several tissues with small blood stains on them and some small plastic parts.

The boxes were all cut open and three of them were neatly packed with smoke detectors. One box had smoke detector parts in it and behind the large boxes were the empty individual containers for about fifty of them.

Harrison picked up one of the dismantled plastic devices and examined it. "Look, they removed something. See here?" he said, pointing to two little holes on the circuit board. "There were screws here, holding something in. It must be that source you were talking about."

"Yeah, the screws are over here. They must have used this table to dismantle them. And here's a bonus—we may just have a DNA sample on this tissue. Mr. Gates, do you have a small plastic bag?"

"Sure, let me run back up to the office." Gates turned and jogged clumsily out the door and around the corner.

In a few minutes he was back with a small plastic sandwich bag. "Is this okay?"

"Perfect, thank you," she said, carefully sealing the tissue in the bag.

"It certainly doesn't look like they're finished here. I'm guessing they'll be coming back to finish the job." Turning to Gates, Laura asked, "Mr. Gates, did they say where they were heading?"

"Wyoming," Gates said immediately. "Well, they never really said that's where they were going, but they asked me if I had a Wyoming map. I keep some road maps lying around."

"Mr. Gates, thanks for your help," Laura said as she watched him snap the lock back on the roll-up door. "Here's my card. Please call me if these men return. Don't tell them that we were here and don't act suspicious or try to do anything heroic. There will likely be an agent watching this place for a while, so don't be alarmed."

On the walk back to the office, Laura flipped open her cell phone and called Bob Williams.

"Williams here."

"Bob, seems like Ali Atif has an accomplice. We believe his first name is Ahmed. I'll have a search run on the name when I get back to police headquarters."

"I'll have a list run for you—it'll be quicker. We can e-mail the results to you. Anything else?"

"We found the stash of smoke detectors in a storage room. Seems like they're still dismantling them. We're going to post a lookout. I have information on a van they rented this morning."

Laura thumbed through the file folder and gave Williams the VIN, license plate number and physical description.

"I'll put out an APB on the van and let you know if we find out anything on Ahmed. What's Campisi doing?"

"He's got his team looking for the hotel where they may have stayed."

"Okay, Laura, keep me posted."

Back at the car, Laura turned to Mr. Gates and thanked him once again.

"Glad to be of help. Good luck." Gates watched them get in the car and drive off.

"Let's get to Billings PD," Laura said.

"Yeah, we can pitch in and help find the hotel—if they're staying in one, that is," Harrison added.

Chapter Twenty-five

Four Sixes Ranch
May 10, 2004

"Okay, run complete. Tool's comin' up," Billy yelled from the back of the truck. Jimmy wrestled two large trashcans up on the rig platform grating. He pulled old rags out of one and wrapped them around the cable as it came up. When a rag became too soiled, he threw it in the empty can, grabbed a clean one and continued wiping the cable before it coiled on the winch. With a hundred feet to go the gawd-awful odor returned. By the time the tool clanged past the lower valve, he was retching uncontrollably. He jumped off the platform and ducked his head as he entered the space below the platform, pushed the red button on the switch box tripping the motor that rotated the big ball valve sealing the well shut.

By the time he emerged from under the platform, Billy was listening to the faint clicking of the Geiger counter. He turned and flashed a thumbs-up, then opened the pressure relief valve. Jimmy reluctantly climbed back up the platform and loosened the clamp holding the rubber boot. The winch hummed again and the nuclear tool rose from the well casing, slinging black slimy goo onto their clothes and faces and into their hair. They both grabbed a handful of rags and started wiping it down while trying not to breathe.

"I can't do this anymore," Billy gasped finally. "Let's just get it in the box and we'll have the techs finish it when we get back to Laramie."

"No argument here."

Billy reversed the winch as Jimmy guided the tool into the shielded case and clamped it shut. They grabbed the handles of the heavy box and loaded it into the back of the truck next to their spare nuclear tool.

"Let me go in and report to the cheese and we can head into town and clean up," Billy said.

"Come in," Brandon called, responding to a rap on the trailer door.

The door cracked open. "I don't think ya want me in there the way I stink, sir."

"Yeah, stay out there. I'll come to you." Brandon noticed that Billy Goller had respectfully stepped about twenty feet down wind.

"We're finished with the nuclear run. Gonna head into town to scrub up. I ain't never smelled anything like this before," Billy explained.

"It takes some hard scrubbing to get that stench off. Dallas and I have some experience at that. Any preliminary report?"

"Well, I have ta run the data, but the rock's real fractured and porous under the cap. I'll start the computer chewin' on it when we get to the hotel."

"Okay, guys, go get cleaned up. See you in the morning."

"Yes, sir."

Brandon turned and walked back to the microscope he had set up on the table. He'd been studying the samples all afternoon after confirming it was indeed soft tissue. He had one of the laborers drive into Cody and buy several large coolers and dry ice. The samples were placed in the coolers so they didn't degrade further.

He tried calling Andrew Burch at the Paleontology Department at Harvard and Kurt Edmonds at the Phillips County Museum in Malta, Montana. Kurt was the Curator of Paleontology at the museum in Malta and ran amateur digs throughout the summer. Brandon had spent his summers up in Malta exploring the exposed Hell Creek formation that yielded so many of the dinosaur fossils that were discovered in the area. He and Kurt had become good friends and Brandon admired the way Kurt handled amateur diggers that came to the area for dinosaur hunts. *Damn, where were all the paleontologists when you needed them?*

"You ready to get out of here, Dallas?" Brandon asked.

"Yeah, Doc. I've got to get me some aspirin for this headache." Dallas had been coughing and spitting phlegm for the last half hour.

Brandon loaded the coolers into the back of the Humvee and he followed Dallas back to Cody. They took the dirt access road off the ranch then turned west on Route 14 and headed into the sunset. The pale yellowish-orange orb of the sun hung low in the sky, half hidden by Rattlesnake Mountain. The mountain gave way to the city of Cody and the glistening blue waters of Buffalo Bill Reservoir.

The ride back to Cody reminded Brandon of the rugged beauty of the Luliang Shan Mountains in China that Mae had called home. Depending on the results of the well logger's tests, Brandon thought he would take a week off to explore Yellowstone National Park and then travel up to Malta to visit his friend Kurt.

They pulled up to their condominium just as the last bit of sun dipped below the horizon. Dallas crawled out of the Hummer and headed to his room.

"Hey, Dallas!" Brandon called after him. "When are we meeting for dinner?"

"You go ahead, Doc. I'm feelin' a bit puny. And last night was a helluva long night."

"You want me to bring you back something?"

"How about some cold medicine? You know, the kind that helps you sleep," Dallas said, coughing.

"Sure thing. I'll be back in about an hour."

Dallas lifted his hand in a half-hearted wave as he turned and walked off to his room. *Damn, Dallas*, Brandon thought. *You need a vacation more than I do*.

Chapter Twenty-six

Billings, Montana
May 10, 2004

"I've got 'em!" one of the off-duty officers yelled. "Comfort Lodge on Minnesota Avenue near the refinery. They have an Ali Atif and Ahmed Halid still registered."

"Jackman, get over there now and position yourself to watch the rooms, unseen. Johnny, let's get Williams on the phone and talk through this. Inspector Todd, do you have someone that can go with Jackman?" Laura barked.

"Sure." Todd looked over his shoulder. "Hey Jim, go along with Agent Jackman." Picking up the piece of paper that the off-duty officer handed to him, he turned back to Jackman. "It looks like they're in 115 and 116. All the rooms are visible from the street."

Campisi threw the keys to the van to Jackman as he and the Billings policeman headed for the door.

"Inspector Todd, is there an office we can use to call Seattle?" Laura asked.

"Sure, Agent Daniels. You can use that one over there. There's a speakerphone and everything," Todd answered.

"We'll be using our cell phones, but thanks for the offer. These are encrypted and secure." Laura pointed to Campisi, then to the office. "Let's do this Johnny—Harrison, you too."

Johnny closed the door behind him while Laura sat the little phone down on the desk as Williams answered. "Bob, this is Laura. I have Johnny and Detective Harrison in the room with me."

"Yeah. Go ahead."

"First off, we believe Ahmed's last name is *Halid.* H-A-L-I-D. We have them registered at the Comfort Lodge in Billings. We just sent Jackman and one of Billings' officers to watch the place."

"Just a second."

She heard Bob whispering to someone on his end of the connection. "Ahmed Halid is also on the watch list. He is an electrical engineer that worked for a German radiation device manufacturer. He came to the United States several years ago to work in the company's Chicago office. Earlier this year he quit, saying he was going back to Iran to be with his family. He never left. He has been suspected, but never implicated in the attempted detonation of a Sarin gas bomb in Westminster Abbey in 2001. The device failed, but reportedly he killed five Bobbies and three MI-6 agents when they trapped him in an alley. Despite all that, he escaped," Williams added. "The notes here indicate Halid is a real bad-ass. Be careful around him. I'm transmitting the file to you now. I'll call Washington to have them send in a tactical team to help you. Campisi, you keep the rooms under surveillance until they get there. Do not move in by yourselves. I'll call with an ETA. The APB on the van hasn't turned up anything so far. Unless there's anything else, I've got calls to make," Williams said.

Laura looked at Johnny Campisi who was shaking his head from side-to-side. "That's it."

"Good enough. Keep it up. And remember, stay at arm's length." The line went dead.

"Johnny, how are you doing on sleep?" Laura asked.

"We're okay, but you look tired. Why don't I drop you and Harrison off to get some food and rest, then I'll take Aldo over to check on Jackman."

Minnesota Avenue was a wide street in an old industrial section of town. The Comfort Lodge was one of the few buildings standing on the block.

"Tell me about this area, Campbell," Jackman asked while driving past the Comfort Inn. Bart Jackman was just plain intimidating. He shaved his head with just a shadowy hint of dark black hair and the same shadow was forever present on his face. His eyes were shielded by the overhanging cliff of his broad forehead. A former Navy SEAL, he was strong, agile and highly trained with explosives. His forte, however, was surveillance.

"The motel is used by contractors working at the refinery. It's a real fleabag," Campbell answered. "How many times are you going to drive by?"

"The location makes surveillance tricky. There's no place within sight of the rooms that we can remain inconspicuous. We'll park around the corner and walk the street. It looks like the rooms are dark."

He pulled the van to the curb. "Let's go, Campbell. We'll walk up the block and settle in next to that half-wall across the street from the hotel. Grab that bag behind your seat. I hope you're used to standing for long periods." Jackman reached back and grabbed the night vision equipment as he stepped into the cool night air.

They headed away from the hotel toward a mostly demolished building directly across the street, then picked their way through the rubble and stopped behind a brick wall that was left standing. Jackman removed a clear bowl-shaped apparatus with a pistol grip from his bag and handed it to Campbell. Then he pulled a set of headphones, plugged it into the directional microphone and handed them to his new partner.

"Put these on and point the dish at the windows. There's a sight just like a gun."

Jackman flipped the switch on his infrared scope and concentrated it on the rooms. No distinct heat signatures.

"This could be a long fucking night." Jackman raised his arms overhead and yawned.

Laura and Harrison dragged their suitcases onto the elevator of the aging Holiday Inn. Laura rested her computer case on the top of her suitcase as the elevator doors closed. The lift started up with a jerk causing her to lose her grip on her computer case. It fell to the floor spilling her notes and pens.

"Oh, crap," Laura said.

They both bent over at the same time to pick things up and almost banged heads. Laura glanced up to see Harrison's face inches away from hers. Their eyes locked for a moment and Harrison's cheeks flushed as he looked back down and handed her the papers he had retrieved. The doors opened on the fourth floor and they made their way to their rooms.

"How about throwing your things in the room and let's go to the restaurant across the street?" Harrison asked.

"Sounds good. Let me hook my computer up to download my e-mail and I'll meet you downstairs in fifteen minutes. I'm waiting for the file on Halid."

"See you in fifteen," Harrison said as he disappeared into his room.

Chapter Twenty-seven

Cody, Wyoming
May 10, 2004

Ahmed peered from the window of his comfortable villa as the pipeline contractors pulled their caravan of trucks and trailers into the Wyoming Inn parking lot. The 1950's vintage two-story L-shaped complex was built with cinderblock walls. A separate office building sat near the street just below the bright flashing neon sign. A sharp red light announcing "vacancy" cut through the darkness, casting an eerie glow on the whitewashed hotel walls.

The two familiar Wyoming Test Lab trucks pulled in front of the office and three men went inside. A few minutes later, they returned to their vehicles and pulled them forward a few feet to parking spaces in front of the first three rooms nearest the office.

"Ali, I am going to take a walk down the street to get a closer look. Right now it looks like we may need to develop an alternate plan. The trucks are too visible from the street and the hotel office." Ahmed's quiet voice masked his concerns.

Ahmed left the warmth of the villa and stepped into the cool evening. He strolled down the sidewalk and crossed the dimly lit street at the crosswalk, then walked back towards the Wyoming Inn. He needed to get a look at the trucks. Turning into the driveway furthest from the office, he covered the short distance to the long leg of the L-shaped building and hid in the shadows. He could see the desk clerk sitting in the window of the office looking out over the parking lot. He had the look of a man bored with life. The trucks were right in his line of sight.

"Damn!" Back near the street, Ahmed raised a small pair of binoculars and read the sign on the office door.

"Office Open 24 hours. Ring bell if door is locked."

Why couldn't this be easier?

Billy Goller dabbed at a runny nose while standing by the truck. Where *the hell are they*, he wondered. He had been waiting ten minutes for Jimmy and Walt. He figured he'd be the last one out considering how long it took him to shower away the odor from the well. "Come on, guys, I'm hungry," he muttered while pounding on Jimmy's door. A long minute passed and the door swung open. Jimmy's swollen bloodshot eyes peered from wild-looking wet hair and beard.

"Hey man, you look like crap. You ready to go to dinner?"

"No way. I feel worse than I look." Jimmy spat a large ball of green phlegm on the concrete. "I'm stayin' in tonight. Maybe I'm allergic to something."

"Yeah, I've been hackin' up shit for a while too. Musta been something in that shitty smelling gas comin' outta the well. I'm just goin' to the burger joint on the corner. You want something?"

"Yeah, can you bring me some fries and a big coke?"

"Sure thing." Billy slapped him on the shoulder. "Have you seen Walt?"

"Nope." Jimmy hugged his gut as wet coughs doubled him over.

"Man, go lay down, will ya?" Billy turned as the door slammed shut and went to the next room. He heard coughing coming from inside as he banged his fist on the orange door. It swung open and Walt stuck his head out.

"Let's go, Walt. It's just me and you tonight. Jimmy's comin' down with something," Billy said.

"Shit, I think most of the welders started choking after you guys doused them with that stink from the well." They climbed in the x-ray truck and drove down the street to the Burger Barn. After getting their greasy burgers and fries from the pimple-faced teenage boy behind the counter, they slid into a booth.

"So how's the pipeline comin'?" Billy asked.

"Done. Tie-ins tonight. Gas'll be ready to flow as soon as you're done. I'm hoping Mr. McAlister will git me some work on his ranch 'til the next job comes along."

"Well, that should be by tomorrow afternoon," Billy nodded. "Based on the scan as the tool went down, it looks like they got a good well."

"Hello, Dr. Brandon. How are you tonight?" A smiling Debbie asked as he sat at his table at the Buffalo Bill Bar. She ran thin fingers through her long auburn hair. Dark eyeliner accentuated blue eyes that were darker than his own.

"Pretty good, Debbie, thanks for asking."

"Where's your partner in crime tonight?"

"He's a little under the weather. He had a long day and I think he just needs a good night's sleep." *This is starting to feel like more than just small talk,* he thought. *But she is easy to talk to.*

"My experience with men like Dallas is that they do better on two hours sleep than eight." She sat in the chair next to him.

"You just described Dallas. But he's been pushing pretty hard the past two weeks. He usually waits until the end of the project before he crashes, though. I guess age is taking its toll." Brandon smiled. "He'd kill me if he heard me call him old."

"I'll bet he would. Getting old is...well, it's a bitch." She frowned as she cupped her breasts and pushed up as she peered down at her cleavage. "Each day goes by, these point more to where I'm at than where I'm going."

Brandon laughed so hard his stomach hurt and tears rolled down his cheeks. *I'd really like to get to know this woman. She's refreshingly natural—and no ring.*

His eyes did a quick sweep. She appeared to be in her mid-thirties and in good shape with a great figure. And then there was that sexy smile.

"Debbie, I'm not usually this forward, but are you married?"

"Divorced, Doctor. And how about you?"

"Same. And please, call me Brandon. I'm not one for titles."

"Why is that, anyway? You probably worked real hard for that title. But I aim to please," she said, staring at his eyes again.

"I don't believe a person should be judged by their titles or education, but how they live their life."

"Wow, that's a great philosophy, Brandon. I wish more people believed that way."

Brandon looked down at the menu before raising his eyes and mustering some courage. "I'm about a week away from wrapping things up out here. I'd certainly like to take you to dinner before I leave." He looked down to his hands. "Look at me, my palms are sweating like a teenager."

"Why, I'd like that a lot. Just not here. I'm not crazy about the food." She reached across and touched his hand. "A little clammy, but I think you'll make it."

"Sounds like a date. You pick the restaurant and we'll go out next weekend if that works for you."

"I'll make it work, Brandon. Now what would you like to eat tonight?" she said, standing up. "I better start hustling or the boss will be on my butt."

Brandon watched her walk off, hips swinging in her Wild West wardrobe, and smiled.

Chapter Twenty-eight

Billings, Montana
May 10, 2004

Laura and Harrison decided on a small Italian restaurant across the street from the Holiday Inn. Dim lighting was provided by the flickering flames of candles stuffed into old Chianti bottles sitting on red and white checkered tablecloths.

"How about a nice bottle of Pinot Noir?" Harrison asked as the young raven-haired waitress approached.

"I'm more a Bud Light girl." Laura grinned across the table at Harrison.

"Well, I had you figured as a wine connoisseur."

"You're not a very good investigator, now are you?" She giggled like a teenager, feeling a bit giddy.

Harrison turned to the waitress. "Two Bud Lights, please." Twisting back in his chair to face Laura, he asked, "So, how'd an attractive girl like you wind up working for the FBI?"

"God, where do I start?" Laura asked back.

"Why not start at the beginning?"

"Geez, first off, I come from a household of men. I have three brothers and was raised by my dad."

"What about your mother?" Harrison asked.

"She died when I was born. Some complication from the anesthetic."

"Damn, I'm sorry, Laura." Harrison shifted uncomfortably in his chair. *Stupid question.*

"It was a long time ago."

"You know, we can change the subject if you want to."

She looked up with a weak smile, "I really haven't told anybody about this stuff—you're probably sorry you asked."

"No, no, as long as you're okay, I'd like to know more about my new partner."

"If you're sure...anyway, my mother was thirty-six at the time and my dad raised us. Two years after I was born, my dad found out Marcus, my oldest brother, was gay. My dad was an ex-marine and a macho guy. He was devastated."

Harrison was trying to absorb Laura's misfortune when the waitress brought their beers and took their orders. He needed the break.

After the waitress left them alone, Laura took a sip from the icy mug and continued, "Ummm, that's good. Okay, so my dad decided his other two sons weren't going to turn out the same way and pushed them into every sport he could. He even coached their teams. Since there wasn't anybody to watch me, I got dragged to all the practices and games and grew up being catcher, goalie, tackling dummy, you name it."

"Well, it showed when Mr. Gates knocked you down with the door. You looked like you were going to kick his ass. So how did you wind up in the FBI?"

"Let's see, in my sophomore year in college I was attacked by two guys while walking to my dorm. They pulled me behind the library and started ripping my clothes. I guess the adrenaline and all those hours wrestling with my brothers kicked in. I managed to double one of them over with a kick to his jewels and sunk my fingernails into the other guy's face. I ran to the panic station about a hundred feet away and the lights and sirens scared them off."

"You fought off two guys? I'm impressed."

"I wasn't going to let them get the better of me. I was able to identify them and didn't back down at the preliminary hearing when the defense lawyer tried to embarrass me into dropping the charges. It turns out those assholes had assaulted a couple of other girls at the school." She raised her hand like a claw showing Harrison her fingernails. "When they realized I had taken some nice skin samples under my nails, they copped a plea to a lesser charge."

"That's amazing, Laura."

"I guess the dean of the School of Criminal Justice was impressed with my...how did he put it...my 'poise and determination.' He asked me to switch majors from biology to criminal justice. After graduation I was recruited by the FBI and took Forensic Science Research in the training academy at Quantico. The agency was pretty depleted investigating the hijackings on 9/11 when the anthrax letters hit. I was assigned as Assistant Special Agent in Charge."

"So how'd you wind up in Seattle?"

Laura looked down at the table. "Congress wasn't pleased when I couldn't solve the case, so they shipped me off to the Seattle office to fill their EEO quota. There aren't a lot of female agents at the office. Of course, all my life I've related better to men than women."

"So how do you like Seattle?"

"I'm not crazy about it, Jim. I hate being a failure and that's how it made me feel."

After dinner, they walked back to the Holiday Inn. A cold wind blew out of the north causing Laura to hug herself for warmth. As if on cue, Harrison pulled off his jacket and draped it around her. She would rather have his arm around her, but the jacket was a nice thought.

Music filtered into the lobby of the hotel from the lounge. Harrison grabbed Laura's hand and said, "Let's go listen to some music for a while. I can use some relaxation and a cup of coffee."

She felt as if a bolt of electricity shot through her at Harrison's touch. The sensation was unexpected but not unwanted. She had been attracted to Jim Harrison from the start. "Sure, why not? It'll be fun," Laura said in an excited voice. "The special operations team won't be here until after midnight."

They walked into the quaint, dark, nearly empty lounge. What sounded like a band was merely a singer with a guitar and a computer back up. Above the small stage, a mirrored disco ball reflected shafts of white light around the room as it slowly rotated.

They sat down and Harrison ordered two beers. The singer welcomed them after he finished his song and immediately sang a slow country ballad. Harrison winked at the singer and reached for Laura's hand. "Care to dance?"

Taking her right hand in his left and putting his other hand around her slim waist, he led her in slow circles. They danced to the music in silence—an uncommonly comfortable silence. Halfway through the song, the formal dance pose turned into a lover's embrace with Laura's arms draped around Harrison's neck as they barely moved to the music.

She was mesmerized by the firmness of his body pressing against her, feeling comfortable and safe in his arms. When the song ended, Harrison kissed her lightly on the cheek and led her back to their table where their drinks waited for them.

"Well," Laura said with a sigh, "that was an unexpected pleasure."

"Yes, it was. You know, Laura, I wasn't sure I was ever going to see you again. You don't know how relieved I was when Chief Reynolds told me I was going with you. It was the best news I heard from him in a long time."

"When he first told me I was going to assist some FBI agent, I never dreamt I'd be working with such a beautiful woman." He paused. "And tough. You handled yourself pretty well when ole Seth's door knocked you to the floor. I thought he was going to pee in his pants."

Laura laughed. "I tried not to show it, but I was shaking pretty badly."

"Didn't notice a thing."

"So, Jim, what's your story?" She squeezed his hand.

"Nothing so complicated as yours. I was born and raised in Spokane. Police work must be in my blood. Both my dad and grandpop were on the force. I went to college for a couple of years, went the ROTC route."

"So you grew up around cops?"

"Yeah, before I got out of college I signed up for a term in Desert Storm as an infantryman, then finished my degree when I got back."

"What was it like in the service?"

"Desert Storm was a big build-up that ended with a little pop. It was pretty uneventful. In retrospect, I'm glad for that."

"So how long have you been on the force?"

"About five years. You see, my dad was the police chief before Reynolds. He was killed outside the courthouse last year in a drive-by shooting."

"Oh my God, I remember reading about that. I'm so sorry."

"That's okay. It seems a long time ago now."

"Jim?" Laura was looking into his eyes. "What do you think about finishing our drinks up in my room?"

"I can't think of anything I'd rather do." Harrison motioned for the waitress to bring the check.

They walked to the elevator with fingers entwined and when the doors closed, they embraced each other passionately with their lips locked as quiet moans filled the air. They walked swiftly to Laura's room and she fumbled with the card key, trying to find the slot while her hands shook in anticipation. Having Harrison's hands on her hips and him kissing her neck didn't help. The door finally swung open and they slipped inside.

Their lips touched once again as their hands explored each other. Her body came alive as his hands traveled down her back and settled on her firm buttocks. He pulled her close and she could feel his excitement build.

She unbuttoned his shirt while he cupped her breasts through her blouse, sparking a passion she hadn't felt in a long, long time. His eyes were closed and his breathing came in slow, deep breaths. Pulling back his shirt revealed an almost hairless, chiseled chest. With her fingers tracing the outlines of his nipples, she pressed her lips to his neck, kissing and licking her way down his chest to his stomach. "My turn," he said, in a low moan as his fingers worked at the small white buttons of her blouse.

Her white silky top and his blue shirt floated to the floor as his rough hands slipped under her bra pushing it up and over the small mounds. Laura reached for his belt buckle, pulling it taut while her other hand slipped between his trousers and his skin. A sudden tingling at her waist was quickly followed by a loud chirp. *You've got to be kidding me*, she thought reaching for the cell phone clipped to her belt.

Her spirit sank and for just a second she thought about ignoring the call, but her training wouldn't let her. She was buoyed by the thought that their relationship had taken this turn. Without saying a word, Laura pulled from his grasp and grabbed the phone.

"Daniels," she said, in the phone's transmitter.

"Laura, this is Johnny. What are you up too?"

He couldn't possibly know. "Uh. Just going over some details. Where are you?"

"At the motel. Where the hell do you think I'm at?"

It took her a moment to realize he was at the Comfort Lodge with the surveillance team. "Sorry, I zoned out for a moment."

"There doesn't appear to be anybody in the rooms. There are no vehicles, no sounds and the infrared isn't picking up anything," he informed her. "I'm heading back to the police department. Can you and Harrison meet us there? I'd like to have a plan before the special ops guys get here."

"You have the car, Johnny," she answered.

"Aw, crap. Okay, I'll swing by in ten minutes."

"Okay, see you in ten." She flipped the phone closed as Harrison finished tucking his shirt back into his pants.

She reached out and put her hands on his face. "I'm so sorry, Jim. Can we continue this later?"

"God, I was hoping you'd say that." He beamed at her. "I'm going to take a real quick cold shower to douse this fire. I'll see you in ten downstairs."

The ride to the police department was quiet. Once inside, Johnny laid out the situation on a white board. It was time to call Bob Williams.

"Williams here."

"Bob, we wanted to run the situation by you," Campisi said. "Atif and Halid aren't in the rooms. There are no vehicles, no sounds or lights and the infrared is negative. We believe they rented the van and are on another mission."

"Couldn't they just be headed back to New York?"

Laura interrupted. "Since they haven't checked out and they seem to still be working on the smoke detectors, we think they're coming back."

"So what do you want to do?" Williams asked.

"We'd like to enter the hotel rooms and plant some bugs. We'll set up surveillance so we can watch the rooms without being spotted. We'll also keep the storage facility under surveillance," Campisi said.

"What else?"

"We think they took the van down to Wyoming. They must be after some radiation devices. Can you get someone researching potential radiation sources that may be in use in Wyoming? Bob, my gut tells me they wouldn't have left the smoke detectors unless there was something better worth going after. It looks like they left in a hurry," Laura said.

"Okay, I'll get some people on it," Williams said. "Your plan is approved. Get started and be careful."

Laura flipped her phone closed and stood up.

"You heard the boss. Let's get going before they return."

Campisi shouted, "Hey, Todd, you got a minute?"

"Yeah, Johnny." Todd pushed himself from his office chair and ambled over to the group. "What's up?"

"How many routes are there into Billings coming from Wyoming?" Johnny asked.

"Hmmm, let's see, there's I-90 from Sheridan. Highway 310 from Powell and 212 from Yellowstone. They intersect south of town. Then there's I-90 from the west. There are two other minor state roads that could be used. Why do you ask?"

"We need some help. We need you to dispatch lookouts on those routes for the white Billings U-Store rental van for the next few hours while my team sets up bugs and surveillance on the Comfort Lodge," Campisi said.

"What do we do if we spot them?" Todd asked.

"Just call it in. We don't want them alerted. That also means your guys have to find a good place to watch without being seen."

"Oh, you don't have to worry about that." Todd's tobacco and coffee stained teeth flashed as he grinned while his hand smoothed down hair that wasn't there. "We have plenty of hidden places to set up radar. Let me call in the troops."

"Thanks. I'll make sure my boss knows how cooperative you've been. When do you think you'll have the men in place?" Campisi asked.

"Give me thirty minutes." Todd turned and headed for the radio at the front of the small building.

Campisi looked at Laura and Harrison, "Okay, we'll leave here in forty-five."

Chapter Twenty-nine

Cody, Wyoming
May 11, 2004

Ahmed and Ali sat in the comfortable confines of the Buffalo Bill Villa's living room. Arranged like a small efficiency apartment, the living room shared space with a dining table and small kitchen on the main level. A spiral staircase led to separate bedrooms on the second floor. Beige grass cloth covered the walls and a hideous bright green carpet spread from wall to wall. CNN's "Larry King Live" played in the background masked by the rush of warm air from the ventilation duct. Ahmed had the drab brown curtains pulled aside and stared at the Wyoming Inn situated across the street.

"Here is the plan," Ahmed said, speaking to Ali without letting his gaze drift from the motel across the street. "You pull the van into the last registration parking space. That will put the back doors of the van close to the well logging truck. I will go into the office. As soon as I do, start working the lock on the truck's back door."

"What if the source isn't in the back? What if it is in one of the storage places on the side?" Ali asked.

"I think the tools are too long to fit anywhere but the back," Ahmed answered. "I will take care of the hotel clerk and put his body somewhere it won't be noticed. Then I'll come out and cut the lock on the x-ray truck while you're picking the other lock. It should not take more than five minutes."

"I'll make sure the bolt cutters are within your reach."

"Good. Then we will drive to Billings and use the store room to dismantle the sources." Ahmed closed the curtains. "I'm going to check the Internet for news of the security guard in Spokane. We will leave at 2:00 a.m."

Ahmed went to the small table where he had his computer hooked to the Internet via telephone line. He Googled for news stations in Spokane and found WKVR Channel Six's website. There was nothing on the front page. Ahmed found a link to headline archives.

Security Guard Found Shot to Death was the fifth headline. Ahmed clicked the link.

Mohammed Atwah was found shot to death, execution style, in his apartment this morning. According to sources, the disturbing method in which Atwah was shot prompted investigation by outside agencies. Spokane Police Chief Henry Reynolds would not comment on the investigation other than saying the police were pursuing several leads.

"Ali!" Ahmed called. "Brother Mohammed was found. It says that outside agencies are investigating. It may not be wise to go back to Billings. Take the van and park it around back. I will look for an alternate place to dismantle the sources."

Ali went out to move the van. As he drove it to the back of the building, a police cruiser drove into the parking lot of the Wyoming Inn. He pulled the van around the back of the villas near a trash dumpster and hurried back to the room. "Ahmed," he called quietly excited. "Come quick. There are two policemen in the parking lot across the street."

A second police cruiser parked next to the first one facing in the opposite direction. The officers had their windows rolled down and appeared to be talking. Ahmed clenched his fists tightly, digging fingernails into the palms of his hands. Heat rose to his face as he watched the policemen sit in the lot for the next hour.

Finally at 2:45 a.m. one of the officers drove off. *Enough is enough*, he thought.

"Get your things in the van, Ali. Pull to a place where you can see the police car. I am simply going to walk up to him from behind his car and shoot him through the open window. As soon as I do, pull the van up to the office and continue with the plan."

"But, Ahmed, that is too risky," Ali protested.

Ahmed turned and growled, "I am tired of waiting. Do as I say. Allah will watch over us."

They gathered their things and put them in Ahmed's rental car. Ahmed slid his handgun in the waistband of his pants against the small of his back. He pulled his shirt tail out to conceal it.

The villa door opened to the brisk night air. He stood at the door until he heard van's engine start. *Just walk calmly to the police car*, he thought. *Act like nothing is wrong*. The blond-haired officer read a newspaper with his elbow resting on the door ledge created by the open window. The orange glow from a lit cigarette came into view as he flicked ashes to the ground. Keeping his head down, Ahmed shifted his gaze and saw the front of the white van in the alleyway of the villas across the street. Everything was set.

He picked up his pace. Twenty feet to go. He reached behind him to grasp the handle of his Jericho handgun. As it pulled free, headlights appeared in front of him. He heard the light squeal of tires trying to gain purchase of the damp asphalt street and the sound of an accelerating engine. He spun and ducked into the shadows of the Wyoming Inn. The car continued accelerating towards him, then braked and pulled into the parking lot next to the police cruiser. It was the other policeman and he appeared to be looking directly at Ahmed.

He began to panic and was about to turn and run. *Wait! Surely he wasn't spotted.* He took a deep breath to steady himself and watched as the newly arrived policeman handed a steaming cup and a small bag to the man who had been marked for death. He could hear the two policemen converse as he remained pressed against the building. Across the street, Ali had backed the van out of sight.

Watching the police officers, he remained motionless until they began talking again. Using the distraction, Ahmed ducked around the corner of the building and took a long detour back to the villas. With the door closed behind him, Ahmed slammed his fist into the grass cloth wall. *That was stupid. Ali was right, it was too risky and he had nearly caused the entire mission to fail.* He collapsed on the couch and put his face in his hands, then threw his fists down against the cushions and stood.

"We will wait until tomorrow and move our schedule up to 1:00 a.m. in case the officers return." Ahmed stomped swiftly to his bedroom and slammed the door.

Chapter Thirty

Billings, Montana
May 11, 2004

The desk sergeant put down the radio and turned to the FBI group. “Agent Campisi, the units have been in place for ten minutes. No sign of the U-Store van.”

With the arrival of the Special Operations Tactical Team, the FBI ranks had grown by five men. They were all dressed in black, except Laura, who ran the operation from police headquarters. She positioned herself at the radio to keep the surveillance team advised. Harrison had asked to tag along to observe and Campisi reluctantly agreed after she insisted. Surveillance was Campisi’s specialty and Harrison seemed interested in learning.

Campisi put the earpiece of his two-way radio in his ear. He keyed it and asked, “Any change in the situation?”

Jackman responded, “Everything still negative—nobody’s home.”

“Let’s go,” Campisi ordered.

The group divided into three teams—one for each of the two rooms and one for long-range surveillance. The vans pulled in front of the Comfort Lodge office and Campisi entered the office with his identification in hand. The details were already cleared with the owner of the small hotel.

Campisi returned with keys to the rooms and the group split up in silence. Harrison followed Campisi and watched as the team efficiently hid a tiny, almost invisible transmitter in the telephone. They placed a fiber optic camera in a heating register in the ceiling. Another transmitter was placed in the bathroom.

Campisi called out to the surveillance van that was now parked well down the street. “Ready to check.”

“Ten-four,” was the response from the earpiece.

In a whisper, Campisi said, “Check, check. You guys hear me?”

Again he heard in the earpiece, “Loud and clear, Campisi—camera is active too, but bend it to the left a hair so we can see the door.”

“Aldo, move the camera to the door a hair.”

Aldo stepped on his small ladder and nudged the almost imperceptible piece of fiber.

"Okay, good. Right there. Let's get out of here."

The team grabbed the equipment bag and left. Campisi hesitated at the door, turning and sweeping the room for any trace of their visit—*nothing*.

Across the street, the third team finished chiseling a hole in one of the bricks of the half demolished wall. They placed the miniature infrared monitor in the opening and placed another brick on top of it.

"Now you can watch in comfort, Jackman," one of the special ops agents said.

"It's a good thing. I'm getting cramps in my legs, squatting like this." He stood slowly, stretching his legs. "Let's get out of here."

Chapter Thirty-one

Cody, Wyoming
May 11, 2004

Dallas lay in the comfortable bedroom at the Vista View Condominiums somewhere between sleep and wakefulness. With the upscale, homey furnishings it seemed he was in somebody's home rather than a hotel. In the distance, a light beeping sound bothered him. It seemed miles away. "Oh, shit," he groaned as he reached over to turn off the alarm. "Feels like a truck ran over me—twice." Fumbling for the travel alarm, he managed to knock it to the floor. "Batteries must be weak."

Managing to roll over, he reached down, fingers brushing against the curled, Berber carpet until he found the alarm on the floor. A flip of the switch and the clock rattled back on the dresser's veneer top. He swung his arm overhead and rolled to his back in an exaggerated exhaustive gesture.

"Damn, I feel like crap," he moaned. Sinuses draining like crazy, he coughed through the night and his head pounded a beat equal to his heart. Pushing himself out of bed with arms too weak to cooperate, he managed to get to his feet. The room swirled and went dark as he felt himself falling backwards. His body bounced on the bed and his eyes snapped open.

After the room stopped spinning, he pushed himself out of bed again, holding onto the wall this time, and stumbled his way to the bathroom. Not recognizing the reflection in the mirror, it shocked him to see the caked dried blood on his upper lip and cheeks.

"What the hell?" He poked his head through the doorway and was stunned by the amount of blood that stained his pillow. His mind flashed back five years. The last time so much blood came from his nose he had been diagnosed with lung cancer. Caught in its very early stages, the chemotherapy put the cancer into remission and the doctors declared him cancer-free two years later. That dreadful morning burned in his memory because it was the last day he ever smoked a cigarette. He never told Brandon the real reason he had given up smoking.

With the blood washed from his face and neck, and five ibuprofens melting in his stomach, he turned on the shower and forced himself to get ready for the trip to the ranch.

Jimmy Buck was having a difficult time as well. Jimmy woke up with lungs full of phlegm and a horrendous headache. He had only slept a few hours. Billy came by the room and told him to stay in bed for the day. He said he would get Walt to help him at the ranch.

Jimmy nodded his head and closed the door. His stomach cramped and a queasy, unsettled feeling washed over him as he scrambled to the bathroom—barely making it in time to throw up in the toilet. When the heaving finally stopped, he reached to flush the stench away and caught a glimpse of the scarlet blood floating inside the bowl.

On all fours, he crawled back to the bedroom, bothered by the blood, but too weak to do anything about it. He struggled to pull himself into bed. Uncontrollable shivers started an hour later as his fever raged. It was all he could do to wrap the bedspread around him in a protective cocoon. Every move, however slight, brought back the shivers.

The jobsite at the Four Sixes Ranch resembled a ghost town. Half the pipeline crew called in sick and all but a few of those that showed up were coughing and spitting.

Sparks flew as welders made the final tie-in weld that connected the well to the Montana Gas Pipeline. The Montana Gas project team was on its way from Billings and was scheduled to be at the site before noon.

While the well logger was making his final run, Jerry Muckler, the rig foreman, worked on the well completion sequence. The last step was to perforate the casing. Jerry prepared the line shaped-charge jet perforator. This was an explosive mechanism originally designed as an armored tank-piercing weapon. Lowered to the right depth, the charge would be tripped, perforating the casing and fracturing the rock surrounding it, allowing oil or gas to flow through it and up to the surface. Jerry would drop the heavy device in the hole as soon as the well logging tool was removed. Brandon instructed him to perforate the casing just below the cap rock.

Billy Goller was too busy to be worried about Jimmy. With his head and body aching, concentration on the task at hand wasn't coming easy. Walt, on the other hand, seemed perfectly healthy. Billy twisted copper wires around lugs and tightened wing-nuts to secure the electronics in the sonic tool to the computer in the back of the truck. Working the valves on the well, the long silver torpedo started its journey down the hole. The sonic run would only take half as long as the nuclear run had taken.

"Hey, Walt, I ran this report on the nuclear run last night. Can you run it over to the trailer and give it to Mr. Stiles or Mr. Wheeler?"

"Sure thing. I've got nothing better to do 'til the welders finish that last weld," Walt said. He took the report and shuffled off towards the trailer.

Billy turned and gazed at the Tetons rising in the distance. Storm clouds swirled around the peaks, casting a dark shadow that moved across the floor of the valley toward him. Hopefully they would finish their work here before it hit.

Knocking on the door first, Walt pulled the trailer door open and walked in. Brandon worked on his computer at the conference table and Dallas had his head down on the desk in the office.

"Mr. Stiles, Billy asked me to give you the well log from yesterday."

"Thanks. How are you guys doing out there?" Brandon asked.

"Well, Jimmy wasn't feeling well and stayed back at the hotel, so I came out to help. I'm Walt, the pipeline x-ray technician."

"Nice to meet you, Walt," Brandon said.

"Billy's running the sonic log now. We should be done before lunch."

"Great. I'll look this over right now," Brandon said, holding up the report.

As Brandon scanned the report, a smile spread across his face. His concern over Dallas's health waned as he looked at the results. Perforating the casing just below the cap rock was the right decision. The sandstone formation was perfect for producing gas flow. If gas production fell off, they could re-perforate it at a lower depth to produce oil.

This well was likely to produce more gas than oil, but even the oil reserves looked extremely promising. There was enough here to get approval to continue sinking wells in this formation.

He began transcribing the highlights into an e-mail that would get enough information back to the main office to estimate the size of the reserves. Jeff could then head to Washington, D.C. to report the news to Senator Macmillan and his energy subcommittee.

The cacophony of Dallas's hacking cough and labored breathing brought Brandon out of his euphoria. He turned in his chair in time to see Dallas disappear from sight. A dull thud shook the flimsy floor of the trailer.

"Dallas!" Brandon shouted.

He jumped up and ran to the desk. Memories of Mae rushed back as the image of Dallas lying on the floor with blood dribbling from his nose and mouth burned into his brain. He shook Dallas until his eyes fluttered open. Sweat beaded on his forehead as he started to shake.

"Hey, Doc," Dallas mumbled with a weak smile, his eyes staring blankly. "I don't feel so good."

"Don't worry, Dallas, I'm going to get someone to help me get you to the Hummer and I'll get you to the hospital. Don't go running off anywhere."

He jumped to his feet and raced out of the trailer. Running to the rig foreman, arms flapping, he yelled, "Jerry, you have to help me! Dallas is sick and collapsed. I need you to help me get him in the Hummer so I can take him to the hospital."

Jerry ran back to the trailer to help. They lifted Dallas off the floor and threw his arms over their shoulders. As they walked him to the oversized vehicle, Brandon barked orders. "Perforate the casing twenty-feet below the cap. Make sure the tie-in gets done pronto. Montana Gas is on their way and should be here within the hour. They'll start up the compressor engine and open the valves."

"Dr. Stiles, I'll take care of it. Half my guys are sick at the hotel and a few others are feeling puny, but we'll get the tie-in done. After Montana Gas takes over, I'm sending the crew home."

"Okay. Oh, and tell Billy, the well logger, to send the sonic report over to the Vista View Condominiums building five, unit B. I want them as soon as possible," Brandon said as he strapped Dallas in the passenger seat.

Not waiting for an answer, he slammed the passenger door and bolted for the driver's side fumbling with his keys. His shaking hands finally managed to find the slot in the ignition switch. "Hang on, buddy, here we go." Brandon threw the big Hummer into gear and tromped down on the accelerator. The powerful engine roared to life and propelled them down the dirt road toward Cody.

Chapter Thirty-two

Cody, Wyoming
May 11, 2004

Lynn Howard sat on the concrete bench watching a group of kindergartners running and howling behind the chain link fence of the schoolyard. Her eyes were honed on a freckle-faced five-year old boy spinning in circles with his tiny hands covering large eyes. He counted, screaming out the numbers as his classmates ran away to find hiding places.

"Looks like he's a real pro out there," Larry Enders said.

"Yeah, he's growing up too damn quick." Lynn turned toward her partner who stood above her with two steaming cups of coffee in his bear-like hands. Larry was a beast of a man, too large to be an Emergency Medical Technician, but he didn't let that stop him from being one anyway. Curly black locks topped a teddy bear face, with full cheeks and extra chin. He was six-foot-three and weighed in at a touch over two-ninety.

"You know, if I didn't know who Bobby was, I could walk right over to him and pick him out as your son. He looks just like you."

"Yeah, but he has his father's stubbornness." Lynn held the coffee to her mouth and breathed in the earthy aroma. "I just wish that jackass would leave once and for all."

"Is Jack back?" Larry asked.

"Shit, I thought I told you." Lynn shifted her body to face her partner who loomed above her. "He showed up with some blond bimbo in tow asking for money."

"What an asshole. Lynn, you didn't give him any, did you?"

"Not much." She shook her head, then brushed back her shaggy brown hair from large brown eyes. The corners of her mouth turned down.

Larry threw his half-empty Styrofoam coffee cup against a streetlight post, startling her. "Dammit, Lynn. When are you going to wake up? Jeeesus! He's going to continue to suck the life right out of you unless you close the door on his fucking freeloading face."

"I know, I know."

"No, I don't think you do. Lynn, you're a smart woman—too smart to fall for his shit. You put yourself through EMT school while raising a kid. You're amazing, and dammit, if you won't do something about it, I will."

"Larry, no." She looked up to Larry's bright red face, then reached out and touched his arm. "I'll handle him."

"Promise me."

Lynn turned back to look at her son as the teacher rounded the kids up to return to the classroom. "I promise."

Jimmy Buck woke to the feeling of bile rising in his throat. He started choking but was too weak to do anything more than roll to edge of his bed. When his head cleared the bed, he felt warm vomit drain from his mouth to the floor. His face contorted from the sour, acidic fluid. Feeling wet, he looked down to clothing soaked in blood and vomit. Spitting out what he could, he reached for the phone next to the bed and dialed "0."

"Front desk."

"Help me."

"I'm sorry, what was that?"

"I need help."

"Help? Sir, can you speak up?"

No response.

"Sir?"

"Shit," the clerk said, setting the phone down and grabbing the master key card. He left the desk, trotted to room 103 and banged on the door. "Hotel management. Are you okay in there?"

There was no answer. The manager inserted the card in the slot and pushed the door open carefully. "Oh, criminy. Oh Jesus. Hey buddy, I'll...I'm calling an ambulance!"

Running back to the office, he dialed 911. "I need an ambulance at the Wyoming Inn on Minnesota Avenue right away. I think the guy's dead or something."

Firehouse Number Two received the dispatch. Chief Paramedic Larry Enders waddled quickly to the front seat of the ambulance when he heard the call.

"Come on, Lynn, let's go," he called.

Lynn dropped her cup into the trash container next to the bench and climbed into the truck. The ambulance sprang to life with a myriad of flashing lights and whooping sirens. Lynn was a rookie EMT and had only been on a few real emergency calls. Each time she heard the sirens, her adrenaline surged in anticipation of the unknown. A short two miles later, anticipation turned to desperation as they entered Jimmy Buck's motel room at the Wyoming Inn. Stinking of puke and feces, it looked as if an axe murderer had run amuck. Jimmy's head hung off the bed—bloody vomit dribbled in long strands from his mouth to the floor.

Hesitating a moment to let the reality of the bizarre scene sink in, Larry drew in a breath of putrid air. His mind snapped into gear. He rushed to the blood and bile covered body to check its pulse. *Surely he was dead.* "I have a weak pulse," he reported to Lynn. "Let's get his vitals."

Fighting the repulsion of the gory scene, Lynn began working on collecting his other vital signs while Larry rolled the rag-doll body from side to side checking for open wounds.

"Where the hell is all the blood coming from? He's got no wounds. We need to get him on the stretcher before I start to puke," Larry said, gagging.

He grabbed his radio and keyed the microphone. "Cody Community, this is unit two."

"Cody Community, go ahead two."

"I have a white male between thirty and forty years old. He's been vomiting blood, a lot of blood. His systolic bp is eighty and weak, temperature a hundred and four. Breathing shallow and raspy. Maybe poisoning, but there's nothing obvious in sight," he said, looking around.

"Start an I.V. and get him here stat. We'll be ready when you arrive."

"Ten-four." Larry let the mic go. "Come on, Lynn, let's get this guy moving. You can put the I.V. in on the way. One, two, three—lift."

They lifted him on the stretcher and rolled him through the door when the police showed up.

"Is he injured?" the policeman yelled.

"No, sick—real sick," Lynn said, slamming the door from the inside.

Larry hustled to the driver's door, and stopped to yell at the officer. "Check the room. If you find anything unusual, call it in."

"What am I looking for?" the officer yelled over the roar of the ambulance's engine.

"Fuck, I don't know." Larry threw the big rig into gear and started the short journey to the hospital.

Ahmed Halid woke to the wailing of sirens. The shrill sound filled the room as if they stopped right outside the door. Reaching under the pillow, he wrapped his hand around his pistol, slipped out of bed, made his way to the window on all fours and peeked through a small slit in the curtains. Across the street was an ambulance with two paramedics scrambling to get a stretcher out of the back. It looked like they were heading into one of the rooms near the manager's office. *Wasn't that where the radiation people were*?

Brandon brought the big Hummer to an abrupt stop, huge tires squealing, in front of the emergency entrance to Cody Community Hospital.

He slammed open the double glass doors and yelled, "Someone help! I have an emergency here. I need a wheelchair or something!"

A man in a long white coat appeared from a curtained trauma room. He ordered a gurney. Stat. Brandon turned to go back to Dallas with the doctor close behind. "What's the problem here?" the doctor asked.

"He's been coughing and wheezing this morning. He collapsed at the jobsite about forty-five minutes ago. Since then, he's been in and out of consciousness. He threw up blood and had a bloody nose. Now he has a fever and he's been sweating and shivering." Brandon's voice quivered explaining the situation, as the doctor and an intern loaded Dallas on the gurney.

"You'll have to move that vehicle. We have another emergency coming in a few minutes," the doctor instructed. "See the nurse at the desk as soon as you do."

Brandon looked on helplessly as they wheeled his friend through the emergency room doors. He climbed into the Hummer and pulled it around the corner into two parking spots, then ran back to the hospital. As he neared the glass doors, the warble of a siren in the distance caught his attention. Brandon stepped up to the desk, nose stinging from disinfectant, where a nurse thrust a clipboard over the counter.

"Please fill out the insurance and patient history forms, the doctor will be out to see you shortly," she told him in a dispassionate, robotic voice.

Brandon walked into the waiting room noticing a group of men that looked like some of the construction workers from the drill site. He picked out a hard, plastic seat in the corner and just started to work on the hospital forms when the emergency room erupted in a flurry of activity.

"Where do you want him?" Larry called to the nurse at the desk, his voice carrying a sense of urgency with it.

"Follow me." She jumped from her seat. "Trauma room two."

"His vitals are weak but stable." Lynn ran alongside the stretcher checking the monitor that lay on Jimmy Buck's chest. "I had a hard time getting the IV started. His veins are collapsing."

Jimmy thrashed, gasping for air on the gurney. Larry stopped and held his shoulders as Lynn bent down and pulled his mouth open, searching for an obstruction. As she did, Jimmy's body retched, spraying bloody vomit like a fountain, the viscous fluid catching her full in the face. She turned and doubled over as her own stomach cramped and emptied its contents on the floor with a splat.

Larry rolled Jimmy on his side to let the blood drain from his throat and patted his back to help eject the remaining thick fluid. "Lynn, are you okay?"

Her body convulsed as she yanked off her shirt to wipe the blood and vomit from her face and neck. "I'll catch up." Wiping the thick fluid from her eyes, she ran to a basket of linens and clutched a sheet, then ran for the scrub room.

In trauma room one, Dr. Alex Weiss heard the commotion and instructed an intern to start an I.V. on Dallas. He ran to room two and was distressed to see the patient lying in blood on the stretcher.

"Let's get him on the examination table," he ordered.

The doctor, the paramedic and the nurse hoisted Jimmy's body from the stretcher to the stainless-steel table. Dr. Weiss probed Jimmy's chest and stomach with his stethoscope.

"Intubate him. Larry, go to the front desk at admissions and tell them to page Dr. Wilcox, stat. We need him here yesterday."

"Yes, sir." Larry dashed for the admittance desk moving quicker than a man of his bulk should have been capable of.

"I'm going to talk to the man that brought in the other patient and try to piece together whatever the hell is going on here," Dr. Weiss said to the nurse. "Get Dr. Jost in here to get this man on a ventilator. He's in room one."

Dr. Weiss strode quickly to the waiting room where Brandon was finishing the hospital forms. As he approached Brandon, he said, "I'm Dr. Weiss. I'd like you to tell me what your friend has been up to or where he may have been in the past week."

Brandon looked up at the small, almost mousy-looking man. Wispy gray hair splayed across his narrow forehead. Thick tortoiseshell glasses with lined bifocals seemed too large for his small features. "We work for Interex Exploration Company. We've been working on an exploration well about thirty-five miles southeast of town on the Four Sixes Ranch."

"Wait—did you say Four Sixes Ranch?"

"Yes."

"Do you have a..." He flipped through his notes holding them close to his face. "Wyatt Construction Company on your site?"

"Yes. Why?" Brandon asked.

"I have eight patients out there with symptoms similar to what Mr. Wheeler has, only much less severe. I don't think it's a flu bug, Mr. Stiles, nor a coincidence. Can you follow me to trauma room two and see if you can identify someone for me?"

"Yes, of course," Brandon said, rising.

The doctor opened the curtains to room two, where an intern was finishing the intubation insertion and ready to hook Jimmy to the ventilator.

"Oh shit. I recognize him," Brandon said, wincing. "His name is Jimmy something-or-other. He's one of the well loggers working at the site. I heard he was sick this morning."

"Thank you, Mr. Stiles. You can go back to the waiting room. I have some calls to make."

"When will I know something about Dallas?"

"You'll know as soon as we do."

Dr. Weiss stood and headed up the hallway. He stopped and turned.

"Dr. Jost," he called.

"Yes?"

"Isolate those men waiting in the corner there. Make sure they don't leave." He pointed to the construction workers huddled in the corner of the waiting room.

"But—"

"Just do it, Doctor."

Dr. Weiss turned and disappeared around the corner.

Billy Goller flipped the switch on the winch. With a buzz and whir, the drum revolved, raising the sonic tool from the depths of the earth. Walt manned the rags, wiping down the cable as it came out of the well. The scene from the day before was repeated as the tool neared the surface.

The cable became coated with thick blackish-grey ooze. The odor became noxious and the two technicians boxed the tool without cleaning it thoroughly, deciding to leave it to lower level laborers back at the home office in Laramie.

Billy called Jerry Muckler over and informed him that they were finished.

"Great news," Jerry said. "The Montana Gas crew has been eager to get the gas flowing."

"I'll go tell Mr. Stiles and Mr. Wheeler that we're done and I'll have his report in the morning."

"They ain't there," Jerry said. "Doc Stiles took Dallas to the hospital. He didn't look very good."

"Aw, damn. That's a shame. Mr. Wheeler's a good guy."

"Damn good guy, for sure. But that reminds me. The Doc told me to have you drop your report off at the Vista View Condominiums building 5B tonight."

"Thanks, Mr. Muckler. We're heading back to Cody to check on Jimmy."

"Take 'er easy, fellas."

Jerry walked over to the group from Montana Gas. They were fidgeting with the controls on a gas-fired booster engine, the size of a small trailer, that would draw gas from the well and compress it for its journey to Powell, Cody and Billings—then eventually to the West Continent Pipeline.

"It'll take me an hour to perforate the well casing. Then you'll be good to go. I just need you guys to hang back here away from the well until I drop the charge into the hole."

"Thanks. We're just hooking up the fuel lines. It looks like the timing is going to work out perfectly."

Jerry walked back to the rig waving his hands at what was left of his crew.

"Let's go, guys," he yelled. "Back away."

Billy and Walt packed the rest of their gear and hoisted themselves into the truck.

"Hey, Billy, you ever known Jimmy to stay back sick?" Walt asked.

"No, never. I'll tell you though—he looked like absolute crap this morning. I hope he feels better tomorrow or the ride home ain't gonna be fun."

Billy slid a cassette tape into the dash and Garth Brooks accompanied them to Cody along the scenic rural roads. They pulled up to the hotel, passing the police car parked at the office. Billy walked around his truck, opened the back and started his computer. It would take hours to run the data. Walt walked over to his truck that remained parked in the lot and checked the locks and placards.

As Billy stepped down from the logging truck, he heard someone yell. He turned to see the hotel manager and a policeman walking toward him.

"Are you Billy Goller?" the policeman asked.

"Yes, sir. What's the problem officer?"

"James Buck was taken to the hospital about two hours ago. The doctors would like to talk with you."

"Hospital? Oh shit, is he all right?"

"I don't have any information. I was told to wait for you and bring you to Cody Community Hospital. It'll be quicker if I take you in the squad car."

"Walt, you wanna come?"

"Sure," Walt said.

Once in the squad car the policeman wasted no time getting them to the small hospital.

Chapter Thirty-three

Cody, Wyoming
May 11, 2004

Dr. Weiss barged into the Cody Community Hospital administrator's office. "Alicia, we have a big problem."

Alicia Manson, Cody Community Hospital's administrator for the past fifteen years, drew in a long breath and leaned back in her chair. She was the first black female doctor to work at Cody Community. Her hair was pulled up into a bun atop a cherub face. She had interned at the hospital twenty-five years earlier and had never left. She was an excellent diagnostician and leader. "Hello to you too, Alex. What's the problem?"

"Possibly the start of an epidemic. Maybe I'm over-reacting, but in the past two hours, we've seen ten cases of varying degrees. All of them from a construction site south of town on a cattle ranch." He tossed two charts on her desk.

"Varying degrees of what?"

"I'm not sure. At first, considering the group, I thought maybe radiation sickness, but I've ruled that out. Now, I'm thinking Anthrax."

"Anthrax? Dr. Weiss, we need to be absolutely sure before we raise a red flag. What symptoms do you have?"

"What I'm seeing doesn't really fit into any one diagnosis. There are distinct symptoms of cutaneous, gastrointestinal and inhalation anthrax. But it seems to be progressing much faster. Fast like Ebola. God, I hate to even say that word. The stress on the respiratory system is a little like what I read about SARS."

"I guess we have no idea whether or not it's airborne?" Alicia asked, already knowing the answer.

"If it is, we're screwed. I mean really screwed. I think we need to call Wyoming Health Services and the CDC now."

"Close the door." Alicia dialed the Wyoming Health Services Department All Hazards Response Program hotline with freshly manicured fingers.

"All Hazards Response Department. This is Jason Smith."

"I'm Alicia Manson, Administrator of Cody Community Hospital. I need to speak to the department chief immediately."

"Please hold."

After a brief pause a new voice hit the receiver. "This is Alan Probert. How can I help you?"

"Mr. Probert, my name is Alicia Manson. We believe we may have a contagious disease emergency here at Cody Community. I am going to put you on the speaker phone with Dr. Weiss, our chief of trauma."

Alicia punched the speaker button and put the receiver in its cradle.

"Are you there, Mr. Probert?"

"Yes."

"We have ten cases of what most closely resembles anthrax. Only it seems to present itself much faster than anthrax, like some type of hemorrhagic fever."

"Dr. Weiss, hold that thought. Please remain at this number. I am going to gather some of my people and try to conference in the CDC. I will call you back in less than thirty minutes."

As the speaker went dead, Dr. Weiss stood and started out the door.

"Where are you going?" Alicia asked.

"I'm going to talk to some of the patients and try to piece together some common thing or event that may give us a clue where this came from. I'll be back in twenty minutes."

The charge went off with a muffled rumble as Jerry tripped the wire line, shaking the earth below his feet. He pushed the button on the winch and started retracting the cable at high speed so the lower ball valve could be closed quickly.

The pressure of the gas flowing up the well blew the rubber boot off the casing and black liquid erupted from the top.

The cable came free and Jerry yelled, "Now! Close the valve!"

The laborer pushed the red button on the lower control box and the motor rotated the valve shut. The rushing of gas and liquid stopped as suddenly as it started.

"Close the upper valve!" he yelled again.

The laborer, stationed at the upper valve control, pushed the button, setting off a loud hum as the large motor sprung to life. He was a few seconds too late and both Jerry and the laborers were standing too close. Smelly black liquid gushed from the well, soaking them.

"Now open the lower valve!" Jerry jumped off the rig, black and smelling putrid. "Good job, men." He wiped the oily gunk from his forehead with a faded red shop towel. "Pack up and get outta here for the day."

Jerry checked the valve seal and hustled to the Montana Gas crew, watching the well completion from a safe distance.

"It looks like it's ready to go," the pipeline supervisor observed.

"Yes, sir," Jerry said. "Do you need anything from me before I go?"

"Nope, we're going to crank the engine up, open the valves on the meters and shoot a pig in front of the gas stream to purge the oxygen from the line. By tomorrow morning Powell, Cody and Billings will be getting a brand new gas supply."

Ahmed and Ali spent an hour watching the ambulance and police at the Wyoming Inn. Ahmed was surprised to see the x-ray truck still parked in front. Through his binoculars, he watched as the paramedics rolled a man out of the room on a stretcher and put him in the back of the ambulance. The man looked to be covered in blood.

They took turns watching the activity. Several hours later, Ali called Ahmed back to the window. The well logger truck had returned to the hotel and within minutes the men got into a police car and drove off.

"What do you think happened there?"

"I don't know, but I pray that those trucks remain there tonight. If there were any way to take the sources now—"

"Wait, it's early afternoon, there is nobody around. Ali, get the truck. Let some air out of one of the tires."

Ali drove the van to the office of the Wyoming Inn and positioned it directly between the two Wyoming Testing Lab vehicles and the hotel office, the passenger rear tire almost flat. Ahmed stepped from the van and opened the back doors while Ali went to the office and asked the manager to use the phone. Ahmed removed the spare tire and jack and threw them on the ground. Reaching for his bolt cutter, he casually walked to the x-ray van, watching for prying eyes. With one swift movement, he cut the lock, grabbed the x-ray device and lifted it into the back of the van. Reaching in his pocket, he produced a duplicate lock and placed it on the truck. Ahmed then walked over to the well logger truck and absently tried the door. *Allah was surely looking over them.* The door swung open.

Inside were three long cases and a myriad of computer equipment. He grabbed the handles of one of the bigger cases and slid it halfway out, quickly realizing it was beyond his ability to transfer the case alone. *Come on, Ali. Hurry.* As if on cue, Ali turned the corner. Speaking softly, Ahmed said, "Ali, open the latches to make sure this is the correct device."

Ali flipped the latches and lifted the lid, allowing a foul stench to rise and envelop them. He reached in and ran his finger along the black-stained stainless steel body and recoiled at the feel of the slimy substance coating the device.

"I cannot tell, Ahmed."

"Close it. We will take all three," Ahmed whispered.

It took less than a minute to transfer the three cases to the van and shut the door of the well logging truck. They jacked up the van and changed the airless tire.

"We must disassemble these devices quickly so we can return to New York," Ahmed said as they got back in the van for the short trip across the street to the Buffalo Bill Villas. "Park in the back."

Dr. Weiss ran up the steps and down the hall to Alicia Manson's office. As he entered the phone rang and the hospital administrator punched the speakerphone button.

"This is Alicia Manson."

"Dr. Manson, this is Alan Probert again. Just a second while I conference in the CDC." After a brief pause, the phone clicked. "Okay, Max, are you there?"

"Yes, Alan."

"Dr. Manson?" Probert asked.

"Yes, Mr. Probert and I have Dr. Weiss with me."

"Dr. Manson and Dr. Weiss, my name is Dr. Max Van Pelt, head of Contagious Disease Research here at the CDC in Atlanta. Dr. Weiss, can you tell me what you have there?"

"Dr. Van Pelt, there's more that I don't know than what I do know, but I just found out I have a fatality. A thirty-eight year old man, named James Buck died ten minutes ago of congestive heart failure." Dr. Weiss leaned forward with his elbows on the desk, staring at the phone as if he could see the doctors on the other end of the call.

"Can you describe his symptoms?"

"He came in about 10:00 a.m. His pulse was racing and blood pressure was low. He had a fever of 104.5. He was vomiting and expectorating blood. He presented with a rash that we didn't notice immediately, because we were busy trying to stabilize him."

"Did you get a chance to get a history of the progression?"

"Symptoms started with congestion, cough and fever two or three days ago."

"You have another serious case?" Max asked.

"Yes, sir, I have a fifty-two year old male, same symptoms. I checked, and he is developing a rash on his torso. We're administering antibiotics while the cultures are cooking—Doxycycline and cCprofloxacin. We're also trying to balance his electrolytes and pushing fluids—he is severely dehydrated. If that's not bad enough, I have eight other cases at various stages. All males, all expectorating some blood and all with low grade fevers."

"What else can you tell us, Dr. Weiss? Have you talked to these men to see what they had, or have, in common?"

"They are all working on an oil well project on a cattle ranch about thirty-five miles southeast of town. All but one of them are staying in the same hotel."

"Any other commonalities, Doctor?" Max asked.

"That's all I had time for."

"What are your diagnostic capabilities?"

"We're a small community hospital—more trauma center than research hospital. We have basic equipment, but we're not equipped for this," Alicia Manson answered.

"Okay, the rash, the blood from the lungs and stomach...sounds like cutaneous, gastrointestinal and inhalation anthrax all together, but the progression is too fast." After a brief silence, Max continued, "Dr. Manson, what is your current patient load?"

"Very light." She placed a small pair of gold filigree reading glasses on her nose and glanced at a computer printout. "Two patients and nobody in the ICU."

Dr. Manson, Mr. Probert—I am ordering Cody Community Hospital quarantined. I'm sorry, I have no other option. When I hang up, I'm calling USAMRIID and then sending for the National Guard to post a perimeter around the hospital. In the meantime you must post your own security and keep everyone in the hospital. It is imperative that nobody—and I mean nobody, leave or enter."

"What kind of help are you sending and when can we expect it?" Dr. Weiss asked.

"Our team will be in the air within the hour. Also, USAMRIID may be sending a team. I'd guess we'll be there in about four hours," Max said. "We'll bring our own diagnostic equipment and set up in negative atmosphere tents. I'll call with an ETA for the National Guard."

"Is there anything I can do?" Alan Probert asked.

"You can call the governor and the mayor of Cody," Max said. "Oh, and Dr. Weiss, any additional information you can get for us that may help identify what we're dealing with would be helpful. Also, we'll need an autopsy room."

"I'll get on it," Dr. Weiss said.

"Dr. Weiss, Dr. Manson, thanks for your cooperation. I'm sure we'll resolve this quickly. I'll be seeing you soon. For now, good luck."

As the phone went silent, Dr. Weiss looked at Alicia Manson. "Is this really happening?"

"Get down to emergency and I'll call security. Let's get this place locked down," she said. "And for now, nobody uses the phones."

After receiving the news that Jimmy died, Walt and Billy left the old, white-painted brick hospital. Walking outside into the darkness, they both stopped at the edge of the parking lot. Walt slapped his forehead with the palm of his hand. "Oh, shit. We don't have a ride back to the hotel and it's a good two miles. I'll go back inside and see if we can get a cab."

"Nah, let's start walkin'. I need some air anyway. Damn, I just can't believe he's dead. I mean, I haven't known Jimmy all that long, but he was a pretty good partner."

"Man, did you see how messed-up he was? Jeez, it looked like a truck hit 'em. And what kinda bug gets ya that sick that fast?"

"Beats me." They came to the intersection and Billy asked, "Hey, do you remember how to get back?"

"Yeah, we make a left here and keep walkin'."

A white Chevy Suburban rounded the corner, stopped at the intersection and waited for two men in the crosswalk. When the men reached the curb, the plain white Suburban rumbled through the intersection and swung into the emergency room parking lot. A tall security guard hurried out of the passenger door, threw a heavy chain around the door handles to the ER and secured it with a large padlock. Hearing the hasp click into place, the guard walked back to the truck and asked his partner, "What do you think is going on inside?"

"Damned if I know, I'm just glad we're out here."

Billy and Walt walked most of the way in silence. The streets were deserted and the clicking of the heels of Walt's cowboy boots echoed off the storefronts as they made their way to the Wyoming Inn.

"So whatcha gonna do, Billy?" Walt asked, breaking the solitude.

"I'm gonna pack up and head back to Laramie first thing in the morning. The sheriff said they closed up Jimmy's room and notified his parents, so there's nothin' to stay for."

"What about that well report we ran today? The rig boss said the Doc wanted it tonight."

"Ah crap, I forgot. Shit, I reckon I'll run it over to the Doc's condo when I get back. It should be done runnin' by now."

Light from the orb of the near-full moon cast long shadows as they turned the last corner into a stiff cool breeze. Billy jammed his weathered hand into the pocket of his tight jeans and extracted a large key ring. Flipping through house and car keys, he found the key to the back of the truck, shoved it into the slot and twisted. *Something wasn't right*. There was no click of the tumbler falling into place. Panic took hold before the door swung open. *Oh, my God, they're gone.*

"Holy shit, Walt!"

"What's the matter?"

"My sources are gone. Fuck, the truck was unlocked. Oh, shit. Walt, my fuckin' sources are gone!"

Billy burst into the hotel manager's office and screamed unintelligibly, "Call the fucking police! Now!"

When he returned to the truck, he saw Walt fumbling with the lock on the back of his truck.

"Shit, Billy, somethin's wrong with the lock. I can't open the back of the truck. I don't think this is my lock."

Billy paced the parking lot behind his truck. *Breathe, Billy, breathe. The procedure. Where's the procedure?* He pulled open the passenger door of the truck and retrieved a crunched-up manila folder. He traced his finger along the procedure to follow if one of his sources was lost or stolen, took a deep breath and flipped open his cell phone. He dialed the first number on the list: the owner of the company, Josh O'Connor.

"Mr. O'Connor, I've got a lot of bad news," Billy said.

"What's going on, Billy?"

"Well first off Jimmy Buck is dead."

"Jimmy's dead? Oh my God. What do you mean Jimmy's dead? I thought he was just sick."

"I ain't seen nothin' like it, Mr. O'Connor. Jimmy got real sick today and went to the hospital. They said his heart gave out from an infection."

"Jimmy's dead?"

"Yes, sir."

"Damn, that's just hard to believe, Billy. I don't know what to say."

"Mr. O'Connor, there's more."

"What?"

"Someone stole my sources."

"Someone what? What the fuck do you mean someone stole your sources?"

"Me and Walt got back from the hospital just now. The back of my truck was unlocked and my nuclear loggers are gone. Walt thinks someone may have fooled around with his truck too, but he can't get the lock off the back."

"You've gotta be shitting me. Where the hell are you?"

"At the Wyoming Inn. Uh, Mr. O'Connor, the sheriff just pulled up. I need to go."

"Okay, Billy, I'm calling the NRC. Don't you leave until you hear from me, understand?"

"Yes, sir," Billy answered.

He went to where the tall sheriff was talking to Walt. He stood, scratching the back of a hairy neck.

"Hey, are you Billy Goller?" the sheriff asked.

"Yes, sir."

"Like to tell me what happened here, and what these, uh, radiation things are?"

"We just got back from the hospital, see, and I noticed that the back of my truck wasn't locked. When I opened it, the radiation sources were gone," Billy explained.

"Okay, you're scaring me, son. What kind of radiation? Can anybody get hurt or sick from these things?"

"If they ain't handled right. Yeah, someone could get hurt. They're in shielded cases, but if someone removes them and messes with the shutter, they'd be real sorry." Billy said as Walt worked on the lock on his truck.

“Let me get my clipboard out of my cruiser and get your statement. I guess we can use the hotel office in there.” He turned toward his squad car and ambled off.

Mike Johnson, the FBI Director of Radiation and Biological Terrorism, picked up his vibrating Blackberry. After reading the email he muttered, “Oh, Christ, this is bad.” He dialed the NRC operator that had taken the report from Josh O’Connor fifteen minutes earlier and received a complete briefing. His next call was to Robert Williams in the Seattle field office. After giving him the details he said, “This has to be related to the terrorists Laura is chasing.”

“It certainly fits, Mike,” Bob agreed.

“So are you still watching the hotel and storeroom in Billings?”

“Yes, with no luck so far.”

“Well, if they just stole these sources, they may be headed back to Billings. From what the NRC told me, it would take two of them to handle one of these well-logging tools. You need to divert some of your people to Cody.”

“All right, how potent are these?” Bob asked.

“They’re pretty powerful—five hundred millicuries each.”

“Ouch. That is quite a bit.”

“Yeah, over the normal limit for those devices. I think there’s a testing lab in Wyoming that’s looking at a hefty fine and the loss of their license.”

“I’m sending Laura Daniels and Johnny Campisi down to investigate. We’ve already put out a BOLO for Atif and Halid and an APB on the van.”

“Okay, Bob. I want regular updates.”

Bob closed his cell phone and looked around the den. He rubbed his temples, flipped open the phone again and scrolled through phone numbers. Stopping on Daniels, he hit the call button.

“Agent Daniels.”

“Laura, this is Bob. Pack a bag—you’re headed for the city of Cody in northwestern Wyoming. We think your bad guys just stole some nuclear sources from a well-logging truck. They pack quite a punch, so be careful. I’m sending you the NRC report by e-mail.”

“Okay, Bob, how do you want to handle things here?”

“Take Campisi and Jackman with you and that detective from Spokane. Leave the rest in place. Atif and Halid may be headed back to you as we speak.”

“Okay, so who were these devices taken from and where exactly?”

“The who is Billy Goller and Walt Nolte from Wyoming Test Labs. They’re staying at the Wyoming Inn.”

“Got it. I’ll be getting out of here within the hour.”

"Hang on a second, my Blackberry is buzzing," he said, picking up the vibrating Blackberry digital messaging device from the cherry wood desk. The last e-mail message read *Cody Community Hospital is being quarantined with potential cases of a highly contagious disease exhibiting the symptoms of anthrax or hemorrhagic fever. Wyoming National Guard is being posted to enforce the quarantine.*"

"Oh shit! Laura, there's something else. It may be totally unrelated, but there's a contagious disease at Cody Community Hospital resembling anthrax or hemorrhagic fever. They're quarantining it and sending in the National Guard."

"On my way."

Laura flipped her cell phone closed and sat up in bed, holding the sheet over her breasts. She turned and shoved Harrison, "Come on, Jim, there's a lot going on and we're checking out in half an hour."

Harrison did his best to stifle a moan. "I was just beginning to enjoy myself."

She rolled on top, straddling him and smacked him on the arm. "What do you mean you were *just* beginning to enjoy yourself, mister?"

"Uh, I meant I was just recovering from the immense pleasure you gave me."

"That's better. Now get your cute butt moving."

She flipped her cell phone back open and called Johnny Campisi.

Dr. Weiss sat down next to Brandon in the sterile setting of the emergency waiting room and looked Brandon in the eyes. "Mr. Stiles, I'm sorry to say but I don't think Mr. Wheeler has much time left."

"What? What do you mean?" Brandon asked. "He just started feeling ill. I don't understand."

"We don't fully understand either. However, Mr. Buck has expired and whatever your friend has, it is progressing rapidly. If you wish to see him or say something to him, I suggest you put on this mask and do it now." Dr. Weiss held out a hospital mask. Brandon took it and nodded. "Follow me."

Dallas didn't look like Dallas. The man laying on the gurney looked more like a living corpse. His skin, pale blue and mottled with maroon patches, hung off his cheekbones like a ninety-year old man's. His eyelids fluttered wildly, revealing a hideous shade of pink surrounding brown pupils that rolled back into his head. Dried blood crusted his upper lip.

Dr. Weiss whispered in Brandon's ear. "He's sedated but awake."

Brandon leaned over and placed a hand on Dallas' shoulder. "Hey, buddy, how are you doing there?"

"Doc? Is that you?" The voice sounded feeble—wet—as if he were under water.

"Yeah, it's me. I'm right here, Dallas." Brandon knew his attempt to sound reassuring would fail. He wasn't sure how long he could pull off this charade before his voice completely broke apart.

"Good. I don't think I'm..." His bubbling words trailed off.

"Stop that, Dallas. You'll be fine."

"Yeah, right, you never could lie." He finally focused on Brandon's face. "Doc, about Alice... do me a favor. Remember, what happens in Cody..."

"Stays in Cody," Brandon finished. "Don't you worry, Dallas, I'll make sure Alice is all right."

The corners of Dallas' mouth ticked up ever so slightly. Suddenly a loud steady high-frequency tone filled the room. The scope traced a flat, ghostly fluorescent green line. Brandon turned to Dr. Weiss with a pleading look. "Aren't you going to do something?"

"Should we start compressions, Doctor?" the attending intern asked. There was a long silence. The intern repeated, "Dr. Weiss, should we start compressions?"

Dr. Weiss removed his glasses and wiped them with his coat. "No. His arterial pathways are shot. There's no reason to, Dr. Jost. Brandon, he's gone. I'm sorry."

They looked at Dallas' lifeless body with a sick feeling of helplessness as Dr. Jost pushed a button on the monitor, silencing the alarms.

Brandon turned and rushed from the room sobbing.

Dr. Weiss looked at the clock and announced, "Call it—time of death, 8:15 p.m. Bag him and take him to the morgue with Mr. Buck. The CDC will want to do an autopsy."

He wandered out of the curtained treatment room into the ER. This sight of soldiers positioned outside the large glass doors churned his stomach. *This is going to be a long, long night. Hell, maybe days*, Weiss thought. *I just pray I'm not lying in the morgue in a week.* Beyond the military vehicles and flashing lights was a band of radio station reporters. Surely the Billings television stations were heading down the highway towards them.

He walked around to treatment room three where Lynn Howard, Jimmy Buck's paramedic, laid. She breathed heavily, sweat beading on her forehead from fever. Her vitals deteriorating, she was slipping fast, rushing along the same deadly course as Jimmy and Dallas. So was Larry Enders, the chief paramedic. *It doesn't make sense—there are eight construction workers whose health is getting progressively worse, but at a much slower progression and they aren't showing all the same symptoms. Where the hell is the CDC?*

He went back to the main waiting room and took a seat next to Brandon. "I'm sorry about Mr. Wheeler. Rest assured he was resting peacefully when he passed."

"Damn." Brandon sighed, putting his face in his hands and wiping his eyes. Swallowing deeply he said, "He was such a good guy, a good friend."

"Mr. Stiles, I'm sorry about being so blunt here, but did you write down everything you could about the project? What everyone had in common or anything that might help us find the source of the illness?"

"I've been wracking my brain. And not a lot is coming."

"What about food?"

"No...No. But about twice a week, Dallas or I brought bottled water from the Safeway here in Cody. You know...the big bottles that go on top of a water cooler. We rented one and put it in the shade outside the construction trailer." Brandon stood and paced the floor. "We also made a big jug of Gatorade every day from the powder. We have a couple cartons of powder packets, different flavors, in the trailer. The rig foreman brings ice from a convenience market every morning."

"But it seems like that would affect all the workers."

"Well, perhaps not. A lot of the guys brought their own coolers with water, tea, soda or God-knows-what."

"We covered the hotels, but let's go through it again."

"I think most of the crew stayed at the Wyoming Inn, but there were some guys from the local union hall too. I honestly don't know which ones are which, but we can get the employment records from the site. Dallas, Jerry Muckler, the rig foreman, myself, and a couple of others stayed at the Vista View Condominiums."

"How about contact with animals or bites?"

"The Four Sixes is a cattle ranch, but the owner stretched barbed wire around the job site. I don't remember seeing any cows for weeks, except in the distance." Brandon continued pacing the floor. "As far as other wildlife, we have raccoons and possums rummaging through the trash, but not much else—and no run-ins that ring a bell."

"Mosquitoes or tics?"

"Of course. We actually have a written procedure for that and we supply insect repellent with the maximum DEET concentration we can find. Fifty percent, I think." Brandon sat back down. "We have a couple picnic tables with a chemical cabinet nearby where we keep a good supply. The workers spray themselves in the morning and after lunch. We require work boots, long pants and encourage long sleeve shirts when it's not too hot."

Brandon continued. "These guys are pretty experienced in working outdoors and know to look for tics every night. We go through the bug spray like water—so I think most of the guys are using it."

"How about rodents? Notice any mice or rats, maybe in or around the eating areas, or your trailer or equipment?"

"Wow, not anything that sticks in my mind. I don't think I've ever seen any, although I'm sure there are some around. We keep the lunch area pretty clean and pack out our trash every other day. We're under pretty heavy scrutiny from the Wyoming environmental people, so we're making a conscious effort to keep up with housekeeping."

"Hmm. You're right, with the exception of the water and Gatorade, there's nothing obvious." Dr. Weiss shook his head straining to think of something that would help. "I'm sure the CDC will put you through a thorough interrogation."

"Dr. Weiss, what do you think this is?"

"I really don't know. My best guess is anthrax."

"But anthrax doesn't progress this quickly, does it?"

"You're right. Normally, it doesn't. Do you know much about anthrax?"

"I'm a paleontologist. I've spent a few years studying infectious diseases and the possible effect on the decline of dinosaur populations. In fact, that was the subject of my doctoral dissertation. So, yes, I know a few things."

"Usually anthrax takes five days to a week to incubate and another week or more to cause this type of damage. And I've never read documented cases that are as devastating as what Jimmy Buck had," Dr. Weiss explained. "Normally you see cutaneous, inhalation or gastrointestinal exposure, but not all three at once. And each one manifests itself in a particular fashion, rash, lung infection or digestive system."

"Obviously, there are other possibilities: Hanta, Marburg or Ebola, Lassa or Dengue fever or one of its variants." Dr. Weiss counted them off on his fingers. "All of those are much hotter than anthrax and would better explain the aggressiveness we're seeing. But between us, I don't want to think about that."

"Do you think it's airborne?"

"I don't know. I have two sick paramedics. One was directly exposed to body fluids from Jimmy Buck. The other may have been exposed, but he couldn't remember."

"Wait, wouldn't that rule out anthrax? I mean it's not very communicable," Brandon asked.

"Not necessarily. Cutaneous and gastrointestinal can be transmitted from human to human. Inhalation anthrax would be rare, but hell, I'm not an infectious disease expert. Based on what you're saying, I see no other connection. Hopefully the CDC can identify the cause quickly when they arrive."

"Any idea when that is?"

"I'm guessing in the next hour or so. They'll be trying to identify the problem and clear people to leave as quickly as possible. It's just a good thing that we have a very light patient load right now."

"Dr. Weiss!" A nurse was running towards them. "Dr. Weiss, you have a call on line one. The CDC just landed and a Dr. Van Pelt wants information on where they can set up."

"Got it." Dr. Weiss rose. "Here we go. Mr. Stiles, keep thinking about this and we'll talk again when the CDC is ready."

"Dr. Weiss," Brandon called, causing the doctor to stop and turn.

"What if there are other guys from the job site that are sick and we don't know about them? Or they're afraid to come to the hospital now that it's been quarantined?"

"One step at a time. Hold that thought and let me get the CDC in here."

Brandon waited until the doctor disappeared around the corner, then unclipped his cell phone. In all the excitement, he'd forgotten to call Jeffery Hargrove and Dallas's wife. First he'd call Jeff and then he'd call Alice and tell her about her husband. He owed that much to his friend. Last he'd call Jerry Muckler and see if he noticed anybody else on the crew that was sick.

"Johnny, do you drive the NASCAR circuit on the weekends?" Harrison watched the scenery whiz by in the dimming light.

"Shit, you want fast drivers, turn and look at your partner there," Campisi said, glancing in the rearview mirror.

"That's enough out of you, Johnny," Laura said.

"No, go on. Tell me more." Harrison grinned at her.

"Did she tell you about her gay brother?"

"Johnny!"

"Uh, she mentioned him," Harrison answered.

"Well, Laura's gay brother just happens to be *the* upholstery designer for the largest classic car rebuilder on the West Coast. The dude's loaded." Johnny glanced in the mirror again to ensure he was properly embarrassing Laura.

"Yeah, go on," Harrison said.

"So it's Laura's thirty-third birthday and she's all in a gloom about being sleepless in Seattle, so the office takes her out drinking. Well, after several Cosmos, this guy comes in, dressed like a police officer, spins her around in her bar stool, and does one hell of a striptease for her."

"No, no, no," Laura muttered, her face in her hands.

"Go on." Harrison was beaming.

"So after he gets through his routine, he hands her a set of keys and drags her to the street. There's this cherry 1967 blue Mustang Shelby GT, 427 big block sitting at the curb. It even has her name embroidered in the seats."

"It's a 428 not a 427, Bozo. That just goes to show what Johnny knows about cars." Laura shook her head slowly.

"Wow! Hot car for a hot babe, huh?" Harrison said.

Laura slapped him on the arm. "My mother gave that car to my father on their first wedding anniversary. My dad gave it to me when I graduated college, after I promised to give it back when I was through with it. I shipped it to him when I left D.C."

"So how did it—?"

"I guess my dad figured it was time to make peace with Marcus, my brother, and they decided to pimp my ride." Laura leaned forward and gave Johnny a shove to the back of his head. "Johnny, you need to keep your eyes on the road and your mouth shut. It's getting dark out there."

After a booming laugh, Johnny Campisi concentrated hard on the road. He took great pride in his driving skills and made short work of the ninety-five mile trip. The sun dropped below the tall peaks of the Tetons much earlier than in the flatlands and he was amazed at how dark the Wild West was without the benefit of streetlights. Beetles splattered against the windshield with a sickening crunch, making it more difficult to see the elk and deer wandering on the road. They were everywhere. *This is a conspiracy*, he thought. *The entire animal kingdom is out here, looming just out of the reach of the headlights, ready to jump in front of the speeding van.* He squinted, trying desperately to see beyond the vehicle's headlights. "I know you're out there you sons-a-bitches. Show yourselves."

Chapter Thirty-four

Four Sixes Ranch
May 11, 2004

Night covered the Bighorn Valley in a wave as the sun disappeared behind the building storm clouds rolling in over the Tetons. Like a death shroud, darkness blanketed the valley. Under large emergency lights, electricians and technicians finished wiring the meters that would measure the gas flow to the new pipeline.

The Montana Gas crew chief, David "Chubbs" O'Brien, retrieved a clipboard with the completion checklist from his truck, then joined the group of laborers under the bright lights. "Okay, guys, let's go down the list and get this job done with before this storm blows in. Let me know the status as I read through it. Compressor engine?" Chubbs yelled over the sound of the generator. His breathe visible as a blanket of cold air settled over the valley.

"Up and running," a technician in the group yelled.

"Okay. How about the tie-in?" Chubbs yelled again.

"Done. X-rays show welds are all solid. The joints still need epoxy coating."

"All right. How about the pig?" Chubbs asked.

Chubbs' nickname was not an oxymoron. With a broad, flat chin and wide face, his rusty brown flattop completed a square head. Some of his newer co-workers dubbed him SpongeBob. He had been working in the gas distribution business for fifteen years and he was still amused by some of the pipeline terminology. Pigs came in many forms and were used primarily for cleaning and inspecting pipelines. Early pigs resembled a legless swine, rounded on both ends.

Pigs were now more sophisticated and specialized. This one, in particular, was a purging pig. It resembled a large bullet about eighteen inches in diameter and three feet long. Made of extremely hard rubber, it was ringed with squeegees to provide a seal against the inside of the pipe.

Once the pig was inserted into a launch station, somewhat like a torpedo tube, a valve was opened and gas pressure was allowed to build behind the pig, which propelled it to the receiving station many miles away. Valves were positioned at the receiving end to divert the pig above ground to the receiving station where the oily debris and rust on the inside of the pipe, pushed ahead of the pig would be removed.

This pig would push the air out of the line ahead of the natural gas to prevent an explosive condition. Three things were required to start a fire, often referred to as the fire triangle: fuel, oxygen, and ignition source. Without all three, a fire was impossible. The pig would eliminate the oxygen from the line and was critical to prevent an explosive mixture that only needed a spark to ignite and cause a catastrophe.

"Launch the pig and radio ahead to the receiving station in Billings. We're in business, folks. Let's wrap up. Remember, don't light up until you're off the property. No mistakes." Chubbs walked up to the pig launcher and turned some valves. Natural gas could be heard rushing through the feeder lines filling the launch tube behind the pig.

As the pressure increased, he heard and smelled gas escaping around the seals of the launch hatch. The cloud of gas hung over the platform until the light breeze carried it away. He felt around the seals. The flow had diminished. The rubber seals in the hatch were seating with the pressure and becoming more effective.

"Wow, that stinks. Hey, Blainey, do you have the odorant turned up too high?" Chubbs yelled to the odorant technician. Normally odorless, mercaptan was injected in the natural gas stream in order to detect leaks and prevent explosions.

"No, sir. The mercaptan is metering-in perfectly. The drill crew told me that I didn't need to be here, because the gas smelled bad enough by itself."

Shaking his head, Chubbs heard a muffled *shloop* as the pig shot out of the launcher on its journey to Billings.

"Okay, guys, the pig is away. Let's get out of here. Tomorrow morning Cody, Powell and Billings will be burning this stuff."

By the time the crews started their vehicles, gas, once trapped below the Four Sixes ranch for millions of years, was almost to Cody, Wyoming, through a six-inch lateral pipeline. The gas silently pushed its way through a series of meters and valves into the distribution lines that snaked under the ground to the houses and businesses of the eight-thousand residents.

Within thirty minutes, the gas made its way to the five-thousand residents of Powell, Wyoming, and an hour later, the pig arrived safe and sound in the Billings receiver. The Montana Gas crew shut the valves, released the pressure and opened the pig receiver hatch.

The foul smelling gas swirled around the crew as they removed the pig and scraped out a number of welding rods and other debris left in the line during construction. The gas made its way into the Billings gas distribution system and was sent to almost half of the eighty-one thousand residents of Billings on the south side of town.

Chapter Thirty-five

Cody, Wyoming
May 11, 2004

Nancy Walker fidgeted around, getting ready for bed when her infant son broke into his hunger cry. She lifted him from the crib and cuddled him close to her breasts.

"Oh, poor baby Joey. What's the matter?" she said in her most motherly tone, while bouncing the baby on her hip. "You sound like you're really hungry. Well, we'll just have to do something about that."

She put the baby in his highchair and stroked her skinny fingers through his light brown curls being careful not to scratch him with her long freshly painted fingernails. She stationed herself at the stove that was much older than she was. "Someday I might have enough money to buy a microwave. Because that mean old daddy of yours sure as heck won't buy one for us."

After pouring water into a pot, she set it on one of the stove's burners and turned the knob. There was a hiss, but no flame. When she turned back to the stove, she yelled, "Damn! The pilot light's out again, baby boy."

She pulled her long blond hair back and wrapped a rubber band around it, opened the drawer and retrieved a box of stick matches. Then, putting the pot on the counter, she pulled on the top of the stove until it broke free of the clips that held it in place.

"Joey, did you just poop in your diaper? Geez, something smells." Shaking what was left of the sleep from her eyes, she bent over the stove to find the small hole that housed the pilot light and heard a hissing sound. She recoiled and yelled, "Shit! I could have burned my face off, Joey! I forgot to turn off the burner."

With the burner off, she waited for the gas to clear, then struck the match and waved it over the tiny hole until the small flame flickered and danced. "I'll have you fed in a minute, baby."

Deep in her lungs, the gas she inhaled went to work. Some of the smallest living particles, a deadly cocktail of spores and viruses, found a new harbor to anchor in and wreak havoc upon.

Nancy Walker had no clue that baby Joey would soon be an orphan. She had just been given a reason for dying.

Maxwell Van Pelt directed the crew on the final set-up of the portable Biosafety Level 4 laboratory. Things were proceeding smoothly just like the regular drills that prepared them for these situations.

The BSL-4 enclosure was a technical marvel. Made in sections for portability, the white opaque structure would have an airtight seal. A portable, but powerful HEPA filter ventilation system ensured the atmosphere in the enclosure was scrubbed free of contaminants. It also had an air-lock entrance at both ends with sterilizing showers and air hookups for the ventilated positive pressure suits, worn by personnel in the BSL-4 lab.

One airlock connected the lab to the hospital emergency entrance. The other connected it to the outside world--a world that had to be protected from the atmosphere that would soon be in the laboratory.

A technician arrived, lugging a large white, high-impact case. "I have your life support suit, Dr. Van Pelt."

"Good. It's time I get in there. Get Dr. Larkin and tell him we're suiting up," Max said. "Where are the oxygen bottles?"

"The bottles are being checked for gas mix and pressure and should be here in less than ten minutes. We'll bring in eight fifteen-minute bottles, two each for you and Dr. Larkin and the rest for your emergency back-ups."

"Okay, go, go, go. Get Larkin," Max ordered, schussing him away.

He flipped open the latches of the large case and carefully unfolded the light blue one-piece positive pressure suit. Protocol required the tedious task of visually checking every inch of the suit for cracks or holes. It had already been pressure tested, but working in a BSL-4 environment required redundant systems. One mistake and the life threat towered beyond personal safety or the safety of the crew—it could threaten all of humankind.

"Hey, Max. I see we're getting ready," Dr. Rivers Larkin said as he entered through the airlock from the outside. Rivers, a thirty-year-old Native American had a ruddy complexion, longish black hair and a broad, flat nose. He grew up on a small reservation in Oklahoma where life was simple and luxuries were few. His father died when he was young and his mother worked two jobs to keep him and his five younger brothers clothed and fed.

After high school, he applied for a job at a grain processing plant on the outskirts of Tulsa. His mother greeted him after his first day at the mill with a letter in her outstretched hand. It was a full scholarship to Oral Roberts University. He spent the night futilely arguing with her. The night ended in a promise that he would make something of his life. After medical school at UCLA he took a job with the CDC. A year ago, he applied to work for Dr. Max Van Pelt, one of the most recognized experts in contagious diseases. This was his first hot zone.

"It's about time you got here. How's the rest of the setup going?"

"They're securing the second airlock now."

"Get your suit checked out and let's get in there. Oh, do you have your instruments for the autopsies?"

Rivers reached down, grabbed his small plastic orange toolbox and held it up, smiling at Max. He lifted his suit from its case and began the visual inspection process. A light breeze brushed by Max's scruffy face as the negative air pressure system pulled air from the open airlock. He turned to see a technician roll in a rack of oxygen bottles.

"Dr. Van Pelt, let me secure your air." The man held up two grayish bottles, each resembling a two-foot tall cola bottle.

Max held his helmet under his arm while the technician attached the lightweight, carbon fiber bottles to a belt holster and secured the regulators that would monitor and deliver germ-free oxygen to the suit. "The regulator will automatically switch bottles when the first one runs out, giving you about thirty minutes. You know the drill, Max. When you reach three hundred pounds, get back here. I'm hooking up the air supply hoses to pressure the suits and conserve the bottled oxygen. When I disconnect you, I'll give this valve a half turn and you're on the clock."

Rivers wrapped duct tape around the seal where the sleeves met the gloves, adding another level of precaution against leaks. He stood as the technician brought a pair of oxygen bottles for his life support system.

"Are you ready to do this, Rivers?" Max asked.

"I'm ready. I don't want to sound morbid, but I'm anxious to get my first look at a real-life level four environment."

"Let's just hope all these precautions turn out to be unnecessary. I've been there and it's not pretty. If I never see another level four virus outside the lab, I'll be ecstatic." Max lifted his helmet over his head.

Locking collars were engaged, sealing the helmets to the bodies of the suits. The technician turned the valve to the air supply hose, allowing the dry compressed air to inflate the suit slightly and circulate around them, raising goose-bumps as it met the perspiration that had beaded on their skin.

Max reached down for his sample kit and the single key that would unlock the unknown, possibly deadly atmosphere inside Cody Community Hospital.

"Testing, testing. Rivers, can you hear me?" Max said into the microphone in his helmet. There was a slight tug on the BSL-4 suit as the technician opened the regulators and disconnected the air hoses. The clock was ticking.

"I hear you." Rivers followed Max into the airlock with his autopsy instrument case.

"You perform the autopsies. I'll take blood and swabs from the symptomatic patients. We'll bring the samples out and see what we have." Max counted off the tasks as they entered the airlock. "By that time, team two will be ready to enter and start sampling the non-symptomatic."

"Sounds like a plan."

"Remember to check your time. Make sure you know how long it will take you to get back to the oxygen hoses in the lab. Then watch your pressure and don't cut the time too short. The monitors on the regulator don't give much warning."

Max put the key in the large padlock and turned it. Microphones on the outside of the suit picked up the snap of the hasp and amplified it. He pulled the chain through the handles as a man in grey scrubs and a long white coat walked toward them.

"Are you Dr. Alex Weiss?" Max asked, pulling the doors open. The speakers in the helmet carried his voice to the anxious man.

"Yes, yes I am. Dr. Van Pelt, I presume?" He paused and shook his head. "Sorry, I just realized how corny that sounded."

"I'm Max Van Pelt and this is Rivers Larkin. Look, we're on a limited air supply, so we need to get started. Can you take me to the symptomatic patients and have someone take Rivers to the deceased?"

"Yes, Dr. Larkin. See the intern standing outside trauma room three?"

"Yes."

"That's Dr. Jost. He can take you down to the morgue. Dr. Van Pelt, please follow me."

Dr. Weiss guided Max to the passenger elevators. "We moved the two patients we had in the hospital to the top floor and moved all the symptomatic patients to the second floor where we could keep them more comfortable. We have eight construction workers and two paramedics with symptoms. The most alarming are the paramedics. They were exposed less than twenty-four hours ago and their symptoms are progressing rapidly. One of them was directly exposed to the body fluids of James Buck, one of our first patients and the first to expire."

"Let's see the paramedics first," Max said, his artificially amplified voice reverberating off the walls of the small elevator.

The doors slid open and Dr. Weiss led Max to the first room. The bluish fluorescent light accentuated Lynn Howard's pasty-white complexion. A bright red rash covered her cheeks, ran down her neck and re-emerged below the sleeves of her thin hospital gown. She labored to breathe and her eyes stared blankly at the tiled ceiling.

"This is Lynn Howard. She was directly exposed to James Buck's body fluids as she brought him into the hospital. James ejected bloody vomit into her face as she bent over to read his vitals," Dr. Weiss said. "That was about eighteen hours ago."

"Okay, Doctor, I'm going to need a vial of blood and a swab from her mouth and nose."

"Let me take the blood samples. No sense in you having a sharps accident," Dr. Weiss said, referring to the needles that could easily puncture the life support suit.

"I appreciate that, but it's not necessary," Max responded.

"No problem, Doctor. Besides it will speed things up. If you like, I can get Dr. Jost up here and we can handle these samples while you start the analysis."

"No offense, but protocol requires us to do these ourselves. Drawing blood will be help enough. It's only been eighteen hours and she's already developing a rash? What are you treating her with?"

"Doxycycline and ciprofloxacin—same for all the patients."

Two floors down in the morgue, Dr. Rivers Larkin was about to begin the autopsy on what was once Jimmy Buck. Both Jimmy Buck and Dallas Wheeler had been moved to the cold basement morgue and now rested in opaque body bags on stainless steel tables. The concrete floor sloped to a large sewer grate at the center of the small room. On the far wall, several push brooms leaned against the white porcelain tile wall next to a coiled garden hose. Several large plastic containers of chlorine bleach were stacked next to the brooms. Rivers squinted against the bright fluorescent lighting.

"Do you need me to assist?" Dr. Jost asked.

"No, you need to leave the area," Rivers answered. "There may be pressure in the body. I can't have you exposed to body fluids."

"Very good. Is there anything you need? We have instruments in the cabinet in the corner."

"Thanks, I'll be fine. I'm going to take samples of Mr. Buck here. The second squad will take the other body."

"Okay, but if you need someone or something, the intercom is here on the wall. Push the red button and talk. We'll be able to hear you in the ER." Dr. Jost turned and pushed through the swinging stainless steel doors.

Rivers turned to the cadaver on the table and pulled down the nylon zipper of the body bag. All the pictures he had seen and all the drills he had been through should have hardened him, but stinging bitter bile rose in his throat. *Oh Christ, Jimmy Buck*, he thought, taking a deep breath trying to relax himself. *You poor son-of-a-bitch.*

Large red welts covered the body. The skin had taken on a grey pallor with large blackish-purple blotches below the surface. The connective tissue in his face had degenerated and skin hung from his skull, giving him the appearance of a very old man. Severe bruising indicated the start of a bleed-out, but it appeared his heart gave out before the process had begun in earnest.

Rivers opened the autopsy kit and set up several specimen holders for tissues samples. He carefully removed a scalpel from the kit and started the long incision that would hopefully reveal the identity of Jimmy's murderer. He had to be careful with the razor-sharp instrument, but there was no time to be neat.

The skin covering his chest and abdomen peeled back without any resistance; the connective tissue here was destroyed as well. He lay open the skin, exposing the chest cavity. *Oh, man, what kind of bug does all this?* The lungs were flat and the outer layers sloughed off into the chest cavity. The stomach and intestines were in the same condition. Jimmy's arteries appeared to be ruptured and blood pooled in the bottom of the cavity.

Rivers went about the task of taking tissue samples from the lungs, heart, spleen, kidney, liver and digestive track. He collected a blood sample from inside the body cavity. The color of the blood was darker than he'd ever seen. Autopsy notes and photos were captured with the digital recorder and camera integrated in the high-tech life support suit.

Carefully securing his instruments in a plastic case, he placed the case in a re-sealable plastic bag and glanced at his air gauge. *Ten minutes left*. With at least four minutes to get to the main floor and two more to navigate the halls to the airlock, he was cutting it close. Rivers hastily placed the post-mortem specimens in the toolbox, closed the lid and secured the latches.

He reached for the zipper on the body bag and pulled it towards Jimmy's head. As the opaque bag closed over the zombie-like face, Rivers whispered, "Adios amigo."

With the nylon zipper closed, he started to turn to pick up his kit, but as he withdrew his hand from the zipper, he felt resistance and a sinking feeling in the pit of his stomach. "Oh crap!"

He immediately stopped his arm motion away from the zipper. The glove on his suit was caught. He grabbed at the zipper with his left hand and pulled gently down. It didn't move.

"Oh shit, oh shit, oh shit!" He fought to stay calm, but adrenaline pulsed into his body and his blood vessels restricted as he trembled with nervous anxiety. His heart pounded and his temples throbbed. The sound of heavy breathing through the mechanical regulator filled his helmet and echoed in his head reminding him of Darth Vader. "Come on, Rivers, get it together," he whispered.

An almost imperceptible voice drifted in the helmet, barely audible above the crescendo of rushing air and pulsing blood. "Rivers, this is Max. I hope you're done and headed upstairs."

"Uh, just ran into a little snag here, Max. I'm aware of the time. Just have that air hose ready for me."

"Whatever you're doing, drop it and get the hell up here!" Max ordered.

"I'm doing my best."

Max's voice brought him back to reality. He leaned closer to see better, but his rapid breathing fogged the face shield. The bulky suit and double gloves made performing minute tasks difficult. Sweat dripped into his eyes, causing them to blur and burn. He tried wiggling the catches on the zipper from side to side with no luck. He increased pressure, trying to pull the catch over the thick glove, but it didn't budge.

Risk being exposed to the virus or die of suffocation? Caution aside, he tugged at the zipper with all his strength. It slid downward and his glove pulled free. He brought the glove to his face and inspected it. No apparent cuts, thank God. A glance at the oxygen gauge told him the pressure was still holding.

His muscles relaxed.

Rivers reached for the zipper again and pulled it shut, this time making sure his glove was free of its jaws. Grabbing his kit, he bolted for the swinging doors to the elevator. He punched the lone button, expecting the doors to slide open. Nothing happened. His eyes moved to the digital readout above the doors—first floor. *Oh shit!* He forgot to tell Jost to send the elevator back down. He fought the urge to use the stairwell—stairs were just too hazardous in the heavy life support suit.

After an eternity, he heard a ding and the doors slid open. They seemed to be moving in slow motion. He slipped into the elevator as the doors were still opening and punched the button for the main floor and then repeatedly jabbed at the close door button.

They hung open for a moment as Rivers slapped the button again and again. Finally, they began to shut and with a slight jolt, the elevator car began its ascent. The short ride to the first floor was torture as the dial on the oxygen meter moved into the red. About two minutes left. He took a shallow breath and held it, trying to calm himself.

With a thump, the doors opened and Rivers ran for the emergency room. The physical exertion caused him to breathe heavily, using up precious oxygen. He looked comedic trying to hurry, yet take careful strides in the cumbersome suit. If he fell, his race would be over. He would be locked on the wrong side of the emergency room doors.

Cody Community Hospital was a blur. He was a drowning man frantically trying to reach the surface. Somewhere in his helmet Max's voice urged him to get the hell out of there. A shrill high-pitched warbling sounded in his helmet. He knew from the drills he had maybe two or three breaths of air left and the emergency room doors looked to be a mile away. He took a deep breath and held it. The warbling alarm became a steady screech as the last wisp of oxygen flowed into his suit.

His left hand hit the crash bar on the doors and he burst into the airlock, collapsing to his knees. Max reached down and attached the air hose to his suit. The hiss of oxygen flowing in sounded like a chorus of angels. Cool air rushed around his face and he took a deep breath.

"Max, you never looked so good," Rivers gasped between breaths. "Thank God."

"You can tell me what went on down there while we start the analysis," Max said, helping his partner off the ground.

After his decontamination shower, Rivers looked around and noticed four other technicians in light blue BSL-4 suits. Electron microscopes were set up and two of the scientists were working on the blood samples and swabs.

"What did your subject look like, Rivers?"

"Looked more like a hemorrhagic fever than anthrax," he said, still breathing heavily. "Most of the internal organs were on their way to soup. He started bleeding out, but his heart failed before it happened. The liver was the worst. Connective tissue in the face and torso had deteriorated and the stomach and intestines were full of dark blood. What about your subjects?"

"It's pretty confusing. There are eight cases that look more like anthrax to me." Max fought the urge to scratch a persistent itch gnawing on his hairy chin. That was the problem with wearing the life support suits, one that he had gotten used to. He concentrated on preparing a slide for his electron microscope trying to forget about the need to scratch. "However, there are two cases that are progressing much too fast for anthrax and taking the same course as the cadaver you examined."

Rivers looked toward the virologist preparing to enter the hospital to take tissue samples from Dallas Wheeler's body. "Before I forget—two things, Jarvis. Tell Dr. Jost or Dr. Weiss to send the elevator back down to the morgue and make sure nobody uses it while you're down there. And watch the zipper on the body bag."

"Dr. Van Pelt, there are people from the FBI at the main security gate wanting to talk to you," a voice said over the intercom.

"Let them through," Max responded.

Johnny Campisi drove to the barricade being patrolled by the Wyoming National Guard and flashed his I.D. The frightened-looking young guard radioed the information from the badge to his command post and a few minutes later, the van was escorted to the hospital parking lot, a safe distance from the quarantine zone.

"You make me nervous as hell, Johnny," Laura said, resisting the urge to kiss the ground.

The scene around her looked surreal. Military personnel patrolled a perimeter of barricades while a crowd gathered around speculating on what was happening. Bright spotlights traced wide arcs on the surroundings and the buzz of helicopter rotors filled the air, giving it the feeling of a movie set.

Laura spotted a uniformed national guardsman in brown camo approaching the group and held out her I.D. badge. "Can you take us to the CDC command post?"

"Yes, ma'am. Follow me, please." He led them to large green tent outside the hospital.

The CDC command center bustled with orange jumpsuit activity. A row of spectacled young men and women typed feverishly on laptop computers. Another group worked a bank of telephones while a third huddled around a large white board building a multi-colored storyline of the current situation. A young lady sitting alone at a long table stood when they entered. "You must be the FBI. Dr. Maxwell Van Pelt has been notified of your arrival, but he's still in the lab."

"Is there any way we can have a brief talk with him?" Laura asked.

"They're pretty busy in there and protocol requires no distractions. It's too dangerous. But I'll try his radio and see if he responds." She picked up a headset and began talking very quietly. "Dr. Van Pelt, there are people from the FBI here who want to talk to you."

"Okay, put them on. I'm between samples." The response came through loud and clear on the radio speaker.

Laura took the headset from the lady in orange and said, "Dr. Van Pelt, this is Agent Laura Daniels with the FBI Seattle Field Office."

"Yes, Agent Daniels?"

"We've been tracking two suspected terrorists in the area. We think, or at least thought, that they were collecting radiation devices in order to build a dirty bomb."

"Okay, do you think this might be related in some way?"

"I can't say for sure except that we believe them to be in the area and now, coincidentally, we have this potential outbreak. It's highly suspicious and I've been directed to investigate."

"I understand. Here's what I know, and it's not much. We have a fairly isolated group of construction workers from an oil-well site that are infected. Preliminary diagnosis points to potential anthrax exposure or some kind of hemorrhagic fever or both."

"Excuse me, Doctor, did you say oil well?"

"Yes, why?"

"Because oil well contractors use equipment with radioactive sources and some of that equipment was just reported stolen from a Wyoming Test Labs truck here in Cody. Is there anybody in there that has knowledge of the oil well that I could talk with?"

"Yes, there is. I believe he's the project manager. Let me look at my notes here." There was a break in the conversation before Max came back on. "His name is Brandon Stiles. He's in the hospital but has no symptoms. You can have Anita call into the hospital and track him down."

The lady with short, straight black hair and black-framed, librarian styled eyeglasses standing next to Laura held up her hand to let her know who Max was alluding to.

"Doctor, when might you know what you're dealing with?" Laura asked.

"Hopefully within the hour—at least we'll have a good start."

"Thank you, Doctor. I understand you have your hands full, but keep the terrorist angle in mind and let me know if you find anything helpful for us. I'll give Anita my contact information."

"Of course. Now you must excuse me. I'm starting a gram positive stain and it's a bit tricky in these suits."

Anita was already on the phone when Laura removed the headset. "Okay, please hold for one moment." She handed the phone to Laura, whispering, "It's Dr. Brandon Stiles."

"Hello, Dr. Stiles?" Laura asked.

"Yes, this is Brandon Stiles."

"Dr. Stiles, I'm Special Agent Laura Daniels with the FBI. I'd like to ask you a few questions about your oil well."

"It's more like an exploration well, but sure, what can I help you with?"

"Are you aware of any equipment at your site that may have had radiation sources in them?" she asked.

"Yes, two of them, actually. We just had well loggers at the site and they have several Americium-241 sources. Also, the pipeline crew was finishing up and the x-ray technician uses an Americium-241 source to inspect pipeline welds."

"Is this well logging company Wyoming Test Labs?"

"Yes, it is. And the x-ray technician is with the same outfit."

"Do the names William Goller or Walter Nolte ring a bell?" Laura asked, referring to the NRC incident report.

"Yes, Billy was the well logging crew chief. The x-ray technician was named Walt, but I didn't catch his last name."

"Are you aware of any problems or thefts?" Laura asked.

"None at all, but I've been here all day."

"Have you noticed any men of Middle Eastern descent around the well site or the hotels?"

"Huh? Middle Eastern descent? No, not that I can remember."

"In regards to either this outbreak or radiation topic, is there anything else you can think of?"

"One of the well loggers, Jimmy Buck, just died in here. Billy Goller was supposed to drop off a report at my condo tonight, uh, last night," Brandon said.

"Who's Jimmy Buck?" Laura asked.

"He was one of the well loggers, Billy Goller's helper."

"Thank you, Dr. Stiles. I may be back in touch with you."

"You know where to find me. From what I see, I don't think I'll be going anywhere for a while," Brandon added.

"Here's my card, Anita. If you can't reach me for some reason, call the office number and ask for Robert Williams." She turned to her team. "Let's go."

"Where?" Johnny asked.

"The Wyoming Inn. Something is seriously wrong here, but I'm not sure what. I'll explain on the way. See if one of these National Guardsmen knows where it is."

On the short ride to the motel, Laura explained what she had learned from Brandon. They pulled into the parking lot of the Wyoming Inn and Laura went to the office with Johnny Campisi.

"Excuse me, sir, do you have a William or Billy Goller registered here?" Laura asked after showing her I.D. to the night manager.

"Yes, ma'am. Room 104. That's next to the boy that was taken out of here today in an ambulance," the night manager told her. "But, ma'am, you know it's pretty late, don't you?"

"Yes, I do, thank you." Laura turned and pushed her way through the door.

It was warm and dry in the portable BSL-4 laboratory. There were incubators, electron microscopes, and projection equipment as well as an assortment of computers and printers, all of it generating heat in the airtight enclosure. A refrigeration unit on the air supply kept the virologists cool as the air was pumped into their state-of-the-art protective suits.

"I have B. anthracis in the pleural fluid for patient number seven," one of the virologists said into the intercom in his helmet. "No sign of spores in the nasal swab, but the fluid is teeming with the bacteria."

The entire conversation in the portable lab was received and transcribed by the computer operators in the command center.

"Okay, record inhalation anthrax in patient number seven. That's a Robert Townley, one of the construction workers." Max reported for the benefit of the recorders while scribbling the information on a white board in the lab. "Rivers, is there anything on your specimens?"

"I've got the RNA/Primer mix incubating for the reverse transcriptase-polymerase chain reaction. That will take about twenty more minutes. The ELISA testing is in incubation for another forty minutes. I'm scanning liver tissue now, trying to isolate any viruses."

"Max! I've got inhalation anthrax in patient six," one of the other men said, getting up from the sophisticated scanning electron microscope.

"Patient six, that's another construction worker," Max said, recording on his white board.

He switched to the radio in his suit. "Anita, can you patch me through to Dr. Weiss in the hospital?"

"Sure, Max, just a second."

A minute later, Max heard a beep on the helmet speaker, then, "Dr. Van Pelt, this is Dr. Weiss."

"We have identified inhalation anthrax in several of the construction workers. Are any of them responding to the Doxycycline and Ciprofloxacin?"

"As a matter of fact, fevers are dropping in several of them and they're breathing a bit easier," he reported. "Do you have anything on the pathology or on my paramedics?"

"Not yet. We're running a few tests that won't be ready for an hour or so. Right now we're scanning for viruses under an electron microscope, which can be slow."

"Thanks for the update. Is there anything else I can do?" Dr. Weiss asked.

"Pray, Dr. Weiss. Pray that this is anthrax. That would make life a little easier." Max turned off his radio.

"Life's a bitch, Max. And God's not answering your prayers today," Rivers said. "We've got big problems."

"What do you mean?" Max asked.

"Come look. I have a filovirus on the screen," Rivers announced.

"Oh crap!" Max's heart sank and his stomach felt like he'd been kicked by a mule.

The entire team jumped up to stare at the projection screen that amplified Jimmy Buck's obliterated liver tissue millions of times over. Thousands of threadlike organisms occupied the screen, interlaced like a writhing ball of snakes.

"Can you isolate one?" Max asked.

"I'm looking," Rivers answered. "Okay, switching now and amplifying."

The image on the screen was that of a single thread with one rounded end. The four virologists stared, mesmerized and terrified at the image on the screen.

"We definitely have Marburg or Ebola. There's the definitive Shepard's Crook. ELISA and RTP should help us pinpoint it," Max added. "I'm getting out of this suit and calling USAMRIID. They have more experience with filoviruses than we do."

Chapter Thirty-six

Cody, Wyoming
May 12, 2004

Billy spent the night getting the crap beat out of him. A line of people waited to kick him in the nuts. First in line was Josh O'Connor, the owner of Wyoming Test Labs. He kicked Billy repeatedly for ruining his company. Each time shouting "You stupid bastard!" Second in line was Billy's wife, Julie. She walked up to him with a contorted face he had not seen before and slapped him repeatedly before jamming the pointed toe of her spike heels into his crotch. He managed to pick himself off the ground only to see the bloated, blue-gray face of Jimmy Buck grinning at him. Jimmy began slamming the oil-slicked well logging tool into his skull. "Thump, thump, thump." Billy threw his hands over his head, but Jimmy kept pounding the heavy instrument into his skull. "Thump, thump, thump."

He woke with a start and abruptly sat up in his too damn hard motel bed. Dazed, he turned to look at the clock radio teetering on the edge of the nightstand and struggled to focus his eyes. It read 1:45 a.m. He heard the thumping again—then a muffled female voice.

"Billy Goller, please open the door. I'm Special Agent Daniels with the FBI."

He swung his feet off the bed, stumbled to the door and peered through the peephole. *What the hell? Three dudes and a babe, what now?* "I'll be right there. I've got to get some clothes on," he called through the closed door.

Did she say FBI? Billy scratched his tussled, oily brown hair. He threw on an old pair of tattered blue jeans and a grey Old Navy tee shirt with a faded American flag, slipped his feet into a pair of chewed up flip-flops and shuffled to the door.

"Special Agent Daniels, FBI Seattle Field Office. These are Special Agents Campisi and Jackman and Detective Harrison. We'd like to ask you some questions about the radiation devices you reported stolen."

"Sure, uh, you want to come in?" he asked, rubbing his eyes.

"Here is fine. Is that your truck?" Laura pointed to the panel van in the parking lot with the magenta radiation placards pasted to the sides.

"Yes, ma'am, that's mine. The yellow one next to it—that's Walt's.

His source was stolen, too."

"Walt Nolte?"

"Yeah, Walt's in that room right there." Billy pointed to the door next to his.

Laura nodded at Johnny. "You want to get Mr. Nolte out here?" Johnny turned to room 105 without a word. "Mr. Goller, can you show me where you kept the sources?"

"Yes, ma'am—right back here." Billy led her to the back of his truck as he heard the other agent banging on Walt's door. The hum of the old Wyoming Inn neon sign was the only sound other than their footsteps. He reached for the door handle. Laura grabbed his wrist, bringing a look of surprise to his face.

"Don't touch that, Mr. Goller. We need to check for prints."

Billy opened his hand displaying a key. "I don't need to touch the handle. I use the key to turn it."

"Okay, go ahead and open it, but be careful not to touch anything."

With a twist of the key in the lock, the door swung open. There wasn't enough light from the parking lot to see details. Billy reached in and flipped a switch near the door, illuminating a small dome light in the ceiling. Laura grimaced. *What part of 'don't touch anything' didn't he understand?*

"I kept the nuclear logging tools right here on the floor. They come in shielded cases 'bout eight foot long." Billy pointed inside the truck. "They even took my sonic tool. I reckon it looks enough like the others, but a bit shorter."

Jim Harrison came up behind Laura, "Was this door locked?"

Billy looked down at his feet. The question struck a chord.

"I...I thought so. But I can't be sure. You see, me and Walt just got back from the job this afternoon and I came back here to start my computer chewin' on the data." He looked back at Detective Harrison. "That's when the cop came up to us and told us Jimmy was real sick. He told us to get in the car with him 'cause the doctor at the hospital had some questions."

Harrison asked again, "So did you lock it?"

"I thought so. Shit, it's a habit. But when me and Walt came back tonight, I put the key in and didn't hear it click."

"Well, Mr. Goller, that doesn't mean you didn't lock it. If someone picked the lock, they could have left it open," Harrison consoled.

Laura looked over to see Campisi and Jackman with Walt Nolte standing at the back of his x-ray truck. Walt was pointing to the cut lock lying on top of the tool boxes.

"One last question for now. Are you sure the devices were back here before you left for the hospital?" Laura asked.

"Yes, ma'am. That much I know. I had to squeeze by them to get to my computer."

"Thank you, Mr. Goller. I suggest you stay in town for a few days in case we need additional information," Laura advised. She turned to

Harrison. "Let's talk to the manager."

A bell tied to the door handle of the manager's office announced their entrance. The burley, unshaven man eyed them as they approached the counter again. Laura asked, "Sir, did you by chance see anything suspicious around those vehicles today?"

"No, ma'am. Quite honestly, I was pretty upset with that man being in such a mess today—I mean the ambulance, the police and now I have to keep the room locked and I have no idea how I'm going to clean it up."

Laura rephrased the question. "Did you happen to notice any foreigners around, like any Middle Eastern men?"

The manager's eyebrows rose a bit. "Yeah...yeah I did. This afternoon, an Arab man came in to use the telephone. Real polite fella. His van had a flat tire and he needed to call someone."

"Did you notice anything about the van—license plate, color, markings or signs?"

"It was a plain white cargo-type van. I couldn't see the tags, but it was from some Montana storage place. They parked right there—kinda blocked my view."

"Montana U-Store?" she offered.

"Sounds right, but I can't be sure. Things were a little messed up around here."

"Do you have surveillance cameras on the premises?"

"No, ma'am."

"Did he say anything about where he was headed or is there anything else you can remember?"

"No, ma'am. That's 'bout it." After a hesitation, he continued, "He did have a buddy. The other guy worked on the flat, while the one in here made the phone call."

"Did they mention any names?"

"Nope."

"Thanks for your help." As she stepped back out into the cold air her cell phone chirped and vibrated. "Agent Daniels."

"Agent Daniels, this is Anita Gabon with the CDC."

"Yes, Anita."

"Is this a secure line? Dr. Van Pelt asked me to call you."

"Yes, go ahead."

"We've identified anthrax in all the victims here."

"Oh shit," Laura said. "Thank you, Anita."

"Wait! That's not all. We've also identified at least one filovirus—something like Ebola or Marburg as well as another potential level four virus, like Lassa Fever or Hanta."

"Oh my God. How can that be?" Laura's stomach churned and her knees went weak. She knew enough about the diseases to know how severe the ramifications could be and how unlikely this is to be a natural occurrence.

"Nobody here knows. That's why Max asked me to call. He suggested you get back here for a conference call. He's also called in U. S. Army Medical Research Institute of Infectious Diseases."

"I'll be there in a few minutes, Anita. I'd like to add a few names to the conference call list." Laura snapped her phone closed.

"Guys!" she called. "I've got to go—now!"

Johnny shook Walt's hand, thanking him for the information and apologizing for dragging him out of bed in the middle of the night. He trotted to Laura with Bart Jackman in tow.

"What's going on?" he asked.

"This is getting more serious by the moment," she said in a low voice. "The CDC has identified anthrax, and several other highly contagious, deadly viruses in the victims at the hospital. This just *can't* be coincidence."

"Do you think our bad guys are preparing a multi-tiered attack?" Harrison asked. "Maybe they exposed these workers to keep us busy while they ran off somewhere to detonate a dirty bomb?"

"That certainly seems like a possibility," Laura said. "But why the hell bother with a dirty bomb when you have the mechanism to unleash a bio-threat like this?"

Bart spoke up, "Maybe they couldn't come up with enough anthrax and virus to cause a panic, so they're using it as a diversion."

"Laura, you said you have to go. Go where?" Johnny asked.

"I have to get back to the hospital. The CDC is hosting a conference call and I want to get Bob and Mike Johnson involved." She glanced at her watch. "Johnny, why don't you and Bart go to the police department and try locating Halid and Atif. They probably ran, but we may be able to get a lead if they spent the night here. Jim and I will go the hospital."

"We'll see if we can't get the local police started and then find a place to shut our eyes for a few hours," Johnny said. "Jacks and I are running on fumes."

"Can you find out if the police have a spare vehicle that we can use and get it out to the hospital?" Harrison asked.

"I'll get you something," Johnny answered.

As Laura climbed in the van, she flipped open her cell phone to call Bob Williams in Seattle.

Laura and Harrison jumped out of the van as it pulled to a stop and made their way through the National Guard perimeter surrounding Cody Community Hospital. Finding Anita, Laura asked where the conference call would take place.

"Follow me." She directed them to a tent in the middle of the hospital parking lot.

"Come in, Agent Daniels," Max said, standing up. "We're just about to get started. I understand you want someone included in the call?"

Max fit the image Laura had in her mind: mid-fifties, average height, average, if not slightly over-weight build, gray-streaked black hair combed back with a salt and pepper beard. The look of a college professor. She had already picked him out in the room.

"Yes, here are the numbers." She handed a piece of paper to Max. "That's Robert Williams, Chief of the FBI Seattle Field Office and Mike Johnson, Chief of FBI Bioterrorism Division, Headquarters."

Max handed the paper to the man sitting next to him who immediately began punching in numbers on the satellite conference phone.

"On my end, I've asked some people at the CDC, USAMRIID and Homeland Security to listen in," Max explained. "I'll wait to get into what we have until we have everyone hooked up."

Minutes later, the man in charge of the phone said, "Dr. Van Pelt, I have everyone on. Is there anything else you need from me?"

"No, that will be all. Thank you." Waiting for the door to shut he continued, "Okay, I suppose everyone is here. I'll start with what we have and be brief as possible."

Max positioned his reading glasses low on his nose and opened a notebook. "To simplify this I will put our cases in four groups. First, we have two deceased. Both male and both associated with a pipeline and well that are being built thirty-five miles southeast of Cody on a cattle ranch. We identified inhalation and cutaneous anthrax and a filovirus that closely resembles Marburg, but with some slight variations in its protein coat. If that's not bad enough, there is another virus—I'll call Virus X—spherical in shape and not responding to our antigen tests."

"Max, this is Lieutenant Phillips, USAMRIID. Both patients had all these present?"

"Yes, sir. We're trying to put all the details together now. We should have it uploaded, with electron microscope scans, to our network within the hour," Max answered.

"Second, we have two paramedics that responded to one of the two deceased patients. One of the paramedics we know had direct contact with body fluids and the other is probable. We have identified the filovirus and virus X in both, but no anthrax." Max took a breath. "Their symptoms are progressing at a rapid pace with everything you can expect from the Marburg-like filovirus. Problem is, the filovirus may be masking virus X symptoms."

Whenever Max paused in his briefing, the tent was silent. Laura wasn't sure it was from disbelief or shock.

"Third, we have eight construction workers from the well site. We have only identified inhalation and cutaneous anthrax in them—no virus. Their symptoms are progressing along the expected course for anthrax exposure and several are responding favorably to treatment. Are there any questions?" Max asked.

"Lieutenant Phillips again—you said four groups, and have you made a determination on whether it's airborne or not?"

"Fourth group, we have at least one man connected with the job site who has no symptoms," Max continued. "However, there are potentially a dozen others from the site that may be affected, but we don't know. With the hospital in quarantine and the fast acting nature of the virus, we're unsure if we have everyone with symptoms. Also, there are no hospital workers that are symptomatic...yet."

"Greg Reilly, Homeland Security here—that last piece is excellent news."

"Well maybe, maybe not," Max said. "Remember, there's virus X. I'm not trying to alarm anybody here, but it may be just as lethal and the filovirus is masking it. We do know that it's not as aggressive as the filovirus, but it *is* multiplying—especially in the kidney and spleen. We may have an airborne virus that hasn't manifested itself in the hospital workers yet. They'll be tested next."

Max took a breath and continued, "I'm having the CDC issue an immediate special health bulletin to all medical centers in Wyoming and surrounding states. The remainder of the country will be included on the regular weekly update."

"Reilly again—this question is for Mr. Johnson of the FBI. Can you fill me in on the information the FBI has."

"I'd rather have Agent Daniels do that. She's closer to the investigation," Mike said.

"This is Laura Daniels, here in Cody. Gentlemen, we have been tracking two Middle Eastern men, Ahmed Halid and Ali Ibrahim Atif. They are suspected to have ties to a terrorist cell in New York City. We believe they killed a security guard in Spokane, also Middle Eastern, and stole a shipment of smoke detectors. We presume to build a dirty bomb. They rented a storage room in Billings, Montana, and we believe they came here to Cody to steal several larger radioactive sources from a testing company working the well site where the outbreak may have begun."

She continued, "Right now, we are trying to find where they are, or were, staying in Cody. My guess is that they are somewhere else by now, but we'll find them."

"That sounds fishy to me. There's too much here to be coincidence," the Secretary of Homeland Security added. "Dr. Van Pelt, three questions. How long before we know if we have this contained and if it's airborne? Do you have any ideas on how the viruses were introduced? And what resources do you need to ensure containment?"

Max tapped his pen on the table. "Secretary, I'm sorry I can't answer your first question with any accuracy—at least not until we can pin down this second virus. Hell, even the filovirus isn't identical to Marburg or Ebola. We're going to have to fly in some lab animals and conduct experiments. It could take days, even weeks to confirm whether or not either of the viruses is airborne."

"As far as your second question, the preliminary information suggests that the exposure started at the ranch. It's the only commonality we have for sure. It could have been introduced a number of ways: water, food, oxygen or acetylene cylinders or even some kind of manufactured delivery device. We can't even discount that one of the workers at the site was working with the terrorists."

"I'll definitely need some people from USAMRIID as soon as possible. They have more experience with filoviruses than us. We're going to need investigators to find the missing construction workers and I'll have to call in some more of my staff to take samples at the ranch and run tests on them."

"Mr. Johnson, can you spare more resources to track down the construction workers?" the Secretary asked.

"I'll cover it," Johnson responded. "Laura, how are your resources holding up?"

"I've got agents in Billings watching the storage facility and the hotel. Unless we get lucky here, I could use some help."

"Okay, I want you and your group to stay on Halid and Atif. I'll bring in other agents to find the construction workers. Williams, call me right after we end here to discuss how to allocate our resources. Dr. Van Pelt, I'll have some of the agents report to you to assist in locating the construction workers. Expect them by daybreak."

"Okay, gentlemen, keep me informed. I'll be personally advising the president within the hour," the secretary said before hanging up.

With the conference call over, Laura looked over to Max Van Pelt. "Doctor, how long will it be before you can release Mr. Stiles from the quarantine area?"

"I'm not sure. We have a team in the hospital right now collecting blood and nasal swabs from the non-symptomatic. But until we know more about this unidentified virus, I can't say with any accuracy."

"Here's my problem—I need more information about the job site. I also need the personnel records. Stiles may have the information."

"Let's get him on the phone and have a chat." Max summoned the guard posted outside and asked him to have Anita get Brandon Stiles on the phone. "Agent Daniels, knowing what you know about these suspected terrorists, do you have any ideas on how they may have distributed the anthrax spores or these viruses?"

"Unfortunately, no," Laura answered. "I heard no mention of gastro-intestinal anthrax which would rule out contaminated food or drink."

"Possibly, yes, but I wouldn't dismiss that possibility yet. Classic filoviruses aren't airborne and only survive a short time in the air. Being blunt with you, this is confusing as hell to me."

"What if Halid and Atif had nothing to do with this situation?" Harrison asked.

"What?" Laura turned to Harrison, eyes wide.

"Seriously. If we blindly make the assumption that these two guys unleashed biological jihad on a bunch of well drillers, we may be overlooking a more obvious reason," he said.

"Wait, you think this may all be a big coincidence?" she asked.

"I'm just saying, I think it would be a big mistake to make any assumptions right now. And why didn't they let this virus loose in Spokane or Yellowstone National Park?"

"You know I can't answer that, Jim. I just can't believe this isn't intentional."

"Then we need to concentrate on finding these bastards," Harrison said. "We shouldn't be worried about how the viruses were released. That's not our job right now. At least not until we capture these guys."

"But there may be something at the well site that could lead us to them."

"Sorry, but I don't think we should be wasting our time there. We need to get back to the station and help find these dirtbags."

The conference phone rang and Max pushed the speaker button. "Is this Mr. Stiles?" he asked.

"Yes, it is."

"Mr. Stiles, I have some people from the FBI with me and we'd like to ask you some questions."

"Call me Brandon, please."

"Okay, Brandon, how can we locate everyone who has worked at the well site?" Max tugged at a stray eyebrow hair.

"Getting me out of here would be a good start."

"I'm afraid we can't do that quite yet, but we're working on it."

"Yeah, I was afraid you were going to say that. Okay, you need to contact Jerry Muckler. He's the rig foreman and he's at the Vista View Condominiums Building 3, Unit A. He can get you the employment records."

"This is Agent Daniels again. Can you think of anything that all the infected people from the well site had in common?"

"Dr. Weiss and I went through this yesterday. Most of the people stayed at the Wyoming Inn, but not Dallas. We rented a water cooler and brought in water from the Safeway Store. We also purchased powdered Gatorade and made it with ice from a convenience store every morning," he said. "The only thing left is that we all worked on a cattle ranch for three weeks—that's all that comes to mind."

"Thanks again, Brandon, we appreciate your help," Laura said.

Pushing the release button on the conference phone, Laura looked at Harrison.

"Let's get to the police station. Dr. Van Pelt, please keep me informed of any developments."

"Of course. It's time for me to get back to work," he said, standing up.

"Damn. We need to find some transportation, Laura," Harrison said.

"If I know Johnny, there'll be a something waiting for us. He can be very persuasive when he wants to be."

They left the makeshift conference room and headed for the barricade. As they rounded the corner of the tent, the crowd of onlookers had swelled with multitudes of news reporters and cameras. Half the population of Cody was trying to find out what was invading their normally quiet town.

As Laura showed her identification at the barrier, the soldier at the temporary gate stopped her.

"Agent Daniels, I have car keys for you. A Cody police officer told me to hold them for you. The car is right over there. The blue Taurus," the soldier said, pointing to the street outside the barrier.

"Thank you," she said. Turning toward Harrison, she smiled and added, "See, I told you. Let's hurry up, it will be daylight soon."

Inside the hospital, Brandon was left thinking about the commonalities of the crew and what might be the carrier of the viruses, but nothing was coming to mind.

Okay, so what was different from other job sites? Think, Brandon.

The pipeline to Billings wasn't completed yet. Most of the crew came from Tulsa, but then they hired guys out of the local union hall. *Wait! There was that unusual smell—that grossly horrific odor. But, that came out of the hole. Or did it?* His mind raced.

Regardless of whether it came out of the hole or not, there were only a few people who had contact with that chunk of organic material and both Jerry Muckler and I aren't ill. He didn't know who was assigned to the mud pit duties when it was found, but figured he could check that out later.

"Oh, well, what else..." he said, as his mind focused on getting out of the hospital.

Chapter Thirty-seven

Cody, Wyoming
May 12, 2004

Johnny dropped back in his chair, threw his muscled arms in the air and stretched his thick body. The Cody police headquarters occupied the back half of the post office building. Cinderblock walls were covered in mug shots, some as old as twenty years. Johnny recognized many of them, especially the mugs of former mobsters. "How many damn hotels are there in this small town?" he asked.

"Not so many hotels, but lots of smaller places to stay. Remember, we're only fifty miles from Yellowstone. The park has over four million visitors every year. We get a lot of the overflow. We've got hotels, motels, bed and breakfasts, dude ranches, lodges and condos," Sheriff Halloran said. "If I wanted to get lost somewhere, this wouldn't be a bad place to do it."

"Johnny, something just hit me," Bart Jackman said, looking up from his list of hotels. "If you wanted to steal something from a truck that was parked at a hotel, the best way you'd have of moving in quickly would be to keep it under constant surveillance, right?" He turned to the tall, rail-thin uniform sitting next to Johnny. "Sheriff Halloran, are there any hotels in visual range of the Wyoming Inn?"

"Let's see. The Buffalo Bill Villas is across the street and down just a bit. That's about it."

"Damn, Bart, I must be slipping. Give them a call."

"You know, they say the mind is the second thing to go, Johnny." Bart used his learned, special agent overly-serious tone. "Have you talked to your doctor about Viagra yet?"

"Just shut the fuck up and get on the fucking phone."

The door to the station swung open and Laura and Harrison rushed in. "How are you guys doing?" Laura asked.

"I'll tell you in a minute," Johnny answered. "Bart just had a brainstorm and is checking it out. If this doesn't pan out, we'll need your help. What's up at the hospital?"

"Not good at all. Pretty soon this town's going to be crawling with agents looking for workers from the well site. There are a dozen or so unaccounted for. We, however, are concentrating on Halid and Atif."

"Hot damn, I knew it! We got 'em!" Jackman shouted, pumping a fist in the air. "Buffalo Bill Villas—the old lady that runs the place says they're paid through tomorrow."

"Great job, Bart. Let's go," Johnny said in his big voice.

The sun peaked above the Bighorn Mountains, fanning out and painting scattered clouds on the eastern horizon various shades of orange and pink. To the west, the new sunshine reflected off the Tetons giving the majestic mountains a golden hue. The air was brisk and Laura was without her coat.

The touch of Harrison's hands as he draped his lightweight jacket over her shoulders brought a quiet gasp. She looked over her shoulder and smiled at him.

"Hey, is there something we should know about you two?" Johnny asked, the corners of his mouth turning up in a grin.

"No," Laura answered curtly. *Damn, overly observant FBI agents.*

"Uh huh, well save that touchy feely crap for later," Johnny added, still smiling. "Besides, Harrison, she could kick your ass. You better be careful."

Once they were inside the van, Laura asked, "You're the surveillance expert, Johnny, how do you want to play this?"

"The van is generic enough, but we'll park out of sight of the rooms. Laura, you and Harrison go talk to the manager and get a key. Bart and I will check out the back of the place."

"Okay so far," Laura said. "Then what?"

"I'd like to see you dress up in a French maid's outfit and knock on their door," Johnny added, looking to get a rise out of her. "You know…the type with the really short skirt and fishnet stockings?"

"Ha-ha very funny. Did you skip sexual harassment training?" she asked.

"I was sick that day," Johnny retorted. "But seriously, maybe we can have the manager knock on the door to check out a gas leak or something to see if they answer. If they don't, we simply go in and check it out. I have a hunch they've moved on."

"We can't put someone in harm's way like that," Laura said.

"Yeah, you're right."

"If they're on the road, I'm surprised that the APB on the van hasn't turned up anything," Harrison said. "The state patrol is usually real good when it comes to spotting something as obvious as a cargo van."

Johnny pulled their van to the curb across the street from the Wyoming Inn and about fifty yards from the Buffalo Bill Villas and killed the engine. "Shit, just think, we were right here last night. Those bastards could have been watching us."

Laura and Harrison headed to the office while Campisi and Jackman went to the alley behind the small complex.

"Hello, ma'am, I'm Agent Daniels of the FBI and this is Detective Harrison." The elderly woman watching television in the back of the room turned and struggled to push her bulky, aged frame out of the recliner—slight muscles fighting gravity.

"Oh my, yes. Someone just called me about some guests I have," she said, breathing heavily as if she had just finished running a marathon. "I suppose you're interested in those two A-rab men that I have registered."

"Yes, ma'am, Ali Atif and Ahmed Halid."

"Well, I only have a Mr. Halid registered, but he rented a two-bedroom villa and said he would be sharing the room. I gave him a very nice unit with three televisions," the old lady rambled.

"Ma'am, I need the key to the villa. They are suspects in a criminal investigation," Laura said.

"Well, I guess that's okay," she said, handing Laura a key ring with a large plastic tag displaying the room number.

Johnny fidgeted with his binoculars as Laura approached. He pointed to the far edge of the small complex where a fraction of a white van was visible. "Look…over at the corner of the building. That looks like our van."

"Halid is registered, not Atif. The manager says it's a two bedroom unit," Laura said, not taking her eyes off the sliver of white van in her view. *Got you, you bastards.* "How about the back of the building?"

"No exits or windows back there. There's only one way out. Do you have the key?" he asked.

"Right here." She held out her hand, dangling the key in front of him.

"Okay. Laura, you and Harrison will be positioned behind me. Bart, you're between the door and the window. I go in first, then Bart. Laura, let us clear the room, then you and Harrison—"

"Uh, I'll take up position behind you, Johnny," Harrison said.

Laura slapped him on the arm.

"Oww! What?" Harrison asked, cradling his arm.

"I can handle myself. Just take your position," Laura said curtly.

They made their way along the building, trying to stay out of sight as much as possible. The old lady in the office peered out of the corner of the window not wanting to miss the show. After assuming their positions, Johnny made eye contact with them and gave the okay signal with his left hand. He pointed to Jackman and then to the left side of the room. Then he pointed to himself and to the right side of the room. Jackman nodded acknowledgement.

Laura stood ready. Arms outstretched, gripping her Sig P-229—maybe a bit too tight—muzzle pointed to the ground. She squinted her eyes to be ready for the change in lighting.

Handguns drawn and cocked, Johnny quietly slid the key into the lock and opened the door a crack. After a quick look around, he slammed the door open.

Johnny rushed in with his gun held high and straight out in front of him, scanning the right side of the villa living room. Jackman rushed in behind him and was down on one knee with his gun at eye level surveying the left half of the room.

"Clear!" Johnny yelled. "FBI, come out with your hands in the air!"

No sounds, no movement.

Johnny pointed to Harrison and Jackman and then to the stairs that led to the bedrooms. Heads nodded in acknowledgment as they started quietly up the steps. He looked at Laura and pointed to the kitchenette and bathroom at the back of the villa. She nodded and followed Johnny to the bathroom doorway.

Leading with his gun, he jumped into the open doorway of the bathroom, crouching down. "It's clear."

"All clear up here." Jackman's voice could be heard from upstairs.

They relaxed and holstered their weapons. Jackman and Harrison trotted down the stairs.

"Nothing," Harrison said. "Beds are made, nothing in the drawers or closets and no suitcases."

"Dammit! Doesn't look like anything down here either," Laura said, disappointed.

"Well, if they aren't here and they haven't shown up in Billings, they're either en route home or on their way to steal another radiation source," Johnny said.

Laura trotted down the corridor to the white van. It read *Jay's Catering Service*. She looked up at the sign in the strip of grass next to Buffalo Bill Villas that read *Jay's Restaurant and Catering Service*. She walked back across the parking lot to the office where Harrison was waiting. The old lady was still peering through the corner of the window.

"Ma'am, when's the last time you saw them or their vehicles?"

"Well, I'm not one to be nosey. But I took some trash out to the Dumpster yesterday afternoon and noticed their cars were gone. I thought they probably drove up to the park. You know it's beautiful this time of year—all the trees blooming and all."

"And you didn't see them last night or this morning?" Laura asked.

"No. You see, I take a short walk at night and I didn't see Mr. Halid's nice car."

"Did you say car?" Harrison spoke up. "You mean van, right?"

The old lady shuffled behind the counter and pulled out a registration card. She put on her reading glasses and extended her hand trying to focus on the handwriting. "No, he had a beige 2004 Buick Century. Now that I look at the card, he forgot to fill out his tag number. I did see a white van in the parking lot yesterday and then parked in the back by the Dumpster."

"You mean the catering van?"

"No, dear, I know Jay's van. I mean way back by the Dumpster. There was a white van back there."

"Did you happen to notice if the Buick's tags were from Montana?" Harrison asked.

"No, I'm sorry, I didn't. But there was something peculiar." She looked down and her forehead wrinkled as if she were straining to jog her memory. "He paid cash for two nights and when I asked him for a charge plate, he said he had lost it. I told him I needed a deposit and he gave me an extra one hundred dollars. But he hasn't come back for it."

The team was quiet on the short ride back to the Cody police station.

"I'm going to have the surveillance teams in Billings go in and check out the hotel room and go through the storage space. I don't think they are going back to Billings," Laura said, reaching for the cell phone on her belt.

Laura called Bob Williams and updated him on their progress.

"Okay, I'll call the surveillance team and tell them to go in," Williams agreed. "I'll let you know what they find. So tell me what you plan to do now."

"We have a lead on Halid's car. He's driving a beige or gold Buick Century. We don't have the license plate number. I'll put an all points on it. Meanwhile, we're going to go through the villa here thoroughly."

"I'll handle the APB. I'll also have Olsen see if she can find the rental agency and a plate number," Williams said.

"Have her start in Billings. Try small agencies first. Their pattern has them using cash and staying under the radar."

"I'll get on it. Good work so far, Laura. We have to get these guys before they get out of sight."

"I know, Bob. We'll find them," Laura said and thumbed the disconnect button. *Damn it, now what? I have no clue where to go from here.* "Get it together, Laura," she whispered.

Turning to her team, she said, "Let's get some rest."

Chapter Thirty-eight

Powell, Wyoming
May 12, 2004

"Let's see what this thing looks like," Ahmed said. He sat on the edge of the couch, bending over one of the long heavy black cases.

"Ugh! The smell is horrible," Ali recoiled from the case. "Close it back up."

Ahmed closed the case as he sat back. "I don't know what stench is on this device, but we have to get some cleaning supplies and deodorizers or someone will report this odor."

"Shouldn't we get rid of the van, Ahmed? It is due back today. If the owner reports it stolen, it is very easy to spot. I can take it someplace where it won't be noticed and leave it while you get supplies."

"I have already thought about that. Until we are able to remove the radiation sources from these cylinders, I would not feel comfortable without the van. Let's wait for the moment."

Ahmed drove to a small convenience store for cleaning supplies and food. In less than an hour, he was back with two bags of various liquids, sprays and paper towels.

They moved the first case into the bathroom. After spraying the room with deodorizer and turning on the vent fan, they lifted the nuclear well logging tool into the tub. It was longer than the tub and it took some jockeying to get it situated.

"This is horrible, my brother. The smell is disgusting and this black stuff looks like it will block the drain," Ali said, wiping his hands on a paper towel.

"We are almost done with our mission, Ali. Soon we will be returning home," Ahmed said, as he spun the faucet in the tub. "We must persevere a bit longer."

"It will feel good to—"

The water spurted out of the faucet hitting the ooze covered curved surface, splattering them both with the blackish-grey slime.

"Agh!" Ali said, spitting the foul-smelling stuff out of his mouth.

Ahmed grabbed a towel and wiped the stuff from his eyes. They set about the task of cleaning the eight-foot long stainless steel probe, filling a plastic garbage bag with crumpled, black-stained paper towels. He sealed the bag and carried it out to the Dumpster in the back of the parking lot. Ali was emptying a can of deodorizer into the bathroom when he returned.

"Ahmed, how will we disassemble this device? Our tools—they are not large enough."

Ahmed examined the long cylinder. Stainless steel plugs were screwed into both ends. He left the room and returned a moment later with a compact tape measure. It would take a three-inch wrench to remove the plugs and extract the radioactive sources.

"We must disassemble these. We cannot go to New York in the van. I am going to try to find some tools to take these apart. Let me help you lift the next piece in the tub so you can continue cleaning."

Leaving the sickly sweet odor of country flowers mixed with the lingering putrescence of the black ooze, he opened the drawer in the nightstand by the bed and thumbed through the phone book.

Ahmed visited two hardware stores and both were closed. He knew this department store wouldn't have a wrench big enough, but it was better than going back to the foul-smelling room.

"Can I help you, mister?" asked a frail-looking old man sporting a white scraggly beard.

"I am looking for a wrench with a three-inch span. Do you have anything like that, uh, Raymond?" Ahmed asked reading the man's Handi-Mart name badge.

"Three inches? My, my no. That's a specialty item. I guess you have a truck or some big machinery you're working on?"

"Uh, yes, yes, a large truck. It broke down and my partner and I are in a bind, Raymond. Do you know where I might find one?"

"Well, let me see," the old man said, running his fingers through the splaying white hair on his chin. "Brown's Hardware on Division Street can surely order one from the Snap-on catalogue, but I'm not sure they would stock something that big."

"Thank you for your help," Ahmed said, as he turned to leave.

"Or...you could just call Smitty's Garage. They can fix anything. Real cheap, too."

He stopped and turned. "Smithy's Garage?" Ahmed repeated, pronouncing the name carefully.

"No, Smitty's. It's on Fourth and Gilbert—just east of here."

"And they would have the tools for a large truck?"

"Oh my, yes. You know, mister..."

"Halid."

"Mr. Halid, you don't dress like the normal long-haul driver."

"Oh, no. I don't drive. I am the owner and I decided to accompany my driver on this trip."

"Ah, I see," Raymond said. "Well, I hope you get it fixed, Mr. Halid."

Back inside the Buick Century Ahmed slammed his fists against the steering wheel. Stupid to have used his real name. "Argggh!" *We need to get home.*

Feeling the need to check out Smitty's garage, he drove to Fourth Street and turned east. The old frame homes were quite quaint and the neighborhood looked very serene. Fourth came to a dead end at Evarts Street forcing him to detour to Fifth for a block, then back to Fourth. A left on Fourth and two blocks down—there it was, Smitty's Garage.

Ahmed pulled the car to the curb and pushed a button. The window slid down with a hum letting the chilly night air circulate around his face. A ten-foot chain link fence surrounded the garage with a sign that warned *Beware of Dog.* Large lights shone down from the corners of the small single-story building and the sounds of barking dogs could be heard in the distance. Across the street, a row of two story homes stood, many with light streaming from their windows.

"Son of a bitch!" Ahmed screamed, as he slammed his fists on the steering wheel again.

With the car in gear, he circled the block. The fence continued around a small junkyard in the back of the garage. *If he could just lure the dogs near the fence and shoot them, then climb the fence...*Ahmed stopped the car and rubbed his forehead. *This is too frustrating.*

After the window thumped up, he drove the short distance back to the hotel, thinking through several plans. All were too risky. First thing tomorrow, he would try the hardware store. If that were unsuccessful, Allah would help him think of something.

Inside the stinking atmosphere of the hotel room, Ali finished the dirty work of cleaning the devices. He found the device that was not covered in smelly slime. In a sour mood, he was not happy at the project Ahmed had given him. *It was his room that stunk and he had to sleep here.* He finished twisting a green wire around the last plastic garbage bag when a rap on the door caught his attention.

"Who is there?" Ali said, squinting to peer through the peephole.

"It's me."

Ali opened the door without saying anything, noticing his partner was empty-handed.

"I am sorry, Ali. I was unable to find the proper tool."

"Brother Ahmed. We can talk in the morning. This job is terrible. I want to shower and sleep, but I can't stand the smell of this room."

"I'm sorry for that. Let me rent another room for the night."

"We have no more money. We don't even have enough for food and gasoline to get back home."

"That is a problem. I don't want to use a credit card yet. You can stay in my room, I have two beds." Ahmed stared hard at Ali. "But you must remember one very important thing."

"Yes, my brother, what is it?"

"You must not snore." Ahmed's serious stare cracked into a smile as he slapped Ali on the back.

"Thank you, brother. You are too kind to me."

"Tomorrow I will try to buy a large wrench to remove the radiation sources. I pray to Allah that this hardware store has what we need. If not, I will have a more difficult job to do."

Ahmed tossed and turned. Sweat dampened his brown skin and he couldn't breathe without coughing up phlegm. This was not a good time to be coming down ill. The trip to New York would take days.

His throat full again, he hacked up a mouthful of sticky fluid. Leaning over the edge of the bed, he spit it out into the wastebasket he had taken from under the sink in the bathroom. Even though his eyelids were heavy with exhaustion, he couldn't sleep. He sweated from the excessive heat in the room, and the anxiety of running into problems preparing the radioactive sources for transport was wearing on him.

They must be ready to travel tomorrow. He wanted to start the nineteen-hundred mile trip back to New York and he knew the longer they lingered in the area, the better the chance was of being caught. Especially after using his real name to that old man today.

In the next bed, Ali Atif was having trouble sleeping also. He had a horrendous headache and couldn't seem to shake the chills that had started several hours earlier. The thermostat was set to eighty degrees and the noise of the old fan clanging in the heat register seemed deafening. Like an ice pick jammed between his eyes, the metallic noise reverberated in his brain.

His breathing was labored and fluid rose with every cough. Already an entire box of tissues lay balled up on the nightstand and floor next to his bed. He struggled out of bed and into the bathroom to retrieve a roll of toilet paper. Clearing his throat, he spit in the sink. In the dim light the thick mucus looked dark. Flipping the light switch, he saw it was streaked with blood. *Probably the dry air from the heater.*

He hobbled back to the bed trying not to wake Ahmed and to keep his body from shivering as he went. Curling into a ball on the bed, the covers offered warm refuge.

Elsewhere in Powell, Wyoming, disaster was ready to strike. Natural gas carrying microscopic agents of death from millions of years ago began entering homes and businesses. The aging rural town had a considerable number of furnaces, water heaters and stoves with leaking pipes and valves and pilot lights that wouldn't stay lit. It was the beginning of a scenario that the CDC, or any other agency for that matter, had never dreamt to prepare for. It was the same deadly scenario that was playing out in Cody and Billings.

Chapter Thirty-nine

Cody, Wyoming
May 12, 2004

After grabbing a few hours sleep on a cot at the police station, Laura decided to go back to the hospital and see if there was any additional information available. The barricade around Cody Community Hospital was being pushed back into the town. USAMRIID Level-4 specialists arrived as well as ten FBI Agents.

She found Max Van Pelt in the conference tent with an FBI Agent, an Army officer and a man in jeans and flannel work shirt. Max looked like hell. She knew she looked the same way. Max stood up as she approached and introduced her to Agent Schaffer, FBI, Washington D.C., Max's counterpart with USAMRIID and Jerry Muckler.

"Mr. Muckler just arrived, Agent Daniels, and we were about to find out about the workers at the ranch."

"Yeah, like I was saying," Jerry continued, "at various times we had as many as fifteen on the drillin' rig and maybe another fifteen on the pipeline crew. Oh, then there was the radiologists and the start-up crew from Montana Gas out of Billings—there was maybe ten of them or so."

"God help us," Max said, running his fingers through silvery hair. "I have the count up to almost forty people exposed and only ten accounted for. We need to corral those people in Billings immediately before they spread this up there—if they haven't already."

"Mr. Muckler, where are the employment records and where can I find these people?" Agent Schaffer asked.

"The records are in a file cabinet in the construction trailer at the well site. It's in the conference room right across from the door, in the middle drawer—should be marked well enough."

"Do you have a key we can use?"

"Yeah, sure, but it'd be easier if I take you out there."

Max interrupted, "Uh, Mr. Muckler, we need you to stay here for testing."

"Any idea how long this will take? I've still got work to wrap up at the site. I need to get the equipment broken down for transport and I have what's left of my Oklahoma based crew at the well. They're good men, but they need watchin'."

The tent door swung open and Brandon Stiles walked through, smiling weakly, with Dallas Wheeler still on his mind.

Max stood and introduced Brandon to the group. No handshakes were exchanged. *Protocol or paranoia*, he wondered? He nodded across the table at Jerry.

"Dr. Stiles was just cleared. It appears he either wasn't exposed or has antibodies that were effective at warding off the viruses."

"I attribute that to thirty-five years of clean living. I can't vouch for the other six years," Brandon added.

"Dr. Stiles, would you go with us to the well site to collect the employment records and workers?" Agent Schaffer asked.

"I'd be happy to do anything that gets me out of this hospital."

"Agent Daniels, why don't you and your crew find a place to rest for a few hours?" Agent Schaffer said. "I'll send three of my men up to Billings to find the Montana Gas crew and take a couple men and Dr. Stiles here to the ranch."

"Sounds like a good idea. We got a few hours on a cot, but it's been a while since I've had a shower or been in a real bed."

"I'm very sorry, Dr. Stiles, but do you need to rest. Could I get you some food or something?" Agent Schaffer politely asked.

"Thanks, but I'm good. Actually, Dr. Weiss and the hospital staff made us quite comfortable, and the food wasn't bad either."

"Very good. If you don't mind then, I'd like to get going."

Max turned to Jerry Muckler. "Mr. Muckler, are you feeling ill in the slightest?"

"I feel fine. In fact, when I left the ranch, none of the guys were complaining. And, I'm tellin' you, if they have so much as a scratched pinky, they call in sick."

Max stood and said, "If you'll follow me, I'll get someone started on your tests."

He escorted Jerry to the door and instructed a CDC worker to take him to the non-quarantine testing area.

When Max returned Laura asked, "Dr. Van Pelt, are there any new developments?"

"Yes, there are. One doctor, an intern, has contracted the filovirus. Five of the remaining six hospital workers having direct contact with either the first two victims or the two paramedics have been infected with Cody. That's the official new name for the virus X. The virus seems to be invading the kidneys and spleen. They're starting to run fevers, but that could be from many things."

"Are either of them contagious?"

"I assume by contagious you mean airborne. There's not enough evidence to conclude that, but we also can't disprove it either. Any one of those hospital workers could have come in direct contact with body fluids."

"How are the paramedics?"

"Lynn Howard is on a ventilator and on the verge of bleeding out. She doesn't have long. Larry Enders has been holding on, but I think it's only a matter of a day or two."

"That's a shame," Laura said, standing up. "Thanks for letting me sit in on this. I'm going to find a place to rest."

She pushed back from the table and headed out the door and through the barricade. The onlookers were still behaving themselves, but the crowd was growing. Laura guided the Cody police car back to the station. She knew the team could only push themselves so long. She felt herself approaching a wall.

At the police station, Harrison and Campisi were in a heated discussion about sleep deprivation and Jackman was still on a cot in the back room.

"Guys, let's find a motel. We need to sleep. We're no good to anyone in this condition."

"That's what Johnny and I were just talking about. There's a Best Western just down the street, walking distance," Harrison said.

"Laura, Williams called with a license number on the Buick Century. They added it to the APB," Johnny said, as he handed her a piece of paper with a license number scribbled on it.

He quietly walked to the doorway of the back room where Jackman was snoring. "Hey Jacks!" he boomed.

Jackman jumped off the desk—looking from side to side with a bewildered look in his eyes.

"Let's go find a real bed, sleepy," he said, stifling a laugh. "God, I love doing that."

After reporting to the sheriff, the four of them headed out the door and down the deserted street toward the Best Western and some much needed rest.

Chapter Forty

Powell, Wyoming
May 13, 2004

Light streamed through the window between the gaps in the heavy, worn drapes. Sunlight splashed across Ahmed's eyes. Rolling away from the light, he looked at the alarm clock on the plastic and veneer night stand—7:30 a.m.

He swung his feet out of bed and sat up. Feeling lightheaded, he bent forward and placed his face in his hands—his head felt twice its normal size. Rising slowly, Ahmed turned on the television and pulled off his night clothes. On the other bed Ali was curled in the fetal position, wrapped in the heavy bed covering.

He turned on the small television and set the volume on low, then went into the bathroom and spun the faucet in the shower to hot. Waiting for the hot water to make its way from the aging water heater to the showerhead, his attention focused on the sound of the television. "This just in, we have breaking news in the city of Cody, Wyoming. Reporting live from Community Hospital in Cody is Karen Vargas. Karen, what's going on down there?"

"Ashley, I'm standing in front of a National Guard barricade. Cody Community Hospital is under quarantine due to a mysterious illness. No one is being allowed in or out, and from our vantage point, we can see a number of tents that have been erected next to the hospital."

Ahmed turned off the water and stepped into the bedroom to concentrate on the television.

"Most of the activity seems to be centered on several white tent-like structures that were erected sometime during the night. Authorities from the Centers for Disease Control in Atlanta have told us that an unknown illness has been identified in several patients at Cody Community Hospital and as a precautionary measure Cody Community Hospital has been placed under quarantine until further notice. The illness may have originated at a jobsite at the Four Sixes Ranch, thirty-five miles southeast of the city. All workers employed at that site during the past two weeks are strongly urged to either come to the quarantine security checkpoint at Cody Community or contact the CDC at 800-555-2543."

"Thank you, Karen. We'll keep our viewers up to date on

developments at the hospital as we learn more. Now for a look at the weather..."

Ahmed scratched his head disbelievingly as the news shifted to the local weather. He went back into the bathroom, turned the water back on, and took a long shower. The steam from the hot water swirled around him, relieving some of the pressure on his sinuses.

Suddenly a hacking cough welled up in his throat and caused him to double over. His throat filled with phlegm and he spit it out toward the drain at his feet. The large wad of thick blood-streaked green mucus swirled with the water but was too thick to drain through the small holes. *No matter*, he thought, turning off the water. He planned to be on the way home later today.

Ahmed stepped out of the shower onto the cool tile floor and reached for the skimpy bath towels hanging on the plastic bar. As he dried himself, he noticed that the hot water had raised red splotches on his arms and chest. They looked strange against his brown skin.

After getting dressed, Ahmed woke Ali.

"Yes?" Ali's voice sounded tired.

"Ali, you do not sound well, my brother."

"I didn't get much sleep. I must have caught a cold or something. I was either hot or cold all night and my head really hurts."

"Then you should rest for our journey. I will go to the hardware store and get the tools we need to disassemble the devices."

"Brother Ahmed, are you sure this is safe?"

"Yes, I have done the research and the sources are sealed and shielded. Do not worry. Allah will protect us," Ahmed said, pacing the floor. "I will wake you when I get back. Oh, I turned on the local news. There seems to be a mysterious illness in Cody."

"I will try to listen to see what is happening. May Allah protect you."

Ahmed grabbed his wallet and car keys. He had less than one-hundred dollars in cash left. *That should be plenty until we get on the road.* He left and drove to Brown's Hardware on Division Street.

It didn't take long to realize that no store in town had the type of wrench he needed. Even though he hated the idea, there was no other choice. He had to take the devices to Smitty's Garage. It was a huge risk. He turned the Buick around and headed back to the hotel, first stopping at a small convenience store to buy some snacks, cold medication and gasoline.

Ahmed returned to the motel and let himself in the room. He was surprised to see Ali's wretched condition—his eyes puffy and face flushed. "Ali, I brought you some cold medication and something to eat."

"Thank you. I will take the medication, but I am not hungry," he said, taking the box of Dayquil from Ahmed. "Did you find something to dismantle the devices with so we can go home?"

"Unfortunately, no. I know you don't feel well, but we have a job to do. My plan is to load the devices in the van and take them to an automotive garage. I am told that the garage has the tools we need. We will explain that we use the devices for business, but our tools were stolen."

"I'll do anything so we can begin our journey home."

"Pack your things and keep your gun with you. We need to be ready if something goes wrong. We will leave in ten minutes to carry the devices to the van."

Ali nodded as he swallowed the pills. He then began packing his bag. As he passed the bathroom, he noticed the trashcan was full of bloody tissues from coughing and spitting blood and mucus. At the sink, he splashed water on his face. Bloodshot eyes stared back at him through the large mirror. The rash on his arms had spread to his chest and had grown bright red.

For the first time, he wondered if the illness that plagued Cody Community Hospital had infected him. Grabbing his bag, Ali left the room and hoped he would be headed home to New York soon.

They loaded the devices in the van and Ali followed his beige Buick on a careful, slow drive to Smitty's Garage. Ahmed knew that all too often fugitives were caught by being careless and breaking traffic laws. Not as much careless as stupid and arrogant. Parking on the street in front of the garage, Ahmed entered and looked around.

The shop was old. Pale yellow sunlight streamed through the small, grime-streaked windows mixing with the bluish hue of the fluorescent fixtures flickering and humming overhead. The air was thick with a mix of motor oil and gasoline. An assortment of tools, auto parts and manuals were scattered on the greasy floor around a variety of cars and trucks setting on jack stands.

"Hello?" Ahmed called.

A balding head with a wrinkled face popped up from behind an old Ford pick-up truck. "May I help ya?"

"Yes, sir. I have a small problem. I have some electronic equipment that I need to disassemble, but we left our tools behind. The wrench we need is very large, about three inches," Ahmed said, politely. "Do you think you can help me?"

"Well, bring it on in here and let's see." The man struggled to get off the floor. "Rheumatism is actin' up a bit."

"I am sorry to hear that. My instruments are in the back of my van and they're quite heavy."

"Pull the van in here and I can work out of the back of it."

"Very good." Walking to the entrance, he waved to Ali. "Back it in and he will look at the equipment."

"By the way, if ya hadn't figured it out already, I'm Smitty," the old man offered as he ambled up to the back of the van in grease-stained coveralls. "Let's have a look see."

Ahmed swung the doors open and unlatched the first case.

"My, my, what've we got here?" Smitty ran his short, stubby, callused fingers along the shiny stainless steel torpedo-like surface. "So it's this plug on the end that you want off?"

"Yes, the electronics in both ends have to be calibrated. They are instruments we use in our well business."

"Okie dokie, let me get my large pipe wrench to hold it and I've got me a great big crescent wrench that should fit right nice."

As the old man walked away, a younger version of the same man in the same greasy overalls came through the side door. "Hey, Pop, I found us a u-joint that should fit that Ford driveshaft."

"All right, Bobby. Give me a hand here for a minute."

"Sure, Pop, whatcha got?"

"Get that pipe wrench on the shaft of that there thing and be careful not to scratch it. I'll take out this plug."

Bobby plopped the u-joint on an old wood-planked workbench covered with pictures of what Ahmed guessed were Smitty's and Bobby's families. He and Ali stood and watched the father-son team struggle, pulling wrench handles in opposite directions. Suddenly the threads lost their grip almost sending old Smitty to the floor.

"Whoa, watch it there, Pop," Bobby cautioned.

Smitty turned the plug with the wrench until the threads ran out. The heavy steel cylinder attached to the plug was labeled with a bright yellow and magenta radiation warning.

"Whoa, buddy, what's that?" Bobby asked, taking a step back. "Hell, Pop, remember Jackie Brown? He used to work with this kind of stuff—said it made him sterile as a castrated pig."

"It wouldn't surprise me if Jackie's wife castrated him for screwin' around on her," Smitty said, setting off a good laugh between them. "Besides, Son, I thought when April had the baby next month, you was gettin' fixed. Shoot, just rub this thing between your legs."

"Naw, Pop. I'm goin' ta Doc Phillips at the clinic."

Ahmed interrupted the banter. "Do not worry—it is safe. The equipment is heavily shielded and the radiation source is small. The sign is merely a precaution." The conviction in his voice seemed to set them at ease.

"All right, Bobby, let's turn this beast around and get the other plug out." Smitty placed the sealed radiation source on the cracked concrete floor.

"My associate and I will put this in the car. We do not want it to slide around back here unsecured." At the car, he turned to Ali and said, "When they remove the last one, kill the son from behind. I will take care of the old man."

"Why bother? They are of no concern to us," Ali said.

"They have seen the radiation devices. We will put their bodies in the van, leave it in the shop and lock up as we leave."

Although Ali acknowledged him by shaking his head, he was barely able to walk, let alone kill anyone. Hopefully he would come through in the name of Allah.

The auto mechanics made short work of removing the other plugs including the sonic probe's electronic package. As Smitty and Bobby were concentrating on the last one, Ahmed nodded to Ali. Guns appeared from under lightweight jackets and aimed at the back of the father and son's heads. A muffled crack and Smitty's forehead exploded and splattered on the white painted steel interior of the van.

"Pop!" Bobby spun around in time to see Ali fumbling with the safety on his Jericho. His knees gave out as he pleaded for his life. "Dear God, mister, please, I've got a pregnant wife and little boy. Take whatever you want, but please don't kill me." He watched Ali with terror in his eyes as the gun barrel came up. His eyes squinted. Nobody wanted to see death coming, but something inside him needed to know. Another crack echoed through the shop as the nine-millimeter bullet entered cleanly into Bobby's forehead. The burning hot piece of metal exploded from the back of his skull, taking bits of grayish-red brain, blood, scalp and hair with it and pasted them on the back door of the van. Bobby's body slumped backwards against the bumper and fell to the greasy concrete floor.

"Let's get them in the van and leave."

On the other side of the street directly across from Smitty's Garage, Betsy Hubbard, a sixty-five year old widow, had just turned off the television after watching her early afternoon soap opera. As she walked back to the kitchen, she heard a muffled noise that sounded like an engine backfire. *There it was again.*

Living across from Smitty's for almost fifteen years, she had heard quite a bit of commotion from time to time. Since there was nothing important waiting for her in the kitchen except a hot cup of tea, she decided to grab her glasses and take her perch in the window above the street and see if there would be anything good to gossip about later with her sister. She suspected that Ole Smitty was seeing Mildred Applewhite. Smitty had been a widower for a long while, but Mildred's husband passed just five months ago.

The closed door caught her eye. That was a bit odd. It was a beautiful day and the temperature was warming nicely. She knew Smitty well enough that he enjoyed the fresh air whenever he could.

Five minutes went by and two dark skinned men left the garage, carrying something heavy. They placed the things in the trunk and drove off in a tan Buick something-or-other. Living next to a garage for so long, she knew her cars well enough, except she wasn't so good on the newer models.

Hmmm, well, nothing terribly interesting. After she figured there wouldn't be anything good to talk about, she went about her day.

Chapter Forty-one

Four Sixes Ranch
May 13, 2004

"Turn in right up here...through the cattle gate," Brandon directed Agent Schaffer as they bounced along on the rutted dirt road. Schaffer saw the drill rig reaching into the sky half a mile from the site.

The van shook violently over the steel bars of the cattle gate embedded in the dirt road. He brought the van to a halt next to the construction trailer, kicking up dust as it rolled across cracked, parched earth.

"Joe, you video the site. Hal, take the camera and look for anything that might help." Schaffer barked orders to his subordinate field agents. "Dr. Stiles, let's go talk to the men over there and then get the files we came for."

"Please call me Brandon." He walked over to the partially dismantled rig where the roughnecks were working with Agent Schaffer following. "Excuse me, guys. This is FBI Agent Schaffer and he needs to talk to you for a minute."

The sound of heavy tools clanging against the metal decking of the drill rig filled the air as the eight roughnecks dropped their tools and approached the two men.

"Gentlemen, I know you have a job to do, but I have been told to escort all of you to the Cody Community Hospital for medical testing. As you know, a number of your coworkers have come down with an illness. Since none of you appear to have any symptoms, you're probably in the clear, but we need to be sure."

A large bear of a worker in a red-checkered flannel shirt and tattered dirty jeans stepped forward. "What kind of illness? I hear the guys got anthrax and the hospital's been quarantined. Is that right?"

"The hospital has been quarantined, but I really don't know anything about the illness. The doctors are taking care of that."

"Well, I ain't goin' anywhere near that fuckin' hospital." He bent over to pick his large wrench off the floor of the rig.

"Sir, this is not a choice. You *will* follow us to the hospital." Schaffer's authoritative tone was emphasized by subtly pulling back his jacket to give the workers a look at his holstered forty-caliber Beretta. "But you needn't be worried, the doctors have a testing area in a non-quarantined area and as soon as you're cleared, you'll be allowed to get back to work."

The gigantic workman took a step back and asked, "Yeah, so when are we goin'?"

"We have some things to do first. We'll come and get you shortly."

The men turned back to the platform, picked up their tools and returned to work. "Let's get this section broke down before we hafta get outta here."

"Just a second," Schaffer said softly to Brandon. He went to Hal who was photographing the water cooler at the front of the trailer. "Hal, keep an eye on these guys. I'm not sure I trust them."

"Sure thing."

Returning to Brandon, he said, "Let's get to those files."

Brandon climbed the wooden steps and opened the trailer door. "Right over there—second drawer," he said, pointing to a small file cabinet on the other side of the conference room. "I'll make sure there aren't any files in the office."

"Don't let me forget the boxes of Gatorade and a sample of the drinking water for analysis," Schaffer said, checking his pocket notebook.

Brandon walked back to his office and rustled through the paperwork that Dallas had been working on just before being rushed to the hospital. Being there brought memories of his friend, and tears started building in his eyes. *Hey, Doc, how ya doin'?* resounded through his mind. Feeling the walls start to close in, he rushed from the office.

"I've got to check on something," he called. The door slammed open and he stumbled down the steps, bent over with his hands on his knees and took a deep breath of the cool fresh air. Out of the corner of his eye, he noticed something odd. "What the heck?" he muttered.

Collecting himself, he shuffled to the back of the trailer, tugged up on his trousers and crouched down to look under the trailer. *What the hell?* As he stuck his face under the trailer, he was met by the glower of shining eyes and bared snarling teeth. He pushed himself backwards away from the onslaught, frantically kicking away from the trailer while waiting for the inevitable attack.

Heart racing, his eyes focused on the opening under the trailer, waiting, ready to ward off the attack. Nothing. Confused, Brandon stood up on wobbly legs. Head snapping from right to left, he found an old broom, approached the opening under the trailer cautiously and began swinging the broom handle at the base of the trailer.

Schaffer came charging out of the door to see what the racket was. He looked to the back of the trailer and saw Brandon comically swinging a broom in the air, beating the side of the trailer.

"What the hell are you doing back there?"

"There's some kind of wild animal under the trailer," Brandon gasped, backing away, out of breath.

Agent Schaffer waved his hand signaling Brandon to back off and cautiously neared the back of the trailer. He slipped his Beretta from its holster and unclipped a small LED flashlight from his belt. Getting on his knees, he approached the hole in the trailer apron shining the light ahead of him. When the bright beam of light hit the hole, Schaffer saw two red eyes staring back at him. Flinching slightly, he kept the light trained on the animal's eyes. There was no movement.

He stood up chuckling, "Give me your broom, Brandon."

After Schaffer fished the stiff corpse of the raccoon from under the trailer, Brandon stood there, shaking his head, feeling like a fool.

"Aw, shit. Those raccoons have been living under there since we moved the trailer in. They manage to raid our trashcans every night if we forget to pack it out with us. Poor little guy."

A loud commotion from behind caught Schaffer's attention. He turned, pulled his Beretta and trotted to a group of pick-up trucks parked near the cattle gate. "Stop right there! Take another step and you won't have to go to the hospital." A wiry, rugged worker had the door to his truck open and was ready to bolt. He stopped and looked down at the three red laser dots dancing on his chest.

"Go back and wait with the other guys. We'll just be a minute." Schaffer watched the man slam the door shut and tromp back to the rig. "Hal, don't take your eyes off them. Let's get going."

Brandon thought about going back inside and decided against it. He couldn't get Dallas out of his mind. *First Mae, now Dallas. I'm cursed.*

Schaffer disappeared into the trailer for a minute before returning carrying a box of files and Gatorade packets. Brandon watched as the FBI agents rounded up the rig workers and herded them into their trucks. Although they didn't seem to be protesting after their buddy had the shit scared out of him, he could sense the apprehension at the prospect of being diagnosed with a life threatening disease.

Chapter Forty-two

Cody, Wyoming
May 13, 2004

"Max! Max, wake up."

Max opened his eyes to see Rivers standing over him. "Don't you know you should always wake somebody up gently?"

"What, do you want me to give you a little kiss on the cheek?"

"I just dozed off, why the hell are you waking me?" Max pushed himself to a sitting position on the uncomfortable cot and stretched his arms with a yawn.

"We may have *big* trouble. In the last hour, we've had five walk-ups from Cody residents complaining of sinus problems, headache and fever. We've also gotten calls from an emergency clinic in Powell, Wyoming, and General Hospital in Billings, Montana with similar cases."

"Oh, shit." Max struggled to get out of the short-legged cot. "Dammit, now what? I thought we had this isolated."

"I have the Cody patients being tested now. But I was thinking, God forbid, if these are level four cases, there's no way it could have spread from the well site workers. Powell wasn't even on our radar."

"Shit, I knew I shouldn't have let the FBI convince me that this was isolated at that damn well site. Goddammit, Rivers, why the hell didn't you convince me that we had to do more?" He put his face in his hands. "Shit, shit, shit."

"Come on, Max, now isn't the time. We don't have the luxury of second-guessing ourselves and thinking about what we should've done. It looks like we need reinforcements."

"I'll say. Well, before we jump into the deep end, we need to get some samples from these people." Max grunted as he bent over to slip on his shoes. "Round up whoever you can. We have the USAMRIID staff now, so you grab one of them and get a chopper up to Billings. Set up an isolation area as best as you can. Get some blood and nasal swabs and have the chopper get them back here stat."

"All right, I'll get my stuff together. But what about Powell?"

"Where the hell is Powell anyway?"

"Not far from here—less than an hour northeast."

"I'll get somebody up there by car."

"Max?" Rivers said solemnly.

"What, Rivers?"

"If this is one of our viruses, how on earth do we quarantine three towns?"

"All I can say is pray, Rivers. God help us."

Max rushed from the makeshift sleeping quarters and found Anita Gabon at the command center. "Anita, I need everybody in the conference room except those who are analyzing specimens from the locals that just came in."

Anita put her hand over the telephone receiver and said, "In a minute, Max. I'm on the phone with headquarters filing the daily report."

"Now, Anita!"

"Yes, sir," she said, then speaking back into the phone. "I'm sorry—I have an emergency issue to attend to. I'll call you back with the rest of the report in a few minutes."

"Anita, this is important. I want everybody, understand? Including the FBI. Let Agent Daniels know I'm starting the meeting without her and I'll fill her in. I'm going to throw some water on my face while you're rounding everyone up."

Laura woke to the chirping of her cell phone. She looked around the room trying to figure out where on earth she was. Shaking the cobwebs, she reached for her cell phone and flipped it open.

"Agent Daniels."

"Agent Daniels, this is Anita Gabon with the CDC. Dr. Van Pelt wants you down here immediately."

"What's going on?"

"He'll fill you in when you get here. We're meeting in a few minutes. He said he'd get you caught up, but you need to get here ASAP and go straight to the conference tent. I'll clear you."

"Okay, thanks." Laura punched the disconnect button then pulled up Harrison's number from the cell phone memory and pushed the talk key.

"Yeah, what's up?"

"Get ready ASAP. We need to get to the hospital."

"Okay, give me five minutes. I'll meet you in front of the hotel on the street."

Laura hit the disconnect button again. *Damn, it's hot in here*, she thought. She turned the dial of the electric window heater-air conditioner combination unit from heat to cool. Thank God I showered before I jumped into bed. She pulled a comb through her tangled hair and splashed water on her face, then rummaged through her overnight bag for the cleanest outfit she had left.

She found a pair of black slacks and a red sweater that weren't too crumpled. Minutes later, with the room card key in hand, she ran down to the street.

"So what's the emergency?" Harrison asked as Laura pushed through the front door.

"I don't know, but it sounds serious. Van Pelt said he'd fill us in on anything we miss, but whatever it is, he wasn't willing to wait twenty minutes for us to get there."

They jogged to the police station in silence. The borrowed police cruiser was right where they'd left it.

"I'll let Johnny and Bart sleep for a while longer," she said.

"It did feel good getting in a few hours, anyway."

"I'll say. My mind was starting to shut down. Although I think I could have slept another twelve hours."

"So have you had any revelations on how to pick up the trail of Halid and Atif?" Harrison yawned, stretching his arms.

"I've got an idea. That guy, Brandon Stiles, said he had an office in Billings that he hasn't been to in a week."

"So what's your point?"

"Halid knew about the well and the radiation equipment. Maybe he got the information from Stiles' office."

"That's a stretch."

"Do you have any better ideas?"

"Not a one. Which makes your idea brilliant."

They hurried through the growing crowd of curious on-lookers to the conference tent. *Something is different.*

"I wonder why these people are lined up on this side of the security zone," Laura asked.

"I don't know. But maybe that's what this meeting is about."

"Please go right in," Anita Gabon said when she spotted Laura and Harrison.

There was a large group in orange jumpsuits, white tyvek suits and military uniforms. Max stood in front of a whiteboard leading the meeting.

"Okay, so Sergeant Givens will take two technicians to the emergency clinic in Powell. Make sure we isolate everyone. We have a couple of Sikorsky Pave Hawks en route from Warren Air Force Base. They'll bring the samples back for analysis. Any questions?"

No one spoke up, so Max continued. "People, this could get real messy real quick, so we have to stay on top of it. We'll start getting results back from the ELISA test on the people here in Cody in about thirty minutes. Based on the growing line outside, I'm expecting the worst. That's all, get back to work."

The people filed out quickly, conversing quietly in small groups. Max waved Laura and Harrison over, "Please have a seat." Max sat down scratching at his balding scalp. "I think we have a worst-case scenario playing out here. I assume you saw the line of residents outside?"

"Yes," Laura answered, giving Harrison a quick nod.

"At last count we had fifty-two people in Cody and over a hundred in Billings who are ill and presenting characteristic symptoms. We also have an unknown number of people in Powell, Wyoming, lined up outside a local clinic."

"Is it anthrax or one of the viruses?" Harrison asked.

"We're about thirty minutes from knowing that. Until then, it's a guessing game. With all the media out there, I expected a few hypochondriacs coming forward, but either we're seeing the beginning of mass hysteria or we have an enormous problem. I'd bet on the latter."

Laura and Harrison looked at each other. "What can we do to help?" Laura asked.

"Besides praying, find those fucking terrorists. I've notified the president, and the military is pulling resources together for a massive quarantine zone. The airfields are already shut down. Bus and train traffic has been delayed. The next step is shutting down the roads. And we still haven't mapped out the Cody virus, so we don't know how bad this could get."

Max continued, "You have to find those terrorists and find out how this is spreading. Now, you'll have to excuse me, I have more calls to make." He motioned to the door.

"We'll do our best, Doctor."

"Agent, I'm not one to criticize, but you need to do better."

With that, Laura and Harrison left the tent. Once outside, she said, "I'm calling Schaffer to see if they found anything at the well site. Then I'll find Brandon Stiles. We need to get to Billings."

Chapter Forty-three

Powell, Wyoming
May 13, 2004

Amy Rosecranz, proprietor of Powell Full of Posies needed her pick-up truck to deliver the morning's flower arrangements. She decided to walk the half-mile from Main Street to Smitty's Garage. The sign out front said *closed*, which was odd, since she just talked to Smitty an hour ago. She tried the door—locked. "Smitty? Bobby? Are you in there?" she called loudly, banging on the old wooden door. "Dammit you guys, I need my truck."

They must be out back. Smitty had been fixing her cars for fifteen years and she was no stranger to the garage. She went to the tall wood plank gate next to the building and entered the side yard. Rufus and Bud greeted her enthusiastically, tails wagging and barking loudly. Ha, those beware of dog signs were a joke, she thought. Rufus and Bud wouldn't harm a squirrel.

"Smitty! Bobby!" No answer. She went into the side door of the garage, "Anybody here? Come on guys, where are you?" She spotted her truck near the front of the garage. There was something odd about the van parked next to it.

"What the devil is this?" she said, as she touched the red streaks on the back door of the van. Greasy. She brought her fingertips to her nose and a familiar coppery smell touched her senses. "Oh my."

She opened the back door of the van and—

"Oh my God!" She turned and ran for the door. By the time she made it outside and slammed the door, she was crying hysterically, hardly able to breathe. Rufus and Bud romped beside her as she raced for the road. Slamming the gate behind her, she ran partway down Fourth Street, finally collapsing in the grass next to the sidewalk. She dumped the contents of her open purse on the grass and picked up her cell phone. Her finger jammed against the "1" button, her speed-dial number for emergencies. "Oh, please answer."

"Emergency response. What is the nature of your emergency?"

"Oh my God, you have to help me. I'm at Smitty's Garage on Fourth and they're dead."

"Slow down, ma'am, who's dead?"

"Smitty and Bobby. They're both dead." She sobbed almost uncontrollably.

"Who am I speaking to, ma'am?"

"My name is Amy Rosecranz. I came to pick up my car and they're dead."

"Where are you now, ma'am?"

"I'm outside the garage just down the street on Fourth."

"One second, please. I'm calling for help. Please hold the line."

Amy heard the dispatcher talking to someone on the radio in the background.

"Ma'am, a police officer will be at your location in about three minutes. Did you see anybody else in the area?"

"No, no one."

Sirens wailed in the distance. "I hear them coming."

"Yes, Ms. Rosecranz. I'll stay on the line with you until they arrive."

"Thank you."

She heard the police car as its tires squealed, rounding the corner at the end of the street. It screeched to a stop in front of the garage. She forced herself to her feet on wobbly legs and rushed to the squad car. Absentmindedly, she flipped the cell phone closed, ending the call.

"Officer, I'm the one that called," she said, waving her hand over her head.

"Are you Ms. Rosecranz?"

"Yes."

"I'm Officer Hanley. Can you show me what you found?"

"I'm sorry, Officer, I can't go back in there." Tears still streamed down her cheeks carrying thick globs of mascara painting her face like Alice Cooper in concert. Her hands continued to shake.

"Okay, I understand. Can you tell me what you saw?"

"I called Smitty about an hour ago to see if my car was ready. He told me to come and get it. I went to the front door and it was locked, so I went around the side." She pointed to the wooden gate. "I saw my truck and went up to it. I noticed something smeared on the back door of a white van next to my truck and opened it up."

Tears flowed down her cheeks again, thinning the black mascara, and her voice broke. "Oh, Officer, it was horrible. Smitty and Bobby were wonderful people..." She cried hysterically and buried her face in trembling hands.

"Okay, wait here, I'll check it out." Amy heard Rufus and Bud barking as Officer Hanley disappeared through the gate.

Officer Hanley opened the side door to the garage with his gun in one hand and flashlight in the other. He crept to the front of the garage and looked into the back of the van. "Oh shit." Holstering his gun and yanking the radio from his belt, he reported in. "Base, this is unit two-nine."

"Two-nine, this is base, go ahead."

"I've got a 901-S here at Smitty's Garage. I need the coroner here."

"Hanley, this is Chief Furgeson. What's going on out there?"

"Chief, looks like we have two shooting victims in the back of a white rental van. Name on the side says "Billings U-store." The victims appear to be the owner and his son."

"What's the tag number on that van?"

"8-7-Alpha-5-7-2-4"

"Wait, the FBI has an all points for that vehicle. Secure the site and don't let anyone in. I'll dispatch the coroner and be there in a few."

"Yes, sir."

Officer Hanley bowed his head and crossed himself. "God help these poor sons-a-bitches." He shook his head and left the garage.

Chapter Forty-four

Cody, Wyoming
May 12, 2004

"The news is bad," Rivers said to Max. "Not only is it bad, it's worse than bad."

"What do you mean?"

"Lynn Howard and Larry Enders died."

"Okay, I hate to sound harsh, but that's hardly a surprise."

"Dr. Jost, the intern that only has the Cody virus is deteriorating rapidly. The bug accelerated at an alarming rate once it got a foothold and it's not responding to treatment."

"Oh, shit. And if it turns out to be able to live outside a host for any length of time, we could very well have a worst-case scenario."

"Yeah, well that was the bad, here's the worse part. The first of the tests are in from the walk-ins this morning. They have the Cody bug."

"Damn! We have to figure out if this is airborne soon. Where are we on the study?"

"The first set of monkeys has been inoculated with Cody. It will take some time for them to become symptomatic and to see if they spread it to their cage mates."

"This is all taking too long. I feel so damn helpless."

"What I can't figure out is how these people got infected if it's not airborne. I mean, what on earth could the medium be that is this wide spread? We have to find out what these people have in common."

"The FBI has to come up with something quickly."

"Max, you said it earlier. We can't wait for the FBI any longer. We have to start interviewing everyone that's associated with this outbreak. We can use the standard questionnaire."

"You're right—I'll call Atlanta to get more help."

The van raced along State Road 294 just north of Powell, Wyoming. Laura and Harrison found Brandon at the condominium complex and were now headed to Billings. Laura's cell phone sprang to life. She looked at the color display and saw the incoming call was from Robert Williams. "Agent Daniels."

"This is Bob, Laura. Where are you?"

"On the road. We're going to Billings with Brandon Stiles to check out his office for leads."

"We've got a lead on Halid. Get to Powell, Wyoming—"

"Wait, Bob." She pulled the phone away from her ear. "Jim, we need to go to Powell, Wyoming."

"We passed the turn-off about fifteen minutes ago," Harrison said. The van pitched forward as he pressed hard on the brakes.

"Okay, Bob, I'm back. We're pretty close. Fill me in."

"There was a double murder earlier today—two auto mechanics. The Billings U-Store van was left behind. It's at a place called Smitty's Garage on Fourth Street and Gilbert."

"Okay, Smitty's on Fourth and Gilbert. Do they have an idea of the time it happened?"

"Not long ago. Maybe around noon."

"Thanks Bob. I'm going to call Campisi and get them headed this way."

"Good luck, Laura. Keep me posted."

"So, wait a minute, where are we going now?" Brandon asked from the backseat, hanging on as the van made a quick u-turn in the middle of the deserted highway.

"Sorry, Dr. Stiles, we just received a lead on the suspected terrorists. We have to follow up on it right away. I'm afraid you're along for the ride," Laura answered as she dialed Campisi's phone number. "I'll tell you more in a minute."

Laura spoke into the receiver. "Johnny, we've got a hot lead. Jim and I are headed to Powell, Wyoming. They found Halid's van at a murder scene."

"Give me directions."

"Smitty's Garage on Fourth and Gilbert. As you get close, call me back. I'll be able to give you better directions. We're maybe fifteen, twenty minutes out."

"Gotcha. We'll be rolling in ten minutes."

Laura snapped the cell phone closed. *Finally, a solid lead.*

"We needed a break," Harrison said.

"Excuse me, you said you'd tell me more?" Brandon asked from the back seat.

"I'm sorry, Dr. Stiles—"

"Brandon. Please call me Brandon."

"Okay, Brandon." Laura gave Brandon a brief history of the case as they entered the city limits of Powell. It didn't take long for Harrison to find Fourth Street and Smitty's Garage. Powell's entire fleet of emergency vehicles blocked the street, all with lights flashing.

As the van pulled to a quick halt, Laura turned back to Brandon and asked, "Would you mind waiting here, near the van?"

"I have no interest in seeing a bloody crime scene."

Laura and Harrison jumped out and trotted toward a group of uniformed officers standing outside the front of the garage.

"Who's in charge here?" Laura asked as she approached the group, holding her badge out for identification.

"I'm Chief Furgeson," a tall silver-haired man standing in the middle of the group said. "Are you Agent Daniels?"

"Yes, sir. Time is of the essence here, so can you show me the scene?"

"Right this way." He turned and led them through the gate and into the garage from the side door.

"Where are the dogs?" Laura asked.

"We tied them up in the back. They seemed friendly enough. I think the sign on the gate is just to keep strangers out."

When they approached the open doors of the van, Laura tried to conceal her emotions. *Ruthless bastards.* Smitty and Bobby were lying on their backs, eyes staring blankly at the white metal roof of the van, blood pooled under their heads. Smitty's forehead was mostly missing, while Bobby's forehead had a small clean hole with a dribble of dried blood trailing down to his ear.

Next to the bodies were three long black cases and three long shiny steel cylinders.

"These must be the stolen devices. But why are they here?" Laura asked.

"Look at the ends of the cylinders, there and there." Harrison pointed at the ends of the long devices. "See the threads on the inside? I'll bet the radioactive sources screwed into these things. Look at the size of the wrenches on the floor, there. It took tools you can't just buy at the local Sears store to dismantle these things."

Laura nodded. "So they came here and asked these guys to help. But why kill them?"

"I can't answer that."

"Hmmm, I wonder..." Laura turned and left the group. She rounded the corner and went through the gate to find Brandon.

"Dr. Stiles, uh, Brandon. How familiar are you with the well equipment that was stolen from the men working at your site?"

"I know a thing or two."

"Follow me, please." She led him back through the gate and into the garage.

"Oh my God!" Brandon turned and gagged.

"I'm sorry, I should have prepared you, but we don't have a lot of time. We're trying to figure out why these terrorists would have killed these men who were helping them disassemble the radioactive equipment."

Brandon turned back and looked at the scene. "The sealed Americium sources are missing on the ends—but then you knew that, didn't you?"

"We suspected it," Harrison answered. "What would the Amer...the radiation sources look like?"

"Hmmm, well, the sources are just heavy steel cylinders with a wire harness attached. There's a shutter device that opens when they're operating. They would, or at least should have had a standard yellow and magenta international radiation warning shield with the conditions of the general permit issued by the Nuclear Energy Commission printed on them."

"Wait! That's it. Halid may have been worried these two would report two Middle Eastern men with radiation devices to the police—"

"So they killed them." Harrison finished her supposition.

The chief's radio cackled. He yanked it off his belt and answered the call. "What is it?"

"Chief, a woman who lives across the street just came forward. Says she saw two men leaving the scene."

"We'll be right out." He looked up at Laura and Harrison. "Let's go see what she has to say. Then we'll come back and check the scene for other evidence." They turned and left the remains of the father and son mechanics in the stuffy garage.

In the middle of Fourth Street a small crowd gathered in a circle around the scene as Smitty's neighbors emerged from their homes for some good gossip. Inside the circle, an elderly lady wearing a flowered bandanna around her rollered hair and a light crocheted shawl that flapped in the breeze talked with one of the uniformed officers, her speech accentuated with body language and hand gestures.

"Hello, ma'am, we're with the FBI."

"Well hello, I'm Betsy Hubbard. I live in that house there across the street."

"You say you saw something this morning?"

"It was just after noon...yes, because I just finished watching *All My Children* and I was getting hungry for lunch. I always get hungry about then."

"What did you see, Betsy?"

"Well, first I heard something. It sounded like a backfire. Living across from Smitty's for so long, I'm used to that, but it didn't sound like a car, really. So I went to the window there." Betsy pointed to the upstairs window in the old frame home. "I was about to go downstairs when I saw two men come out of the door and get into a car. I thought it was odd that Smitty had the doors shut, because it's such a beautiful day."

"Can you describe the men?"

"Let me see..." she put her finger to her forehead as if to dig the information from her head. "They had black hair and were dark. I don't think they were black, maybe Mexican, I couldn't see their faces very clearly."

"Could they have been Middle Eastern?"

"You mean like A-rabs?"

"Yes, like that."

"Well, I guess so."

"Okay, Betsy, you said they got into a car. Can you tell me what color?"

"It was a tan Buick. I'm not sure which model."

"Could you see the license plate?"

"Oh, my, no. I didn't pay much attention to that."

"Is there anything else you can recall?"

"Just that they seemed to be in a hurry."

"Okay, Betsy. Here is my business card. Please call me if you can remember anything, anything at all, no matter how small."

Laura turned away from the old woman and spotted the Cody police cruiser as it screeched to a stop just outside the police barricade. She watched as Johnny Campisi and Bart Jackman trotted towards them with Jackman's small forensics kit.

"Well?" Johnny asked as he walked up to the group.

"Chief Furgeson, this is Agent Campisi and Agent Jackman from the Seattle field office," Laura introduced them, as the men exchanged greetings and handshakes. "Chief Furgeson, if you were headed to New York City, what route would you take from here?"

"There are only two real ways to get to Interstate 90 East. State Route 14 to Sheridan is the shortest route, but you'd have to go through the pass. There are a bunch of secondary roads around Yellowtail Reservoir. The other route is way longer—Route 310 to Greybull, then south to Worland. Once in Worland, you'd probably go east to Buffalo." The chief hesitated and then asked, "Is there some connection between this and what's going on at the clinic? We've got a hundred people lined up over there."

"That's a distinct possibility. I have another favor to ask."

"Name it."

"We need to find out where these two may have spent the night. It's important that we check the room."

"Sure. That shouldn't take too long."

"Good, we're looking for Ahmed Halid and Ali Atif," she said, writing their names on a page in her notebook. She tore it off and handed it to the chief. "It's likely they would have paid cash."

"I'll call this in."

"Thanks, Chief. Johnny, I'm going to check in with Williams. The bodies are in there." Laura pointed to the gate on the side of the garage. "Oh, Johnny, make sure we check every nook and cranny in that van for anything that may be related to the viruses.

"I'll show you," the chief said, as he grabbed the radio off his belt.

Chapter Forty-five

Cody, Wyoming
May 12, 2004

Rivers sat with Max in the command tent adjacent to the BSL-4 lab. The whiteboard was covered in lines, circles and arrows of various colors detailing what was known of the situation. The Native American doctor, his shiny black hair slicked back, reviewed a printout just handed to him by a research assistant. "They're all coming back positive with Cody, Max. We have the odd case of anthrax and a couple with the filovirus, but most of them have Cody."

"Yeah, we have over seventy here in town, fifty-two so far in Powell and over a hundred-sixty in Billings. But there are a lot more specimens from Billings yet to be tested. We need to get Secretary Reilly on a conference call." Max punched the intercom button on the phone and told Anita to get General Carmichael with USAMRIID and Agent Schaffer and meet them in the conference room.

"How long has it been since you slept, Rivers?"

"About twenty hours."

"That's what I thought. Right after this call, we need some down time. I'll check on the lab progress and then we'll go to the dorm tent."

When they arrived at the conference tent, Anita was waiting. "Get Greg Reilly from Homeland Security on the phone. And where are Carmichael and Schaffer?"

"General Carmichael is on his way. Agent Schaeffer is out finding the construction workers with his staff." She opened her book of contact names and started dialing.

The speaker phone rang as General Carmichael pushed through the door.

"Sorry, Max. I was just in the hospital and had to go through decon. We're moving all the Cody residents that are testing positive into the hospital. So far they're scared, but cooperative."

"Reilly here," the secretary of Homeland Security's voice rose from the speakerphone.

"Mr. Reilly, this is Max Van Pelt with the CDC."

"Yes, Max."

"I have my associate, Rivers Larkin, and General Carmichael of

USAMRIID with me."

"Is there any good news out there, yet?" Reilly asked.

"No, sir, quite the opposite. We have a worst-case scenario playing out here. We have almost three-hundred confirmed cases of this new virus we're calling Cody."

"Three-hundred? Good Lord!"

"There are a few cases of anthrax and a filovirus, but it seems this new bug is of most concern."

"What are we doing with the infected people?"

"We're moving them into the hospital here in Cody. In Billings, the general hospital has been quarantined and we're using the high school gymnasium in Powell."

"Have we made any progress on identifying the viruses?"

Max turned toward Rivers and nodded.

"Sir, this is Rivers Larkin. We've analyzed the anthrax. It doesn't match up with any lab developed strains that we know of. The filovirus, while very similar to Marburg and Ebola, has subtle differences in the protein coat. It's a variant we haven't seen yet. The Cody virus is most similar to the Sin Nombre Virus in structure—"

"Sin Nombre Virus?" Reilly asked. "I've never heard of that."

"Sin Nombre means 'no name' in Spanish. It's in the *Bunya Virus* family and a variant of Hantavirus. Our first close look at Sin Nombre was in the Muerto Canyon area on the Navajo Reservation in Arizona. The Navajo Nation didn't want us to call it Muerto Canyon, so we refer to it as Sin Nombre. It causes severe Hanta Pulmonary Syndrome or HPS—a particularly deadly one with a mortality rate of 50% or more. You may remember it as the Hantavirus outbreak in the four corners region of the U.S."

Rivers glanced down at his notes. "Anyway, it's a lot like Sin Nombre, but there are slight differences. It's possible those differences make it more virulent and increase its ability to survive outside a living organism, making it airborne."

"So it *is* airborne?" Reilly speculated.

"We still aren't sure, but there's a high likelihood that it's either airborne or waterborne to have spread so quickly and so broadly."

"I think it's waterborne. I fail to see how so many people could have been exposed any other way. These bastard terrorists must have found a way to deliver this through reservoirs or in the water supply," General Carmichael added.

"The bottom line, Mr. Reilly, is that we have to quarantine these cities. It may be too late already, but we need to take immediate action, regardless of the affect on the economy or any other factor," Max said. "Call it a natural outbreak or spin it anyway you want to avoid panic, but do it now, and do it quickly."

"I understand what you're saying, Max, but you have to be absolutely sure."

"By the time I'm absolutely sure, it will absolutely be too late."

"Okay, I'll call the president. And I'm advising him to raise the threat level to orange."

"Won't that cause a panic?"

"Gentlemen, the country instituted this system for a reason. It's only prudent to raise the level and awareness. General Carmichael, you need to be kept in the loop on the military's involvement."

"I'll make sure that happens, Mr. Reilly," Carmichael responded.

"Very well, Secretary Reilly, we'll be in touch." Max reached across the table and pushed the disconnect button on the speaker phone. "Rivers, get a couple of technicians to go to the addresses of some of the infected residents and pull water samples, get samples of the food, drinks, and whatever else might jump out at them. Have them inventory drinks and food by brand and lot number."

"Okay, I'll get right on it."

Max left the tent and headed toward the secured perimeter. Teams of reporters and cameras pressed against the barriers with hundreds of simultaneous conversations. As soon as they saw him, the cameras pointed in his direction and reporters began excited chatter into microphones. On the other side of the street stood the friends and relatives of the people that had been placed under quarantine. Everyone was looking for answers—answers he couldn't provide.

Soon, all these people would be prisoners.

Chapter Forty-six

Powell, Wyoming
May 12, 2004

Harrison brought the white van carrying Laura and Brandon to a stop in front of a small motor lodge not far from Smitty's Garage and the brutal killings. Campisi and Jackman stayed at the scene trying to glean whatever clues could be found.

"Okay, Brandon, we're running back to the police station to see if we can locate these bastards," Laura said. "Enjoy your stay at this luxury hotel. It's on the government."

"Yeah, it looks cozy," Brandon teased.

"Here's my card if you need to reach us."

He grabbed the card and slid it in his shirt pocket, then took his computer case and disappeared into Room 1004 at the Comfort Lodge. The disturbing image of the father and son lying in a pool of their own blood replayed in his mind. *What kind of monster could execute innocent people like that? Those ruthless bastards!*

As Laura hoisted herself back into the van, her phone vibrated at her hip. "Agent Daniels."

"Daniels, this is Chief Furgeson, I think we found the hotel."

That was fast.

"We're on our way." Laura disconnected, then pressed the speed dial for Campisi. "Johnny, get to the police station, we may have the hotel located."

"On our way."

Laura heard Campisi yell for Jackman before the line went dead and Harrison already had the accelerator floored as they raced to the nearby station. *Maybe, just maybe, we're catching the break we desperately need.*

The van pitched forward as Harrison jammed on the brakes in front of the station. Once inside the small building, Laura spotted the tall police chief immediately.

"Over here, Agent Daniels," he called, waving his big hand. He stood in front of the city map, pointing to a small building on the corner of Division and Colter Streets. "The clerk at the Huntsman Inn reported that he rented two rooms to a dark skinned foreigner. He used an ethnic slur I don't care to repeat, but I took it to be a match for Middle Eastern. He said the man paid cash and would not sign the guest register."

"Thanks, Captain. We're going to need some assistance. When we leave, I need four of your men to quietly cover the back of the building, here, on Douglas Street," she said, pointing to the map. "Call the manager on duty and make sure he has the keys to those rooms ready. The rest of my team should be arriving any moment."

"Agent Daniels, I think I can get us a search warrant from Judge Parker in an hour or so."

"No time for that. This is a national security issue. The paperwork will have to wait. Captain, instruct your men that we need these terrorists alive. Shoot to disable, but that's it. Make sure they have weapons ready. They are extremely dangerous and have no regard for human life. You've seen what they are capable of."

"Yes, ma'am. I'll get my men ready to go."

Five minutes later, a white van and two squad cars carrying Laura's team and four Powell policemen quietly rolled to the curb on Douglas Street, behind, and out of sight of the Huntsman Inn. The new building was a simple two-story design with all the doors facing the outside. One large window to each room. The rough staccato finish was painted a light green with dark green doors and trim. There were about two dozen pick-up trucks, vans and cars on the parking lot.

"I want you two on the northeast corner of the building and you guys on the southeast corner," Laura said quietly, pointing to the local cops. "Johnny and Bart—you two open the doors and toss in the flashbangs. I'll back up Bart. Jim, you follow Johnny."

Laura's team rounded the corner and met the manager outside the office. After giving her the keys and pointing out the two side-by-side rooms on the first floor, he ducked back inside.

"The curtains are closed tight. Let's go," Laura whispered, handing the keys to Johnny and Bart.

They crept close to the building, and quickly made their way to the rooms. Johnny and Harrison crawled against the air conditioning unit that thrust below the large curtain-covered window of the nearest room. Keys were slowly and quietly placed in the door handles.

Laura counted down with her fingers, then pointed. Both doors slammed open. Flashbangs detonated with a brilliant light and loud blast. Moments later, the agents stormed the room, guns at arm's length. "FBI, drop your weapons!"

Laura's heart sank as she released pressure from the trigger. The twin beds were rumpled but empty. She could see into the small bath at the end of the room and it too was empty.

"Dammit! Let's give the place a once over." She *really* wanted to empty the magazine of her forty-caliber Sig into the empty bed.

From the other hotel room she heard Harrison yell, "God, this place stinks."

Johnny stuck his head around the corner and reported, "There's a bunch of used cleaning supplies and a horrible stench in the room. I'm not sure what the hell went on in there, but sure as hell nobody slept in that bed."

"Laura, check this out," Jackman called, pointing to one of the beds. "There are blood stains all over the bed and bloody tissues and toilet paper everywhere."

She studied the bed and the pile of tissues on the floor next to it. "Looks like maybe a bad cut? Well, grab some of these and we'll see if it matches the blood from the storage room."

They were traveling east on Alternate 14 heading towards Sheridan, Wyoming. Ahmed and Ali left the garage three hours ago and were traveling through the low mountains.

Ali turned to Ahmed. "I don't feel well at all. My head hurts and I am either hot or cold. I can't stop my nose from bleeding and blood keeps draining down my throat."

"Try to rest, my brother. I am not feeling well either. I too have a bad headache and my breathing comes hard."

"You don't think we have contracted the disease that they talked about on the television, do you?"

"I don't know, but it is better not to think about it."

"Do you think Saif will be proud of us for bringing back the large sources from the construction site?" Ali asked in a raspy voice, straining to talk.

"Yes, he was supportive of the idea. We will be held in high regard. My brother, look at the scenery around you. It is quite beautiful. The sun is shining on the mountains and they are taking on a golden glow. It's as if Allah is giving us a sign."

Ali wheezed, "We need to find a place to stay. I'm afraid that I cannot travel much further."

Ahmed glance across the car's interior and winced at Ali's ghostly pallor. He too felt sicker by the hour. "All right, Ali, I will get off at the next exit. We'll find someplace to stay. Somewhere off the highway. If our car was spotted at the garage this morning, it would be better not to stay at a hotel."

"Thank you, Brother."

"Allah will watch over us. Tonight we will pray for his blessing. Look, there is a sign for Dayton—the exit is two miles ahead. I'll buy some gas and more medication then we will find a secluded home and get some rest."

Highway 14 narrowed becoming a city street as it wound through the small Wyoming town. Ahmed pulled the Buick into a gas station and settled it next to the pump furthest from the attendant. The sign on the gas pump read, *Cash customers prepay inside.* There was still some money left, so he went inside the store.

"Is there a pharmacy in town?" Ahmed asked him.

"Sure is, make a right on Third and then another right on Broadway, 'bout two blocks down. Can't miss it."

"Thank you very much, sir," he said, handing the clerk twenty-five dollars.

"Sure thing, Brother."

You are not my brother, you idiot American, Ahmed thought, shaking his head almost imperceptibly. He returned to the car and filled the tank, then drove to Broadway Drug Store and bought some protein bars, bottled water and cold medication. This would be the last of the cash. From here, they would be at risk using a credit card. At the cash register, an old lady behind the counter seemed mesmerized by a small television. "That's some mess they have over in Cody," she said, looking up.

"I'm sorry—I have been traveling all day, what mess is that?"

"Oh, my, the news folks said that people have anthrax or Ebola or some such nasty disease. Now they're saying the military is surrounding the town and all of them are trapped."

"That sounds very serious."

"One of the stations said the Homeland Security people might raise the threat level to orange and it might be terrorism." The old woman looked at Ahmed. "Where you coming from, mister?"

"I am driving from Cheyenne toward Seattle. I seem to be catching a cold, so I thought I would stop and get something."

"Well, I hope ya'll feel better."

"Thank you, ma'am," Ahmed said, hurrying back to the car.

"Here, Ali, take some medication and have a protein bar. You need some strength."

"Thank you, Brother Ahmed."

Ahmed turned left on Dayton East Road and drove about four miles, looking for an isolated place. He spotted a lone driveway with a small home set back from the road. Turning into the driveway, he brought the car to a stop and instructed Ali to rest. He reached under the dashboard and pulled the engine compartment handle springing the hood with a muffled pop. Grabbing his gun from under the driver's seat, he slipped it into his waistband and pulled his jacket over it. He shivered as the cool steel touched the fevered skin of his back.

There was a lone pick-up truck parked next to the small single-story frame home. No toys or bicycles in the yard—no children. *Good.* After opening the hood all the way, Ahmed climbed the steps to the front porch and knocked on the wooden screen door.

"Hello, is anyone home?" he called out, as his eyes scanned the landscape around him. A strange scent of apple pie mixed with fish floated through the screen door. A bump and a thud preceded the door swinging open, revealing an older lady dressed in jeans and a sweatshirt. Her black hair was streaked with a few strands of gray and pulled back in a bun. "Can I help you?"

"I am terribly sorry to bother you, ma'am, but my car seems to have some problem. I was hoping I could use your telephone to call a tow truck."

"Why, yes, I guess," she said, eyeing the stranger warily. She turned toward the interior of the house and called, "Honey, there's a gentleman at the door. Says he needs a tow truck."

"Would your husband know a place in town that could help me?"

"I'm sure he does. Come on in and I'll go get him. He's just cleaning up from a fishing trip down on Tongue River."

He followed her inside and began to reach for his gun when he spotted a fillet knife on the counter. There were fish in the sink that had just been gutted and cleaned and a steaming apple pie on the counter. As she turned away from him, Ahmed picked up the fillet knife with his right hand and reached around the lady's head with his left. Clasping his hand over her mouth and jerking her head back in the same motion, he brought the razor sharp fillet knife to her exposed throat and sliced deep.

Blood coursed from the gaping gash onto the counter, coating the apple pie in thick maroon topping. Ahmed held her tightly and muffled her cries for help. Even though he couldn't see her eyes, he knew they would be open wide, not yet understanding what was happening or why her time on earth was ending. *She should be thanking me*, he thought.

The vibration of her body next to his, twitching as death overcame her, aroused him in an almost sensual way. A slight smile spread across his face as she quit struggling and went limp. He lowered her lifeless body to the floor and placed the knife on the blood-soaked counter.

Killing with a knife was more personal, more satisfying than with a gun. It brought back memories of his days at training camp in Afghanistan. It had started with animals. They were easy to kill. No resistance, no fear, no soul. They never realized that they were dying.

He remembered his first human kill. A peasant family had been taken from a local village. Ahmed was told that his reward for exemplary performance was first choice. He grabbed the arm of a dirty little girl of maybe fourteen years of age and pulled her from the arms of her mother. As he stood behind her and held the knife to her neck, he smelled her fear and heard her parents as they begged for her life. They wailed for mercy as he pulled her close so he could look over her shoulder, into her frightened eyes. When he pulled the blade across her neck, her eyes were wide with the shock of seeing her blood splash on her pleading, crying parents. He kept her close to him until the warmth drained from her body, then let her collapse to the ground. It was a powerful feeling he had almost forgotten.

The faint sound of water running brought him back to the present. He reached behind him for the gun in his waistband and walked through the house quietly, in search of the husband. The sound of water took him to the master bedroom and a partially closed door, leading to the bathroom.

He carefully peered through the doorway and saw the outline of a man through the shower curtain, humming some sort of tune.

"Honey, is that you? Why not come and join me?"

The shower curtain opened abruptly. The man's jaw dropped when he saw the muzzle of a gun pointed at his head, instead of his playful wife.

The sharp crack of the gun bounced off the tight confines as the man's body slammed against the back wall, quickly slumping down into the tub on the slippery surface. Ahmed heard the crunch of the man's skull as it hit the side of the tub. Dark red blood streaked the tile wall and was quickly washed away by the hot water spitting from the showerhead. Red tinted water swirled around the drain and disappeared.

Ahmed reached in and turned off the hot water, leaving the cold water to wash the remainder of the blood off the body and out of the tub. He went back to the bedroom and unplugged the telephone cord. Confident he had control of the house, he headed to the car to get Ali.

Chapter Forty-seven

Washington D.C.
May 12, 2004

Greg Reilly, Secretary of Homeland Defense, led the discussion in the cabinet room in the West Wing of the White House. Sitting with him were the secretaries of defense, transportation and health and human services, the directors of the CIA and the FBI, the chairman of the joint chiefs of staff and the chiefs of staff for the army and the air force. They were joined via videoconference by the president and the secretary of state, who were campaigning in Atlanta, Georgia.

"Okay, Gentlemen, let's get started," the president said. "I've already talked a bit with Greg and the situation sounds serious. Greg, give us a rundown on what's going on."

"Yes, Mr. President. First, this is what we know. Less than a week ago, the FBI began investigating a series of radioactive material thefts. The first, in Spokane, Washington, was a shipment of smoke detectors with very small sources. Several days later, three much larger sources were stolen at an oil and gas exploration site near Cody, Wyoming." The White House technician projected file photos of Ali Ibrahim Atif and Ahmed Halid on the projection screen.

"These two Middle Eastern men with suspected links to al-Qaeda are known to have been in the area of the thefts. The trail has led the FBI from Spokane, Washington, to Billings, Montana, to Cody, Wyoming, and now to Powell, Wyoming. At the same time the radioactive sources were stolen in Cody, the drill crew came down with severe illnesses. The CDC has identified not one, but three deadly and serious Biosafety Level-4 agents: anthrax, a filovirus similar to Ebola, and a new virus similar to a very virulent Hantavirus." Reilly paused as the projection changed to a highly magnified image of the two viruses.

"There have been at least five deaths and a number of others are in critical condition. As far as we can tell, roughly sixty-percent of the crew was infected by one or more of these agents." Reilly let that number sink in for a moment, and then continued. "Today, approximately three hundred residents of Billings, Cody, and Powell have been diagnosed with same the viruses. Although, the CDC and USAMRIID haven't confirmed it yet, they are extremely concerned that the viruses are airborne and they are asking that we quarantine the three communities before these diseases turn into a worldwide pandemic."

"Greg, do we have projections on what would happen if we are unable to contain this threat?" the president asked.

"Based on a mortality rate of fifty percent, the projection is in the millions in the U.S. alone. If just one international visitor gets out of the country, it could be tens of millions. The Ebola-like virus is extremely hot and the mortality rate is eighty percent or more, but it presents itself and kills quickly, making it slightly easier to contain. The new virus, which the CDC is calling the Cody virus, takes longer to present and then only seems like a common cold. If, in fact, this virus is airborne, the worst-case projections are much more likely to occur."

"When will we know whether or not they are contagious?"

"We know they are all extremely contagious, but I assume you mean airborne, sir. The CDC may not be able to verify for at least another day, maybe longer and by that time it may be too late. It may already be too late. Cody, Wyoming, gets considerable tourist traffic due to its proximity to Yellowstone. Thank God school is still in session or we'd have a stream of tourists that could spread this beyond our ability to contain it. We have already shut down air, bus, and train traffic to these cities, but we obviously couldn't close the interstate yet." A map of the Wyoming-Montana area with the three cities highlighted was now on the projection screen.

The joint chief's chairman joined the conversation. "The manpower required to secure an area this large is beyond anything we've ever seriously considered. It may take five to ten thousand troops. And then there is the issue of closing down Interstate 90 which is a thoroughfare to Washington and Oregon."

Reilly watched the room erupt in sidebars and whispers as the various government heads shared concerns. The president could also be seen having a private discussion with his chief of staff and public relations director.

"Is there anything else that is critical to making this decision, Greg?" the president asked.

"No, sir. I know there are a thousand questions and few answers, but you all have the pertinent information as we know it."

"Okay, I know that this may bring on widespread panic, which we will somehow have to avert, but I see no other course of action than to quarantine the communities and deal with the fallout. Greg, raise the threat level to orange, but I want the government and utilities infrastructure on high alert just as if the threat were severe. Does anybody disagree?"

The room fell silent as the cabinet members and officials exchanged looks.

"Okay, USAMRIID will have the lead on the quarantine. Start mobilizing troops immediately. I'll address the nation in an hour as a first step to calm the fears of the people. Greg, you need to get law enforcement officials throughout the country ready. Get to work, people, and pray to

God we get this thing contained."

The screen went blank as Greg Reilly began discussing specific details of the quarantine plan.

Alan Booker had been Reilly's aid since the formation of the Homeland Security Office and was experienced enough to take the cues from the meeting and set things in action.

He left the Cabinet Room and went to one of the private offices in the West Wing to call his office.

"Audrey, put me through to the government and utility red team."

He heard a series of clicks and then voices.

"Ginstead here."

"Halloran here."

"This is Booker. Mr. Reilly has just bumped the threat level for the public to orange. However, he wants the government and utility infrastructure raised to severe."

"I assume this has to do with the activity in the Northwest?" Halloran asked.

"Yes, it does. Mr. Reilly feels certain that the nation is under terrorist attack and we need to button things down without causing a panic."

"So we're locking down utilities?" Halloran questioned.

"We don't know how the terrorists are distributing the viruses. Until we find out, we need to take the conservative route. They may somehow be using our utility infrastructure against us."

"All right Alan."

Halloran hung up the phone and swiveled his chair to face the desk which was dominated by four large flat-panel monitors—one for electric utilities, another for oil and gas, the third for water and sewers and the last for communications.

Although some of the utilities were still upgrading systems, when the utility sectors went on high alert, it generally meant that control rooms were locked down and communications with the outside world were cut off. Until the level was lowered, all orders came from the Office of Homeland Security.

Halloran pulled out the keyboard drawer and initialized the sequencing program that would alert all utilities of the increased threat level. *Sort of like the old* Star Trek *series when Captain Kirk would order the destruct sequence for the Starship Enterprise.* A bright red dialog box popped up in the middle of all four screens that read SCAN ID CARD NOW.

He disconnected his ID card from the lanyard he wore around his neck and swiped it through the reader on the keyboard. Another dialogue box popped up. *ID accepted. User: Simon Halloran. Use Retinal Scanner Now.*

Halloran put his forehead against the retinal scanner and fought to keep his eye open as the bright red light swept across it. When the light went out, he turned his attention to the screens. The previous dialog box disappeared and was replaced by another. *Retinal Scan Accepted and Verified. User: Simon Halloran. Place Thumb on Fingerprint Reader.*

He put his thumb on the fingerprint reader next to the keyboard and after a series of quiet beeps the last dialogue box appeared. *User Simon Halloran Verified.*

"Yeah, yeah, I know who I am." He keyed in the series of codes necessary to alert utilities nationwide. They were now locked down and under a state of high alert.

In the underground control complex of West Continent Pipeline Company in Seattle the computer screens were suddenly filled with bright red alert warnings. *Utilities are now ordered to initiate Homeland Security Threat Level Red protocol. Continue with this operating condition until further notice from the Office of Homeland Security.*

The phone in the director of operations office began ringing immediately.

"Steve Bryce."

"Steve, you received the alert?"

"Yeah, it just came across. Do you have any idea what's going on?"

"Just what I heard on the news. Go ahead and put things on automatic. Everything's programmed for the next few days, including the new supply line from Montana Gas which is scheduled to come on-line in two days. Then lock down the phones. No calls in or out."

Chapter Forty-eight

Dayton, Wyoming
May 13, 2004

Ahmed's eyes opened slowly, his body shivering. He had fallen asleep only an hour ago after wrapping the man's body in the shower curtain and the woman in trash bags. He dragged them outside to the large garage. Had he felt better, he would have taken more care in hiding the bodies, but his strength was drained and he could barely move.

Reaching down to the foot of the bed, he grabbed the hand-stitched quilt he had kicked off and pulled it to his chin, clutching it around his body for warmth. The television on the other side of the small room was on, but muted, and Ahmed could see that the cable news station was still broadcasting scenes from the cities they had fled. He reached for the remote control to turn the volume louder, fighting off the chills that wracked his body each time he moved.

"...new developments and growing concerns surrounding three cities in the Northwest. This is a live shot of the city limits of Cody, Wyoming. As you can see, the military is moving in and forming a perimeter around the entire city. There have been announcements over a loud-speaker that the city is being quarantined and that residents are encouraged to go to their homes and stay inside. Right now there appears to be no way out of Cody. We noticed the military taking up positions about an hour ago. There are helicopters flying overhead the residents of this small community are on high alert."

Fully awake now, his bloodshot eyes were riveted on the television.

"Okay, Jack, we'll get back to you in a bit. Right now we're going to Camden in Billings, Montana where the scene is similar. Camden, what are you seeing there?"

"Joanne, it's been about an hour since we first noticed the military amassing at the outskirts of town. The local broadcasts have been transmitting a quarantine notice, advising people to remain inside their homes unless they have flu-like symptoms, in which case they are to report to General Hospital immediately."

"On your last report, you told us the line at the hospital was several blocks long. What's the situation now?"

"There are fewer people in line now, but the bad news is that not many people are coming out of the hospital once they go in."

"Thanks for that update, Camden. Although we do not have a reporter in Powell, Wyoming, we did receive a report that the city of Powell was under the same city-wide quarantine. Hours ago, the president addressed the nation and spoke of a viral outbreak being reported in these three cities. The president also stated that the military and CDC are working together to maintain control of the situation and that quarantine zones are being erected to protect the nation and other countries from further outbreaks. He also reported that the CDC is working diligently on a treatment.

"Although the president stopped short of identifying the source of the outbreak, our sources have reported that the FBI is investigating a bioterrorism attack in the area. Apparently two Middle Eastern men are being sought in connection with the outbreaks—"

Ahmed turned the volume back down and struggled to get out of the bed. Wrapping the quilt around him and walking gingerly, he went into the living room where Ali was lying on a sofa sleeper.

The light on the end table next to the sofa was on, illuminating the pale complexion of his Islam brother. His normal brown complexion had been replaced by a yellowish cast in sharp contrast to the bright red blood that streaked and crusted beneath his nose and down the sides of his face. The sheets were stained with bloody black vomit and the stench in the room smelled of death.

"Ali, wake up," Ahmed said, shaking his partner.

Ali's arm was hot to the touch and he didn't respond to Ahmed's prodding. His eyes were mere slits revealing bloodshot scleras rolled back in his skull.

Ahmed made his way back to the bedroom and turned on the bedside lamp, squinting as his eyes slowly adjusted to the brightness. The sudden light brought on a blinding pain as if someone had thrust a spike in his skull. He made his way to the dresser, retrieved his cell phone, and pushed a speed dial number.

"Yes?"

"Saif, this is Ahmed."

"Ahmed, my brother, I have been worried about you. You don't sound well. What is your situation?"

"I fear the worst. We are resting in a home in Dayton, Wyoming. I think we have contracted whatever illness they seem to be blaming on us. Ali is bleeding from his nose and mouth and is near death. I think I will be close behind him."

"I have been listening to the situation and find it ironic that they are blaming us. Can you travel in your current state?"

"It is possible, but not far."

"I have an idea, Ahmed, but I have to make a call first. I will be back in touch with you soon. Godspeed to you, my brother."

Saif pushed the disconnect button on his cell phone and went to the bathroom to splash water on his face. It was 3:10 a.m., but he knew who he needed to call.

Retrieving a different cell phone, he scrolled through names until the display read *Dr. Reed Bates*. It had been some time since he talked to the doctor from Fort Detrick and it was time the doctor was put to good use. Hopefully he would remember their last encounter and cooperate as he insisted he would.

After four rings the sleepy voice said, "Hello?"

"Dr. Bates, this is Sam Yasin. I assume you remember me?"

"I remember you. What do you want?"

"What do you know about the situation in the Northwest?"

"I'm not privy to that information."

"Don't insult me, Bates. That would be a mistake you will regret."

"Look, I'm telling you, I know very little."

"Then you are of little use to me, so I will be making a visit to your wife first, then you."

"Wait, no, you've got to believe me, I've only heard rumors."

"What rumors have you heard?"

"There's supposed to be some anthrax cases and Marburg. I've also heard something about an unknown virus. I figured you had something to do with it."

"No, we have not. Marburg, that's like Ebola, correct?"

"Yes, it's a strain of filovirus—level four, same as anthrax."

"If we had a person who died of such a virus, is it possible that their blood could be extracted and used as a weapon?"

"As long as the body fluids were collected in a reasonable time frame, yes. But I don't know what you would use as a delivery system, unless the virus could survive a short time outside a host. Marburg and Ebola typically can't survive outside a host for any length of time."

"Doctor, you are going to repay the debt you owe me. After this, we will leave you alone."

"What do you want me to do?"

"Get whatever items you need to collect two infected bodies safely. You will then harvest the body fluids and help us preserve it until we can put it to use."

"I'm not sure I can get those kinds of supplies."

"You had better figure it out fast. I will be calling you within several hours with further instructions, but you have to be ready by mid-morning. Goodbye, Doctor."

Saif turned on his computer and began looking for flights that would get him close to where his infected cell members were. He could fly into Casper or Gillette, Wyoming, without too much delay. Now he had to find a rendezvous point that they could reach by car. Somewhere no one would stumble on them.

Saif booted his computer and searched for maps of the Wyoming area on the Internet. He was searching for a location where he could send Ahmed and Ali that would be close enough for them to drive to, but secluded. It didn't take long to find one: Arvada, Wyoming.

Ahmed and Ali had become incubators for a devastating weapon of mass destruction against the United States.

Chapter Forty-nine

Washington D.C.
May 13, 2004

Mike Johnson awoke to the sound of the small alarm clock. In complete darkness, he reached to hit the snooze button, but in his early morning grogginess he managed to knock it to the floor. Reluctantly, he reached to turn on the small lamp.

"Mike, wake up. Your alarm clock is going off." A groggy voice trailed up from under a bundle of blankets.

"Sorry, honey. I've got it. Go back to sleep."

He looked to the floor to find the clock. His Blackberry messenger lay next to it. Damn! It must have vibrated off the table in the night. He vaguely remembered switching it to the vibrate mode for his staff meeting at the end of the day.

He grabbed the clock and Blackberry and headed for the bathroom. It took a minute for his eyes to adjust to the bright lights before he could make out the messages he received during the night. The very last message caught his attention.

"Due to the events in Wyoming and Montana, the secretary of Homeland Security has raised the threat level to orange. However, all government offices will be operating at high alert."

"Oh, crap," he whispered. Of all times to miss a message. He pushed the "next" button and kept reading.

"Mike, with the elevation in the threat level, make sure the cell monitor stations sync the keywords with the latest intel. Also concentrate on New York, Wyoming and Montana and the corridor between."

He splashed water on his face, grabbed his cell phone off the dresser and headed down the stairs to his home office. His mind raced, trying to put in order all the tasks he had to do before getting into his car. The laptop computer was already open on the desk and after logging in with his secure identification, he pulled up the keyword list that had been worked up for the current situation.

First the locations: Spokane, Billings, Cody, Powell, Wyoming, Montana. Then the names Ahmed, Ali, Ibrahim, Halid and Atif. Last were the other keywords: radiation, bomb, virus, smoke detectors, well, loggers... The last list went on and on. These would be loaded into the database of keywords for the voice recognition software that ran on the cell phone monitoring system.

He grabbed his phone and dialed the section chief for cell phone monitoring.

"Jack Moniham here."

"Jack, this is Mike Johnson, bioterrorism. I have a new list of priority keywords for you. I uploaded it to your directory. The file name is 'Cody.'"

"Okay, Mike, you know the alert has been bumped, which means we're in overdrive here."

"I know. This list of words gets the highest priority. The focus needs to be put on New York, Montana and Wyoming. You should also monitor the driving corridors between Wyoming and New York."

"I've got it, Mike. You know I won't be able to run these keywords on past calls. With the increase in monitoring, we have to recycle the drives every hour."

"Just get the keywords uploaded ASAP."

"I'll get right on it. It'll just take a few minutes. Do you want all the high probability call transcripts routed to you?"

"Absolutely. Thanks, Jack," Mike said, hitting the disconnect button.

The cell division would have some long days ahead of them. Even though the computers scanned all cell phone calls for certain keywords and converted the conversations into printouts with the phone numbers and tower locations, the clerks still have to read the transcripts and determine whether it gets bumped for further investigation. By adding a long list of keywords to the system, the number of hits would rise exponentially.

Chapter Fifty

Cody, Wyoming
May 13, 2004

"We may have peaked here in Cody, Max. That's the good news. We haven't had any new cases in the past six hours. The bad news is we don't have any more places to put anybody if they do come in. The hospital and Cody's high school gym are full," Rivers said as Max pulled a chair to the conference table.

"How many cases do we have?"

"One thousand twenty-four."

"Let's see, there are about eighty-four hundred people in Cody, so that's about twelve percent. Of course we don't know how many were exposed. How many cases do we have in Billings and Powell?"

"Almost three thousand in Billings. Both hospitals are full and they're starting to set up in the high school gym. Last I heard people are still filing in." Rivers scanned his notepad. "Powell has about nine hundred, and more are waiting for testing."

"Any more fatalities?"

"Two of the construction workers that had anthrax are improving, but the rest aren't responding to the antibiotics. Three hospital workers that contracted Cody expired last night. No fatalities in Powell or Billings yet, but this Cody bug looks like it's going to have a very high mortality rate. Nobody is responding favorably to the antibiotics."

"You know, we've got half the government on the edge of their seats waiting to learn if Cody is airborne."

"I just ordered another blood test on the monkeys. We should have results in a couple of hours." Rivers got up to leave, made it halfway to the door, hesitated, then turned back and said, "We haven't had any luck on the surveys yet. There seems to be no connection at all between the infected. Has the FBI reported any progress yet?"

"They just missed the bastards in Powell. Apparently the S.O.B. terrorists killed a couple of people and ran. Agent Daniels thinks they're driving back to New York. Roadblocks are in place, but no further news yet."

"I'm heading back to the lab. I'll let you know as soon as the tests on the monkeys come back." He turned and exited the tent. The pounding beat of helicopter rotors and the continuous curfew announcements on the public address system were a reminder of the war zone he resided in now. It wasn't a conventional war of epic proportions against a mighty enemy, but the enemy was just as deadly—maybe more so. This was guerilla warfare at its best, since the virus was invisible and not selective in its attacks. This was a hidden viral assassin capable of destroying an entire species more efficiently than any army and just as deadly. No mechanized troops, just hand-to-hand combat.

The tent door opened and General Carmichael entered with a haggard look, unshaven face and sunken eyes. "I'm really too old for this, Max," he said. "If we get through this I may just move up my retirement date."

"We'll get through this. I just received some encouraging news from Rivers. It seems the cases here in Cody have peaked."

"How about the other cities?"

"Not yet. But, hopefully we're over the hump. What worries me most is that we've got the quarantine zone too tight and someone outside will get sick and be afraid to report in."

"I've got forty-five medical corps blanketing the surrounding towns with thermo scanners. Anyone with a fever is being brought to the nearest testing facility."

"When did this happen?"

"Overnight, Max. Sorry, there's been too much going on and I forgot to tell you."

"Is there anything else I should know?"

"There are ten Apache Helicopters with infra-red thermo cameras flying. We've got them calibrated to read heat signatures inside buildings. If they get a hit, non-medical units with portable scanners move in."

"I'm sure we'll get a lot of false positives, but it's a damn good idea."

"I've just got a bad feeling about this, Max. Did you know half the Americans that died in World War I weren't killed by the enemy? They fell to the Spanish Flu."

"I knew it was a large number, but I never thought about it in those terms."

"The most recent thinking has the 1918 pandemic starting at Fort Riley and Camp Funston in Kansas. In other words, Americans may have been responsible for spreading a flu that wiped out up to forty million people."

"Well, we're not responsible for this. Some cowardly, sick bastards without a conscience are responsible and will pay."

"I pray you're right, Max."

Chapter Fifty-one

New York City
May 13, 2004

All the arrangements were made. Saif reached for his cell phone and dialed Ahmed.

"Yes?" The voice on the end of the connection was weak and didn't sound at all like Ahmed.

"Ahmed? Is that you?"

"Yes. Do you have instructions for me?"

"Go to the secure website. I left directions for you there. The doctor and I will meet you this evening."

"It will be good to see you again, my brother."

"Turn off your phone, remove the battery and sim chip. This will be our last communication until I see you. May Allah watch over you."

Saif turned off his phone, picked up his overnight bag and ran out the door. He had a plane to catch and no time to lose.

The cell phone monitoring department was a large theater-like control room with hundreds of desks lined up in rows. The stations were divided by tower groups. The lower Manhattan FBI technician was snacking on a sandwich when a pop-up box appeared on his computer monitor along with an audible alarm. "Probable match....two priority keywords."

He frantically typed commands as he yelled "I have something here."

"Put it on the big screen and speakers."

The large plasma monitors on the front wall of the control room lit up. "Keywords matched, Priority: Ahmed, Allah. Secondary: secure. Yes? Ahmed? Is that you? Yes. Do you have instructions for me? Go to the secure website. I left directions for you there. The doctor and I will meet you this evening. It will be good to see you again. My brother. Turn off your phone, remove the battery and sim chip. This will be our last communication until I see you. May Allah watch over you."

The recorded conversation played on the speakers.

"Did you get locations?" the section supervisor asked.

"I've got tower locations, but there wasn't enough time for GPS lock before they switched them off."

"What towers?"

"Originating tower is in lower Manhattan. The tower identifier is on-screen. The receiving tower is in Dayton, Wyoming."

"Website...website," the supervisor pondered aloud. "Find out if Dayton has broadband service of any kind. Start monitoring all long distance calls from their phone switch for any internet service provider. Also, check with the satellite television companies to see if anybody in the range of that cell tower has satellite broadband."

The supervisor picked up the phone and buzzed Mike Johnson.

"Johnson here."

"We have a cell phone match. I'm sending the transcript to your workstation. There was mention of a website. We're checking to see if Dayton, Wyoming, has broadband and monitoring outgoing telephone calls for internet service providers."

"What else?"

"There's a meeting this evening with a doctor, that's about it."

"Do we have a location?"

"Just the two cell towers, we couldn't get a GPS location on the phones before they switched them off."

"As data comes in, put it right through to my workstation."

"Yes, sir," the supervisor said and looked up at the sea of people and desks. "Come on, people, I want some answers."

"Sir, cable service is limited to the town and no broadband service, no DSL either."

"How about outgoing ISP calls?"

"We're monitoring, but nothing yet."

"Damn, I almost forgot. Monitor that cell tower for ISP calls."

"We're watching for the cell phone to reregister with the tower," the technician assured him.

"They may have another phone, dammit."

Ahmed had to retrieve his laptop computer and Ali's briefcase with his cell phone. He parked the car in the back of the house where it wouldn't be visible from the road. As he left the house, he saw a police cruiser in the distance headed his way.

"Damn," he mumbled, stepping back into the house. Letting the screen door slam shut behind him, he purposely let the old heavy wooden front door open. After retrieving his gun from the kitchen table, he pressed his back to the wall next to the open door.

The sound of gravel being crushed beneath tires announced the arrival of the squad car. The uniformed officer swung the door of the dusty white Crown Victoria open and tugged at his neatly pressed khaki shirt before approaching the house.

Perspiration dripped in Ahmed's eyes as he heard the officer's heels clack against the wood steps of the porch. His arms hung in front with both hands cradling the butt of the Jericho handgun, his fingers lightly touching the cold steel. Ahmed found comfort in the slick, cool curvature of the trigger.

A dark shadow lengthened across the hardwood floor as the bulky officer blocked the sunlight filtering through the screen door. A loud rapping on the frame of the door alerted Ahmed.

"Mrs. Summerfield! Grace! Anybody home? Your phone must be off the hook."

A quick reflex touch to see if the safety was released, then Ahmed sprung the trap as he quickly stepped out from the heavy wooden door and raised his weapon. The surprise in the unsuspecting officer's eyes brought a smile to his lips.

Crack...crack.

Hot lead blasted through the wire mesh screen. The first one found the officer's forehead instantly twisting him around so the second bullet entered through the right temple. He fell backward against the railing of the porch, flipping over it and landing in the flower garden where newly planted day lilies were beginning to bud.

Ahmed calmly put the gun back in his waistband and strolled to the car to retrieve the computer and phone. Five minutes later he had the modem hooked to the cell phone and was dialing the toll-free number to an offshore ISP in the Bahamas. The familiar handshake buzzing announced the opening of the connection as the laptop modem and internet server agreed to talk to one another.

The connection was slow, but within two minutes, Ahmed was looking at a home page for Ebay. Navigating to the correct Ebay store, he used the touchpad mouse to point to the logo at the top of the page and then held the ctrl and shift key and left-clicked.

The screen went white for a moment and then the message within Internet Explorer came up: *The page cannot be found.* After another two minutes, the screen jumped to life and was automatically redirected to the secure website run by his cell. It looked like a child's school project. He scrolled down to a seemingly blank area of the screen and carefully moved the mouse until he found the invisible link to the directions Saif had left for him. A map started building on the screen with directions to an abandoned strip mine outside Spotted Horse, Wyoming. He pulled the cord from the modem and turned off his phone, then took out a pad of paper and copied the screen. It looked to be about ninety miles away on State Route 14.

He hurriedly shut down the computer, gathered their things and helped Ali into the back seat of the car. Ali was on the verge of meeting Allah. They needed to get on the road before the policeman was missed.

"I've got a cell call from the same tower in Dayton, Wyoming, connecting with an offshore ISP." The technician frantically typed commands into his system to get a fix on the call. "In the Bahamas."

"Patch it in and follow his tracks."

"I'm in. Looks like he's at an Ebay store selling goods out of San Francisco."

"I'm sure he'll link to something off that page."

"Nothing. I'm guessing there's a script or something blocking us from seeing where he's going."

"Probably, but keep watch."

After a few minutes the cell phone disconnected.

"He's off the line."

"Okay, get our computer geeks up here to help us figure this out. Put the site on the main screen."

The large plasma screen displayed a household goods store with pages and pages of bedding, linens, towels, and gadgets. The logo showed a bed with sheep jumping over it and the name *Comfort Sleep Shop*.

A young, acne-faced man with wire-rim glasses barged through the door to the control room and ran to the supervisor's desk.

"You can use that workstation right there," the supervisor said, pointing to an empty cubicle. "Direct the information to station 110."

He hustled over and logged into the system, then popped open the CD drive and inserted a disc he had brought with him.

"Okay, you have the website on your station." The technician that tracked the call stood behind him to see how this was done.

He watched as the kid typed commands that opened a series of dialogue boxes with computer code racing by. It looked like a scene from *The Matrix*.

"This may take a few minutes," the kid said, looking back over his shoulder. "It depends on how deep the link is embedded into the html on the page."

Another box appeared on the screen with more computer code.

"Well, lookey here," the kid said, smiling.

"What's that?"

"Embedded in the JavaScript for the logo is our hidden link. All we have to do is this..." he moved the cursor on top of the logo where the cartoon sheep tirelessly jumped over the bed, held the ctrl and shift keys down and clicked the mouse.

To their surprise, Internet Explorer now displayed the familiar *the page could not be found* screen.

"Crap!" the technician said, turning around.

"Wait, this could be a red herring," the acne-face kid replied.

"What do you mean?"

"Chill, dude. This could be a dup to reroute traffic or blow the impatient. Or, it may be a diversion..."

The screen changed again to an amateurish looking child's home page.

"Hmmm. Now what?" the kid said, as he scrolled around the screen. "Where, oh where are you, little link? This will be faster if I do it the modern way."

He moused the start button and ran another program from the CD.

"I wrote this one for my master's project at MIT."

The screen flashed again with no apparent change. The kid took off his glasses, put his nose to the screen and inspected the entire website.

"There you are," he said, pointing to a tiny black dot on the screen. "The program I just ran converts the link properties to display all links in black. They embedded a tiny link using the same color as the background so it was invisible. Only someone who knows exactly where to place the cursor would be able to find it."

He carefully positioned the cursor and clicked. The plasma screen displayed a map of north-central Wyoming with directions and then suddenly went blank.

"What the hell happened?"

"I don't know," the kid said. "It was likely booby trapped."

"What do you mean, booby trapped? How the hell do you booby trap a website?"

"IP address. Or some script that needed a certain identifier off a cookie they have on their machines. There's still a chance I can reassemble the data. We try to trap all the data as it streams through the firewall. It depends how fragmented the data is, but I may be able to put it back together. I'm going back to my desk to get some help."

Chapter Fifty-two

Powell, Wyoming
May 13, 2004

Something had been nagging at Brandon all night. *Something was not quite right. What was it about the current state of things and the way the FBI was operating that didn't sit well with him? Everything fits.*

He woke up early at the small hotel in Powell and looked out the window in time to see a caravan of military vehicles parade by. *What the hell had he missed?* Turning on the television, he discovered that he was again in a quarantine zone. The public service announcement was urging people in the zones to stay indoors unless they were exhibiting one or more of the symptoms. Nowhere in the announcement did it stress how deadly this outbreak could be.

Surprisingly, the hotel had broadband service. He flipped open his laptop and started surfing the web. The CDC website had information on all the major disease outbreaks. The newest was the sprinkling of bird flu in Asia. In the U.S. there was West Nile and AIDS was worldwide. Of course, there was SARS in China, for which there was little information other than renewed statistics. Hantavirus, Mad Cow, Ebola, Marburg, Dengue Fever and then there were an infinite number of influenza strains.

Hantavirus seemed to have originated in Korea. Brandon began to read. *The hantavirus was originally discovered in Asia during the Korean War, Hantaan River, mid-May of 1993, when several healthy young members of the Navajo Nation in New Mexico died within a short period of time. Later that year, the virus itself was given a name: Muerto Canyon Virus, which was eventually changed to Sin Nombre virus. The disease was thusly called Hantavirus Pulmonary Syndrome.*

Muerto Canyon…why did that ring a bell? He hooked into Interex's computer network and downloaded the large historical spreadsheet of worldwide oil and gas exploration sites. Nothing. He Googled Muerto Canyon. That's odd, it was right near Canyon De Chelly National Monument. Pretty close to his gas field in the Four Corners Region in early 1993.

The sharp pitch of his ringing cell phone startled him. "This is Brandon."

"Hey, Brandon, this is Jerry. I wanted to let you know we're on hold indefinitely here. Things are pretty bad. Where the hell are you by the way?"

"Hey, Jerry. Looks like I'm quarantined in Powell, Wyoming."

"I thought you were headed to Billings."

"I was, but the agents I was with wound up getting diverted to Powell to investigate a murder by the terrorists. In fact, we found Billy Goller's missing equipment without the Americium."

"I'll be a son-of-a-bitch! So there are terrorists running loose out here?"

"Yeah, ruthless bastards too. You should've seen what they did to this auto mechanic and his son. Hey, I've got a question. Do you remember seeing rodents around the site?"

"Rodents?"

"Yeah, mice or rats?"

"I know what a rodent is, Brandon. Why do you ask? I mean the CDC asked me that a couple of days ago."

"Probably for the same reason. I'm trying to keep busy here."

"Not a one. Just those raccoons that lived under the trailer."

"Damn, funny you should mention them. They're dead and scared the crap out of me when I went out there to retrieve the employment files."

"How can a dead raccoon—"

"Don't ask. Not one of my better moments. Any new news down there?"

"Nope. No news about getting out of here either. But I'm fine, and thanks for asking."

"Sorry, man. My mind isn't exactly all together yet. Hang in there, buddy. It'd be easier to tolerate if Dallas was here."

"I'll say. I'll sure miss that guy."

"Yeah, me too. See you soon, I hope."

Brandon turned back to his computer, closed his internet browser and opened his e-mail. He opened the confirmation from West Continent Pipeline Group. The new gas tap would become operational tonight at 7:00 p.m. He opened the attachments and looked at the site plans and locator map.

Well at least something is going right. He forwarded the e-mail to Jeffery Hargrove with a note that he was alive and well and a prisoner in Powell, Wyoming.

Laura's cell phone chirped as she reviewed the case file on her laptop.

"Daniels."

"Laura, this is Mike Johnson. We may have a lead."

"Great," she said, grabbing a pen from the desk. "What have you got?"

"We intercepted a call from New York to Dayton, Wyoming, between two Muslim men. The message indicated that a Muslim from New York and a doctor were meeting with a man named Ahmed this evening."

"Where? In Dayton?"

"No. Well, probably not. The directions were on a secured web site. We're trying to reassemble it now."

"I don't understand, Mike."

"We tracked the call to a website, but when we opened the site, it erased itself. The computer staff is trying to reassemble it. Apparently, it was a map of north-central Wyoming."

"I've got a big problem, Mike."

"I know what you're going to say, Laura, and I'm working on it. I've got a call into the DOD to get you out of the quarantine area and have a helicopter at your disposal. How are you feeling?"

"Anxious, but physically great, thanks, and don't forget Jim Harrison and Brandon Stiles."

"I'll see what I can do and I'll let you know as soon as we get the info we need."

Laura hung up the phone, turned back to her laptop and continued working on her files.

Chapter Fifty-three

Spotted Horse, Wyoming
May 13, 2004

There were no signs on the highway, just the shells of a few old buildings that were once the center of the small bustling western town of Spotted Horse, Wyoming. Ahmed slowed the car and made a right turn on a gravel road at the old post office.

Glancing at directions he had copied by hand from the web site—*six more miles to go*—he didn't have much left in him. The pressure behind his head was unbearable and the medicine he took had no effect. With arms that were too heavy to lift, he dabbed at the perspiration dribbling down his face with a paper napkin he took from the house. Bloody tissues littered the seat next to him. *Just want to close my eyes and rest.* His watch read 2:30 p.m. Saif and the doctor should be there in about three hours.

A moan drifted up from the back seat. Ahmed turned to look at his partner and barely recognized him. He was pale and thin rivulets of blood drained from his nose, down his cheek and soaked into the car's beige, cloth upholstery. Surely death was imminent.

The Buick lurched forward as Ahmed pushed down on the accelerator. He guided the car down the little traveled, narrow path. After three miles, the gravel gave way to hard-packed dirt. The rearview mirror didn't reveal a rising trail of dust behind him. As the road rose steadily, it became heavily rutted, raising concern about getting the car stuck. Small trees formed a canopy above him as the path became narrower. Sunlight filtered through the leaves causing Ahmed to squint as he drove, heightening the pain behind his eyes. He began to think that he might not make it all the way to the abandoned mine.

If Saif's directions were correct, he had less than a mile to go. The road ahead turned sharply in a series of switchbacks climbing the steep hill. He stopped the car at the crest and saw the gates lying on the ground, likely torn down by vandals.

The car rolled over the gate toward the old dilapidated office building two hundred yards ahead. He pulled alongside the building and shut the engine off. Relief washed over him. Now all he had to do was wait.

Chapter Fifty-four

Washington D.C.
May 13, 2004

"Where the hell is that map?" Mike Johnson yelled through the phone at the tech division chief.

"We collected all the data points. Now we're reassembling them."

"When will you have it?"

"Mike, there are almost seven hundred thousand pixels that we're putting together without any reference points. It takes time."

"We don't have any time, dammit. It's been three hours already."

"Hold on, Mike, let me check on something." He put the line on hold and punched his intercom and dialed a station number. "How far are you?"

"About sixty percent, but the data is scattered and we can't make anything out of the picture yet. The good news is the process is speeding up with each data point placed."

"How long?"

"An hour, maybe sooner."

"As soon as you have any kind of image, let me know." He pushed a button on the phone, "Mike, give us an hour, I'll call you as soon as we have an image."

"Thanks." Johnson punched the button for his second line and dialed Laura's number.

"Daniels."

"Laura, get ready to move. Go to the main quarantine gate, north on Absoroka Street to 14th. See Major Lee—he has the paperwork to get you out. They have a Black Hawk helicopter and pilot waiting for you. We should have a location in less than an hour."

"Great. I'll gather the troops. I'm getting cabin fever being cooped up here. What's the word on the epidemic?"

"New cases are slowing, but deaths are mounting. If the quarantine successfully contains the virus, casualties are projected to be less than fifty thousand."

"My God! I didn't know it was that bad."

"Most of them are from Billings. Oh, Laura, they're going to scan your body temperature before they'll let you through quarantine. If you have any kind of fever, you won't be allowed out."

"We're fine."

"You may want to take a couple ibuprophin now. That may lower your temperature just in case. I need you on that helicopter."

"All right, Mike. I'll be ready to go by the time you call."

"I think you should leave Mr. Stiles behind. I don't see any good in taking him with you."

"If this doesn't pan out, Mike, I may need him. Besides, he was already released from quarantine and I feel responsible for him being trapped here.

"Okay, I trust your judgment. Good luck and I'll be in touch."

Laura put the phone down, pushed back from the small desk in her hotel room and went to the closed bathroom door. Hot steam and the clean scent of soap hit her when she pulled open the door.

"Hurry up in there, Jim," she said, pulling the shower curtain back, making Harrison jump. "We need to get going."

Her eyes moved down his body, surveying his tight muscular frame. A not-so-innocent smile formed on her face as she turned to call Brandon Stiles. He picked up the phone on the first ring.

"Hello."

"Are you ready to get out of here?" she asked.

"The voice of an angel. You bet, where are we going?"

"I'm not sure yet, but we need to get to the north perimeter of the quarantine zone in the next half hour."

"No problem, I'll be ready."

"We'll meet outside in twenty minutes."

As she sat the phone back in its cradle, Harrison grabbed her from behind.

"I guess we don't have time for one more round?"

"Get dressed, Harrison. We have a job to do," she said as she spun around in his arms.

Twenty minutes later, Laura was driving Harrison and Brandon to the northern city limits. As they approached the quarantine line, Laura took a deep breath. She had never seen a military display like the scene they were facing now. Armed guards, tanks and troop carriers were patrolling a barbed-wire fence and gate. Helicopters were flying low, keeping vigil on the outer limits of town. As they approached the gate, they heard a voice on a loud speaker.

"Unidentified vehicle, stop where you are or you will be fired upon!"

She stomped on the brake and stepped out of the car holding up her FBI ID.

"Approach the gate on foot and present your identification!"

She walked tentatively toward the gate, still holding her badge in the air. As she neared the checkpoint a dozen red laser dots danced on her chest. *Keep walking.*

When she was within twenty-five feet of the gate, a guard shouted, "Identify yourself!"

"I'm FBI Agent Laura Daniels. I'm here to see Major Lee. He is expecting me and my partners."

"Come forward and let me see your ID, ma'am." The guard keyed his radio, "Major Lee, there is an FBI agent at the north perimeter here to see you, over."

"I'll be right there. Send her through after a temperature scan."

"Yes, sir," he said, then turned back to Laura. "Stay right there for a minute, ma'am, while I scan your temperature."

He looked into a thermo-camera where he made out a blue and green image of the woman.

"Okay, please proceed."

"What about my companions?"

"They can stay put until Major Lee gets here."

Laura spotted the jeep speeding towards them from a group of tents about two hundred yards away. It came to a quick halt and a soldier jumped out and trotted towards them.

"You Agent Daniels?"

"Yes, I am," Laura answered, showing her badge. "I have Detective Harrison and Dr. Brandon Stiles with me."

"Yes, we're expecting you," the major said, then turned to the guard. "Sergeant, bring Agent Daniels' people through and escort them to my tent."

He waved Laura to his jeep. "You can wait in my conference room, ma'am."

"Thank you, Major."

Chapter Fifty-five

Gillette, Wyoming
May 13, 2004

Saif climbed down the narrow metal stairway to the tarmac outside of the small terminal at Gillette-Campbell County Airport. His head throbbed from the constant vibration and noise of the turbo-prop plane. At the luggage carousel, he spotted Dr. Bates waiting with two large suitcases.

As he walked past the doctor without making eye contact, Saif mumbled, "Follow me."

The doctor struggled to collect his bags and followed Saif to the Avis Rental desk.

"Mr. Sam Yasin?" the lady behind the counter asked with a polite smile as she looked at Saif's New York driver's license. "Did I pronounce that right?"

"Yes, perfectly."

"We have your SUV waiting for you in space C-19. Right through these doors and to your right," she said, handing Saif the contract and keys to a grey Chevy Trailblazer.

"Thank you very much." Without looking at the doctor, Saif turned and went through the doors, walking very quickly.

"We have a stop to make on the way, Doctor. Put your equipment in the back and let's get going."

"Where are we going?"

"That is none of your concern." The SUV roared to life as Saif guided it out of the parking lot and south, toward town. He headed south on Douglas Highway and pulled into a Wal-Mart parking lot.

"You wait here. I need to make a purchase."

Less than ten minutes passed and Saif returned to the car carrying a bag. He opened the door and hoisted himself into the driver's seat and removed a plastic package containing a fillet knife from the bag. Saif sheathed the knife, slipped it in his waistband and covered it with his jacket.

"What's that for?" the doctor asked nervously.

"Shut up! I have another stop, then we will be on our way." Saif started the SUV and drove to Fourth Street and Miller Avenue and pulled to the curb in front of the Easy Money Pawn Shop.

"I'm leaving the engine running. Don't even think of doing anything stupid."

He stepped to the sidewalk, adjusted his jacket to conceal the handle of the fillet knife and entered the old musty-smelling building. He heard a buzzer ring in the office alerting the shopkeeper of a potential customer. A short, heavy man of about fifty years limped through the door.

"Howdy there. What can I do for you today?"

Saif stepped up to the counter and pointed to the rifle mounted on the back wall. "Is that a Colt M4A1 there?"

"Yes it is. It's semi-automatic and legal."

"May I have a look at it, please?"

"You have a good eye. The previous owner had the scope calibrated just before he brought it in." He pulled a key ring off his belt and unlocked the gun rack on the wall.

Saif grasped the Colt's stock and inspected it as if he were interested in its features. His eyes scanned the shop, looking for the handguns and ammunition.

Setting the Colt carefully on the counter and pointing to another rifle on the back wall, Saif asked, "What's that rifle there?"

"Now that one—"

As the shopkeeper turned, Saif pulled the fillet knife from its sheath, grabbed the man by the hair and jerked his head back, exposing his neck. The fillet knife came up in a swift efficient motion and slashed through the arteries in the man's neck, spouting dark red blood on the back wall.

He held the man's hair until his body quit struggling, then let him fall to the floor behind the counter. He quickly retrieved the key ring and helped himself to a nine-millimeter Glock handgun, the Colt rifle, several boxes of ammunition and a large pair of binoculars. He loaded the Glock and found a case to put the rifle in. He slid the case in the back of the Trailblazer with the doctor's suitcases.

"Now we will finish this job." He put the vehicle in gear and drove north on Highway 16 towards Spotted Horse, Wyoming.

"Where are we going?"

"We are going to a location about thirty-five miles north of here to collect my comrades who are giving their lives for our cause."

Chapter Fifty-six

Washington D.C.
May 13, 2004

"Come on, baby," the young technician urged the computer that was assembling the scattered data points into vital information. "There it is! Hot damn!"

He picked up the phone and called the section chief. "I've got it."

"Send it to Mike Johnson in the terrorism group immediately."

"It's already on the way."

Mike was about to pick up the phone to call the Tech Center again when the message came up on his monitor with the location of the meeting in Wyoming.

He punched the speed dial for Laura.

Laura grabbed the cell phone from its holster and saw it was Mike Johnson, then turned to Harrison and gave him a thumbs-up signal.

"Yes, Mike."

"We have it. They're meeting at an abandoned strip mine six miles south of Spotted Horse, Wyoming. Spotted Horse is about thirty miles north of Gillette."

Laura located Gillette on the map hanging on the tent wall.

"I've got Gillette."

"Follow Highway 16 north until it turns west, about thirty miles. You should see Spotted Horse—it looks to be a ghost town. The strip mine is six miles south of there."

"Shit. There's not enough detail on this map." She looked around the room. "Major, do you have more detailed maps?"

"Sure, U.S.G.S. quads. Let me see where you're at."

He ran over and looked to where Laura was pointing, then rummaged through a stack of maps on a cabinet in the corner.

"I've got it." He laid it on the table and pointing to a marked strip mine.

"Okay, Mike, we've got it. We'll be off the ground shortly."

"Don't fail us, Laura."

"No way, Mike," she assured him as she flipped her phone closed.

Major Lee keyed the radio barking orders to the S70-A Black Hawk helicopter pilot.

"There's a fifty-millimeter cannon, eight Hellfire missiles and two gunners on-board, although I hope you don't need them. Take these radios with you to communicate with the crew. Your pilot has the coordinates and is ready to go."

"Thank you, Major."

"Good luck, Agent Daniels."

As they ran to the helicopter, Laura turned to Brandon and yelled over the noise of the rotors, "Brandon, perhaps you should stay here. This could be dangerous."

"Not a chance. But I'll stay with the chopper. If you get any information from the bad guys, I may be able to help. I've got a pretty good background in infectious disease."

"Okay, your choice."

The Black Hawk lifted off, leaving Laura's stomach behind. She'd been in helicopters countless times, but had never gotten used to takeoffs.

"Good afternoon, I'm Captain Mazilli. I'll be your pilot today. Over to your right is First Gunner Dykhouse and to your left is Second Gunner Nash. There are some barf-bags under the seat if you're so inclined."

Laura fought the urge to vomit. Just the mention of barf-bags churned her stomach to the edge. The vibration was fierce as they climbed. *Thank God for the cool wind that whistled through the open doors.* Mazilli took the chopper to two-thousand feet, pointed the nose down slightly and headed due east. The two gunners that were strapped in with safety harnesses and manning machine guns mounted at the doors swayed and fought to maintain their footing.

Seeing the small historical marker for Spotted Horse, Saif slowed the Trailblazer. When the wood-façade Post Office with a carved wooden sign hanging crooked and swinging in the wind came into view, he turned the SUV onto the gravel road and accelerated toward the strip mine.

"We're almost there, Doctor. You've been quiet for the last half-hour. Do you know how you're going to preserve the virus for us?"

"How long does it have to be preserved?"

"I'm not sure. I have another expert working on an aerosolized delivery system. If he is successful, it may not be too long."

"I think the virus will survive in the bodies for a while. But I may need laboratory supplies and an incubator—unless you can get me a cryogenic freezer."

"I'm afraid that would be impossible. We have a source that can get certain medical supplies in New York. You'll have time during the car ride home to make your list. I'll have it waiting when we arrive."

The grey SUV hurtled forward, bouncing on the rough road. Suddenly, the gravel gave way to hard-packed dirt and Saif slowed down. He now had to navigate deep ruts in the road.

"We should be getting close. I'm going to stop about a quarter mile short of the mine and survey the situation before we drive in."

"Do you actually think someone else could find this place?"

"Never underestimate the United States Government. They may be arrogant, but they aren't stupid."

The road switch-backed on itself as it led up the hill towards the gate. Saif pulled the SUV under a large tree, some fifty feet off the road and shut the engine off. "I'm going to the top of the hill. You wait here in the car."

He opened the lift gate and removed the Colt carbine from its case, loaded thirty rounds of ammunition into the magazine and snapped it in place. He pulled back the bolt of the Glock nine-millimeter handgun, chambering a round and slid it into his waistband, then slung the strap of the binoculars around his neck.

Saif scrambled up the steep hill to the edge of the large pit, dislodging rocks as he went. Scrubby brush dominated the terrain around the large gaping mine. Bringing the binoculars to his eyes, he scanned the scene in front of him.

There. Next to an old tin building was a beige Buick. Even with the high powered lenses, Saif could not see his comrades. *They might already be dead.*

Wait. What was that sound in the distance? Saif scanned the skies and spotted a helicopter approaching from the west. It was flying low and seemed to be slowing down as it neared the mine. He watched as the military helicopter slowed to a hover over the center of the open pit.

"Damn you, fucking Americans!" he shouted, slamming his fist on the ground.

"There, Agent Daniels—a beige car next to that building," the first gunner said into the Black Hawk's audio system. He pointed to the remains of a metal building. "But I can't make out if anybody is in it."

"Do you see any other vehicles?" Laura asked into the headset.

"No, nothing."

"Get us on the ground."

"I'll set it down right there," Mazilli said, pointing. "About fifty yards south of the entrance and building, where the scrub brush isn't so thick."

"If they start moving, we have to stop them without killing them," Laura explained. "They have vital information."

Harrison pulled out his pistol and checked the magazine—full load.

First Gunner Dykhouse tapped Laura on the shoulder. "Agent Daniels, clip the radio to your belt and the microphone to the collar of your shirt.

Push that red button. It will keep the channel open so we can hear everything. If you need assistance, just holler and we'll get in the air."

"Okay."

"If you need a response from us, you'll have to close the channel by pushing the red button again. Otherwise, you won't be able to hear us."

The Black Hawk touched down. Laura and Harrison jumped out and ran towards the beige vehicle, keeping the building between them and the car.

"Head around the other side of the building and come up from behind," Laura instructed Harrison.

"Okay, Laura, be careful."

Harrison quietly made his way around the metal building and peered around the corner at the back of the vehicle. He pulled his pistol, then signaled an okay sign to Laura who was peering around the other end of the building.

The car appeared to be empty. Staying low, he crept toward it, trying to suppress his nerves. He made his way to the passenger door, staying out of sight by keeping below the windows.

Laura approached the driver's side. When she was in position, she jumped up with her gun at arms length pointing it toward the window. "Don't move!" she yelled at the figure reclining in the driver's seat.

Harrison covered the back seat when he heard Laura shout. "Laura, the guy in the back looks dead."

She yanked open the door while keeping her gun trained on the still body.

"Ohhh." Ahmed opened his eyes slightly.

"Oh my God!" she said, when Ahmed rolled his head towards her. He looked like a zombie with a gray pallor and blood staining his nose, mouth and cheeks.

"They're infected with the virus," Laura said, into the microphone. "Are you Ahmed Halid, or Ali Atif?"

"I am Ahmed." His voice was weak.

"How did you spread the virus?"

"I do not know what you mean. We are not responsible for this." Ahmed eyelids fluttered and bloodshot eyes rolled back—looking like pools of blood.

Brandon heard the conversation through the headset. *They aren't responsible.*

"They aren't responsible," he mumbled to no one.

The well, his thesis. *Oh my God!* It was clear now. The viruses were coming from the well—the same viruses that laid waste to countless species millions of years ago. Africa and Ebola, China and SARS, Hanta and Muerto Canyon. *Oh shit, he was responsible for this, not terrorists.*

The e-mail from West Continent—the valve that will send the deadly viral-laden gas to the west coast will be opening at 7:00 p.m., tonight.

Brandon turned to Dykhouse. "It was right in front of me. It was right there in my computer. I did this. We've got to stop it before it gets to the West Coast."

"What?" Dykhouse asked.

"The virus! I have to tell them," he yelled as he ripped off his headset and jumped from the Black Hawk.

"Wait!"

Saif lay in the weeds and watched as the two people approached Ahmed's vehicle. He could see the helicopter off to his right and the gunmen positioned at the open doors. He had no choice—take out the two near his comrades, then take out the gunmen on the helicopter before it left the ground.

He carefully put down the binoculars and picked up the Colt M1 Carbine and looked through the powerful scope. He trained the crosshairs on the woman who had pulled open the driver's door and seemed to be questioning Ahmed.

There was little wind and the shot was relatively easy for someone trained as a sniper. He exhaled as his finger began to squeeze the trigger. *Wait!* Something in his peripheral vision moved. Someone had jumped out of the helicopter and was running toward the pair at the car.

They must have seen me and are trying to warn them. He swung the rifle quickly, centered the running man in his sights.

Brandon was running towards Laura when his world went dark. It felt as if someone shoved a hot poker in his side, buckling his knees. His head hurtled towards a large rock on the ground. A thud resounded like a thunderbolt through his skull as he crashed into the rock, opening a large cut on his forehead. Light was turning to dark as he lost consciousness. *It's my fault...*

Saif swung the carbine back, searching for the woman.

"Where did you go, bitch?" he mumbled.

Hearing the loud report from the carbine bounce off the walls of the quarry, both Laura and Harrison instinctively ducked for cover. Laura heard the rotor of the Black Hawk speed up as it prepared to lift off.

Saif heard it. The helicopter. He swung the rifle back to the helicopter, centered the nearest gunman in his sights and squeezed the trigger twice.

Two shots echoed through the strip mine. One of the gunners collapsed, hanging in his safety harness. The carbine swung slightly, and two more shots sounded. The remaining gunman fell back in his harness as the Black Hawk lifted off the ground.

Saif shifted himself to get a better view of the building. He scanned the area and saw that he had the woman pinned down behind the car. But where was the man that was with her?

Harrison was shielded from sight by the scrub brush that had grown up over the years. Laura was still behind the car.

"Laura, are you all right?" Harrison asked, just loud enough for her to hear.

"Yes. Where is the gunfire coming from?"

"I saw a muzzle flash about forty yards away along the rim of the mine—about eleven o'clock."

"I'm going to try to circle behind him. Give me some light cover."

"Okay, go."

Harrison watched as Laura brought her gun up and fired two rounds in the general direction of the gunshots.

Saif watched as Laura raised her gun and fired in his general direction. *She doesn't know where I am*. He continued to scan for her partner. *Where was he?*

Dr. Bates heard the gunfire, ducked down below the dashboard of the Trailblazer and peered out. For a while, he didn't see anything, but heard the gunfire again and again.

Movement in the bushes up the hill and to his left caught his attention. There was a man making his way towards Saif.

"Don't go that way!" he shouted.

The man didn't hear him. Bates reached over and smashed down on the horn.

Harrison lifted his head when he heard the car horn blaring and turned to see where it was coming from. The sound died off and was replaced by a cold voice.

"Drop your gun, raise your hands and walk straight forward."

It came from the bushes to his left.

"Now! Do it now or you're dead."

Harrison dropped his gun and raised his hands. "Where are you?"

"Walk towards my voice."

"Who are you?"

"That's a detail you shouldn't be concerned with. All I want is to collect my friends and get out of here."

"Give me a break, asshole."

"Shut up and walk. Now!"

Harrison slowly walked forward. He could hear the Black Hawk circling as Mazilli searched for the sniper. Saif stood as Harrison got close. He had the business end of the Glock pointed at Harrison's chest.

"Turn around."

As Harrison started to comply, Saif grabbed him around the neck and shoved the gun against his head.

"We're taking a stroll over to your friend."

Laura watched as Harrison stood and raised his hands.

She saw another man rise and grab him.

"No, don't, you idiot. He's going to kill you anyway. Shit!" she mumbled. Then remembering the radio, she said, "Mazilli, call for back-up and cover me."

Mazilli saw the scene playing out in front of him when he heard Laura's order.

"Base Ten, Base Ten. This is Black Hawk 210. I have three men down and a situation developing. Request support."

"210, this is Base 10. Request received and understood. Sending support. We have two Apaches spooling up and on their way to you."

Mazilli had Harrison and Saif in the sights of his fifty-millimeter cannon. If he opened fire, he would kill them both and he had to assume that Laura wanted the terrorist alive for questioning. But with her radio on "send," he could only assume.

Harrison and Saif were less than ten yards from the car and Laura's cover when Saif asked, "What's her name?"

"Blow me, asshole."

Saif pressed the muzzle of his gun harder against Harrison's head. "I said, what's her name?"

"Agent Daniels."

"Agent Daniels! Show yourself or your partner will die!" Saif had to yell above the roar of the Black Hawk's jet-powered rotors. He used Harrison as a shield from both Laura's position and from the Black Hawk's cannon.

Laura stood up slowly with her gun aimed at Saif's head.

"Put your gun down now," Saif ordered.

"First tell me how you spread this virus."

"You think we did this? Ha. That's ironic. I wish we could take credit. However, we *will* use this to our advantage."

"What do you mean?" *Come on, you bastard, lower your guard for just a second.*

"We will harvest the virus from our fallen brothers and strike a deadly blow against America."

"Your brothers are still alive."

"They're willing to die for their beliefs. Something you insolent Americans can't understand."

"It's time for you to go to hell, you bastard."

The ground erupted around Saif as the Black Hawk's fifty-millimeter cannon fired a short burst into the ground near them.

Saif ducked and his eyes shifted upward toward the helicopter. With Harrison so close, she only had one shot. She drew a breath and squeezed the trigger. This Sig bucked in her hands, raising the sights by six inches up and back. The crack resonated off the steep quarry walls. The forty-caliber round grazed Harrison's ear and entered Saif's head through his cheek bone. He fell back and hit the ground as Harrison grabbed his ear. Laura kept her gun pointed at Saif's chest as she walked towards him. She glared into his lifeless, disbelieving eyes.

"I understand that you're dead, you bastard," Laura said, and then turned toward Harrison. "Jim, are you all right?"

"Alright? You shot me, dammit." He straightened up, bringing his fingers in front of his face to look at the blood that was oozing from his ear.

She went over to him to take a look.

"Quit whining. You'll live." She pushed the red button on the radio and keyed her microphone. "Thanks Mazilli. Your timing was perfect. Did you call for support?"

"Yes, I see the two Apaches in the distance. I have two badly wounded men on board and I need to get them back to base."

"Okay, we're going to get Stiles and get him on board."

"Wait, Laura. There's a car down the hill with someone in it. They blasted the horn."

"Get Stiles on board that chopper. I'll check it out."

"Be careful."

Harrison ran to where Brandon went down.

Laura ran the other direction. She saw a man standing next to an SUV with his hands up in the air. Keeping her gun aimed at the man she yelled, "You come up to me, quickly."

"Don't shoot. They held me captive. I'm unarmed." Bates ran as fast as he could up the rocky slope.

"Who are you?"

"I'm Dr. Reed Bates. These men threatened to kill my wife and me unless I cooperated. They wanted me to help them make a biological weapon from their virus infected friends."

"So you concur that they had nothing to do with the current outbreak."

"I don't think so. They seemed surprised by it."

Laura lowered her gun.

"Dr. Bates, wait here until my backup shows up. They will bring you to the base camp for questioning."

"Yes, ma'am."

Laura ran back to the Black Hawk. Harrison had Stiles draped across his shoulders and was lugging him back to the landing site as the chopper put down. The air filled with dust from the rotor downwash. Mazilli still had the rotors turning full tilt so they could lift off quickly. Once inside, the Black Hawk was nose down heading full-speed back to Powell Base camp.

Mazilli spoke into the microphone. "Put pressure on the wounds. Dykhouse took a hit in the stomach. He's bleeding badly. It looks like the civilian was hit in the sternum."

"Okay, Jim, help me here. You tend to the gunner."

"Base 10, this is Black Hawk 210. Come in."

"210, this is Base 10. Has your back-up arrived?"

"Yes, they're coming in now. There are two terrorists that have contracted the virus in a beige car. There is one terrorist down, near the car and there is a hostage near the entrance road."

"Apache 5 copied. We will secure the infected terrorists and wait for transport. We will also track down the hostage and secure him."

"Base 10, this is Black Hawk 210. I have casualties. Three men down—two crew, one civilian. Gunner Nash is dead, the other two will need immediate medical assistance."

"Base 10 copy, we will have USAMRIID doctors and a medical corpsman waiting."

"What was Stiles doing running out there anyway?" Laura asked into the headset when Mazilli was finished.

Mazilli flipped the switch from radio to intercom. "After he heard the terrorist deny accountability, he started yelling that he knew where the virus came from."

"What?" Laura and Harrison both looked up.

"Let's see, he said, it was right there in his computer right in front of him. Then he said he had to stop it before it gets to the West Coast. I think he said that *he* was responsible for this. Dykhouse maybe heard it better than me if he gains consciousness."

"Stiles said that *he* did this?" Harrison asked.

"I think so."

Laura wadded up her jacket and pushed with all her might on Brandon's wound.

"Don't you die, dammit."

Minutes seemed like hours.

"There's the base. Hang on, we're coming in hot," Mazilli warned them.

Laura saw the land racing toward them faster than it should and closed her eyes. *Oh, shit, this guy's crazy.*

At the last possible moment, Mazilli pulled the nose up and the runners hit hard, jolting the passengers. Medical corpsmen ran towards the Black Hawk and immediately tended to the wounded.

"You've got to save that man," Laura shouted at them. "He has critical information regarding this outbreak. I need him alive."

"We'll do our best, ma'am."

"I need to know the second he gains consciousness."

"Yes, ma'am," he answered as they carried Brandon off.

Harrison walked over to her.

"Now what?" he asked.

She looked up suddenly. "I have an idea."

She turned and ran towards Major Lee's conference room.

"Where are you going?" he shouted, running after her.

Laura raced into the tent and grabbed Brandon's backpack. She unzipped it, pulled out his laptop computer and opened it up. The screen flickered and went dark. He must have closed it in a hurry and forgot to switch it off, sending it into hibernation. She plugged it in and switched it on.

"What are you doing?" Harrison asked when he caught up to her.

"Praying he doesn't use a password to log in," she answered, holding up her hands with her fingers crossed. "The pilot said it was on his computer, right in front of him."

"How do you know where to look?"

"I don't."

The Windows Logo appeared as the computer screen came to life. When his Jurassic Park wallpaper lit up, she let out a long sigh. *Okay, Brandon, talk to me.*

"Let's see." She opened Internet Explorer and clicked on the history button. Links to the Centers for Disease Control website were the only thing in the history for today. She clicked the link and got nowhere.

"Damn! Major, do you have an active network cable that I can tie into the Internet?"

"Yeah, we have an unsecured line for the CDC people who aren't on the dot-mil system. It's that blue cat-5 cable there," he said, pointing to the far wall.

"Can you see if Stiles is conscious yet?"

"I'll check."

Laura carried the laptop to a table in the corner and plugged in the cable. *Halleluiah! It worked.* She began clicking the links in the history folder.

The history of Hantavirus Pulmonary Syndrome caught her attention. She read through it quickly, then opened Word and clicked on the file menu. The four most recent files were at the end of the menu. All four were access agreements for right of entry—*dead end.*

"Agent Daniels, Stiles is critical," Major Lee reported. "They've got him in surgery, but there's no way he'll be conscious for a while—if he lives."

"Shit. Okay, thanks."

Next she opened Excel. The first file was a long list of historic wells. She went back to the menu and chose Edit/Find. The word *Muerto* was the last thing he searched on. *Muerto, wait, that was the origin of the Hanta outbreak in the U.S. in 1993.* She hit the OK button—no results.

She clicked back to the web browser and centered her cursor on the Google toolbar. At the top of the history was *Muerto Canyon.* She clicked it and scrolled through the web sites. Most referred her to Canyon de Chelly National Monument. She went back to the Excel spreadsheet and typed *Canyon de Chelly* into the search box. One result. A gas field in 1993—Interex Exploration, Dr. B. Stiles. *Holy shit!*

She opened Outlook and checked his recent e-mail. At the top was an e-mail from West Continent Pipeline. The message said that the gas from the well would be pumped to the main transmission line on May 13, 2004, at 7:00 p.m. There were two attachments. She opened one and it was a drawing of a meter station and connection to the main transmission line. The other was a section of a topographic map showing the location of a meter station.

"Jim! I think I know what's going on." She looked at her watch. "Oh my God, it's 6:35. She grabbed her phone and dialed Mike Johnson.

"Laura, it's about time, what—"

"No time, Mike. I think the virus is coming from the gas well and it's about to be pumped into West Continent's main transmission pipeline to the west coast. We have to tell them to stop."

"We can't. Utilities are on Threat Level Red. They're automated and it'll take time to go through protocol to get them set back to manual. You have to find another way."

"You've got to be shitting me."

"Laura, I'll try to get through to West Continent, but you have to do whatever it takes to stop that valve from opening."

She disconnected the phone.

"Major, I need that Black Hawk right now."

"Why?"

"The virus. It's coming from the gas well. And the gas is about to be pumped into a main gas transmission line to the West Coast. I need to find this meter station. Can you tell where it is?"

"Let's see. It's the Billings quad." He went to his maps and pulled one out, grabbed his radio and gave instructions to Captain Mazilli.

"Your chopper's spooling up. What are you going to do?"

"I'm not sure, but I have to stop that valve from opening. Are you coming, Jim?"

"Right behind you."

They ran to the Black Hawk, jumped in and put on their headsets.

"Did you get the coordinates from Major Lee?" Laura asked.

"Yes, ma'am, it'll take about fifteen minutes."

"You've got to hurry. If we don't stop this from happening, it could start a worldwide epidemic."

Mazilli lifted the Black Hawk and pointed it north. The airframe shook violently under the heavy thrust of the jet engine spinning the rotor. Laura looked to the west where the sun was disappearing below the peaks of the Teton Mountains. Her mind was racing when she heard Harrison's voice over the intercom.

"Do you have a clue what you're doing, Laura? Because I sure don't."

"No, I guess I'm hoping there's a big on-off button on this valve."

"Maybe there will be a power switch that we can shut down."

Laura's started thinking about the ramifications. There was no telling how many towns were supplied by that main gas pipeline on its way to the west coast. Even a household or two could cause an epidemic if not contained properly.

"There it is," the pilot said into the intercom. "I can set it down on the right-of-way next to it."

Mazilli let the Black Hawk drop out of the sky quickly and slowed it down just as the runners touched the grass. Laura and Jim already had their headphones off and were jumping out of the open door.

The site was partially surrounded by a tall chain-link fence, which hadn't been completed yet. There were two small metal buildings with a heavy padlock on the doors. The pipe jutted from the ground, went into the metal shacks, one at a time and then disappeared once again below the ground.

Jim arrived at the first building with Laura right behind him and pulled futilely on the heavy lock. Yanking his pistol from its holster, he aimed at the lock wincing, then hesitated. He was looking right at a sign on the door.

Warning Natural Gas Pipeline. No firearms, fireworks, smoking or open flames.

"Oh shit, Laura, now what?"

Laura already had her gun drawn and fired at the lock. The impact spun it in the hasp before it fell to the ground. She glanced at her watch—6:55 p.m.

The building was dark and the dangling explosion-proof light fixture was a sign that construction had not been completed yet.

"I can't see anything," she said.

"There, against the far wall—that looks like and electrical panel of some sort."

There was a chart recorder and pressure gauges, but nothing like an on-off or open-close switch.

"This looks like measuring equipment. The valve must be in the other building," Jim said as he turned around to see Laura running out the door.

Before he made it to the door of the next building, he heard Laura's gun fire again.

"This is it."

In the center of the room was a large valve with a motor control alongside. She frantically scanned the dark room for something that would help her, something that looked familiar—wishing her eyes would adjust faster. *Come on, come on.*

Next to the valve was a large green steel box.

"This must be the electrical control. But there's no door and the wiring looks like it's below ground," Jim yelled.

Laura pulled her cell phone off of her belt. As she flipped it open, she saw the time—6:59 p.m.

"Shit, shit, shit," she repeated, as her shaking hands pushed Mike Johnson's speed dial number.

"Johnson here."

"Mike, any luck?"

"We reached West Continent through the Office of Homeland Security. They're trying to reset the system to manual, but it will take time..."

"Laura? Laura?"

A loud clicking noise sounded from the green steel box. Then the motor next to the valve started turning with a loud hum. Laura flipped the phone shut when she noticed the arrow on the top of the valve moving, turning toward the word *Open*.

"Let's go, Jim."

She sprinted back to the helicopter with Jim following close behind, waving her hands at the pilot and pointing up to the sky. The powerful rotor started picking up speed as they jumped in the door.

Diving for the headset, she yelled, "Mazilli, get this thing in the air and get ready to fire one of those missiles."

"What?"

"We're taking out that second building."

"Agent, I can't fire without authorization."

The helicopter lifted off and headed up and away from the meter station.

"I'm giving you authorization. Just do it!"

"I can't."

Laura pulled her handgun and pointed it at Mazilli.

"I told you we have no choice. Fire the fucking missile."

He pulled the Black Hawk back around and hovered about three hundred yards from the buildings, armed his missiles and held his thumb over the fire button.

"Are you absolutely sure?"

"No. Just fire the goddamn missile!"

When he pushed the button the Black Hawk lurched backward. Laura watched as the Hellfire Missile flashed across the sky toward the buildings.

There was a blinding light and a huge fireball erupted. The Black Hawk rocked backwards as if a giant hand pushed it away from the explosion. Laura slammed against the back wall of the small compartment, knocking the air from her lungs. The Black Hawk tilted sideways as the pilot fought for control—alarms sounded and flashing console lights warned of impending danger.

Jim grabbed the gunner station strap managing to push his arm through a loop as his feet cleared the doorway, leaving him dangling a thousand feet over the ground. Laura, stunned from slamming into the wall, slid helplessly toward the large opening. Mazilli overcompensated on the collective swinging Harrison back into the chopper and sending Laura tumbling toward the other open door. She scratched desperately at the floor trying to grab onto something—anything. Spinning in the gunner's harness, Jim reached out and snagged the sleeve of her jacket as her feet cleared the edge of the door.

"Don't let go," she gasped.

Finally gaining control and leveling the Black Hawk, Mazilli climbed away from the growing column of fire. Even at their distance, the heat from the maelstrom reaching hundreds of feet into the evening sky scorched their skin and singed their hair.

"God help us," Laura said.

Alarms sounded and red lights flashed on monitors in West Continent's control bunker.

"We have a pressure loss in mile four-ten mainline two. Temperature sensors are showing we have a fire!" the gas control technician shouted.

"That's the Billings, Montana, Gas Meter Station we received a call about, isn't it?"

"Yes, sir. The gate valves on either side of the blowout are closing."

"Okay, call the authorities in the area and notify them of possible fire. Tell them the source has been cut off, but gas in the lines will continue to fuel the fire for another hour or so. Let them know our recommendation is to let it burn out on its own."

"Yes, sir."

"Are you okay back there?" Mazilli shouted into the intercom.

Harrison answered, "Yes, a little shook up, but we're okay." He was leaning over Laura helping her catch her breath, distraught that he almost lost her.

"Base 10, Base 10, this is Black Hawk 210."

"Base 10 here."

"Base 10, advise the unit in Billings that we have a large fire about ten miles south of town. I'm guessing they already know something's happened."

"210, this is Major Lee. What the hell happened out there?"

"I had to use a Hellfire on that pipeline to stop the gas from getting to the main transmission line, sir."

"You fired a missile at a natural gas pipeline?"

"No choice, sir. I'll be landing in a few minutes—Agent Daniels will explain it to you."

"She'd better."

As the Black Hawk touched down at the base camp, Major Lee was waiting with armed guards.

"Well, let's face the music," Laura said grimly, looking at Harrison.

They climbed from the chopper, walked a safe distance from the spinning rotors and were immediately surrounded by guards as they faced Major Lee.

"Get Mazilli and take him into custody," he ordered.

"Wait. I'm responsible," Laura said. "I forced him to fire that missile. We had no choice."

"What do you mean, you forced him?"

"I had a gun to his head."

"Take this woman, disarm her and place her under arrest."

As the guards grabbed Laura and pulled her arms behind her, Harrison yelled, "Major Lee, are you fucking crazy? This woman's quick thinking may have saved the United States from a major outbreak and panic. You can't arrest her."

"I can and I will."

"It's okay, Jim," she said, as the guards secured the handcuffs. "Major, at least allow me to call Mike Johnson with the FBI in Washington D.C. and report what I did."

"Okay, take Agent Daniels and Detective Harrison to my conference tent. Then take those cuffs off of her and post guards. I'll take her firearm." Major Lee turned to Mazilli who was approaching the group. "Captain Mazilli, why did you fire that missile without authorization?"

"Because it was the right thing to do, sir. There was no danger to anybody in the area and if there was one chance in a thousand that a missile could stop the virus from hitting the west coast, it was worth it."

"Did Agent Daniels aim her gun at you and force you to fire?"

He glanced towards Laura and said, "Agent Daniels convinced me it was the right thing to do, sir."

"Mazilli, you're confined to quarters until further notice."

"Yes, sir." Mazilli saluted the major, turned and saluted Laura, then left for his quarters.

Once in the conference tent, Laura dialed Mike Johnson.

"Laura, what's happening there?"

"I did the only thing I could, Mike. I blew up the valve."

"Well, it worked. You caused a hell of a mess, but it worked. West Continent told me that sensors on the automated system detected a pressure loss and shut the system down, isolating the section of pipeline where the virus was entering."

"Thank God, but I'm in a bit of trouble here. I've been arrested for forcing my pilot to fire a missile without authorization."

"Don't worry, we'll straighten it out. I'm sending a jet to get you in the morning and bring you back here for debriefing. So get a good night's sleep—you've earned it. I'll see you tomorrow afternoon. Great work, Laura. Now let me talk to whoever's in charge there."

"Thanks, Mike." She handed the phone to Major Lee.

After a brief conversation, the major handed the phone back to Laura and said, "I was asked to put you up for the night and release you to FBI custody in the morning."

"Thanks, Major Lee."

"Oh, I'm sorry to say that Dr. Stiles didn't make it."

"Oh my God," Laura said looking down. "He seemed like a really good guy, but I'm not sure he could have lived with himself knowing that he actually caused this outbreak."

Harrison came over and took Laura into his arms. She relaxed as she held onto him.

Chapter Fifty-seven

FBI Headquarters
Washington D.C.
May 20, 2004

"It seems we have things under control." Secretary of Homeland Security Greg Reilly addressed the videoconference attendees. "There haven't been any new cases of Cody, Marburg or Anthrax since the well was shut down. The bad news is the death toll is up to seventy-two hundred and still climbing."

"Has the CDC come up with a cure for any of these viruses?" the president asked.

"Sir, this is Max Van Pelt with the CDC. We are still trying to map the Cody virus and we've tried several vaccines with little success. The mortality rate is upwards of sixty percent, which puts it right up there with the deadliest viruses we've seen."

"So these viruses really came from that well?" the president asked again.

"Yes, sir. We sampled the gas and it was heavily contaminated with several viruses. We're still trying to understand how these dormant bugs survived, but they may have been harbored in what scientists call Extremophiles or even Archaea," Max stated.

"What's that?"

"Extremophile is a generic term for microorganisms that can live under extreme conditions. For example, Thermophiliac bacteria can live in extreme heat and are found in steam vents and geysers. It's just a guess, but we're working on it."

Max continued, "We also went through the late Dr. Brandon Stiles computer files. He was onto something that we never imagined. He was starting to link outbreaks with oil and gas exploration. I've had my staff working on it and we found out that Stiles completed a gas well in early 2003 two weeks before the SARS outbreak was reported. The first cases came from the villages surrounding the well."

"That could be coincidence, Dr. Van Pelt," the president countered.

"There's more. We have evidence linking oil and gas wells to Hanta in Muerto Canyon and Mexico, Marburg in Germany and Ebola in the Congo. There may even be a correlation to an off-shore well and West Nile virus. And, the deadly Spanish Flu Pandemic of 1918 may have been caused by a new gas well dug to supply Fort Riley and Camp Funston in Kansas."

"Wait, now you're stretching beyond reality, Doctor," the president said. "I'm a bit of an expert on World War I and that flu came from Asia."

"There is strong evidence that the flu started at Fort Riley and was carried overseas by soldiers going abroad to fight in the war. It may have mutated in Asia, but it came back to us when the men started returning to Camp Devens near Boston," Max hesitated. "We found out there was a well drilled on a pig farm next to Fort Riley to supply them with heat and light while they were training. The men started getting sick soon after."

"So what do we do? We need the energy from that field."

"John Joplin, Department of Energy here—we recommend flaring the gas and retesting each week. The flare will kill the viruses and hopefully the viral activity will deplete itself over time."

"Dr. Van Pelt, will the flare kill the viruses?"

"Yes, sir."

"Very well, Mr. Joplin, proceed with your plan." The president picked up another folder from his desk. "Okay, the last order of business today is to congratulate the FBI and especially Agent Laura Daniels on stopping the terrorists and stopping the virus from spreading to the west coast and possibly saving the world from a major pandemic."

"Laura, I've got news for you. Come in and sit down," Mike Johnson said.

Good he left out the 'close the door' part. "What's the news, Mike?"

"Close the door."

Here we go again.

"The terrorist you killed at the strip mine was Saif Yasin. We had absolutely no file on him. He must have been a sleeper and in the States for a long time."

"Okay."

After interrogating Dr. Reed Bates and going through Yasin's New York apartment, we discovered that it was his cell that launched the anthrax letter attacks. We found a hand-written letter in the apartment with a vial of anthrax."

"Oh my God."

"Bates admitted to stealing the anthrax from Fort Detrick. Apparently he was supposed to supply them with four hundred grams and he could only confiscate six."

"So they did plan a larger attack?"

"Yes, they were going to launch two attacks, both at football games, one in a ventilation system and one with a crop duster. Anyway, congratulations, you solved your first big case, even if it was a little late."

"Thanks, Mike," she said with a huge smile.

"I've got an offer for you," he said.

"What's that?"

"We'd like you back at headquarters heading up the bioterrorism group again. That includes a nice raise, too."

"Thanks, Mike, but I'll have to get back to you. I have some unfinished business in Washington to take care of."

"Your detective friend?"

"How did you know about that?"

"We're the FBI, remember?" Mike winked at her. "Campisi filled me in."

That ass.

"Can I have a week to think about it?"

"Sure, you've earned that much."

Laura stood up and turned to leave Mike's office.

"Laura?"

She turned back to see Mike lean forward with his elbows on the desk.

"I really want you back here."

"I'll think about it, Mike. Really." Laura turned and walked out of the door, a large smile spreading across her face.

Epilogue

Sometime in May, 2004, packages containing frozen specimens were received in Malta, Montana and New Haven, Connecticut.
"Dr. Burch, a frozen box came in for you from Dr. Brandon Stiles. We put the sample in the lab's freezer, but here's the letter that was with it."

Dr. Burch opened the envelope and unfolded the letter.

My Dear Friend Andrew,

I have sent to you what may be the most interesting find of my life. I believe the enclosed sample to be the soft tissue of an unidentified dinosaur.

I'm too busy solving the world's energy demands to investigate, but I know you'll find good use for the specimen. Perhaps you can use it in one of your classes. Enjoy and keep me informed.

Your friend,
Brandon Stiles

"Well, it sure is nice to hear from an old friend. The specimen will have to wait until I get back from Europe, but perhaps I'll drag it out and have some students investigate it in the fall."

"Kurt, look at this! It's a package from Dr. Stiles."

Kurt Edmonds, the curator of paleontology of the Phillips County Museum, grabbed the envelope that was attached to the package and ripped it open.

"This is amazing. Brandon thinks this may be soft tissue from a dinosaur. Hmm, it's interesting that he doesn't mention where he found it."

Edmonds sat the letter down and opened the package. He untied the wire keeping the plastic bag shut and—

"Oh my God, that stinks..."

Wilfred Bereswill was born and raised in St. Louis, Missouri. He graduated in 1980 with a bachelor's degree in Civil/Environmental Engineering from the University of Missouri - Rolla. He worked in the natural gas industry from 1980 through 1991, which plays a large part in A Reason For Dying.

While many people stereotype engineers as anything but creative, Wilfred begs to differ. Engineers push the limits of creativity to bring architectural masterpieces, such as, Ero Sarrinen's dream of the St. Louis Arch to fruition among other things. He is a believer in research and organization.

Since 2001, Wilfred has traveled extensively through China, a wonderful and fulfilling chapter in his life. Even though travel was restricted during the SARS epidemic, he still made connections and returned to China after things cooled down a bit.

He was encouraged to try his hand at writing by his aunt and uncle, Mildred and Bob MacGuire, after he sent them a journal of his travels through China. A retired college professor, his uncle's advice, "write what you know" became A Reason For Dying.

Wilfred lives in a house full of women. He has a beautiful wife, Linda and three wonderful daughters, Kelly, Kristen and Kaitlin. In order to bring balance to the estrogen/testosterone levels in the household, he purchased a male Soft-Coated Wheaton Terrier named Fraiser. It wasn't long after he arrived that the imbalance was restored with a quick and painless (HA!) neutering.

Wilfred grew up reading Stephen King and other horror and Science fiction works. He moved on to thrillers, reading Tom Clancy, Michael Crichton, Robin Cook and others. He placed third in the 2005 James Nash Memorial Short Story Contest with a historical short fiction about the Spanish Flu Pandemic, In Flew Enza. He is an active member of the St. Louis Writers Guild and Sisters in Crime.

Visit Will at his website: www.wbereswill.com

Printed in the United States
139695LV00004B/63/P

9 781591 332626